To Be Sung Underwater

Tom McNeal

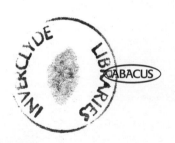

ABACUS

First published in Great Britain in 2011 by Little, Brown
This paperback edition published in 2012 by Abacus

A CIP catalogue record for this book
is available from the British Library.

ISBN 978-0-349-12363-9

Typeset in Garamond by M Rules
Printed and bound in Great Britain by
Clays Ltd, St Ives plc

Papers used by Abacus are from well-managed forests
and other responsible sources.

MIX
Paper from
responsible sources
FSC® C104740

Abacus
An imprint of
Little, Brown Book Group
100 Victoria Embankment
London EC4Y ODY

An Hachette UK Company
www.hachette.co.uk

www.littlebrown.co.uk

for Laura
and in memory of Bill Gerard

To Be Sung Underwater

Prologue

The man sits hidden among pines on a bluff overlooking the grid of farms and county roads lying north. It is hot. Several times now the man has moved his three-legged camp stool to maintain full shade. That is how long he has been waiting and watching and drinking. He watches through a scope, a 3×9×40 Bushnell, the one he has used in his lifetime for large, wary prey—deer, for example, and sometimes antelope.

The first sign of the car is the distant moving cloud of dust that rises behind it. The dust plume is denser than most; the car is moving right along. When it slows to take the hard right turn at Bethel Church and its length presents itself, heat vapors distort the image—the car seems almost a mirage. But it is yellow. It is definitely yellow. So it is her. It is very probably her. A hand takes hold of the man's heart, and its rhythmic squeeze and release causes tender but actual pain.

The car falls out of view for a time, then turns south, onto the creek road. The man raises himself and lumbers to another position. He sits, mouth open, waiting for eveness to return to his breathing. Then he scales down the scope and follows the glimpses of the yellow car as it passes through the cottonwoods and ash that line the road. There are three creeks to ford. This all takes time. Finally the car splashes through the last creek and rolls up into the space the man has had cleared for that purpose. For several seconds, no one gets out of the yellow car. Then the passenger does—a woman, carrying a soft-sided leather bag. She leans into the car to speak to the driver, perhaps to satisfy herself on some point or other, then she steps back so the driver can execute a three-point turnaround.

She watches the car go. Her back is to the man in the pines looking down. Finally, when the car is beyond the creek and out of view, she turns toward the trail. She does not at once begin to walk. She stands with the slouchy leather bag at her feet, looking up and scanning the hills. For a second or two she seems to fix on the shaded spot where the man sits hidden. She cannot see him, the man is sure of it, but he can see her. Through the rifle scope, he can see her clearly. It has been a long time since he has seen her, a very long time, but he would have known her in a second. A fraction of a second. For a moment he feels he might soon waken from a dream, but for once, at last and after all, it is not a dream.

It's you. This is what he thinks. It is all he can think. *You, you, you, you, you.*

Part One

1

The swerve (to use Judith's own term) that slipped her outside the customary course of her life derived from one of those offhand moments in which odd circumstances and amplified emotions invite an odd and overcolored response. Amusement was the presumed objective, whatever the actual result might be.

"It was strange," she said when she spoke of it, which was only once, and much later, to her friend Lucy Meynke. "My life had utterly settled into itself and then this little . . . *swerve* occurred, or maybe I meant it to occur, maybe I'd actually plotted it out in one of those corners of your brain or heart you access only in dreams." She gave Lucy Meynke a look of actual bafflement. "I really don't know."

At the time, though, it seemed simple. Judith was renting a storage garage for some old furniture and when, late in the transaction, she was asked her name, she gave one that was not her own, a name that in fact she hadn't thought of in years. A few hours later, Judith, who was not a loser of keys, lost a key.

—⚉—

Prior to this so-called swerve, Judith Whitman had reached the age of forty-four without serious casualty or setback. This was not mere luck. All her life she'd constructed plans for her life sturdy enough to weather the seasons but skeletal enough to allow for necessary modifications. Without seeming to step carefully, she'd stepped carefully. She'd built not just a formidable life, but the very one she'd wanted. At the moment she gave a clerk in a ministorage yard a name not her own, Judith had a successful career, a smart, socially capable daughter, and a husband who loved her.

She also had two secrets.

Judith held the conviction that above the more routine types of love formed—and, she believed, diluted—by blood ties or economic pragmatism or even geographic proximity, there existed the kind of love that, as she once explained it to Lucy Meynke, picks you up in Akron, Ohio, and sets you down in Rio de Janeiro. ("The Rio Variation, we'll call it," Judith said. Lucy Meynke remarked that she herself had most often experienced the kind of love that picked you up in Minneapolis and set you down in St. Paul.) Judith believed in the Rio Variation because she had herself experienced it, but only once, and that with a boy she'd thereafter abandoned, and yet never quite left behind. This boy was her first secret.

They'd become fully acquainted during her senior year in high school in a town of medium size on the high plains, where she was living with her father and constructing those plans that would take her first off to college and then to Los Angeles to somehow help in the making of movies. The boy was a few years older than Judith, a carpenter whose pale blue eyes and mixed scent of sawdust, sweat, and alcohol could exert an insistent pull on her from ten feet, and when at the end of their summer together he had suggested marriage, Judith had said, *Oh, yes, the answer is yes, definitely yes,* she did want to marry him, only later, when she came back from college. But she hadn't come back from college. She met someone else, an older, urbane, tennis-playing boy enrolled in the business school, a genial and impressive boy with whom she slept in his slender twin bed, establishing in their sex and their sleep an easy unforced synchronicity that they learned to apply to their daylight dealings as well. Although uncertain how much— or even if—she loved him, it was Judith who suggested that someone like him might want to marry someone like her. Malcolm Whitman's hair was fine and long and beautifully groomed, his wrists were thin, his smile small but playful. "Is this a proposal?" he said, and Judith said yes, come to think of it, it probably was. Malcolm Whitman said, "Then I accede with enthusiasm." He gave her a kiss of surprising length and intensity, after which he leaned back and became again his Malcolmish self. "Marriage," he said. "I had no idea you were so intrepid." This was the way Malcolm Whitman spoke, with a quick, slightly distanced wryness that Judith had always found attractive, and still did, up to a point.

At Judith's suggestion, the newlyweds moved to Los Angeles, where Malcolm converted his competence and connections to significant positions and income, and where Judith eventually found work in movies. She worked first as a personal assistant to an actor-director, whose help, over time, afforded her the chance to apprentice in editing, the field that attracted her. She waited nearly eight years before bearing a child—a healthy daughter christened Camille—and thereafter avoided pregnancy. She lost none of her confidence in shaping her life, but at some point she began to grasp that achieving one's ends was no guarantee of happiness, at least not happiness of the unadulterated variety. Judith didn't have the appetites that lead to such things as obesity, casual infidelity, or credit card problems. She and Malcolm lived in a good neighborhood, they had respectable careers and pleasant friends, their daughter was enrolled in the Waterbury School. Judith wrote these and other assets in a long column one afternoon in hopes of improving her mood—this was before the swerve—then stared at the list without any feeling whatever. On another occasion, while searching for unbruised bananas at Vons, she suddenly stopped and thought, *If for one year all the movies were based on lives like mine, the industry's kaput.* This was not a completely random thought. Judith habitually considered her living days in terms of something she privately called *My Movie*. For example, even as her first editing job was receiving praise from the director, Judith was thinking, *Okay, this scene is going into My Movie.* More often she thought things like, *My Movie should be tossed from the nearest pier.* Or, if tired, something simpler, as in, *My Movie is crap.* Fairly often she wondered whether the chief character in her movie could be considered sympathetic.

So she had forgotten the boy in the high-plains state. After meeting Malcolm, she stopped writing letters to the boy and stopped answering the telephone. She would later tell herself she'd needed to be cruel. She'd seen that, upon returning from Rio, life attached to the boy would not in any way resemble the life she'd planned for herself. She had just one photograph of him, and kept it hidden in her wallet between pictures of her daughter. From time to time, Judith took the photograph out and stared at it. She had snapped the picture during one of their picnics, and its image of his relaxed attitude was calming, and allowed her to imagine his forgiveness.

When she'd known the boy, he lived with his parents, and for many years she would dial their telephone number, which she knew by heart. The boy (by then factually a man, though she could only vaguely think of him as such) never answered. It was always his mother, and often Judith would linger before hanging up so that his mother might say hello again in her gentle voice. Judith felt comforted by this. But one night the boy's father answered her call. He had always seemed to Judith a stony, redoubtable man, and so on this day, when a few seconds of silence had passed and the boy's father said in a small, almost pleading whisper, "Is that you, Willy?" Judith, with the phone to her ear, felt as if a hatchway had just been opened into deepest space. She put down the receiver as gently as she could. There *had* been yearning in the father's whisper, she was sure of it. It seemed clear that something had separated Willy from his parents, some kind of estrangement that his father found regrettable. Judith resolved to telephone again, this time identifying herself so that she could inquire about their son and unravel the mystery, or at least prize free some useful hints, but by the time she actually did call again, the boy's parents had acquired an answering machine with a leaden message noting that whatever the caller had to say was very important to them, so please leave a message. But Judith left no messages. Finally—this was perhaps three years ago— Judith, after dialing, heard a recorded voice report that the number was no longer in service.

The other of Judith's important secrets was her fear that she hadn't properly inhabited her role as a mother. She knew she loved her daughter, but it was a love with a strange insulating distance built into it. Judith had delivered Camille without so much as a Tylenol. She hadn't screamed. She'd worried about screaming, and about flatulence or even voiding, and of losing her inhibitions and throwing off her clothes, all of the things she'd heard delivering mothers might do, but when the time came she'd gone to war. She'd clenched her teeth and grabbed a nurse's hand with her right hand and Malcolm's with her left, and she had, as she described it afterward only to herself, fucking gone to war. When it was over she turned to the side table where the nurse was quickly wiping the bloody little Camille clean while Malcolm (woozy as she was, Judith knew what he was up to) discreetly checked for malformation and missing digits, and at the moment the nurse held up for view the cleaned pink bawling baby, the thoughts that came unbidden to Judith's mind were these: *Could that possibly have been inside me?* And, *Could that possibly be mine?*

Other mothers seemed to immerse themselves in their mothering lives without a wayward thought, but from the beginning Judith had dreams of extrication. She missed only two weeks of work before leaving Camille in the hands of Sunova from Denmark, the first nanny. For a time, Judith dutifully pumped milk at work, but she gave up morning-and-evening breast feedings when Camille (whom already they were often calling Milla) cut sharp teeth. The child grew and the nannies came and went. It had been true in those early years, as Judith told friends, that she never failed to thrill with gladness at seeing Camille's beaming face when she returned home in the evening, but the complementary, unspoken truth was that she never failed to feel relief each morning when she left the child behind. Even as Camille's beauty and precocity took form, when pride alone might have nurtured proprietary feelings, she never seemed quite the child Judith was meant to call her own. Malcolm began to care for Camille on weekends, and, over time, more and more became the intermediary agent with the nannies and schoolteachers and Brownie troop leaders. Friends would often remark on Camille's physical resemblance to her mother, but in attitude and expression, the girl grew less in Judith's image than in Malcolm's.

—◆◆◆—

From an early age, Judith heard a number of gloomy aphorisms applied to marriage, nearly all of them by her own mother. All marriages come with a pinhole leak, her mother once said. Marriages swallow love and excrete grief. Marriage is a house a woman can't leave and a man merely visits. (Or, as a variant: Marriage is a house with a woman locked inside.)

One morning, sitting at the kitchen table—this was after Judith's father had left them in Vermont to take a teaching position in Nebraska—her mother said to Judith, "Our marriage, like all marriages, was happy until it wasn't." It was a pronouncement, like many of her mother's, that Judith could neither quite believe nor forget. Later, without really wanting to, she would occasionally hold her own marriage up to her mother's stark vision, but when she did, it was like those x-rays her dentist sometimes clipped up to a light panel—she was never quite sure what she was seeing.

True, there were whole hours and even days when Judith was visited by a dull ache that in spite of its unspecific origin seemed symptomatic of yearning, but there were also whole hours and days of productivity, good cheer, and reasonably warm fellow-feeling that she presumed she should, to be fair about it, call happiness, or something within inches of it. She averted her eyes from marriages—and they were everywhere—that had lost their fondness, but that wasn't Judith and Malcolm's circumstance. Their sexual relations were often routine but occasionally weren't, and they were otherwise at ease with each other—they laughed, touched, talked, did all the things couples in good standing do. Once, when all the diners at a small party were asked to name the one aspect of their marriage of which they were most proud, Malcolm said, "We can travel significant distances together in a car without annoyance." It was both ironic and true. They rarely argued.

There were points of disagreement, of course, and the bird's-eye maple bedroom set, handed down to Judith's father by his grandparents, and by Judith's father to Judith, and by Judith to Camille, was among them. The three-piece grouping comprised a bed with a tall, ornate headboard, a high, narrow chest of drawers that Judith—like her father, grandfather, and great-grandfather—called a chiffonier, and a marble-topped washstand that the family had always called a commode. Judith took possession of the furniture after her father's death eleven years before, and shipped it home along with his personal papers. "The venerable pater's venerable papers," said Malcolm, casting a doubtful eye on the cardboard boxes lining an entire wall of their home office. (After two or three stifling conversations, he and Judith's father had kept their distance. Judith believed this was because they both wanted to occupy the same irony-dense space.)

Judith loved the look of the bird's-eye maple furniture, though this feeling might be confused with her pleasure in its family history, whereas Malcolm didn't like the furniture in the slightest (it might, he said once, be coveted in Croatia), and, probably as a consequence, neither did Camille. When Camille was nine she glued multicolored sparkles to the veneer (Judith spent an entire Sunday cleaning them off), and then this past year, nearing age sixteen, she began angling for a canopied cherrywood bed, which, without Judith's advance knowledge, arrived one day along with a companion dresser and nightstand.

"Where did all this come from?" Judith said. She'd been led to the room by Camille, with Malcolm following behind.

"Thomas Moser!" Camille sang out.

The bed was so tall it came with matching cherry step stools for either side.

Judith turned to Malcolm. He was still an imposingly handsome man, though she'd begun to notice that his clothes and grooming were carrying more of the load. His thinning hair and flyaway eyebrows were trimmed weekly, and expensive clothes weren't wasted on him—even now, at the end of a summer's day, his gray trousers and white shirt were perfectly creased.

"A birthday present," he said. "I let her choose. I said, 'The bed or a hollow artificial celebration?' She chose the bedroom suite. That's why the occasion of her birthday will slip by without the usual extravaganza." He eyed Camille. "Ain't that so, Miss Pie?"

As with most bright children, in Judith's opinion, Camille's was a calculating nature. By pretending to be so overwhelmed by the furniture, she managed to avoid the question of the forgone party. To Judith, who was on to her daughter, this indicated that in Camille's mind it was not quite forgone. The girl—thin, long-limbed, often mistaken for an athlete, which she was not—climbed onto the bed and lay there smiling up at the beribboned canopy. She said that the bed was very *deluxe,* her father's word, spoken with her father's ironical inflection.

Judith said, "*Precious* is the word I'd use."

Camille's expression, already bright, brightened to something like glee, and Judith realized too late that her sour response was exactly what Camille had hoped for.

Judith—she knew she shouldn't—said, "Pity the poor Joe who marries you, Camillikins."

Camille held her smile even though she hated the term *Camillikins.* Malcolm slipped Judith a look. He'd brought up this kind of talk when he and Judith had made their single foray into family counseling. Malcolm and the counselor agreed that remarks of this type could weaken Camille's self-esteem. Judith said that was fine by her. Camille had oodles of self-esteem. What was in short supply were the odd little commodities like empathy, charity, and humility. Malcolm and the counselor had fallen momentarily quiet, then begun to talk as if she weren't there. Judith hadn't gone back.

Camille hugged a pillow to her chest. "This bed is *titanic.* What if for my birthday I just had two or three friends for a sleep-over? We could all sleep sideways on the bed, like we did at Lauren Hartman's."

Malcolm smiled. "Lauren Hartman! Lauren Hartman! Must we always play catch-up with Lauren Hartman?"

"Yes!" Camille said, and dropped ten years from her voice. "Catch-up and mustard, too!"

This was a game they played, an exclusive little tea party of father-daughter silliness (and of denial, too—Camille had been wearing bras for four years now, and a few months back Judith had discovered several lacy, vividly colored thongs tucked into a deep corner of the bottom drawer of the chiffonier), and Camille and Malcolm laughed easily, lost in each other's needs, hers to acquire, his to provide. It was no surprise when he said, "Okay, then, Miss Pie, but the maximum guest list is two."

Camille's smile dried up. She seemed capable of crying. "What about Torry?"

The barest moment passed before Malcolm complied. "Okay, three. But that's it—three, tops."

Camille plopped back into the fluff of her duvet, thinking.

Judith asked something she'd been wondering since entering the room. "So what did you do with the bird's-eye maple?"

Malcolm nodded toward the window.

Judith pulled back the French lace curtains. Down at the edge of the bricked pool deck, her father's old furniture stood clustered in the glaring sun, the bed's rails, headboard, and footboard sandwiched between the backsides of the commode and chiffonier.

It was not as if something snapped inside Judith. It was more an unfolding, a slow blossoming of resentment. She couldn't have expected more from Camille, Judith understood that, but what about Malcolm? He was a grown-up, wasn't he? If he needed to present this whole deal as a fait accompli, couldn't he soften the fait a little? The unmatched oak stuff they had in the guest room was no better than average, for example—why not put the maple in there and set the oak out to warp and split in the freaking sun?

Though, when she thought of it, that would've annoyed her, too, shunting the maple to the guest room, where every day it would be eyed for replacement by Malcolm.

Judith took in three short staggered breaths, which, together, deeply filled her lungs. She held the air a moment before slowly releasing it, and then she repeated the process. This was the only lesson learned in her Lamaze class that she regarded as worthwhile.

When finally she spoke, she was surprised at how calm she sounded. "I'm afraid they'll blister out there," she said.

"You're right," Malcolm said, "they might. I'll cover them up." Within the hour—before he set off in his whites to the tennis club—he'd neatly wrapped the furniture with old bedsheets and bound them at the base with green gardening twine, tied off with a bow knot, a knot that Willy Blunt, long ago, seeing it used by a traveler trying to fasten a tarp, had stepped in to replace with something sounder.

2

Judith's father had been a quiet man with a great ruddy slablike face. His nose, which Judith as a child had loved to kiss, was crooked at the spine and flat at the nostrils—the nose, she would think later, of a brawler, though to her knowledge he'd never been in a single fight. He'd been raised by his mother in San Francisco and then, after her death, by his grandparents in northwest Nebraska. At Rufus Sage High School, Howard Toomey was reclusive, capable, and stolid, qualities that kept schoolmates and even teachers at a respectful distance. He was Howard. No one called him Howie. He read books all the time, even when walking. He rarely spoke, but when he did, it was with a deep and resonant voice that attracted the attention of the school's musical director, whose invitations to join the school choral group Howard stiffly dismissed. He didn't play sports or join clubs, and when he won a scholarship to study literature at the University of Chicago, there was almost no one in Rufus Sage, other than his grandparents, to whom he was obliged to speak a parting good-bye. While doing graduate work in eighteenth-century English literature, he paid his bills by taking assistantships and found he had an aptitude for teaching. In the stillness of the classroom he would recite long passages of poetry and prose in a baritone so musical it afforded even listless students a glimpse into their own untapped capacities for exaltation. Girls sometimes responded extravagantly; one of them, Judith's mother, married him.

When Kathleen Peebles walked into Howard Toomey's class on "The Age of Johnson," she was a Delta Gamma girl wearing a long pleated plaid dress, white bucks, and a V-neck sweater, with fresh copies of *Clarissa* and *Tom Jones* held against her chest. Judith has a black-and-white photograph of her mother six months later, on her wedding day, astride a motorcycle behind Judith's father. He is wearing work boots, dark denim pants, and a plaid flannel shirt over a black turtleneck. His flattened nose is seen in profile, but he doesn't seem to be holding a pose—he's simply looking forward, in the direction the motorcycle will go, and he seems anxious to be done with the silliness. Judith's mother, however, seems to want to hold on to the moment. She stares into the camera from behind dark glasses. She's wearing a tight light-colored sweater and black capris. Her chin tips up; her head is wrapped in a scarf that in the photograph appears merely dark but which Judith, because she now owns it, knows to be wine red. Her mother looks so unlike her mother that Judith has always simply taken her identification as a matter of faith. "That's you trying to look like Audrey Hepburn," she said one night to her mother when, as adults, they came upon this picture while going through her father's boxes of old photographs. Her mother, drinking Pimm's Cups, said, "Unless it's Audrey Hepburn trying to look like me."

Premaritally the relationship between Judith's parents had been ardent and turbulent, but the ensuing marriage turned gradually sullen. Judith's father never spoke of its disintegration—it wasn't his nature—but Judith's mother, by then already collecting grim metaphors for marriage in general, offered various pronouncements specific to her own failed attempt.

"Your father seemed happiest living in rooms the rest of us weren't permitted to enter," she said.

And: "Your father was a strict monogamist, until the second drink."

She also said, with an unhappy smile, "Few marriages are presented with an actual crossroads."

She referred to a two-way stop in Dade County, Florida, where Judith and her parents were vacationing one summer with another couple. Dale Irwin was a comp. lit. man in Howard Toomey's department at Middlebury College in Vermont; his wife, Vanessa, was a nurse. The Irwins, like the Toomeys, had a single child, a girl less than a year older than Judith, who was then thirteen. This was the families' second shared vacation, and to this point it had been as pleasant as the first. Among the group there was an easy compatibility that, for the adults anyhow, took a mildly frisky turn after 5 P.M., when Dale Irwin began blending rum, ice, and fruit nectars in the stainless steel blender he'd packed for just this purpose. When he presented his concoctions in tall beading glasses, he used a rough approximation of John Wayne's voice to say, "Try this libation on for size." He made separate rum-free drinks for the girls, whom he addressed, again John Wayne-style, as little ladies.

Toward the end of the week, the couples left the girls home with pizza and the motel television so they could have an adults' night out. The evening ran late. After dinner at an oceanside restaurant, they took the tip of a busboy and went to a remote roadhouse named Lefevre's. The two couples danced and drank and stayed longer than they intended. As the evening wore on, allegiances among the couples blurred. A little before 2 A.M., Howard Toomey was driving them all home along the dark two-lane highway. His wife was on the front seat, leaning against her door, staring at him. The Irwins sat in silence at opposite sides of the back seat. An unlighted crossroads presented itself. Howard Toomey swung the car abruptly left. In the sweep of their headlights he saw a car bearing down on them with its headlights dark. He tried to break off the turn, but the tires struck something and wrenched the steering wheel from his hands. The car lurched across the narrow shoulder and down an embankment before a glancing collision with a banyan tree. Some seconds passed. From the back seat, Vanessa Irwin said, "Are we all right?" Judith's mother wanted to say yes, because this was what she wanted to believe, but she couldn't make a voice. She was also surprised that her eyes were closed. It seemed now that she couldn't open them, no matter what she did, and when finally she managed to part them slightly, she saw her husband with his head slammed into the steering wheel, looking as dead as could be. Blood slid from his forehead and covered his face. Judith's mother, pushing herself away from him, spilled out of the car and dislocated her shoulder on the hard ground.

This, it turned out, would be the most serious injury incurred in the accident. Howard Toomey was not dead, or even seriously hurt. Vanessa Irwin expertly stanched the blood while Dale Irwin and Judith's mother stood a distance apart, watching. Judith's father, dazed but not incoherent, said, "What happened to the other car?" and after the other three exchanged blank looks, Vanessa Irwin said, "What other car?" The vertical gash running down the left side of Howard Toomey's forehead was bloody but shallow. At the local emergency room, it was stitched and bandaged. It would knit, the doctor told him, but scarring was inevitable.

When Judith's parents returned to the motel, her father's forehead was bandaged and her mother's left shoulder, manipulated back into place after an injection of Novocain, was supported by a sling. The Irwins were tense but unhurt, which created for Judith the sense that there had been a fight, which her parents had lost. This impression was reinforced when the Irwins, tight-lipped, hurried their daughter off to their own room, where they packed and departed for Vermont, the early-morning hour notwithstanding.

"What happened?" Judith said.

Her mother told her to ask her father.

"We had a minor accident," her father said, and that's all he would say.

They returned home, but for Judith's parents, it was as if the accident had caused in their marriage a decisive shift in its weights and ballast—it lost its precarious equilibrium. Her father didn't even look the same. The scar ran vertically from his hairline toward his left eye and caused a bald divide in his left eyebrow.

One morning after he walked out the door for work, Judith's mother rinsed out her coffee cup, set it into the drainer, and said, "Glenda says she can't look at his face anymore. She says it's like a slashed painting." Glenda lived three doors down and was her mother's afternoon coffee friend.

Judith didn't know what she thought about the scar, except that she'd begun hardly to see it.

Judith's mother said, "I think Glenda's wrong, though. She thinks it defaced the picture. I think it just completed it. He was always scarred—now it just shows."

"I don't get it," Judith said.

Her mother looked out the kitchen window. "No, I suppose not." Then, after a moment: "You know what marriage is like?"

Judith said nothing—these questions had become as stifling to her as knock-knock jokes—but her mother went on anyway. "It's like picking the place you're going to live for the next fifty years by using a wall map, a blindfold, and what you really, truly, deeply believe is your lucky dart."

Sullenly Judith said, "I don't believe I have a lucky dart," and her mother cast an unhappy smile her way and said, "You will, though."

—⁂—

Judith's parents had separated the summer she was fourteen, more or less beginning with the June afternoon her father came into the living room, sat down in the overstuffed floral armchair that was his favorite, and said he'd been offered a position at a state teachers' college in Rufus Sage, Nebraska.

"*Nebraska?*" her mother had said.

Judith was in the room at the time. Her father had smiled. "It sneaks up on you," he said, and her mother said, "So do most kinds of cancer."

"You'll like it," he said. He let his eyes fall on Judith. "We'll all like it."

Judith's mother gazed out the window with what Judith thought of as her Elsewhere Look. Her mother often sang to herself while washing or drying dishes. When she stopped singing to stare out the window was when the Elsewhere Look would appear.

"Kathleen?"

When Judith's mother turned and spoke, her voice had a chill in it. "I thought you were just using this interview as a way to revisit the cheerless site of your cheerless youth."

"I thought so, too," her father said.

When he didn't elaborate, Judith's mother said, "Does this have anything to do with the house?"

The house was one that his grandparents had owned and, upon their death, left to him. It stood on a good-sized residential lot in town. Judith's mother had never seen the house, but when he inherited it she'd shuffled through a few photographs of the property and seen a tallish blockish house painted bright yellow and trimmed in a Kelly green that made her laugh. "Good taste takes a holiday," she'd said good-naturedly. "How soon can you sell?"

He hadn't sold, though. He'd kept and rented it, and now, on this June afternoon, sitting forward in his floral armchair, he said, "The renters moved out last month, so yes, that adds an element of convenience, but no, that's not why we'd be going."

Judith's mother gave him another severe look and left the room, but a few seconds later she abruptly returned and said, "If you take that job, Howard, Judith and I are not going with you."

Before her mother's sentence was complete, her father's gaze had begun turning toward Judith. Their eyes met for an instant, then his slid beyond her and he did something characteristic. He brought his fingertips together in front of his face, rested his chin on the joined thumbs, and set his joined fingers gently against his lips. It was his habitual attitude of contemplation, and though to a younger Judith it had suggested silent prayer, she now thought of it as the cage where he kept his thoughts locked.

And so he had gone to Nebraska, but Judith heard, or overheard, no talk of divorce, and there was no separation of goods (her father packed only a few cardboard boxes of clothes and books in the trunk of the Bonneville before leaving). These observations allowed Judith to view the change as temporary. Still, it was during these months that she began to plan her own life, how it might be constructed, of what kind of job, of what kind of house, and of what kind of husband, if any at all.

In her father's absence, Judith's daily routine evolved in unsettling ways. Meals were more haphazard; the house was a mess; bills lay unopened on bookcases and bathroom cabinets. For fourteen-year-old Judith, that her mother seemed happier didn't count for much. The telephone was intermittently out of service, and if Judith and her friends came to the house after school and found that Central Vermont Public Service had cut off the electricity, the only thing more mortifying to Judith than the unpaid bill was her mother's cheerful adaptation to it: as she lighted candles and fixed them in melted wax on pottery saucers, she would be chattering on about how, except for washing machines and possibly stereos, we'd all be better off without electricity anyway. Her mother was enthusiastically shedding her former life. She took a part-time job waitressing at the Satellite Coffee Shop and enrolled in an evening drama class, and when Judith and her friends exchanged their skirt-blouse-and-sweater combinations for miniskirts and tights, or T-shirts and thrift-shop Levi's, her mother began borrowing Judith's clothes. She let her hair grow long and straight as a folksinger's, and that spring, as the Vermont winter finally gave way, she stopped wearing hose and bras.

Judith had seen boys ogle her mother, and even wait to get one of her tables at the Satellite and leave twenty percent tips, and girls with whom Judith wanted to be friends—girls whose elevated status allowed them to look sportively upon girls like Judith and their mothers—were happy to report what boys might say about her. Judith laughed and pretended amusement, but she fooled no one. The stories kept coming, and her resentment swelled.

One day Judith approached a boy named Mack Stanton in the school cafeteria. Her body felt at once burnt and brittle. Mack Stanton was sitting among friends when Judith walked up and said, "So, where would your hands have to be at the time?"

Mack Stanton was known as a cool customer. He gave her a quizzical look and said, "Hold on, now. Where would what have to be when?"

Judith said, "You told Marjorie Williams you could get a hard-on just thinking about my mother, and when I heard that, I wondered where exactly your hands would have to be at the time."

The other boys at the table were suddenly one in their expectant grins. They looked at Mack Stanton, who tore a ragged section from his sandwich and popped it into his mouth. "Look," he said mildly, "this is the kind of thing that ought to be discussed in private, don't you think? Besides, it was, you know, kind of a *compliment*. I didn't mean anything by it."

Judith was unmoved. When Marjorie Williams had told her the tale in the C Wing bathroom, two girls she didn't know had stopped their own conversation and turned to listen, which just about doubled the humiliation factor. "Behind your back?" she said now to Mack Stanton. "Could you get a hard-on thinking of my mother with your hands behind your back? How about folded on top of your head? How about with a thumb in each ear, wagging your fingers like a jackass?"

Laughter worked the table, with Mack Stanton, red-faced, trying to join in.

"Because if you can get a hard-on thinking of my mom with a thumb in each ear, that would be a prime example of something definitely worth demonstrating."

When Mack Stanton didn't speak, she was satisfied. As she left, the laughter at the table turned raucous. She heard someone whoop, "Where would your hands be at the time?" and she understood that without question this would not be the last time these words would be flung her way. They would float with her through the school corridors and probably beyond.

As she walked, her skin felt like pudding. It was the sweat, she guessed. When she glanced down at her white top, she saw that the wetness under her arms had radiated halfway down her rib cage and was tinted a brackish yellow. Oh, she thought. Oh, how she hated Marjorie Williams and Mack Stanton and his sniggering friends and what they'd turned her into.

It took over an hour to walk home. Her mother sat on the front stoop wearing cut-off Levi's and a man's white sleeveless undershirt, painting minute blue flowers on her toenails. She sat in dappled sunlight that sifted through the just-leafing elm tree. She seemed happy. She looked pretty. She didn't remark on Judith's early homecoming. "Hi, princess," she said, and Judith, with just a flick of her eyes, said, "Couldn't you at least wear a bra when you're outside where anybody can see you?"

—⁓—

To prepare for the jibes and simpering grins she knew she'd be receiving at school, Judith stood before her bureau mirror and practiced a drop-dead look while saying things like "Are you a half-wit or just easily amused?" and "If I was the weatherman I'd call you a pocket of fog," phrases she imagined Don Rickles might use, but her heart wasn't really in it. She sensed something she would later be able to put into words: that her adolescence wasn't meant to play out in the spotlight; it was meant to be quiescent, transitional, pupal. She didn't want unpaid electric bills and she didn't want boys ogling her mother and she didn't want friends telling her that her mother had given them cigarettes and free fries at the Satellite and she didn't want boys using her presence as an excuse to ask someone nearby where their hands would have to be at the time. She didn't want attention of any kind. She wanted to lose herself in the book she was reading, or in the movie she was watching, or in the plans she was laying for the life she would one day lead.

What Judith decided was that her mother needed to start acting like her mother again, and this would occur only if her father came back and started acting like her father again. To this end, Judith arranged to spend the summer with her father in order to bring him back to Vermont—not that she said so.

"Is there some point to this visit?" asked her mother, who knew that with Judith, there was a point to everything.

"I just want to see him, that's all."

Her mother studied her a moment, but she was late for her shift at the Satellite. She began looking for her keys, which Judith found under a catalogue for summer recreation classes. At the door, her mother looked back. "You can visit if you want, but Judy, sweetie, don't do any plotting on my account."

"I'm not," Judith said in a peevish tone. She felt her skin flushing. "I just want to see him. Is that so terrible?"

Her mother smiled and said that nobody said it was.

—⁓—

The father Judith found in Nebraska was not quite the father she'd had in Vermont. He'd gotten slightly bulkier, for one thing, and he'd become a surprisingly good cook. He loved baking bread, especially challah, the braiding of which Judith herself quickly learned to enjoy. He'd taken up photography—black-and-whites of abandoned farmhouses and outbuildings were attached with clothespins to a line hung in the basement, where he'd built his makeshift darkroom—and he'd planted a tidy garden in the backyard. "You garden?" Judith said when he led her out to it, and he smiled and said, "Yes, well. It surprises me, too."

She regarded the house itself. It was her first good look at it—she'd arrived after dark the night before. "I thought it was bright yellow with green trim." The yellow now was pale and the trim was white. The shutters were painted a mossy green she found pretty. The work looked fresh.

"I only finished yesterday," he said, and brought the back of his hand close to his nose. "I still smell like turpentine." Then, looking again at the house: "Do you like it?"

Judith did, and said so. She also made a mental note to send a picture of it to her mother in Vermont. Her mother would like the house better now that it wasn't those garish colors. Maybe she would want to move here, if Judith's father couldn't move back home. One element was common to both houses. Here, as in Vermont, her father liked to read in an overstuffed armchair covered with red floral fabric. Judith thought he might have bought it because it reminded him of his chair back home, but no, he said this chair had belonged to his grandparents and in fact he'd bought the one in Vermont because it had reminded him of this one.

Judith and her father fell easily into a routine. In the morning, her father sliced fresh bread for cinnamon or French toast, and when she saw him pouring cream from a little tin pitcher into his mug of percolated coffee, she wanted that, too, though she preferred such a large proportion of cream that it turned the coffee cool and caramel-colored. Her father also consumed a small dish of prunes every morning for regularity, which he prized. (Judith said she'd take constipation over prunes any day of the week.) Before the morning turned hot, they went out to the garden to pull weeds and hand-pick snails and harvest tomatoes and butter lettuce as well as beets, which her father had learned to pickle. They cleaned house together and marketed together and for lunch ate bacon, lettuce, and tomato sandwiches on toasted bread. Afterward they napped and read for an hour or so. Midafternoon, they walked to the pool in War Memorial Park, where Judith swam laps and sunned and covertly watched older boys while her father sat in the shade and read, sipping iced coffee, hunching close to his text, bracketing phrases and making marginal comments in a tight, tiny hand. College girls would come to his table, often in wet swimsuits, and Judith would wonder what her father might be saying that could make girls who at the other end of the pool seemed to jingle with laughter turn so still.

Before Judith had arrived, her father had sought out information about various activities she might be interested in—youth programs in dance and gymnastics; a drama camp at Fort

Robinson; a three-day teen archeology dig at Toadstool Park—but Judith wasn't interested in mingling, and in fact soon came to rely on her father's regimen. Monday nights they went to Brun's Coin Laundry (though she didn't like the commingling of their clothes and having to fold her underthings in public), and because Judith loved movies, they went to the Eagle Theater every Wednesday and Sunday night, when the movies changed, unless it was something Judith guessed would make her queasy watching with her father (she ruled out *Carnal Knowledge,* for example). Tuesday nights her father taught a summer course on Jane Austen, during which time Judith read or walked or, most often, watched reruns of *I Dream of Jeannie, Bewitched,* or *Truth or Consequences* on Channel 11 from Denver. Normally she didn't answer the telephone, but once or twice, when she did, a girl's voice would register surprise and say, "Oh, I was trying to get Professor Toomey." Occasionally her father would answer the ringing phone and listen a few moments before saying courteously, "Let me give you my office hours. We can discuss it then." Other evenings he made a single large gin and tonic (usually with complaint about the hard-skinned limes available locally), brought it to the living room, and sat in his look-alike chair, where he read *Pride and Prejudice* to her in his low rich baritone. One night, after he finished a chapter and marked his place, Judith said, "Will I ever be like Elizabeth Bennet?" and her father released a puff of air through his lips, his version of a laugh. "Once, when you were ten or eleven, you asked your mother if you would ever be a bathing beauty." He let his eyes settle calmly on Judith. "This is a much better question."

She was stretched out barefooted on a sofa upholstered with worn green velvet. Dusk had come on during the reading, and the room was dim and cool. She said, "Did you used to read to Mom?"

He had, he said, before they were married, and afterward, for a while. "But then . . . things intervened." He smiled. "Parenting, for example."

"I like it when you read," she said, because she did, but then, with the same innate calculation she would later notice in her own daughter, she said, "You know, if we bought a washing machine, we could read Monday nights, too."

Her father smiled and sipped his gin and said maybe he would start watching the classifieds.

—⁂—

Judith slept in the large concrete basement of the house, where several rooms, including her father's darkroom, had been improvised through construction of partitioning walls. When Judith arrived, the room allotted her was bare except for a worn Persian carpet on the floor and a cot and some old wooden crates, recently cleaned. A promotional calendar from Eitemiller Oil Company featuring a hunter and his dog before a local butte hung on one wall above a two-tiered glassed bookcase, its upper shelf half filled with a dozen or so old copies of books acquired secondhand for her by her father—*Pride and Prejudice,* for example, *Anna Karenina, Tess of the D'Urbervilles.* After breakfast on Judith's third or fourth day in the house, her father led her to a lean-to shed built onto the rear of the garage. He cleared cobwebs with a broom handle and shined a light inside so that Judith could get her first glimpse of the bird's-eye maple bedroom furniture. Plastic sheeting meant to protect the chest of drawers had yellowed and somehow become an encrusted part of the veneer. Elsewhere the layering dust on the furniture's flat surfaces had darkened to grime and was dotted with rodent droppings.

Her father said, "Needs some help, doesn't it?"

Judith said, "What it needs is some blind men to haul it away."

She leaned in and was met by the thick fusty smell of dead rodents. "Blind men who are also hard of smelling."

It took them most of two weeks to restore the furniture—filling the scars and tiny holes, sanding, finishing, sanding, finishing, sanding again. They drank lemonade. Sometimes they would talk, but often they were quiet. Judith broke one of these silences by saying, "You lived in this house when you were in high school?"

"Yes." Her father looked up at the house. "It hasn't changed that much. The color now is close to what it was then." His gaze shifted toward his garden. "The garden's right where my grandmother's used to be."

"Did you like it here?" she said, because she knew he had not.

Her father took a sip of lemonade. "As much as I could've liked anywhere I'd been at the time."

"I thought you hated it."

He seemed amused by this assertion. "Did I tell you that?" he said, and Judith knew he knew he had not. It had come from her mother, as almost all the authoritative assertions did.

"A student of mine said it was a *sincere* house, and that seemed the right word." He pointed out the foundation and back porch made of red sandstone blocks cut by stonemasons in Hot Springs, South Dakota. "You don't get work like that anymore," he said. "The rock's still there, but the stonemasons are gone."

Judith, on the verge of sulking, said nothing. What bothered her was the almost certain fact that the student who'd commented on the house was a girl. No boy would call a house *sincere*.

Judith and her father worked on quietly for a quarter-hour, and he said, "Did you know that this furniture has a history?"

Judith's sourness hadn't lifted; she gave a bored shrug.

The story, which Judith initially pretended to ignore, was this. In 1879, the furniture before them had been crated by A. A.

Copeland & Sons of Philadelphia and shipped to Rufus Sage by rail. Harry Toomey, Judith's great-great-grandfather and the town surveyor, had hauled the packing crates from the station to a farm owned by a friend, where the furniture was stowed in a barn. The furniture was identical to the set his young wife had seen while visiting a family friend in Des Moines. She'd gone so far as to write to the company, whose response she had handed with trepidation to her husband. He had looked at it long enough to memorize what it said, then folded it and dropped it into the fire. He was sorry, he said, but buying furnishings they couldn't afford wouldn't give their marriage a good beginning. Harry Toomey was an absentminded man. He forgot birth dates, he forgot names, and he was not above playing this forgetfulness to his own advantage. When the day came that marked the first anniversary of his marriage to Christianna Gardner, he let most of the day pass without notice. Early evening, Christianna carried the *Rufus Sage Record* and a covered dish to her great-uncle, a widower who lived three doors down the street, something she did every night of the week. While there, she visited perfunctorily, straightened the house, and washed the day's dishes. This generally took thirty to forty minutes. During this time Harry Toomey and two friends set to work. They took away the Toomeys' crude bedroom furniture and replaced it with the fine bird's-eye maple. By the time Christianna returned from her great-uncle's, the bed was made, all of their clothes were neatly folded into the drawers of the chiffonier, and Harry Toomey sat by the fire reading, just as he had been when she'd left forty minutes before. Christianna went into the bedroom to put down her purse, as he knew she would. He didn't speak or follow her into the bedroom. She was in the bedroom perhaps five minutes. When she came back out, her face was pink and discomposed, as if she'd been crying. She said one sentence: "I knew you wouldn't forget."

33

When he was done, Judith's father waited a second or two and said, "Do you like that story?"

"I guess," Judith said.

Her father made the smallest nod. "I do, too."

"That man Harry Toomey who bought the furniture for his wife," Judith said. "Did they stay happy and married?"

Her father shrugged. "I hope so. They stayed married, I know that."

A breeze stirred. A truck could be heard downshifting on Highway 20, a few blocks north. Judith said, "You haven't once asked how things are at home."

Her father smiled but didn't look up from his work. "How are things at home?"

Judith didn't like being made sport of, and it gave her response a sullen edge. "It's like she wants to be my age."

In a mild voice her father said, "Whereas Judith wants to be hers."

Judith didn't think this was fair at all. "She borrows my clothes," she said. "She asks my friends to call her Katie. She offers them cigarettes. She buys Grand Funk Railroad albums."

Something just short of a chuckle escaped from her father, which incensed Judith. "She doesn't wear bras. A boy at school told someone he gets a hard-on just looking at her."

"Ah," her father said, and if he was shocked, as Judith had intended, he didn't reveal it. He was quiet for a while, and then he said, "People separated from their spouses . . . they're almost like stroke victims. They have to learn everything over again." He refolded his sandpaper and stared at the wood he was working on. "I can tell you from personal experience that the way we get around at the beginning isn't always pretty."

What was he talking about? What was he saying? "But this is just temporary, isn't it? You being here and us being there? Either

34

you're going to come back home or Mom and I'll come out here, isn't that right?"

She was glad he had the sandpaper in one hand so he couldn't put his fingertips together and make the cage he kept his thoughts in, or at least she thought she was glad, but then she wasn't, because when he couldn't look into his thoughts, he looked instead at Judith, and she saw in his eyes more uncertainty than she had ever seen there before.

"Maybe," he said. "I don't know."

"You don't know? If you don't know, who does?"

His eyes slid away from hers and he began again to sand. Judith stalked into the house. A half-hour later she peeked out. Her father was still seated in the same place, in the same attitude, evenly sanding the bird's-eye maple.

—m—

Once they'd refinished the bedroom set, carried it to the basement room, and purchased a mattress from Midwest Furniture, Judith and her father began scouring farm auctions for the kind of quilt Judith wanted as a bedspread, and one Saturday morning, on a farm southwest of town, they found it, a like-new quilt intricately composed of blues, yellows, and greens in thirties prints. Judith had read enough about quilts to know their patterns had names, and when she asked the auction's cashier about the quilt's history, she was directed to the widow who was selling the house and farm in preparation for a move to the retirement home in Rufus Sage. She was sitting by herself at the fringe of the crowd, eating pie from a paper plate.

"It's called Young Man's Fancy," the woman told Judith. "I made it for my husband the winter before we were married." She lifted a corner of the quilt and brought it within an inch of her eye for a last inspection. "It's a nice tight stitch," she said in a whispery voice, "better than six to an inch." Judith felt a sudden sense of intrusion, and her father seemed to feel it, too, because he said, "We'd like for you to keep it," but the woman quickly dropped the quilt from her hands and raised her eyes. She squinted, as if from an unexpected introduction of light. "It turned out my husband didn't care for the quilt—he thought it was too prissy. My husband . . ." She smiled, shook her head, and stared off, as if trying to compose the sentence that might set before them the exact nature of her fifty-three-year marriage. "He was a good provider," she said, then paused again and finally gave up. She said, "I'm glad you'll have it, missy."

When Judith spread the quilt over the bird's-eye maple bed, it was so beautiful that as she stepped back to look at it composed with the blond furniture and the deep reds and blues of the Persian rug, she began secretly to hope that this was what her own honeymoon cottage might someday look like—a notion she revisited throughout the summer, even though she knew the idea was embarrassingly conventional.

3

In Toluca Lake, the furniture still stood at the edge of the pool. It had been there a week now, and every day Judith vowed to make the time to do something about it, but the season was off to an ominous start—already they were reshooting scenes, shortening the time between the shoot and air dates—and she had worked long days right through the weekend. The bedsheets covering the furniture were now littered with fading bougainvillea bracts. Before Malcolm left for work this morning, he slid a note under Judith's cup next to the coffeemaker: *Re the bird's-eye maple, shall I call in the army?* His joke term for the Salvation Army.

Judith had a schedule. She would sleep until Malcolm's 5:50 departure for the gym or tennis club, the two sites of his daily pre-banking workout, then she would put on her robe and, before Camille and the nanny were up, poach an egg, section a pink grapefruit, toast a thick slice of artisan bread, and drink Peet's coffee from a delft blue china cup set on a delft blue china saucer. This was her ritual, one that positioned the day for good effects. But now there was this note, and Judith's response was resentful.

The Salvation Army?

This was where Malcolm thought the furniture should go? Why did he loathe the stuff so much? She'd once asked him that very question, and when he'd looked at her with calm eyes and said, "Why do you love it so much?" she'd had the sudden alarming notion that his reason for hating it and hers for liking it might be one and the same. That he knew nothing of the furniture beyond its general family history wouldn't necessarily keep him from sensing that its importance to her went beyond that to something more specific.

Judith flipped over the slip of paper and wrote, *No need, I'll make arrangements,* and hurried off to the studio.

For the past three years, she had been working on a critically respected television drama about an earnest yet winsome college girl with a social conscience and lots of problems with her great-looking boyfriends and roommates (Judith never knew which was more stunning, their god-and-goddess looks or their disinterest in the most basic acting technique). She loved the job, especially when she was tucked away in the editing room, but it wasn't as if she didn't have to look over her shoulder. She was answerable not only to the director of the episode at hand, but also to Mick Hooper, the wiry, semimanic, and omnipresent associate producer who ran the post department, and Leo Pottle, the show's producer, with whom she'd previously worked. Pottle in fact had been the one to bring her on, and Judith in turn had brought on Lucy Meynke.

The morning's work proceeded efficiently, and a noon-hour sound-spotting session with the sound supervisor went so quickly that, with Lucy on the Avid burning a DVD for the director of the last episode and both Mick Hooper and Leo Pottle off the lot, Judith saw her chance to investigate the storage yard she had telephoned a few days before. It was a clear day, with actual massed clouds, unusual for Los Angeles in July, and as Judith wheeled out of the studio parking lot, she felt at once released. *No joy like the truant's joy.* Willy Blunt had said that.

On La Cienega, she turned up the CD in the changer. It was

Warren Zevon, a personal favorite. Judith kept singing along as an accompaniment, but it was just as she sang "gorilla" she saw, at a stoplight, a nearby driver—a man in a suit—seemed to be wondering if she were deranged, so she fell quiet until the light changed and the man was safely beyond her. Then she began to sing again, though not as freely as before, and finally she gave it up and listened to NPR for the duration of the ride.

Red Roof Mini-Storage, it turned out, was a two-acre compound of pink cinder-block buildings that plenty of sun, salt air, and neglect had given a blasted look. The iron frontage fence was blotched with rust, Bermuda grass grew from cracks in the asphalt, and the red of the metal roofs had dulled to something faintly orange. But Judith was paying for storage, not curb appeal, and besides, places like this held a kind of noir charm for her. Red Roof Mini-Storage, she thought, was the kind of place you'd be happy to find if you were driving around with a body stuffed in your trunk.

Judith was dressed as she normally dressed for work: light-weight cotton and flax in beiges and blacks, sandals without hose, and just enough jewelry—a double-chain gold necklace that looped over her chest—to indicate legitimate economic standing. As she got out of her car, a seagull screamed. She hadn't seen the gull, and it wasn't an actual scream, she knew that—it was just the shrill call of a common shorebird—but it had entered her ear as a human scream would. She waited for the sound to come again, and when it did, in a series of staccato bursts, it sounded like mimicry of raucous laughter.

Inside the Red Roof office, a slim, slouchy boy with combed-back black hair watched her approach the counter and waited for her to explain herself. She wanted storage space for some old furniture, she said. She wasn't exactly sure for how long or of what size, but it shouldn't be too small.

The boy looked at her and nodded. His eyes were deeply brown, nothing like Willy Blunt's pale blue, and yet their peering-in-from-a-distance quality reminded her of Willy Blunt. The boy was faintly handsome—every boy who reminded Judith of Willy was faintly handsome (or maybe it was even more gymnastic than that; maybe any boy Judith could think of as handsome had first to remind her in some slight way of Willy Blunt).

The boy lifted a hinged section of the counter and led her outside to a faded red golf cart to show her what was available. The cart was shabby, but its quietness pleased Judith, and the little cooling breeze that slipped into her clothes caught her off-guard, hinted at some past childhood sensation—coasting barefooted on a bicycle, maybe.

The boy wore khaki slacks and shoes of an intricate weave of soft leather, without socks. His bare ankles were brown and smooth, like a Pakistani's, Judith thought (though she knew no Pakistanis). She extended her legs, relaxed into a position just slightly more recumbent, and gazed at the sights. Most of the doors were locked and closed, but in one building, a man in a sweat-darkened T-shirt was packing neon-colored teddy bears into plastic bags; in another, a group of boys wearing huge earphones stood amid a tangle of wires playing electrified guitars and keyboards only they could hear; and, further along, an obese woman was silkscreening dancing bears on aprons. If any of these people were happy, it would come as a surprise to Judith.

She said to her driver, "Did you hear about the woman who killed her husband and stashed him in a mini-storage in San Bernardino?"

The boy kept his eyes straight ahead and said no, he hadn't.

Judith said, "She had him there three years." The boy said nothing, but she could tell he was paying attention. "She got caught when she forgot to pay the rent."

The boy gave a muffled snort, then stopped and pointed up to storage compartment 142C, which he described as a twelve-by-twelve-by-twelve overhead.

The story about the stored husband was true, or at least Judith presumed it was true. She'd heard it this past winter when she, Malcolm, and Camille had spent a skiing weekend in Big Bear. They'd gone up on a Friday, and the next morning they were driving to Snow Summit when the story was reported on NPR's local news. Malcolm laughed and said, "If that's not made for a made-for-TV movie, I couldn't say what is."

Judith, in holiday spirits, said, "Really? It sounds like Merchant and Ivory to me." (The truth was, she thought the Coen brothers could probably do something with it.)

Camille sat in the back seat. She'd been silent for perhaps five minutes when she said, "Do only stupid people kill people?"

Immediately Malcolm said, "That's right, Miss Pie. Only really stupid people kill people. Smart people talk, and if they can no longer talk, they walk away."

It was a perfectly good answer, Judith had seen this at once. In Camille's worldview, nothing was worse than being stupid, unless it was wearing clothes purchased at Ross Dress for Less. Malcolm understood this and had tried to fit a sturdy moral into Camille's Tinker Toy value system. Who knew what Judith, alone and upon reflection, would have said? *Of those who kill and get caught, a higher than normal percentage are stupid?* Or (as, to her surprise, she really believed), *Only stupid people get caught killing other people?*

The faded red cart was heading up an alley toward the office. They'd looked at five different storage units, several too small and one, the one she kept thinking about, too big. When they'd gone back to look at that unit—17C—she'd noticed an electrical outlet, and the boy said it was a small, something-amp circuit. Twelve, maybe. Now, to make conversation, Judith said, "So what do you do if you break into a delinquent unit and find yourself faced with a cadaver?"

The boy said, "Besides ask for a raise?"

Judith laughed, which in no way affected the boy's expression. "Yeah," she said. "Besides that."

The boy let a second or two pass, then said, "Dead bodies never came up during orientation."

Judith laughed again and turned to look at the boy in profile. "That's funny."

The boy gave a bland nod that made Judith realize he hadn't been going for humor and wondered why she might think he had. It was true she was feeling a little odd.

When they returned to the office, Judith surprised herself by saying she would take the twelve-by-twenty walk-in, the big one, bigger than she really needed. When faced with the price, she said, "Yikes," in a voice meant to be playful.

The boy took it for actual resistance. "There's a five percent discount for six months' advance rent," he said. "Ten percent if you pay cash."

He pushed the registration form in front of her. Judith hadn't given her name when she'd come in, hadn't given the boy her card. She was carrying cash. She didn't need to write a check. A name came to her, and Judith watched with a kind of surprised amusement as the blue ink flowed from the pen in her hand.

The boy spun the card around, scanned it, and looked up.

"Edie Winks?"

"That's right," said Judith, aware that her whole body had stiffened. (This, she thought later, is why lie detectors work on your typical citizen.) "I mean, technically it's Edith," she said, recovering a little, "but I always go by Edie."

The boy nodded, but kept looking at the signature.

42

Judith heard herself say, "We've traced the family back to the isle of St. Kilda." An island Camille had wanted to visit, where the people once lived on puffins.

Judith thought she saw the boy flick a glance at her left hand.

"It's my husband's name, actually. My maiden name is Winterbottom." She'd known a Winterbottom once, but really, where was all this coming from? "You can imagine the fun my school chums had with that."

Here the boy's eyes rose from the registration form and took on a long-distance glaze—maybe it was *school chums;* who under the age of sixty said *school chums?*—and just like that the boy was gone, off to that place where bored teenage boys go, a place, Judith guessed, chock-full of cars with loud engines and girls with big breasts.

Judith opened her purse and started counting out money. The boy opened a receipt book and began copying the name from the application. He said that the first time the circuit breaker threw, there was a fifty-dollar charge; the second time, seventy-five. "So don't try any microwaves or anything."

"How about a lamp?" Judith said, and the boy said, "Two sixty-watt bulbs, max." He looked at her blandly. "If you need more juice, you'll need to go to a different unit."

Both were then silent until Judith pointed to one of a set of five different padlocks mounted on a wall behind the boy. "And I'll get that big Master lock," she said, pointing.

The boy pulled a fresh box from beneath the counter. He slid out the lock and displayed it to Judith, who nodded and pushed another twenty-dollar bill into her cash pile.

Two keys were attached to a thin spring ring, along with a promotional red plastic tag in the shape of a roof. The boy said, "Some customers like us to keep a key in case they lose theirs."

Judith had no intention of leaving the key to her storage unit

43

in the hands of this boy, or anyone else, for that matter. "It's okay," she said, taking the ring with both keys. "I don't lose things."

The boy, letting his eyes fall on Judith, blinked so slowly that Judith imagined it in film slowed to thirty frames, so subtly stretched that the viewer could hardly notice. Certainly in her movie that's how she would shoot it, to acknowledge the unconscious traps we set for the opposite sex. But that was her own editorial tinkering, because the boy merely said, "No worries, then," and began counting out her change.

—m—

After taking a last look at her storage unit and securing the door with her new lock, Judith walked to the parking lot, turned on the engine, and let the air conditioning pour into the car. From the moment she'd gotten on that golf cart, something had come over her, an expansion of possibility, something odd and enlivening. *Vivifying.* Malcolm had said that to her once. *You are strangely vivifying.* Judith flipped open her cell phone, thinking to call him, but she didn't. She dialed 411 and heard herself ask for William C. Blunt, possibly in Nebraska. After the barest moment, the operator said in a flat voice, "I have that number in North Platte. May I connect you?"

Judith said she could.

A woman answered on the second ring.

"I'm from the Rufus Sage Chamber of Commerce," Judith said, "and we're contacting past residents regarding next year's Fur Trade Days. Is Mr. Blunt in?"

"He'll be back in a bit," the woman said. "Did you say Rufus Sage?"

"Right, Rufus Sage. Did Mr. Blunt ever live in Rufus Sage?"

"Not that he mentioned, but ..." The woman caught herself up. "Who is this again?"

44

"Did he ever go by the name of Willy?"

"His name's William," the woman said. "We call him Bill. Now who are you again?"

"Edie Winks."

"And what's your number?"

Judith idiotically said, "Thank you," and hung up, feeling terrifically slimy. She speed-dialed Malcolm, who answered with a calm "Hello."

"It's me," she said. "Feeling lonely. What're you doing?"

"Miss Metcalf and I are touring tilt-ups in the industrial cityscape."

Tilt-ups, Judith knew from past conversations with Malcolm, were warehouses and office complexes whose sides were composed of poured concrete and then tilted up into place, or something like that. As for Miss Francine Metcalf, Judith had met her many times. She was the bank's chief loan officer, a position she'd held in every bank Malcolm had run. She evidently did good work—Malcolm often referred to her as "the exemplary Miss Metcalf"—and Judith had thought that if she were the jealous type she could imagine Miss Metcalf as attractive, but Judith wasn't, so when she thought of this woman, she thought only of the loud geometric designs Miss Metcalf favored in clothes and the coarse, mouse-colored hair that seemed always to have the mashed look of the just-awakened. "How important is this field trip you're on?" Judith asked.

"Not terribly. Why?"

"Lucy's doing dailies and Hooper and Pottle are putting out other fires, so I wouldn't exactly be missed for the next two hours." Judith glanced at her watch, and in a slightly friskier voice, one not quite her own, she said, "I could meet you at One Pico at three, and I could have a room key." One Pico was a tony restaurant attached to a beachfront hotel called Shutters, to which

45

they'd been given a good-sized gift certificate by the bank board at Christmas.

Judith expected Malcolm to regretfully decline—he wasn't the type either to ditch work or to expend a luxury-room chit for an impulsive hour or two—but he surprised her.

"It's possible you're a telepath," he said with perfect equanimity. "That's a property I've been dying to see."

Judith didn't speak for a few seconds, during which a blooming excitement allowed her to cast herself as Edie Winks on the phone with a wry, handsome man of means, a man not her own husband but someone else's. "Let's make it two forty-five," she said, "and forget the restaurant. Just come up to the room."

Half an hour later, Judith was wearing a white hotel robe, lying on a four-poster bed in a breezy third-floor room overlooking a wide white-sand beach, wondering how this had all come about. She wasn't sure and she didn't care. She'd slipped outside of her life, that was all she needed to know. A door had swung open and she had stepped through. She'd thought of lying naked on the bed when Malcolm walked in, but a few minutes of waiting without clothes on had made her feel too self-aware (her thighs felt suddenly heavy, and when she glanced at her stretch marks, they seemed like white scars), so she put on the plush terrycloth robe hanging in the bathroom. She opened the balcony doors, tied back the drapes, and left the sheers to flutter. She checked the hotel's spiral-bound informational notebook to determine her emergency exit route, flipped through an in-room magazine—*Islands*—then lay back and closed her eyes. The hum and calls of the beach crowd floated lazily through the open balcony doors. She thought she heard a girl say, "I just saw Patrick Swayze," and a boy seemed to say, "Whose Uzi is this?" In the outside corridor, a cart rolled past the door. Two women spoke in Spanish and laughed. Later she would wonder how she had lazed so freely when she should have been at work, but at the moment it all felt slightly and pleasantly foreign.

Outside, a shrill commotion of seagulls erupted (she imagined someone lobbing remnants of a sandwich), then a general suspension of voices, the solid *ka-whump* of a wave, and the calls and happy screams resumed again. But the seagulls. In *The Birds,* weren't they all seagulls? Rod what's his name, and chilly Tippi Hedren. Hitchcock's chilly girls. Chilly Tippi Hedren and chilly Eva Marie Saint and chilly Grace Kelly and chilly Kim Novak, everybody in the darkened theater, man and woman alike, hoping the leading man would melt her down. Rod *Taylor.* That's who. After somebody bigger wanted too much money or something. Cary Grant, maybe.

Her mind moved to the plastic red-roof key tag, which pleased her in some way she couldn't explain. She sat up and felt for the keys in her purse. She unfolded the receipt that enclosed them— *Edie Winks, Unit 17C*—and turned over the red plastic tag in her hand, the Red Roof address and telephone number on one side, the company motto on the other: *Your Safe Under the Red Roof.* Was that a typo? Or did it mean that your storage room was your safe? *Postage Prepaid. Mail to Red Roof Storage.* The keys themselves were sturdy, and for a few moments she gently sawed the toothed side of one across her bare arm and let her mind go empty. She was in this state when the quick click of a key card at the door gave her a start. She slid the receipt and keys into the gap of the hotel's spiral-bound directory, then—the door still hadn't opened—she lay back, closed her eyes, and pretended composure.

She listened to the solid latch of the door, the tap of heels on the hard floor, then soft footsteps on carpet. This reminded her of a time with Willy Blunt, a time she had waited for him in her basement room, and then it reminded her of nothing else at all. These could be anybody's footsteps. This occurred to her.

47

Everything turned still then, completely still, except for the rising pulse of her own heart, and finally it was too much for her—she had to open her eyes.

Malcolm stood looking down at her.

She was surprised how deflating his presence was. She felt she could smell his smell before she actually smelled it, could hear his voice before she heard it.

"Do I have the right room?" he said. Relentlessly wry. She had said this to someone. *My husband is relentlessly wry.*

"You need a scotch," she said.

He made a thin smile. "I do? I didn't think I drank scotch."

She found a single-malt in the minibar, poured it into a tumbler, and, after sampling it herself, handed it to Malcolm, who said, "I not only drink it but drink it neat."

He sipped the scotch and while loosening his tie said, "I'm afraid your telephone call effected a certain *tumefaction* that I feared would become observable and perhaps misconstrued by the exemplary Miss Metcalf."

Judith smiled but didn't laugh. She rearranged herself on the bed and closed her eyes, and when he again started to speak she said, "Don't talk."

She felt the depression of his knee on the mattress. She detected the faint smell of scotch. She did not open her eyes. As he loosened and laid back the folds of the robe, she felt a rising expectancy that seemed almost tidal. Things started quickly and moved easily past the usual restraints. She was not quite herself. She had an unusually good time.

Afterward, Malcolm said, "Indeed."

Judith laughed, and said, "Sound to the deaf, sight to the blind." Words she'd spoken before to Malcolm, words borrowed from Willy Blunt, not that Malcolm needed to know that. They lay quiet for a few minutes—it seemed to Judith like the reluctant waking from a pleasing dream—then Malcolm leaned from the bed and slipped his phone from his coat pocket. He glanced at Judith. "I'm not calling work," he said. "I'm calling Sonya."

Sonya was the latest nanny (though Malcolm called her their *familial assistant*), but Sonya didn't answer the phone. Camille did, and Malcolm's expression brightened. "Miz Milla," he said. "It's your pop figure. What're you literally doing?" A pause, then: "And what literally is cooking? I think I smell meat loaf. Do I smell meat loaf?"

It was Wednesday. Sonya was from Hutchinson, Kansas, which in conversation she abbreviated to Hutch. Every Wednesday Sonya made the most delectable meat loaf, a scheduling pattern that Camille had detected before anyone else—she would have no trouble seeing through her father's present ruse. Into the phone Malcolm was saying, "That's not true! It's because of my highly evolved sense of smell. Can I not, for example, smell a Baskin-Robbins from five hectometers?"

Judith walked naked toward the bathroom. Possibly her backside was her better side—she still had the long legs, and her bum (Malcolm's term, and now hers) was still pert. She sensed a break in Malcolm's patter and dimly felt his gaze, but it meant nothing now. She drew a bath—the tub was set in white marble and separated from the bedroom by hinged windows she left closed—and added a bubbling agent from a surprisingly heavy glass decanter. By the time she turned the water off, Malcolm had called the bank and was in discussion of somebody's loan application. "Of course we want the loan, Henry, but we have to have her K-1s," he said, and Judith quit listening.

A minute or two later, Malcolm appeared fully dressed in the door and said he had to go, smallish crisis but crisis nonetheless. Judith smiled. He looked happy, dapper, businesslike—blue coat, red tie, gray pants, all just so. He kissed her on the forehead and said, "Loan committee tonight, so I'll be ten-ish." He glanced back into the room before returning his eyes to her. "Sorry to leave the love nest."

When she heard the door shut, she let her eyes close. Baskin-Robbins, pink and brown, always reminded her of the first time she laid eyes on Willy Blunt, though at the time she didn't know his name—he was just a roofer whose smooth brown arms flowed from a sleeveless red T-shirt so old it had faded to pink. She had been with her father then, on Cordelia Guest's farm. A long time ago.

From the phone by the tub, Judith dialed room service for the applewood smoked salmon and creamed spinach. "And I'm in the tub," she said, "so I'd appreciate your sending the tray up with a girl."

They sent a lanky boy whose heavy black-framed glasses were a terrible mistake. She slid down below the suds and allowed him to set the food where she wanted it, on the marble that edged the tub. When she looked up from signing the slip, she caught him glancing into the water. This made him blush, which Judith found disarming. Behind his glasses, his eyes had the watery diffusion of someone fighting a cold. She nodded toward her purse and asked the boy to hand it to her. It took her a few seconds to find a five-dollar bill. When she extended the money to the boy, he was glancing again. "You know," she said, "you should be paying me."

His face pinkened.

Again Judith found herself thinking that something had come over her. She felt happy, playful, not sexual—clearly that had been an earlier element, but Malcolm had taken care of that. No, she felt like an escapee. She again closed her eyes.

"Thank you, ma'am."

"You're welcome."

She listened for the solid clatch of the door closing behind him on his way out. With his big eyes and big bobbing Adam's apple and big black-framed glasses, the boy didn't fit her idea of a psychopath, but then, if this were a movie of a certain type, that would have been the very hint that he was—who didn't suspect, for example, that Norman Bates was more than merely shy? In this type of movie, the boy with the big black-framed glasses would have opened and closed the door *without leaving*, would at this moment be standing very still within the next room, realizing that he'd just done something all but irreversible and wondering what exactly he meant to do next.

"Hello?" Judith said experimentally, and heard nothing in return.

A cheerfully whistled version of "Ob-La-Di, Ob-La-Da" carried from the boardwalk. And then something else, or so she thought. A subtle rustling sound.

Judith slipped lower in the tub, held her breath, and again tried to detect a living presence in the other room, someone who, standing there perfectly still and with eyes wide open, might be trying to guess at her exact location, condition, capabilities—in other words, her emotional whereabouts. *Good luck,* she thought. *Good fucking luck.*

A noise from the other room. A sniffle. A faint truncated sniffle. Was that what it was?

Judith sat rigid, listening, until she convinced herself she'd heard nothing at all.

Sometimes she worried that it was the movies that made us view the world this way, movies and the local news. At a party she'd once stood in a small circle of people that included Janet Leigh, who said that since the stabbing scene she'd never again taken a shower behind a transparent curtain. Janet Leigh had seemed used to an attentive audience, and she seemed used to telling this tale. Someone, a small-time producer, a woman, mentioned having heard that Hitchcock gave his leading women a tiny ivory comb for use "on the nether parts," and Judith had receded from the circle. And yet she couldn't quite shed the implication of Janet Leigh's words. How images manufactured by others, perhaps for the sake of artistry, but more usually as a commercial necessity, could manipulate your expectations of the real world.

Again the sniffling sound, or something like it.

Oh for God's sake, she thought, and rose from the tub. She wrapped herself in a towel, took the heavy glass decanter in hand, and crept into the other room. There was no one there, of course. The sheer curtains billowed and shushed. She checked the narrow balcony beyond the doors. There was nothing, no one. Though a slight surprise did occur. When a peripheral movement drew Judith's attention, she found herself staring into her own startled expression. The woman in the mirror, wrapped in a towel, decanter in hand, seemed like someone interesting, and for two or three seconds she stood perfectly still, not even breathing, trying to get a lasting look at this woman, whoever she was, before she again disappeared.

Judith put on the hotel robe and took her tray of food to the white wicker table on the balcony. The sounds of the ocean and children at play, dimmed somewhat within the room, here were full-throated. When her spinach bowl was finished, she sopped up the last of the cream sauce with French bread. She felt as if she'd been dropped into the hypervivid world of commercial advertisement, where all the senses seem dilated, all tastes and sensations emboldened. She wished she'd ordered coffee, and was thinking of ordering it, along with a scoop of strawberry ice cream sprinkled with slivered almonds, when her cell phone rang.

It was Lucy Meynke, talking in a lowered voice. "The Pothole's on site and wondering why you're not," she said. The Pothole being Lucy's joke name for Leo Pottle. "He seems actually kind of pissed off."

Judith glanced at her watch. Pottle knew she was a go-to cutter, no job too hard, no hours too long, and good value besides—but still, what was she thinking? She had had no idea it was this late. She hurried into her clothes, grabbed her purse, and gave the room one quick look before closing the door. Several hours would pass before she would realize that she'd left behind the keys to Unit 17C of Red Roof Mini-Storage.

4

Judith's father found the classified ad for a washing machine one night while reading the *Rufus Sage Record* in his red floral armchair. "Seventy-five dollars," he read aloud to Judith, "like new," and two days later they were driving west on Highway 20 toward the farmstead where the washer was for sale. Judith gazed out at the farms, green with alfalfa, yellow with wheat, and said, "It's pretty flat, isn't it?"

Her father smiled and said, "That's what they said to Columbus."

Judith didn't think much of the attempted humor, but still, he was in a good mood, which was the only time to bring up serious subjects. "But don't you miss Vermont?" she said.

"I do," he said. "Sometimes keenly."

Just like that, what had been sunny in his face was now somber. Judith made her voice small. "Do you miss us?"

"Mmm. I miss you especially."

"And Mom?"

He stared straight ahead for a time before letting his face soften slightly and turning to her. "Yes. I miss your mother, too."

Not exactly a posted Notice of Intention to Reconcile, Judith thought, but it was better than nothing. She said, "So what's your favorite single memory of Mom?"

A silence developed, and Judith was wondering if he'd heard

the question or was just ignoring it when he said, "Once, soon after we met, we were in the Reynolds Club"—he smiled—"where every Wednesday was Shake Day, all milkshakes thirty cents, and your mother set aside her straw and said, 'Sometimes I think of a cover of a book as a door to another world . . . but other times I think of it as an escape hatch from this one.' And then she blinked and said, 'I guess it's the same thing.'" He gave Judith a mild glance. "I always thought it possible that I fell in love with her within the space of that blink."

Judith took the story and held it tight as a child might hold a found smooth stone.

Then her father, glancing ahead, said, "We're looking for a green mailbox marked *Guest*."

When they sighted it, they turned up a straight dirt lane that pointed past two or three neglected outbuildings toward a dirty white farmhouse. Beyond it a red barn loomed, with an extension ladder propped against its eaves. The southern half of its roof was stripped to bare rafters and partly sheeted with new plywood.

The moment Judith's father parked in the shade of a cotton-wood, a squat, bristly brown dog came skulking out from beneath the wooden porch of the house. What looked like an old aluminum saltshaker hung from its rope collar, and as Judith's father stepped warily from the car, the dog charged to within three feet of him and stood there barking furiously until Judith's father, in a peacemaking gesture, held out the back of his hand for sniffing—not an easy thing for him to do, Judith knew, given his general aversion to the entire canine family. The dog quieted for a moment, then abruptly lunged forward in a renewed flash of snarl and teeth. Her father found himself pinned against the door, yelling what sounded to Judith like, *"Gwan! Gwan now!"*

The bristly dog merely receded a step or two and gave up barking for a low throaty growl.

Judith leaned over, rolled down her father's window, and said, "I think he's scared."

Without moving, her father said, "I think he's psychotic." Then, in a low, deliberate monotone, he said, "In the glove compartment there is a gun."

"A gun?" Judith said. Her father had never in his entire Vermont life carried a gun.

"Wrapped in a cloth," her father said. His whole body was still and his eyes were fixed on the dog. "Under the manuals."

Judith said, "I'm not getting out a gun so you can shoot a dog so we can buy a used washing machine."

"Judith," he said, tight-voiced, and with his eyes still trained on the dog he reached an open palm into the car. She found a flashlight in the glove compartment and gave him that instead. "Conk him with that if you have to."

Her father had just said, "Judith, get me the gun *now*," when a two-note, high-low whistle carried from the house and the bristly dog at once relaxed and sat and looked over its shoulder. A woman now stood in the door of the mud porch. She wore Levi's and a plaid shirt, tails out. Her hands were evidently wet, because she pushed the hair away from her eyes with the back of her hand before she said, "Did Roscoe bark?"

Judith's father recovered himself. "Quite a lot," he said. "Excessively, even."

The woman laughed. "You here about the washing machine?"

Judith's father nodded. He was now watching the woman almost as intently as moments before he'd been watching the dog. From the front seat of the car, Judith felt like she was watching the kind of play where the meeting of two strangers was clearly significant. She popped out of the car and said, "My father wanted to shoot your psychotic dog."

This seemed only to amuse the woman. She'd written

something on a slip of paper, and bent now to unscrew the little metal saltshaker dangling from the dog's collar, an activity that provided a view of the white cleavage and lacy black bra within her loosened cotton shirt that Judith did not believe unintentional. After the woman put the paper into the saltshaker, she screwed the lid back on and, finally standing back up, said in a robotic voice, "Git Jim."

The dog shot off past the barn and out of sight.

"Who's Jim?" Judith said, but the woman seemed not to hear. "It's hot out here," she said. "Would you like some iced tea?"

"No, thanks," Judith said, but her father said, "Iced tea sounds good to me." He shifted the flashlight to his left hand and extended his right. "I'm Howard Toomey."

The woman said her name was Delia Guest. Strands of premature gray streaked her hair, but there was no getting around the fact that men might find her attractive. Judith guessed she'd been a creamy high school beauty, prom queen probably, or at least part of her court. Not that she was an old maid or anything now. What she'd lost in youthful smoothness, she appeared to have picked up in know-how.

When her father released the woman's hand, he said, "And this is my daughter, Judith."

Delia Guest gave Judith a quick smile before returning her gaze to her father. She nodded down at the flashlight in his hand. "Were you going to shoot Roscoe with a flashlight?"

There was something undeniably frisky in her voice; Judith heard it loud and clear. She said, "He was going to conk your psychotic dog with it."

Again the passing smile at Judith before returning to her father. "Well, you can put it away now, unless there's someone else you intend to conk."

Her father set the flashlight on the front seat of the car and the woman disappeared into the house. Judith leaned on the front right fender and said, "This is a prime example of a place that gives me the creeps," and when her father didn't say anything but took a few steps this way and that, regarding the abandoned roofing project on the barn and then directing his gaze here and there as if this were a property he was thinking about investing in, she said, "If we have to buy a used washer from a place like this, I'd rather keep going to the laundromat."

She felt at once this was one rude remark too many, and so wasn't surprised when her father turned and said, "Stop it now, Judith."

A second or two later the mud porch door swung open and the woman appeared with a tray containing a pitcher of iced tea, a plate of cookies, and a nested stack of tall metal cups, all of which she set out on a crude table that stood in the shade of the cottonwood. She'd also run a brush through her hair.

The iced tea was okay, Judith thought, but the cookies were peanut butter, which she knew her father couldn't stand.

"Yum," her father said.

The woman said, "I get sick of peanut butter myself, but it's about all the boys'll eat."

Judith's father looked at the woman and said, "I doubt I would tire of these cookies."

Judith began to cough and kept coughing until she could finally retch up a brackish liquidy mix of cookie and bile. She expected her father's arm around her, but the woman got to her first.

"You okay, darlin'?" the woman said. She smelled soapy clean, or maybe it was perfume.

"I'm just shaky," Judith said, and gave her father a weak look. "Maybe we should go home."

He was looking at her thoughtfully when a noise took his

attention, and they both turned toward the barn, where a pickup truck approached with a rumble. There were two cowboy hats in the cab, and in the truck bed stood something large wrapped with a tarp. The dog was also back there. He seemed now to be grinning.

"There're the boys," the woman said.

Judith watched them coming and said, "So which one's Jim?"

The woman said, "Those two are both mine, though I don't always like to say so. The big cute one behind the wheel is Patrick and the little cute one beside him is Petey." Then she offered Judith's father another peanut butter cookie, which he accepted. Who Jim was Judith still didn't know.

The boys really were boys—the driver looked thirteen or fourteen, and his passenger was even younger—but they both wore boots, denims, long-sleeved shirts, and cowboy hats so big their heads looked small. They got out of the pickup slowly, almost somber, like smallish men on big business. The driver went back and pulled the tarp from the washing machine, which looked new.

"This is it," he said.

The other boy silently climbed into the back, sat on the wheel well, and began to scratch the dog, who pushed close with craving.

Judith's father put down his iced tea and walked over. He stepped onto the running board, opened the lid of the washing machine, and stared into the tub. It must've appeared as unused on the inside as it did on the outside, because he said, "You manufacture it yourselves?" and it came as no surprise to Judith that the farmboys took the question at face value.

"No, sir," the younger one said. "We took it in trade for some work we done."

The other one said, "From a man who'd himself taken it in trade for work he done."

Judith's father glanced at the half-finished barn roof and said, "Are you sure you don't want to use it to pay for the work someone else does?"

The boys silently turned to their mother, who said, "Things are tight. We've decided to sell it."

Judith couldn't stand to watch these proceedings, and couldn't stand not to. At one point, when she'd tilted her head away so she could simultaneously listen and appear bored, she felt the older boy's eyes creeping all over her, and when she turned suddenly and drilled him with an ice-cold look, he blushed and took his cowboy hat off but kept his eyes on her all the same. His hair was short on the sides, longer on the top and, as was the peculiar local male style, brushed forward into bangs. Living here, she'd thought more than once, was like living in a town full of Captain Kangaroos.

"I don't own a truck," her father said. "Any chance you could deliver it?"

The older Guest boy turned to the question. "Yes, sir. Hook it up, too."

Judith's father was nodding agreeably when the sound of an approaching vehicle drew Judith's eyes to a station wagon rolling up the dirt lane in front of its own rush of dust.

The older boy said, "It's like Grand Central Station around here today."

Judith looked at the boy and said, "Have you ever been to Grand Central Station?"

The boy stiffened slightly and shook his head.

"But you know where it is, though, right?"

The boy lowered his eyes. Judith expected her father to say something to save the situation, or maybe the boy's mother, but nobody saved him, and in the silence she felt a twinge of remorse.

The station wagon, a finny, late-fifties Dodge Sierra, was heavily freighted in the rear with plywood, which gave the vehicle's front lines a sharkish upward cant. The driver, a tall boy with a full sandy blond beard, pulled close, pushed his cap up a bit on his forehead, and took in the gathering with what appeared to be an amused grin.

He was twenty or twenty-two easy, Judith guessed, maybe even older—he already had the beginnings of crow's-feet around the eyes. He was wearing the T-shirt that had faded to pink; it was of the sleeveless type that Judith associated with ripe, unfiltered body odor. *I suppose this is the roofer,* was her first thought, and her sole positive observation was that he at least didn't have bangs.

"We're all set, Mrs. Guest," he said to the woman, and gave her a little more of his good-humored smile. Judith wondered whether maybe the crow's-feet came from all the idiotic smiling he felt the need to do. Though the gray-blue eyes were an okay feature, she had to admit. By this time, the roofer turned his attention to the boys. "You amateurs ready for a little sweat and toil?"

The older Guest boy sneaked a last look toward Judith, then slapped his hat on and headed off toward the barn, with the littler Guest trailing right behind.

Mrs. Guest turned to Judith's father. "I've got the warranty and stuff inside."

Judith watched him follow her in and didn't stop watching until the door closed behind them. When she turned back, the station wagon was still there and the bearded roofer was looking her way. The red brim of his Purina seed cap was stained dark with sweat, and his amused expression seemed to suggest he knew

61

a little bit more about this county and about this farm and possibly even about her than she ever would. It was quite an irritant. With all the hostility she could muster, she said, "What're you looking at?"

The roofer made dropping his gaze seem like an act of deference. "Well, I was looking at you," he said, then raised his eyes again and let them settle even more fully on Judith. "And I'll bet I'm not the first." He was smiling again.

Judith gave him a stony stare and said, "Are you half-witted or just easily amused?"

She expected this to send the roofer into retreat, but it didn't. His smile in fact loosened slightly. He raked his fingers through his beard and said, "Just exactly how old are you, anyway?"

"Seventeen," she lied.

He nodded, stared off for a moment, then turned his face to her again. "Well, then, I'd call you dangerous."

His eyes, reaching in, exerted on Judith what felt like a subtle but actual pull, which alarmed her. She put an edge on her voice and said, "What's that supposed to mean?"

He shrugged and smiled and was pulling at her again with his eyes, which seemed oddly, pleasantly *wintry*. She wanted in the worst way to say something to splinter the moment, but she couldn't, she couldn't think of anything at all to say, and a not-unpleasant stillness materialized, the kind of quiet calm in which snowflakes might float.

"Hey!" the older of the Guest boys called out, and the spell was broken. The boy was perched halfway up the ladder leaning against the roof eave. "Barn's over here!"

This, like everything else, seemed to amuse the roofer. He shrugged, tapped the bill of his cap back into place, and, after a final look at Judith, began to ease the truck away.

"Hey!" she said, and he braked and looked back. She had no

idea what she meant to say. "That grin of yours," she said. "I would have to call it baboonish."

If anything, the roofer's grin stretched a fraction wider. *"Peligrosa,"* he said with an unhurried drollness nothing in this part of Nebraska had prepared her for. *"Muy peligrosa."*

He drove off then, and Judith went through a quick set of adjectives—*unsettling, odd, arrogant*—and came to rest on *unpleasant,* because that's what he was, and what those little cowboys were, and what Mrs. Guest was, too.

Judith got into the Pontiac, intending to use the horn if her father didn't appear soon. He did, though, pushing through the screen door with the farmwoman right behind. Judith studied their faces as they came toward the yard gate, but there wasn't much to see. Her father carried his checkbook and what looked like an appliance manual in its plastic sleeve.

At the gate, her father said, "Thank you, Mrs. Guest."

Mrs. Guest said, "You're welcome, Mr. Toomey."

Two blank pages, Judith thought. That's what they want me to see.

She leaned out the window and said, "Is that roofer named Jim?"

Mrs. Guest seemed confused for just a second, then said, "Oh, no, darlin'." She set the gate into its catch. "His name's Willy."

Judith settled back in her seat and noticed Mrs. Guest kept her eye on Judith's father when she raised a hand in good-bye.

As her father wheeled the Bonneville around, the older Guest boy was sliding a sheet of plywood up the rails of the ladder toward the littler Guest, who waited above at the roof's edge. The brown-armed roofer was further up, with his back to the car, pulling a sheet of plywood into place with the claw side of his hammer. The older Guest boy, having gotten his plywood to the roof, gave a wave that Judith pretended not to see.

"God!" she said, which seemed enough for a while. Then, when her father had turned the car off the dirt lane and onto the relative smoothness of the highway, she said, "So who do you think Jim is?"

Somebody who wasn't there, her father guessed.

Judith said, "I'd say those who were there weren't all there."

Her father smiled and said, "I noticed one of those little cowpokes kept his focus on you. Though I don't suppose that alone would certify him as crazy."

"That's rich, Dad," she said, and stared out at the passing fields. She thought of telling her father that the bearded roofer had called her *muy peligrosa,* which she was pretty sure would amuse him, but some protective instinct—of what, exactly, she wasn't sure— warned her off. She thought of her father and the farmwoman, and then of the farmwoman's lacy bra, which, Judith would bet anything, was no everyday farm bra. She said, "Did they know we were coming today?"

Her father nodded.

"And did they know you're a professor?"

"Mrs. Guest recognized my name when I called, if that's what you mean. Why?"

After a second or two, Judith said, "Because she just seemed kind of careful about how she presented herself." She paused. "How she spoke and stuff."

Her father said he hadn't noticed that. Judith gazed out at the buttes to the southwest and said, "So did you think Mrs. Guest was pretty?"

Her father seemed to consider it. "She wasn't conventionally pretty, was she?"

"But you thought she was kind of pretty?"

"Yes, I thought she had aspects of beauty."

"Kind of pretty, then, in other words."

64

Her father nodded.

A row of sparrowlike birds rose from the roadside fence and peeled away in a curving line. Judith said, "Prettier than Mom?"

Her father turned now for a moment and gave her the face that had always been her face to touch with little fingers and to kiss on the nose. "No," he said, "not prettier than Mom."

Judith nodded and turned away. At the base of the buttes, massed pines turned the landscape green. It was more scenic here than she'd expected, and she liked riding along like this, staring out and knowing that her father still thought her mother was more attractive than that farmwoman, Mrs. Guest, who, Judith had to admit, wasn't a bad total package.

When another set of the sparrowlike birds peeled off a fence at their approach, Judith asked what kind of birds they were.

"Lark buntings," her father said. "I think so, anyway." Then, a mile or so farther along: "So what did you make of that amusable roofer?"

Judith tensed slightly and said what did he mean, what did she make of him?

"Well, here he is, driving an old clunker wagon and about to climb onto a steep roof in stupefying heat and humidity with nothing but green kids for help, and he acted like he was on his way to a picnic."

What Judith thought was that the roofer was probably a prime example of somebody who hadn't given his life enough thought to know how unhappily he ought to view it. "Maybe he's a simpleton," she said.

"You think?" her father said, and Judith said yes, she did.

And so the Bonneville carried them away, and left behind Mrs. Guest, Patrick Guest, Petey Guest, a dog named Roscoe, and a smiling brown-armed roofer who had called Judith dangerous but didn't otherwise occupy another moment of her thoughts until one morning a week or so later, when she awakened from an exotic dream with the odd sensation of having seen his pale gray-blue eyes staring down at her, watching her sleep.

—⁓—

That Wednesday, Judith's father had to go up to campus in the morning for some kind of meeting. As he left he said, "Those Guest boys might come by with our washing machine. If they do, show them where it goes."

This was alarming news. "When're you going to be back?" Judith said.

Her father, already at the door, shrugged. "An hour or two."

Patrick and Petey Guest appeared a half-hour later. She saw them through the kitchen window and watched as they unwrapped the tarp that covered the washer, but when they knocked and she opened the door, she hitched her chin a little to let them know she regarded them warily.

"We're here to set up your washing machine," the older brother said. He was wearing his big hat and a newish-looking yellow-and-black-plaid cowboy shirt, neatly ironed. Judith didn't speak. The boy said, "I'm Patrick, if you don't remember me." He cast a quick glance at the other boy. "He's Petey." When Judith still didn't speak, his eyes drifted beyond her, and he said, "So where does it go?"

Judith led them downstairs to the basement. Patrick looked at the hose bibs and drainpipe and said they'd do. A few minutes later they were easing the machine down the wooden stairs. The younger brother had his face turned, hugging the side of the machine, while the other looked steadily over it.

When they got it roughly situated, the older boy sent his brother off to the truck for specific tools and fittings.

66

Judith, standing at some distance, said, "Do you know what you're doing?"

The boy grinned and said, "Oh, that would be taking it pretty far." He looked around the basement and saw the door to the partitioned bedroom. "That your room?"

Judith, who wished she'd closed that door, didn't say anything.

The boy said, "I like a basement room. Cool in the summer and warm in the winter. At least ours is. We got a boiler in ours." He gazed around. "You're fuel oil, I guess."

He looked at Judith, who had no idea what he was talking about. She said, "How old are you, anyway?"

The boy pushed his cowboy hat back and revealed an arc of white skin the sun never hit. "Almost fifteen."

"How come you can drive?"

"School permit." He grinned. "Also 'cause nobody stops me."

Overhead, the front door was heard to open and close, and a moment later the younger brother came down the stairs carrying a wooden tray of tools and fittings. Patrick looked at them and said, "You forgot the ball valves," and the little brother again disappeared.

Patrick began to work. Judith wanted to leave, but she didn't want him snooping around in the basement, peering through the door to her room. There was an old rowing machine down there, parked at the base of the concrete wall near one of the window wells. She sat on it and began idly to row.

Patrick raised his head from behind the washing machine, watched her rowing for perhaps ten seconds, and said, "Now that's something."

Judith said, "That pronoun had no antecedent."

"What?"

"When you said, 'that's something,' what was the *that?* The machine, or me, or what?"

The boy's face flushed slightly. "I don't know. I was just trying to talk to you."

Judith softened at this. "It's just . . ." She paused and then heard herself say, "that I have a boyfriend. He'll be a senior this year."

Patrick took this in.

Judith suddenly remembered how she'd grilled him about Grand Central Station. She said, "I'll tell you this, though. I think it's amazing that someone fourteen years old can set up a washing machine by himself. I couldn't do it in a million years."

Patrick looked at what he was doing, then looked back at her and said, "Yes, you could."

The little brother appeared with two valves, one red-handled, the other blue. Patrick looked at Judith and said, "Where's your water shut-off at?" and when Judith gave him a blank look, he turned to his brother, who went off to find it. "Look on the south side first!" Patrick yelled after him, then, softer, to Judith, "That's the usual place." A minute or two later, the younger brother yelled down that he'd found it. "Okay," Patrick called back, "turn it off and leave it off till I tell you!"

Patrick resumed work. It was quiet except for the occasional clink of a tool laid on concrete. After a while, Judith said, "So did you finish your barn roof?"

The boy stuck his head up from behind the washer. "Yep. We were done a day or two after you were there. That roofer flat *worked*. My mother had him do some other stuff, he was so good. He'd wake you up with his hammering about ten seconds after the sun was up."

"And you paid that roofer with the money from this machine?"

The boy gave his head a shake. "We were going to, yeah, but he wouldn't take money. He said eating my mother's cooking and enjoying the bountiful vista from up on the roof was pay enough. I think he knew we were up against it."

Judith went through this in her mind. "He said he was enjoying the *bountiful vista?*"

The boy nodded. "It was a funny way to put it, that's why I remember it. At night he'd go up on the roof and sit and drink his beer. I didn't see the attraction. You can see almost as far from the hayloft and it's lots more comfortable."

Judith, trying to imagine all this, had a thought. "So what did he do with the empty beer cans?"

"Bottles," the boy said. "Heaved them."

"Heaved them," Judith repeated.

Patrick Guest nodded. "Heaving the beer bottles seemed to be part of the fun. He heaved them down toward the rhubarb. My mother didn't like beer bottles in her rhubarb, so in the morning he'd go around and pick them up."

Judith said, "Now there's someone who knows how to have fun," and Patrick, after smiling and nodding, said, "You know, though, in a way he did."

The amusable roofer, her father had called him. She said, "What was that roofer's name?"

"Willy Blunt," the boy said, and Judith said, "So who's Jim?"

The boy cocked his head as if to say, *What?*

"That day I was at your farm, your mother told that psychotic dog to go get Jim."

"Oh," the boy said, "he was my stepdad."

"Was?"

"Yeah, he got hit by lightning last summer. Petey found him. He was still on the tractor going round and round." He stopped for a second. "It's kind of embarrassing. I'm surprised you didn't hear about it."

"What's embarrassing about somebody getting killed by lightning?"

"There was an umbrella over the driver's seat and it was thundering."

Judith waited and when the boy still said nothing, she said, "So?"

"A metal umbrella that he'd clamped to the seat for shade. It was like he was driving around sitting on the bottom of a lightning rod."

"Oh."

"He was dead but the tractor kept going in a tight little circle. He wasn't a farmer. He was from Portland, Oregon, and came here to teach school. Band and stuff. I guess he loved my mother, so he tried to be a farmer is all. Lots of people thought it was kind of funny. At the coffee shop I heard a farmer say, 'Well, maybe a foolish man can last in Portland, Oregon, but he won't last long in this country.' I hated that man for saying it. I mean, he was maybe right and all, but I still hated him for saying it."

A moment or two passed and Judith said, "So if Jim was your stepdad and he died, how come your mom says 'Git Jim' to the dog when she sends him for you?"

"Roscoe was my stepdad's dog, but now he just kind of thinks me and Petey are his Jims."

Another pause, and the boy went back to work behind the washing machine.

"What about your real father?"

The boy poked his head up and said, "He wrecked on a horse."

"A horse wreck? Like a car wreck?"

The boy nodded.

"You say *horse wreck?*"

He stared blandly at her for a second before saying, "I do, yeah." Then: "My mom said that marriage was about up anyway. After what happened to Jim, she says she's about through with marriage."

Judith said, "My mother says stuff like that, too," and for a second she and the boy stared at one another, she seeing him and he seeing her. Then the boy ducked his head down and went back to work.

When the job was finished and Patrick Guest and his brother had packed up and were ready to go, the boy abruptly removed his hat and extended toward Judith a slip of paper on which he'd written his name and telephone number. "Would you call me?" he said. "I mean, if you have any problems with the washing machine or anything," and then, his face stiff and pink, he made for the door.

It was funny what episodes and images you remembered in a life. Over the next year or two, Judith exchanged letters with Patrick Guest, and even saw him in fallen circumstances, and yet years later, living in Los Angeles, she could still close her eyes and see him as he had been the day he installed her father's washing machine. She could see the black-and-yellow plaid of his snap-button cowboy shirt, and she could still call up a clean image of his earnest, stolid face and recall how, when the talk turned to marriage, he couldn't quite keep the hopeful element from his eyes. On these occasions Judith would always wonder whether Patrick Guest had found a place in the world that honored his ability to do things carefully and well, and whether, too, he'd found a marriage that hadn't depleted that secret cache of hopefulness he'd been accruing all the way from adolescence, and probably before, Judith guessed, if he was anything like the rest of us.

—␍ɰ—

July passed, and much of August. Mr. Darcy had won Elizabeth Bennet, and the nights were turning cool. The light had begun to change, and late afternoons, Judith and her father began taking rides in the Bonneville, traveling east or west along Highway 20 before turning onto one of the graded dirt roads that cut through pastures and fields. Her father would stop to photograph abandoned houses and barns, and while he moved from one outside location to another, hunting for the right subject and light, Judith would step warily through a door and into shadow, where she would often find artifacts of extracurricular life——cigarette butts, empty bottles, Dairy Queen wrappers, used condoms, words written on walls. On one old plaster wall, someone had written *LLR + ZLL* and then partially enclosed the joined initials within a valentine-style heart left incomplete because the artist seemed to have run out of the pink fingernail polish she (he?) was using for the project. On the wood post in the middle of another building, someone had etched the words *Why are you here?* She felt vaguely accused and left quickly, but when she later mentioned what she'd seen to her father, he released a small puffing laugh. "What we're here for—there's a question nobody sober tries to answer."

Judith's failure to think of it as a Big Question annoyed her, and so did the fact that her father made light of it, which somehow felt as if he were making light of her, too.

"So I suppose you don't think about what you're here for," she said.

This seemed to chasten him. "I do," he said. "We all do. I should've called it the question nobody sober tries to answer *in public.*"

"Now I get it," Judith said. "You *think* things, but you won't *say* them for fear they might make you look silly."

"Something like that, yes."

They drove awhile in silence.

"So you're not going to tell me."

"No."

"Because . . . ?"

72

"Because they would be personal ideas, Judith. I'm the only one for whom they might hold even the smallest significance. And hearing myself say them out loud will only debunk them for me."

As they drove on, Judith tried to poison the atmosphere with a steady expulsion of heavy sighs, which her father ignored (he slipped in an opera tape and at selected points sang along). When Judith noticed a looming one-room schoolhouse, she said sulkily, "I need to pee."

She used the outhouse and her father used the weeds at a corner of the fence line. As they reconvened at the Bonneville, he said, "You drive."

When she just stood staring at him, he said, "Millions do it." He gave her an encouraging smile. "Within a minute you'll be driving better than the average Italian."

Judith slid uncertainly into the driver's seat. He pointed out the pedals and levers, suggested the adjustment of seat and mirrors, and told her to turn the key. She did, and the first quiet firing within the engine's cylinders sent a vibratory thrill through her fifteen-year-old body.

"Now what?" she said.

He told her to take her foot off the brake, to gradually depress the gas pedal, and not to forget to steer. She inched onto the dirt road.

"Now what?"

He sat back and looked out the window. "Go faster."

Judith hunched over the steering wheel, and eventually her adjustments in course and speed grew less abrupt. The spell of sullenness had been lifted from her completely. "This is fun," she said, and her father, staring off at the wide horizon, said, "Yes, it is."

This, then, became the customary method of their afternoon excursions—he drove the blacktop highways, she drove the back roads—and the hours passed in this way, Judith exulting in her assumption of responsibility, her father serene in the shedding of it.

—⁓—

Following these afternoon drives, Judith and her father often stopped to eat a cheeseburger or French dip sandwich at places called the Covered Wagon Inn or Grandma's Apron or the Food Bowl. Judith had begun collecting menus to commemorate her summer in Nebraska, marking the items she'd ordered with a one-to-five ticking system to denote quality (fives were rare, but so, too, were the ones). Afterward, she would ask the help of a passerby to photograph her and her father standing side by side in front of these establishments, his stout arm slung over her slender brown shoulder.

One Friday night, in a town thirty miles east of Rufus Sage, Judith and her father stepped out of the Two Sisters' Café and heard the dim sounds of a marching band carrying from the north. The first pedestrian passing by was an accommodating rancher who seemed to view the thirty-five-millimeter camera he was handed as something newfangled. After he hesitantly snapped two shots, the second with Judith holding her commemorative menu in front of her chest, her father, nodding toward the band music, said, "Football game?"

"Local boys and Hemingford," the rancher said. He seemed happy to hand the camera back. Then, grinning and giving a little show of looking over his shoulder: "I wouldn't bet on the locals."

Judith felt a sudden shrinkage of spirit. The drifting sounds of this football game made specific an ending she'd kept vague. "It's only August," she said.

"They end school early in the spring," her father said, "so they start early at this end."

74

A sense of actual disconnection came over her, a strange floating sensation. In her mind she saw a red kite rising with a cut string trailing behind. The feeling terrified her, and she did something she hadn't done for several years. She reached over and took her father's hand.

He received her hand as if it were an everyday occurrence, and they began walking toward the game. Of the band music, the throb of drums was most pronounced, and now there was cheering, too, evenly spaced, as if introductions were being made. By the time they arrived, the game was under way. They paid their admission and walked around the end zone to the visitors' bleachers. Many of the visiting Hemingford fans gave them a full stare—nobody had to tell them that whoever Judith and her father were, they weren't from Hemingford. These looks turned Judith to stone, but her father smiled and nodded as they climbed to the last row, to a spot apart from the small, seated crowd.

"We are the visitors' visitors," her father said, low, to Judith, and settled back against the pipe railing. Judith watched milling boys for a while, then the cheerleaders, then looked idly at the menu she was still carrying (inside, in green ink, the waitress had written, *Don't be a stranger! Your waitress, Darlene*). She wished she'd brought a book (or, even more, that they were home and her father was reading to her from *The Mayor of Casterbridge,* the new book they'd started), but finally she sat back and looked without interest at the game while keeping a peripheral watch on her father, in the hope that he might become bored, too.

But her father didn't speak or seem even to move until time ran out on the first half, and then he leaned forward and gave a strange half-smile. He looked off, and Judith followed his gaze past the flagpole, where the last sun had turned a broad expanse of brittle cornstalks a buttery yellow. He turned to Judith and said, "Who could sit here and look at this and not believe in the good intentions of the world?"

Broad strokes of this type vexed Judith, so she said, "Which in English would mean what exactly?"

"This." Her father vaguely swept a hand across the field of vision in front of them. "It's all so winsome and . . . unarranged."

Judith regarded the halftime marching band and thought that at least some of the unarrangement came from not practicing enough.

Her father said, "There's an exquisiteness here, Judith, and the visitors' visitors have a good seat for seeing it."

Judith gazed past the band toward the cornfield, trying to find the exquisiteness he was talking about. She didn't, but turning back to him, she wondered if she saw something else: that he was here now for good. It began as just a thought, but after a second or two it had become factlike in its hardness.

She said, "You're not ever coming back to Vermont, are you?"

He'd touched his fingertips together and rested his chin on the touching thumbs, but he turned to her now and said in a gentle voice, "Probably not, sweetheart."

There was another, unspoken part of Judith's question, the part about whether her father wanted Judith and her mother to join him so they could be a family again, but she knew he knew that part of the question, and the fact that he wasn't answering it told her what his answer was. He wasn't going to talk her mother into anything.

The second half of the game had by now commenced, and suddenly the Hemingford fans whooped and rose to their feet: their team had scored. Shortly thereafter, the kicker flubbed the extra point.

"Shanked it," a farmer in front of them said, and another man got a round of laughs by saying he could kick a dog farther than that.

It was a one-sided game, but Judith and her father stayed until the end and afterward walked toward their car slowly, among the locals.

Nearby, a man said, "I love watching that Ross Ray tackle."

There was a three-quarter moon in the sky. As Judith and her father drove west along Highway 20 through the night, neither of them spoke, and the dashboard lights gave a ghostly phosphorescent cast to her father's white shirtsleeve when he leaned forward to put on *La Traviata* (this was okay by Judith—she'd grown familiar with the opera, and more or less looked forward to the big choral party scene).

East of Rufus Sage, where a timbered area stretched south just past the highway and seemed to draw dark curtains to each side of the blacktop, her father said quietly, "At dusk there are deer through here."

The Bonneville's high beams formed a tight tunnel of light in the blackness of asphalt and pines, and it reminded Judith of the place in movies that always came with ominous music and preceded some sort of terrible collision.

"Dad?"

"What, sweetheart?"

"What happened that night you and the Irwins were in the accident?"

After a few seconds, he said, "That was a long time ago."

"But what happened?"

Her father exhaled heavily. "It's not straightforward." He shook his head so subtly she wasn't sure he had. She presumed he would then fall silent, as he'd always done when the subject came up, but she also understood that in telling her that he wasn't coming back to Vermont he'd taken something away, which might make him more willing to give something back. And she was right. He began to speak. "We'd been out to dinner, then dancing and that

77

sort of thing, and were on our way home. We got to a crossroads. Nobody seemed to be coming in the other direction, and as I made a left turn our headlights caught a black sedan moving toward us with its lights off." A pause. "I saw that black sedan. I saw it clearly." Another pause. "The collision with the banyan tree followed."

"The other car had its lights off? I never heard that."

Her father didn't speak.

"But the Irwins blamed you. Mom did, too."

"I was driving."

"What about the black car? What happened to the black car?"

Her father said it kept going, he guessed. Then he said, "I was the only one who saw that black sedan."

"What?"

He said, "We'd been drinking, so the others thought I was seeing things. But I hadn't been drinking much. Everyone was drinking Cuba libres, but after my first one, I took the waiter aside and told him to bring me straight Coke." A pause. "I went through a period of my life when I found it more interesting to pretend intoxication than actually to allow it. But the point is, if I was seeing things, it wasn't from drinking."

The Bonneville broke free of the dark timber. Again the moon illuminated the fields and threw shadows from haystacks and fence posts.

Judith said, "Why was the black sedan driving with its lights out?"

Her father didn't answer. Instead, he slowed to turn onto a county road, then accelerated to a moderate speed and, without a word, switched off the headlights.

In the moonlight, the flat dirt road suddenly seemed a floating white ribbon, and the fields slipping by were shaped by different shades of darkness. Gradually the Bonneville picked up speed.

Something small and dark—a rabbit, probably—darted in front of the car and registered a decisive thump on its undercarriage. Judith had the sensation that the road was rising from the horizontal, that they were moving upward through a disorder of black shadows and shapes. Everything—the car, her own face, the shadowy landscape—felt stretched out of one form and into another. She felt violent dread, and yet when her father finally lifted his foot from the accelerator and switched the headlights on and the dirt road was itself again, what she felt was not just flooding relief, though she felt plenty of that, but also the exultation of the unmarked survivor.

Her father, sitting forward, two hands on the wheel, was quiet.

Judith said, "You've done that before, haven't you?"

Her father seemed to nod.

"And you like it?"

"I don't know if I like it. But I am interested by it."

An idea formed in Judith's mind: that this would be how her father would die.

She said, "Please don't do that again."

Her father again seemed to nod.

"No, I mean it."

"I understand," he said.

Twenty minutes later, lying under her tight-stitched quilt in her basement bed, Judith would wish she'd extracted an actual, iron-clad promise from her father regarding this kind of driving, but they hadn't spoken again for the duration of the ride home, and they hadn't spoken at the house, other than to say parting goodnights as they moved off toward their rooms.

Judith's premonition of the style of her father's death would turn out to be false. Her father would die of a massive heart attack that occurred in the bathroom of his grandparents' home. "Evidently while straining at stools," a paramedic told Judith, a fact that she kept a long time from her mother, and one that she herself would have preferred not to know. A man who ate prunes every day. Better, much better, she thought, that he'd missed a curve on a dark country road, at night, in the midst of the mysteries that occupied him.

—m—

On the first Saturday of September, Judith packed her bags for the plane ride east. From the door of her room, she turned to look at her bird's-eye maple furniture, perfectly restored, and she went back to tug smooth a ripple from the quilt that seemed now to have been purchased a long time ago.

She was to fly out of Rapid City, a two-hour drive north on Highway 385, and Judith's emotions stretched thinner with every mile that passed. She and her father chatted for a while and then fell silent. At one point she sensed he was about to speak, but he didn't. He put on *La Traviata*. The Bonneville swept past the turnoff for Mount Rushmore, Violetta wondered whether Alfredo might steal her heart, and then her father said, "The other day, when you asked what I thought we're here for and I didn't answer . . ."

She turned in her seat. "The kind of thing no one sober tries publicly to answer."

A slight smile formed on his lips. "Yes, that kind of thing."

She waited.

He switched off the opera. "I was going to make a list. Most of them . . . I couldn't bear even to see them on paper. But there is one I am going to tell you." He drew a full breath and expelled it. "I am sure one of the things we're here for is to make certain that those whom we love fall asleep each night assured of that love."

There was quiet in the car. His eyes were fixed on the road before them. "I love you, Judith," he said. "You must know that—

it would kill me if you didn't know that. I love you utterly." And then—what impulse to brutal honesty carried him further?—he said, "And if I could do what I think you've come here this summer to ask me to do, I would, Judith. I would, but . . ."

Judith, like her father, had been staring forward, but she now turned suddenly toward the side window. She thought she might cry. The fences and farms slid by, and she thought she might cry because her father had just given the name of love to his feelings about her, and she might cry because of her futile reflexive desire to tamper with this fact, to expand it to include someone he couldn't include. She willed herself away from saying, *You love me, but not Mom?*

An increase in highway billboards signaled their approach to Rapid City. After a minute or so, her father said, "One other thing. Remember when you asked if you'd ever be like Elizabeth Bennet?"

Judith said she did.

"Well, I just want to say that in all the important respects, you already are."

Her father's soft baritone seemed to crack just a little, or did Judith just imagine it? It didn't matter. She so suddenly began to cry that it humiliated her, as if it were a bodily leak. She told herself to stop, and finally did, and turned back to her father to say, "I'm glad you think so." She made a smile. "Except Elizabeth Bennet wasn't so weepy, was she?"

He said, "We've all done our share of weeping, including Miss Bennet, I'm sure."

At the airport, her father helped her check her bags, then they waited in silence for her flight to be called. When finally it was, neither of them moved for a second or two. She rose only after he did, and took a few steps toward the boarding ramp, but when she reached the line she stood aside and looked back.

He stood where he'd been, stiff and still, as if the slightest movement might cause breakage.

A voice from a loudspeaker again called her flight, and after two or three more seconds, Judith stepped into the line of departing passengers.

5

When Judith and Malcolm had first come to Los Angeles, she'd contacted all the studios in search of an entry-level job, without luck (one human resources woman said, "You don't want to work in food services, do you?"), but one night during a loan committee meeting, Malcolm listened as Miss Metcalf described an application from a man who worked in movies, which, it turned out, was part of the problem with his file: over the past five years, his income had bounced from peak to valley, suffering from, as Miss Metcalf put it, financial mood swings.

"What does he do in movies?" Malcolm asked.

"Finds locations required for certain scenes. A string of three-story commercial buildings built before 1927 was one example he gave me. Another was a cemetery with vertical monuments and no perimeter fencing."

Malcolm, like the others in the committee room, stared at Miss Metcalf.

"And he makes money doing this?" one of them said.

"Quite a lot, actually, when he's working," she said, and without checking his file, she ticked off the names of three directors for whom he'd recently worked.

Malcolm wondered who these people were and what it meant that he hadn't heard of them, but one of the other committee members asked something specific about the subject property, and the discussion switched directions. Afterward he called the man.

"You've been approved for the loan on your rental property," Malcolm said, "but that's not the reason I'm calling." He explained that his wife was looking for an entry-level position in a production company. The man gave a quick laugh and said, "Who isn't?"

"Yes, of course," Malcolm said, and thanked him all the same.

But the man said, "Your wife isn't an English-major type, by any chance?" and Malcolm said indeed she was.

"Organized?"

"Would be an understatement," Malcolm said.

The man laughed again. "I had me one of those," he said. "She's now the ex." Then: "Okay, no promises, but let me have your number and I'll check something out."

Two weeks later he called back. The position was as a personal assistant to an actor-director whose name even Malcolm recognized. During the interview, the actor-director sat squirming in his chair while three of his employees peppered Judith with questions. After a few minutes of this, the actor-director rose and said, "She's fine," and left the room. Once the door was closed behind him, one of the three interviewers turned to Judith and said, "This is of course probationary."

When, later, Judith was asked to describe what the actor-director was like, she answered, "Distracted eighty-five percent of the time, pissed off at somebody ten percent, and friendly the rest."

"How friendly?" someone sometimes inquired.

"Never overly." Some of the hotshots felt entitled, but her hotshot wasn't one of them, which made her respect him all the more. Still, this answer seemed to disappoint people and force them to ask what she actually did.

"Correspondence over his signature," she said. "Speeches, articles, prefaces to books." The work was neither boring nor gratifying, but its proximity to the production of movies led to the deep-in-the-bone conviction that she wanted to edit, wanted to break a scene into its tiniest parts and stretch and shape them in ways so subtle that the viewer could never quite identify the source of their effect. When she worked up the courage to mention her desire to edit, the actor-director seemed pleased. He called it "a good fit." Editing was hard to break into, he said, but if she'd wait until he directed his next picture, he'd get her a position. The next picture was a metaphysical baseball movie, and Judith's minimal editorial participation in it slipped her into the editors' union and out of her actor-director's immediate sphere of influence. It took three years of documented experience before she could become an assistant. The first scene she edited by herself was an alternative ending to a movie about a dog named Hooch. In Judith's scene, Hooch didn't die. In the released movie, he did. Still, her scene turned out competently enough ("Quiet and deft," the director told her, "and every bit as good as the let's-leave-them-weeping thing, which is the thing we'll of course use"). Judith's career had found traction and fitfully ascended to a level of dependable employment. She did TV from roughly July to April, midbudget movies during hiatus. It was through one of these movies that she'd caught the attention of Leo Pottle, who had hired her for several television shows, including the one on which she now worked.

After her interlude with Malcolm at the beachfront hotel in Santa Monica, Judith returned to the studio just as Pottle was leaving it. He walked slowly across the parking lot, a large, slope-shouldered man whose body was so limp it suggested a shortage of bones. Judith lowered her window and threw him a friendly grin. He grimaced, sighed, and looked at the sky, a combination

Judith took as a signal to stop. In a dour voice he said, "If this episode were a ship, the words would be *glub glub glub*." Judith thought of Pottle's comic shtick as Eeyorish, with brains. She obliged him now with a laugh and said she thought the actual words would be *glug glug glug*, and laughed again. Pottle kept his long face, gave Judith a deliberate chest-level glance, then, raising his eyes to hers, said, "For you, with the excellent flotation devices, it might be funny."

Judith laughed, not much of a laugh, but enough to let him know she wouldn't be going to the Labor Relations Board over the remark.

"And did you hear the studio has cut our ad budget?"

She hadn't heard, and probably wouldn't have worried if she had. The accepted wisdom was that the show was less about ratings than about bringing respectability to the network, something to counterbalance the teen garbage that was its bread and butter. For a while, the show had had it both ways—a nice smattering of Emmys and Golden Globes *and* solid ratings— but then they'd been moved to Sunday night, and last year, in the third season, the writers had struggled for story lines, and based on the last couple of scripts Judith had read, things hadn't improved much this year, not that she would say so. Of the cut in the advertising budget she said, "That's not so good, is it?"

"Not so good?" Leo Pottle said. "If being air-dropped into the burning wasteland without food or water is not so good, then all right, it's not so good."

Judith shrugged and grinned, then wished she hadn't. It wasn't the response he wanted, or even one that was appropriate—it was her job, too, after all. Leo Pottle gave her one last morose look and slouched off toward his car, in search, Judith supposed, of fresh sources of gloom.

In the darkened cutting room, Lucy Meynke sat before a Panasonic monitor showing a stilled shot of a single hand breaking a single egg over a stainless steel sink.

"You missed the Pothole," she said as Judith slid in beside her.

"Not quite. We spoke long enough for him to refer to the show as a sinking ship and to my smallish boobs as excellent flotation devices."

Lucy made a short, snorting laugh. "It was weird—he seemed even more than usually grim today, as if the problems he's been expecting all year have finally become real." A pause. "You'd have thought it would make him happy."

This did not seem wrong to Judith, especially the part about Leo Pottle's grimness. There *had* been something stauncher about Pottle's apprehension today, and what should she be reading into that?

"What about Hooper? Has he been snooping around?"

"Only every thirty seconds or so, but he's fine. Just Hooper being Hooper." Then: "So where ya been?"

As Judith told her about the episode at the hotel in Santa Monica, Lucy's eyes grew bright. "Assignation at Shutters!" she said. "Saucy courtesan! Little tramp! I am completely green."

Judith couldn't help but laugh. "It was so *different*, you know? I kept having the crazy feeling that I was someone other than Malcolm's wife and he was somebody else's hubby."

"My God!" Lucy said. "You know what you did, don't you? You used your husband to cheat on your husband!"

This seemed to Judith clever but not necessarily true.

"It's kind of a breakthrough marital move, really," Lucy was saying. "Guilt-free cheating."

Judith said, "It's possible you're overreaching here, Lucy."

The editing room was small, dim, the walls hung with buttoned sound baffling. Its one window was covered with bamboo and then velvet, so nearly all the room's light came from the monitor in the center of a wall-to-wall work counter. The wine red scarf Judith's mother had worn when photographed behind Judith's father on the motorcycle the day they were married was loosely tied over the knob of the closed door. To Judith, there was something about editing rooms that caused the kind of intimacy that quickly bred alliances and animosities. In Lucy's case, it was alliance. They both liked books, and they loved movies, and when it came to the editing, they fed each other's energies, very often saw eye to eye, and when they didn't, Lucy could be deferential without truckling. Lucy had never married, loved traveling, and had found that assisting television editors meant interesting company, a living wage, and a little money left over for travel to the more far-flung but less expensive tourist destinations. Most recently she'd been to Macedonia, where she'd stayed at a small mountain inn and formed a brief affiliation with a widowed tobacco farmer, whom, with affection, she now referred to as her doddering Slav.

"The thing is," Lucy said, "to me and most of the girls in the chorus, Malcolm looks like a yummy grown-up boy toy, and yet to you . . ." She threw up a hand and smiled. "This is just one of about three dozen reasons why connubiality scares the shit out of more than a few of us."

Judith, who usually enjoyed Lucy's riffs on general themes and other people, found she wasn't enjoying this particular riff quite so much. That Malcolm could seem interesting only when regarded as somebody else's husband didn't seem to her like good news. She made a laugh and said, "Let's not overdo it. I had some fun with the hubby, sweetie, and that's all."

She was ready for the next thing, and turned her attention to the monitor. "So what's up with this shot?"

Lucy forwarded from the one-handed egg break to a following

shot showing the finishing touches of what was supposed to be the same egg break, but this one was two-handed.

Lucy, watching Judith's face, exploded into gleeful laughter. "There's some cinematic magic for you," she said, but Judith barely heard. Already she was scanning the interceding frames for ways to patch things up.

There were times when Judith wondered if this explained her inclination to edit—how in film, unlike real life, you could always go back, and by deleting this and adding that, you could change the tone, change the outcome, change even the consequences. If such an act could be performed in real life—she had often thought this—how many crimes of passion might go undone, how many marriages might be saved?

—∿—

By 5:30 Judith had worked her way past the two-handed egg break, and at 6:45 Lucy left for a first-time dinner with someone she would refer to only as John Doe (Lucy called all male companions John Doe until they became serious, which they almost never did). An hour later, Judith was mired in a scene between the show's two male leads. She leaned close to the monitor, trying tiny, frame-by-frame cuts, sitting back, sipping Earl Grey tea, undiscouraged by the small failures, talking in a low, gingery voice, just as if Lucy were still there.

"Whatever happened from this angle is over," she said. "Too much indicating from that jasper . . . I don't want to be in this angle . . . Whoops . . . God, that's a nice reading . . . Nope, I like him better when he's throatier."

A pleasant, immersive satisfaction resulted from this process, and when Judith next held her watch close enough to the monitor to read, she was surprised that it was nearly 9 P.M. She checked what she had after nearly five hours of editing: a little more than seven minutes of finished tape. She was surprised it had gone that well—four would have been a fairly normal yield.

She pushed back from the monitor and went outside. She'd gone into the cutting room when it was light; now it was fully dark, and she brushed across the feeling of emerging alone from a Saturday afternoon double feature, something she'd done often as a child. Usually the studio hummed with activity; now it was quiet. She leaned on a breezeway rail and, listening to the hum of traffic beyond the studio, caught the pleasant, faintly dieselly smell she associated with buses. She felt good. Stretching felt good. Inhaling felt good. She wished Lucy were here—they could run down to Tom Bergin's, order a filet, drink a manhattan. Judith had never smoked, but moments like this suggested to her why a person might. A little slice out of time, you and your tar, nicotine, and floating thoughts. The operator placing that funny phone call to North Platte, the woman saying, "His name's William, we call him Bill, now who are you?" Judith had to laugh. And then one thing leading to another, the SOS to Malcolm, that breezy hotel room at the beach. And what was Malcolm up to now? Speaking at his loan committee meeting, or listening, or pretending to listen while thinking . . . of what? And Camille. What was Camille doing right now? She was home, Judith knew that much, but your daughter being home was a consolation of yesteryear. With the Internet, Camille might as well be leaning against a lamppost in New Orleans or São Paulo.

Judith pulled out her cell phone, dialed home, and spoke briefly with Sonya of Hutchinson, Kansas, who delivered her standard line—"It's all good here"—before intercomming Camille in her room. "Pick up, Camille!" Judith heard her yell. "It's your mom!"

During the summer, Camille worked mornings as a receptionist in a restaurant owned by the family of one of her friends, and she'd volunteered at the public library, helping with the summer reading program, but that was tapering off. Judith had the feeling she was now spending most afternoons with friends by the pool or in front of the TV.

"Yes?" Camille said instead of hello.

Judith said, "I'm cutting and it's going slow, sweetie, so I'll be a little late."

Camille said nothing. In the background, Judith heard a faint papery crinkle.

"I rented a storage place for the bird's-eye maple today."

Still nothing from Camille except more rustling. It was annoying to Judith, which she supposed was the intent. She said, "The storage place was creepy. I think the Coen brothers are the absentee owners."

Camille sighed audibly and turned the page of whatever she was reading.

Judith said, "Did your father tell you we've decided to send you to the Citadel next year?"

This at least provoked Camille to speech. She said, "That's hilarious, Mom."

Judith waited a second or two. "Want to tell me what's wrong, sweetie?"

"Other than being stuck alone in a house under the supervision of a religious zealot and both your parents calling to say they won't show?"

"Dad called, too?"

No response from Camille other than the papery sound.

"What're you doing besides talking to me?" Judith said, trying to keep her voice in the coaxing mode.

"Reading."

"Reading what, princess?"

"*Spin.* The new one with, as Sonya put it, the slut on the cover. And don't call me princess."

It was Judith's turn for silence.

Camille said, "You know what Sonya asked me to do tonight? Have popcorn with her and watch one of her eight-year-old videos of *The 700 Club*." She paused to let this sink in. "If you guys aren't ever going to be here, couldn't you at least get a baby-sitter who isn't an Anabaptist or whatever she is?"

Judith wasn't going to be drawn into this general line of discussion. This was America, and Sonya was free to worship whatever false gods she pleased. Besides, there was something in Judith that made her yearn for belief pure and simple, not that the Pat Robertson stuff was that. She said, "What time did your father say he'd be home?"

"Didn't. He just said later." A pause. "He tried to jolly me, but I wouldn't be jollied."

"No, I'll bet not," Judith said. Odd, though: Malcolm liked to wrap up loan committee no later than ten. After that, he thought the decision-making got sloppy.

Camille broke the silence by saying, "That Miss Metcalf woman called, wanting to know where Dad was. I told her the bank." More background page-turning. "That was before Dad called to say he'd be late."

To Judith's ear, the tone here seemed a creepy mix of calculation and aloofness, and it made her suddenly tired. She said, "You're fifteen, Milla. When you're fifteen, you're supposed to believe in the good intentions of the world."

A phrase, she realized after speaking it, of her own father's.

Camille said, "On one of Sonya's Anabaptist shows I heard a man say that when teenagers are home alone, a moral vacuum develops. I think it's when I'm in that moral vacuum that it's hard to believe in . . . what you just said I ought to believe in."

"The good intentions of the world."

"Yeah. That."

Judith exhaled heavily. "Bye, sweetie. I'll kiss the sleeping you when I come in."

"That's fabulous, Mom," Camille said. "It'll mean the world to me."

Judith resisted the bait. "That's okay. It'll mean something to me. I'll find a nose or ear to kiss."

She waited, and then, for the first time in the entire conversation, she heard a smaller, more endearing voice, the voice of a girl more ten than fifteen. "Promise?" Camille said.

Judith's voice softened, too. "Sure," she said. "Sure I do."

After Judith hung up the phone, she stared off toward a new commercial building that rose above the studio. Some of its windows were still lighted, but none of the rooms seemed occupied. She took a deep breath. Camille was fifteen—the same age Judith had been when she met Willy Blunt with his brown arms and pink shirt. She should go home, she should go straight home and sit up with her daughter in her ridiculous new canopy bed and watch an old movie with her, something black-and-white, simple and substantial—*On the Waterfront,* maybe, or *High Noon,* or maybe even *Pandora's Box,* the erotic one with Louise Brooks following her wayward impulses down the tortuous path that would finally lead to Jack the Ripper. That would give Camille something to fill that moral vacuum she was worried about.

"Hello, Mrs. Judith."

The voice gave her a start. She turned to say hello to Sergio Rocha, the studio's Mr. Fix-It, who was at the moment carrying in each hand small metal boxes that suggested electrical matters. He was already past Judith when she had a thought. "Sergio?"

He turned.

"You don't have a truck, do you?"

Sergio had heavy facial lines and a stiff mustache grayer than his dark, combed-back hair. He gave a nod that suggested formality. "It is with the mechanic, but I will have it next week," he said, and within minutes Judith had arranged the transport of the bird's-eye maple furniture to its new home at Red Roof Mini-Storage the following weekend. Sergio nodded and disappeared around the corner.

Farther down the breezeway a door opened and someone she didn't know left the building whistling "Somewhere Over the Rainbow."

Judith's mind drifted to the hotel room overlooking the beach, and suddenly, without logical prompt, she remembered.

The keys. She'd forgotten the Red Roof keys.

In her movie, there would be a close-up of the black spiral-bound notebook that contained the hotel directory.

—⁓—

Judith checked her purse to be sure, but found only the key card for the room. A telephone call to the hotel was unproductive. The maids hadn't been into the room, she was told, because the room hadn't been vacated. "But it has," Judith said. "My husband and I were there, and now we're not."

The man said, "Yes, but the room is still yours. No one checked out."

How this changed things, Judith wasn't sure. "But couldn't you still just check the room for me?"

The desk clerk excused himself to confer with someone, then returned to say, "I've talked with our manager and she has sent someone up to look now, Mrs. Whitman. Shall I call you back or would you like to hold?"

Judith said she'd hold, and waited a surprisingly short time before the man came back on the line to say, "We found nothing tonight, Mrs. Whitman, but we'll look more thoroughly in the morning. Shall I call on this line?"

Why not look more thoroughly tonight, you freaking slackers? Judith thought, but what she said was, "Yes, this number is best."

She went back to the cutting room and took her place in front of the monitor, but her thoughts kept sliding toward the lost keys, and finally she gave in to it. She had the key card—she would check for herself.

Twenty minutes later, she pulled up to Shutters and asked the attendant to keep the car close by. The moment she stepped into the lobby, it seemed a different hotel from the one she'd visited earlier in the day. The lazy afternoon feel had given way to a more expectant temperament. The restaurant emitted a rich hum of easy conversation and sportive laughter, the clink of silver and the ring of crystal. There was a lot of skin and skimpy fashion on show here, and Judith guessed that among these men you could find a surprisingly high per capita rate of silk socks and Berluti loafers. Women flicked only passing glances at Judith, who tonight had nothing to offer in terms of fashion, but a man at the bar swiveled to let her know his attention was full frontal.

It was while waiting for the elevator that Judith began to feel a little funny about being here. True, the room was still hers. She'd taken it this afternoon. But this afternoon seemed like two days ago.

A muted *ding,* the elevator door slid open, and Judith stepped aside as a man and woman passed her. In the elevator the residual smell of the woman's perfume, some too-tangy shade of citrus, seemed not just to hang in the air but displace it. It was dizzying—Judith could see in the elevator's mirrored walls a long line of ever-dwindling images of her own oddly stricken face—and when the door quietly opened onto her floor, she stood for a time in the corridor, taking in fresh air before heading to the room. She didn't feel herself. As she moved toward the room, she felt she was lifting and setting her feet carefully, as if on black ice.

At Room 314, Judith inserted her key card into the door, saw the tiny green light flash, and had started to open the door when, within the room, a change of smell and light and ownership told her to stop. To stop and yet to look. In the next three or four seconds, her eyes skittered from one image to another. A stilled red *X* against a black background on the TV screen. A naked woman wearing earphones and sitting on the bed in a meditative position, her composed face tilted slightly down, eyes closed, breasts floppy and so smoothly white that in the dimness of the room they almost shone. A pair of gray trousers folded over the high-backed chair. The silhouetted upper body of a man brushing his teeth behind the frosted windows separating the bedroom and bathroom. The man's voice—watery, distorted, as if he were talking through toothpaste—said, "Francine?" Was that what he said? The woman on the bed raised her head and began to lift off her earphones.

Judith closed the door.

Her heart was beating wildly.

From within the room, the indistinct sounds of the woman's voice calling someone's name.

Malcolm? Had the woman just called Malcolm?

Judith stared at the room number, 314, and then at her unmarked key card. It must be the right room. Her card wouldn't open any other room.

Again, muffled voices within the room. The woman calling, "What?"

Judith nearly ran to the elevator. Inside, in the mirrors within mirrors, she saw a diminishing line of ashen Judith impersonators. The citrus smell still hovered. Her hands were trembling, so she held one with the other, which merely seemed to redirect their current to internal circuits. From the elevator she hurried through the lobby to the street and her car. She jolted into traffic, a horn honked, and Judith, glancing in her rearview mirror, saw the attendant stepping into the street to get a better look at her erratic progress.

What had she just seen and heard? She had the reflexive need to rewind the scene, slow it, watch it again and again, frame by frame. It was certainly Miss Metcalf. That was the one given. The man was the variable. He wore trousers like Malcolm's. In silhouette he looked a little like Malcolm. His voice through toothpaste might've been Malcolm's. And the way the gray pants were hung over the chair—waist on the seat side, legs over the back—that was Malcolm, too.

—⁓—

When Malcolm came in, shortly before midnight, Judith was sitting knees-up in bed pretending to read *The New Yorker*. "Home at last," she said in a neutral voice, and peered at him over her reading glasses.

He smiled, used the walk-in closet for changing into his pajamas, then crossed to the bathroom to brush and floss: his usual routine. Judith waited until he was brushing to say, "Bad meeting?"

"What?"

His voice through toothpaste could've been anyone's voice. Judith said, "I asked if it was a bad loan committee meeting."

Malcolm rinsed, spat, and came out dabbing his mouth with a hand towel. "Meeting was canceled. Neil, Dan, and Ivy were all sick with one thing or another, so we postponed until tomorrow night. I stayed late because I was behind and it was my chance to catch up." He gave a subtle wag of his eyebrows. "You might recall that I was detained this afternoon."

Judith offered a polite laugh, waited, and said, "So you'll be late tomorrow night?"

He shrugged. "Not too late. Why?"

"I was thinking of Milla. She was peevish about neither of us being home tonight."

Malcolm nodded and said, well then, he'd just cut the meeting short tomorrow night.

In bed, he put on his glasses and shook out the front pages of the *Wall Street Journal,* and when he began to read with what seemed like his customary casual interest, Judith asked the question she'd told herself not to ask.

"Did Miss Metcalf stay and help?"

"No. She had a dinner date." Prompt in delivery, decisive in tone. Then, more reflectively, "With someone she may well be interested in."

Judith considered this. "And he in her?"

Malcolm's eyes stayed fixed somewhere in the middle of the newsprint. "I'm not sure." Then: "Perhaps."

Judith turned a page. So, after a few seconds, did Malcolm. She said, "Where were they going?"

Malcolm turned. "Who?"

"Miss Metcalf and the someone she may well be interested in."

"Oh," he said. "Someplace in Santa Monica." He touched a finger to his tongue and turned a page. "I told her if they went to One Pico, she could have our room key in her pocket in case he got lucky."

A faint unpleasant shock moved through Judith. What Malcolm was saying could explain Miss Metcalf's presence in Room 314, but even if true (and she couldn't help doubting this), it merely shifted her attention from a greater offense to a lesser one: an easy familiarity with Miss Metcalf's personal life that Judith had never before imagined. "And she responded how?"

Malcolm turned toward her with his wry little smile. "She blushed . . . and took the key."

Judith nodded. She heard herself say, "Ah."

And who knew? This might be true, might very well be true. The man Francine Metcalf was interested in might wear gray pants like Malcolm and look in silhouette like Malcolm and sound with his mouth full of toothpaste like Malcolm. That was the problem with marrying someone as facile and circumspect as Malcolm. Without much effort, he could have you believing this had all been some kind of R-rated Lucy-and-Ricky-style muddlement. And yet.

Malcolm was regarding her. "Did I commit a faux pas in giving her the room key?"

"No," Judith said, almost to herself, then put some spine in her voice. "I think it was considerate of you. It's probably why she's so willing to move with you from one bank to another."

"That," Malcolm said, "and the raises she receives with each new position."

The possible ambiguity of these words wasn't lost on Judith, but Malcolm was a banker, he believed in risk-yield ratios, and what could risking discovery through idle wordplay yield him? Nothing. Absolutely nothing. Still, she said, "Do I get a raise with each new position?"

An appreciative chuckle from Malcolm. "That would be expensive," he said.

A few seconds passed in silence. Then Judith said, "Does Miss Metcalf's new beau have a name?"

Malcolm lowered his newspaper and looked off, as if searching for something hidden in the palm tree outside the window. "Milton," he said. "I think it's Milton. I don't know his last name."

Through a closed door, *Milton* could sound a lot like *Malcolm*. "He's Jewish?" Judith said.

Malcolm gave her a blank look. "What? Is Milton always Jewish?"

They were looking into one another's eyes.

"Maybe not," Judith said.

The smallest smile, a smile so small it might not be a smile, seemed to form on Malcolm's lips. "It wouldn't be the question to ask, would it? 'This new fellow in your life, Miss Metcalf—would he be Jewish?'"

"No, I suppose not," Judith said, and meant to stop there but couldn't. "Though when you think about it, that question wouldn't go much further than asking her whether she'd like a room in which to fornicate."

Malcolm looked actually abashed. "So I did commit a faux pas."

"Maybe," Judith said. "I'll know better in the morning, when I'm less tired."

She leaned over and switched off her light. Malcolm on his side did the same. But she lay in the darkness, awake, as Malcolm fell into the slower, heavier breathing of sleep. She wished he would snore so she could elbow him awake, tell him to turn over, go to another room, whatever people told snoring spouses to do. But of course Malcolm didn't snore. He would never snore. He was too discreet a man for snoring.

Judith thought peevish thoughts like this for a while, and then more reasonably sour thoughts, and then she remembered her promise to kiss the sleeping Camille. The girl's room was not quite dark; a slender illuminated moon hanging from the far wall cast a faint light. When Camille was twelve or so and showed a passing interest in the planets and constellations, Malcolm brought home several astronomy-based gifts. Of them, the one that remained was this craggy wall-hung moon, which, with a remote control, could be clicked through four phases from full to crescent. When she was expecting her mother to look in on her, as she was tonight, Camille would leave the crescent moon lighted, and Judith, after kissing Camille's ear so lightly it wouldn't awaken her, would turn the light off. Tonight, having done that (Camille didn't stir), Judith walked from room to room, looking into some, entering others, sitting occasionally near a window to stare down the canyon past the darkened houses to the shimmering lights of the freeway.

She had distrusted Malcolm once before, and with surprising results. It was in Palo Alto, soon after they'd fallen into the habit of seeing each other nightly, but the Wednesdays had become problematical. Prior to meeting Judith, Malcolm had had a standing Wednesday afternoon tennis date with a girl named Izzy Tisdale, a fact that bothered Judith not at all until she began to notice a gradual lengthening in the tennis matches. Every Wednesday night Malcolm would arrive a little later at Judith's dorm, and with each added minute, Judith's thoughts darkened. She said nothing, even when Malcolm, in conversation with a former fraternity brother, agreed that Izzy was "a leggy number," but finally—this was the sixth or seventh Wednesday, and Malcolm was more than an hour late—Judith bicycled to the courts in a sleepy neighborhood south of campus. As she approached, she heard a volley of hooting laughter, and, dismounting, she crept to a better vantage point. Leggy Izzy Tisdale was nowhere to be seen, but there was Malcolm, hitting ball after ball to a small Hispanic boy dressed in old shorts and new white shoes. His black hair was thick and shaggy; he looked to be eight or nine. Two even smaller boys were racing around fetching stray balls and running them over to Malcolm so he could keep steadily hitting balls to the first boy, all the while giving him gentle repetitive instruction. "Up and through," he droned, "up and through, step straight forward, then up and through." Suddenly he stopped and his voice rose: "There! Did you feel that? Did you feel that? Didn't it feel just *perfect?*" and the small beaming boy was nodding, and then, when Malcolm said, "Ready position," the boy began again dancing lightly at the baseline in his new white shoes.

Then everything began to stop, as first one of the ball boys, then the boy at the baseline, and then Malcolm himself turned toward Judith. It was Malcolm's expression that broke first with recognition. "Huzza-huzza," he said. "It's you." His tone was droll, but his smile seemed a little brighter than usual. He turned to the boys. "Hey, *compadres.* This is my *amiga.*" Then, looking back at Judith: "My *muy* delectable *amiga.*"

The boys circled Judith when she stepped onto the court. "You're Mr. Malcolm's wife?" one of them said.

Judith said no.

"You're his girlfriend?"

Judith laughed and looked toward Malcolm, who said, "Well?"

"Yes," Judith heard herself say. "His girlfriend."

"He's nice," the smallest boy said. "You should marry him."

Judith smiled at the boy. "You think?"

"He gave Eduardo the tennis racket and the shoes."

These words caught Judith by surprise—they seemed to hover suspended for a few extended moments—and she felt something go out to that little boy, and to Eduardo, and most of all to Malcolm, whose nonchalance seemed genuine.

"He was playing with a *badminton* racket, for Chrissake. I thought I'd see what he could do with the proper equipment."

"He's going to teach us, too," one of the younger boys said. "We're going to be Pancho Gonzales."

Malcolm, smiling his thin smile, said he didn't see any reason why not. Then, glancing at his watch, he said, "Yikes. So that's why you're here." He turned from Judith to the boys. "Okay, kiddos, gather them up."

But at once the boy with the new racket and white shoes said,

"Ten more, okay, Mr. Malcolm? Just ten more?" and when Malcolm glanced uncertainly at Judith, she nodded and said, "Sure. Why not?"

It hadn't been that night, or even the next, that she'd first slept with Malcolm Whitman in his slender bed, but it was soon thereafter. And what had happened to those sweet boys? Over the next few years, Malcolm had taught all three of them, and she remembered with pleasure the solid repetitive *thwock* as they delivered one solid backhand and forehand after another. Where did they go? What had they grown into? Were they as different from their younger selves as she and Malcolm were from theirs? Malcolm had received one handwritten letter from the oldest boy, saying he'd made the freshman tennis team, but after that, nothing.

Judith looked at her watch—it was nearly 3 A.M.—and returned to bed. Malcolm didn't stir, but the thought of him and those boys on the tennis court had done its work. Her spirits loosened and released her to sleep.

She awakened two hours later with Malcolm's arm slung over her shoulder, as limp as something dead. His face lay close. His skin seemed coarse and porous, and his breath was stale. Judith pushed his arm away, slid from the bed, and went to the window. The hills were silhouetted now, and the first hints of sun tinted the predawn gray with a faint pink that as she watched grew pinker.

"You okay?" Malcolm's voice from behind her, a little groggy.

She turned. He was still in bed. "Mmm."

"Were you up in the night?"

Judith nodded. "I'd promised to kiss Milla after I got home. And then I was awake."

He said, "You were cross last night."

"I was nonplussed last night. I don't know why. But it's come and gone." She looked out the window. "The sunrise really is lovely, if I can change the subject."

103

"What it really is is early," Malcolm said.

He flipped on his light and sat on the edge of the bed, taking his bearings. He didn't have to say he was going to the gym—today was Wednesday, and Mondays, Wednesdays, and Fridays were gym days. Malcolm's day would be filled with meetings from 7:15 this morning until the seven o'clock loan committee meeting tonight. Judith knew this because during her nocturnal wanderings she'd gone to the study, opened his briefcase, and flipped through his daybook. She'd also noted that his Thursday and Friday were just as tightly planned. Though she knew if time were needed with Miss Metcalf, time would be found.

"I had funny dreams," she said.

Malcolm had eased into a calf stretch. "I love funny dreams," he said. "There's something about being awakened by one's own laughter."

She gave him a look.

"Tell me," he said.

She remembered only one of the dreams, and all she remembered of it was a landscape that seemed green and English, and a rampant stream of small rattlesnakes that came wriggling out from under the wet hedges, across the wet lawns, and onto the wet stone walks. Malcolm, young and handsome, amused others by calling the snakes vipers. No one feared them. Parents called for their children to come out and play with them, and why not? The little rattlesnakes had no rattles. Only Judith realized they were actually rattlesnakes.

"That's because it was your dream," Malcolm said. He'd finished his stretching and was gathering his gear. "When it's your dream, you get to make even the smallest decisions."

Judith thanked him for his insights.

"Not at all," Malcolm said. His keys jingled as he waved.

After he was gone, Judith glanced back through the window.

Already the luminous pink was giving way to a dull yellow. A minute or so passed, and then, as she stared distractedly out, Malcolm's black Jaguar came into view between houses, soundless, dreamlike, disappearing again. From one of her sitting locations during the night, she had calculated that she was now the same age her father had been when he'd given up his teaching job in Vermont for a lesser position in Nebraska, where he'd begun to garden and bake bread and take photographs of ramshackle buildings and drive at night on country roads without headlights.

6

Upon returning from her summer in Nebraska, everything in Vermont seemed odd and unfamiliar to the fifteen-year-old Judith. Her girlfriends seemed younger than when she'd left them, and her mother had collected a new set of friends from the community theater group she'd joined in Judith's absence. These men and women dropped by nearly every night in twos and threes, bearing wine that her mother poured into jelly jars. As the evening wore on, the group seemed to move through predictable phases, from expectant to exuberant to mildly coarse.

There was a man named Jonathan, tall with a drooping mustache, who wore a western-style leather coat with plackets and sleeves trimmed in dangling leather strips. He spoke in a rolling voice and enforced his remarks with sweeping gestures that made the leather fringe dance. This generally drew an approving look or laugh from Judith's mother. It wasn't just Judith's and her mother's friends who seemed foreign, though. Judith realized that her room didn't feel like her room, or her bed her bed, or really, when she thought about it, her life her life. She couldn't keep herself from thinking about Nebraska. She confessed this to her friend Annalisa Williams, who stared at her for a few seconds and then said, "I refuse to take this seriously." But Nebraska was where Judith's mind kept drifting. Nebraska was where her father grew tomatoes and baked bread and kept a gun in his glove compartment, it was where teenagers put roofs on barns and installed appliances in basements, and it was where she'd driven a car down dirt roads and drunk coffee and refinished furniture and learned what to expect next in *La Traviata,* and it was where a brown-armed roofer had called her dangerous. It was where, without really meaning to, she'd gotten one foot into adulthood.

She waited almost a month for these feelings to subside, but when they didn't, she told her mother one night out of the blue that she wanted to go back to Rufus Sage. Her mother made a soft sound of surprise—Judith would always associate it with the movie image of a bird shot in flight. "Oh, Judy, no," she said, and Judith thought her mother's wounded feelings might make her change her mind, but they didn't. Nor did the other arguments her mother made in succeeding days—the better schools in Vermont, the lifelong home and neighbors and friends she would be leaving. The appeal that might've worked—that she needed Judith, would be lost without her—was the one appeal she wouldn't make. Judith's mother had embraced a freer course for herself, and she wouldn't keep her daughter from doing the same, however misguided she believed her daughter's thinking might be.

So in late October Judith was saying good-bye to friends. The night before she was to leave, her mother made chicken enchiladas, Judith's favorite. It was an attempt to brighten the evening, but her mother kept failing at conversation and at last fell silent. She cut her enchilada into bites she didn't eat. Finally she said, "Once when you were little, too little to remember, we visited a second cousin of your father's on his farm in Pennsylvania. This second cousin's name was Wynn, and he had a colt—at least I called it a colt, but Cousin Wynn kept telling me it was actually a filly—whose mother had died. Wynn had bottle-fed the colt, who decided Wynn was her mother. The little horse followed

Wynn everywhere. For entertainment, Wynn liked to get on a bicycle and let visitors watch the colt trotting along behind him. Wynn and your father and everybody else just about laughed themselves sick over it. But when I saw that colt running after a man on a bicycle, my heart sank." She stood and took her plate to the sink. She was wearing a loose flannel shirt, borrowed, Judith knew, from Jonathan, and a long denim skirt with rainbow trim at the hem. When she turned, she laid her eyes softly on Judith. "To me, Professor Howard Toomey looked like the sun and the moon and the stars. To you, he looks like a father. But sooner or later you'll see he's just a man on a bicycle."

When Judith deplaned in Rapid City and followed the other passengers into the small, sleepy terminal, she spotted her father standing off to the side, his hands in the pockets of a camel-hair coat she recognized—her mother had found it for him at a Junior League sale the year before the separation. A navy blue scarf was draped around his thick neck and tucked into the lapels of the coat. He looked to her like an old-time prizefighter, one of the successful ones.

He gave her a long hug, then stood back, grinning. His eyes were bright. "Well, well," he said. "Aren't you a tonic for the troops."

She grinned. "And aren't you the dashingest man on the premises."

Her father scanned the half-empty building and said something about the lack of stiff competition, then fished coins from his pocket and pointed Judith toward a row of pay phones. "I promised your mother you'd call as soon as you'd landed."

Her mother answered on the first ring.

"Hi, Mom. I'm here, and I'm fine. Dad's wearing that Burberry coat you bought him."

"And you're okay?" her mother said. "The flight was okay?"

"It was fine, but kind of bumpy. I sat next to a woman who'd never flown before. She kept nibbling saltines and every few minutes she would say, 'You think they're fixin' to set down yet?'" Judith expected a laugh from her mother, but didn't get one. She turned to look out the plate-glass window at gray skies and ridges of sooty snow ranging over brown grass.

In a sudden rush her mother was saying, "Oh, Judy, sweetie, I already miss you so much," and Judith said, "I miss you, too, Mom," and at that very moment she did, but thirty minutes later, moving south on Highway 385 alongside her father, with the heater churning and snow patches on each side of the highway set off prettily by the beige fields and behind it all a soundtrack of *Don Giovanni,* Judith felt herself shedding weight she hadn't known she carried. A highway sign for Mount Rushmore—*Borglum Blasting Movie Every 2 Minutes!*—made her want to laugh. That night, lying under her quilt on her bird's-eye maple bed, she thought one word: *happy.*

Around town, Judith felt a pleasant fly-on-the-wall anonymity, but at school other students seemed to regard her not only as strange but as deaf. "Where'd she come from?" she heard a girl say in an unlowered voice, and someone else said, "How come she dresses like that?" (Before her move, Judith had decided on a modified North Woods look: loose Levi's, square-toed Frye boots, and a rotation of crew-necked sweaters.)

Teachers praised her for work she knew to be routine, and one or two boys tried to get her attention, but it was hard to take them seriously with their Captain Kangaroo bangs. (She began thinking of them as *roo do's,* and sometime during this period she had a frightening dream in which these bangs, when parted, revealed a third eye, a premise she used for a submission rejected by the school literary magazine, *The Harvest of Words.*) She didn't want

109

to ask about Patrick Guest—and who would she have asked if she'd wanted to?—but she kept a lookout for him. Her thought was to befriend him so he could play a protective role in discouraging unwanted inquiries from other boys, but she never saw him. One day a boy wearing a letterman's jacket introduced himself and asked if she was a foreign exchange student. Judith looked at him a second or two and said, "Yah, dawt iss me."

"Where from?" the boy said.

"Vermont," she said, and for the next few seconds the boy regarded her as if she were a dog whose nip hadn't quite broken skin. This wasn't Judith's only occasion to establish aloofness, and by staying beyond the currents of activity and keeping her eyes impassive and her thoughts more or less to herself, she was soon regarded more as an unwanted furnishing of the school than as a member of the tribe.

Throughout her earlier school years, Judith had always had one particular friend whose subordination to her vision of the world was so subtle that neither of them had to acknowledge it as subordination at all. In Middlebury, this had been Annalisa Williams, and before that Heather Lowe. Later, in Los Angeles, it would be Lucy Meynke. In Rufus Sage, it was a girl who one day approached Judith as she was walking away from school and said, "Do you know Patrick Guest?"

The girl had lustrous red hair that fell below her shoulder blades, but the narrowness of her chin and a slight yellowish cast to her eyes thwarted any notions of real beauty. Judith said, "Who?"

"Patrick Guest." A pause. "He said he put a washing machine in your basement." Another pause. "He said the basement is where your room is."

There was a calculated note of provocation in the girl's voice, as if she hoped to prompt from Judith a revealing response, a strategy Judith recognized because she sometimes used it herself. "It's true my room's in the basement," she said, "but I have a wall between me and the chained sex slaves, if that's what you're wondering about."

This pleased the redheaded girl—her lips relaxed into a smile.

Judith said, "I don't really know Patrick Guest, though. I talked to him while he was putting in the washing machine is all."

The girl nodded. "Well, he said to tell you he moved to Woolcott." When Judith looked at her blankly, the girl said, "Southeast part of the state."

She and the red-haired girl were moving now along the coarse concrete sidewalk on Seventh Street. "Do you know his address?" Judith said.

The girl gave Judith a look with mischief in it. "How come you want it?"

Judith said she was thinking of writing him a one-line postcard asking him about his Jim-getting dog.

"His what?" asked the red-haired girl, and Judith told her about Mrs. Guest and the whole "Git Jim" story, during which the red-haired girl laughed at all the right places. Then she said, "Just put his name on the postcard and the town. He'll get it. It's not that big a town."

At the corner of Seventh and King Streets, the girls' paths diverged. As they separated, Judith said, "What's your name?" and the girl came to a full stop and turned back around.

"Deena Schmidt," she said, and broke into a smile that suddenly broadened her face, and made it seem prettier.

―――※―――

That night, Judith wrote a postcard that said, *You should not have moved. What'll I do now if my appliance needs attention?* (Mrs. Vastine, her English teacher, a pretty woman whose luminous blue eyes were often brimming with fun, had just introduced the class to double-entendre, and Judith was trying her hand.) She addressed it *Patrick Guest, Woolcott, Nebraska,* and when she dropped it in the mailbox the next morning on the way to school, it felt like a message in a bottle.

Ten days later she received a return letter written on lined notebook paper. *Dear Judith,* it said. *I'm glad you wrote me. That washing machine's pretty good so it shouldn't need fixing, but if it does, I'd call Jerry at Western Auto or Marv's LP in Crawford. We're in Woolcott because we sold the farm or I should say the bank did because by then it wasn't ours anymore. I'm glad you wrote because I wanted to let you know I was hoping you'd come back to live here because I had decided if you did I would ask you to a movie or something, not that you would have, I just wanted you to know. Yours sincerely, Patrick Guest. P.S. My address is 242 Adams Avenue.*

When Deena Schmidt read this letter, she shook her head in wonderment. "Well! I can think of three girls right now who would've gone into a dark room with Patrick Guest if he'd shown the slightest interest, which he never did. I'm impressed."

Judith wasn't so sure. Though it was true that the Patrick Guest she remembered was calm and competent and perfectly okay-looking, except for the bangs, which could be cut off in a minute. She looked again at the letter. "Was he smart in school?" she asked.

"I think so, but it was hard to tell. He missed half his tests because of farm work."

Judith folded the letter back into its envelope, and an odd correspondence soon developed between Rufus Sage and Woolcott. Judith's notes played on their shared status as outsiders in new schools (*Do you think it's a moral failing for me to secretly root against our football team?* And: *This is the first school I've ever attended where I don't have a crush-worthy male teacher. Do you like any of your teachers?*) She found Patrick Guest's responses endearing (*I don't just hope my supposed team will lose, I hope they'll lose by 50 points.* And: *I don't like any of my teachers here male or female, except for maybe my Spanish teacher who at least tries to act human.*)

What Judith may have liked best about her new home life was its lack of irritants. The rooms were tidy, the bills were paid, the freezer was full. She enjoyed her father's company when she had it, but she enjoyed, too, the Tuesday and Thursday evenings when he was teaching and she could stay home reading by the fire or just staring into it. Her father often came home late from his night classes, and he was otherwise far busier than he'd been in the summer, but he seemed to enjoy the close proximity of their separate worlds. He'd purchased an old mahogany partners desk that he set in the front room, not far from the fireplace, so that on those evenings he was home he would put one of his favorite composers on the stereo at low volume and they would read and do their work while enjoying the music and each other's silent company and the warmth of the fire.

One night she found herself drawn to a song so evocative it seemed almost haunting. "What's this?"

Her father had been absorbed in his reading and had to catch up with the question. He looked at her, then tilted his head to the music. "Samuel Barber."

"No, I mean what is this particular song?"

Judith heard him say, "'To Be Sung Underwater.'"

She liked the song, and she liked the title. She closed her eyes and imagined singing mermaids and humming whales. So it was a disappointment to her when, drawn closer to the strange music, she turned over the cassette case and found she had misheard. Its correct title was "To Be Sung on the Water," a good title, better than the one she'd heard, which, now that she thought of it, was preposterous.

Scotch was her father's winter drink, either Dewars or J&B, whichever was cheaper at Lariat Liquor, and he generally liked a small tumbler while cooking dinner and another as he sat with his schoolwork. Conversations with him were pleasant and calming, filled with easy silences, and they afforded Judith beguiling glimpses of adulthood's wider field of vision. Once, at a sudden shift and crackle from the fireplace, she looked up from a geometry problem and found him watching her.

"What?" she said.

He turned toward the fire. "I was just thinking how odd it is that I came here against my wishes to spend my teenage years, and how at roughly the same time in your life, you've come of your own accord."

Judith said, "I read in *Seventeen* that most teenagers want to be either someone else or somewhere else, or both."

Her father released one of his small puffing laughs and looked again at the fire. "I underappreciated what my grandparents provided me. I knew my grandmother was fond of me. She was always adjusting a collar or smoothing a hair so she'd have a chance to kiss me on the forehead"—Judith's father smiled—"which was her particular specialty." She was a homemaker, he said, and if that wasn't enough for her, she didn't show it. Once, when he asked her what she liked best in the whole world, she said baking in the winter and gardening in the spring. She belonged to PEO, Republican Women, and the Children's Home Auxiliary, whose shoe drive she organized every autumn. A smile formed on his lips. "All day long she hummed to herself, a low tuneless drone, and when she stopped for a moment I took it as a sign she might be passing gas."

Judith laughed, then waited, and after a second or two, he said his grandfather was more aloof, a gray kind of man. "He worked for Stockmen's Bank and had seen enough droughts and hailstorms and failed farms that he'd armored himself with a somberness so complete that to a teenage boy he could seem not quite human. He was so stiff in his walk I used to think he had mechanical hinges at his knees and elbows." A pause. "I thought my grandparents were indifferent to my progress—they never, for example, asked about my schoolwork or what I intended to do after high school, and they were as surprised that I was going to college as they were that I'd been offered a scholarship to do it—but I think now that what seemed like inattention was an intentional gift. They knew enough to leave me alone. Nobody said, 'Go play football,' or 'So-and-so needs part-time help.' They saw I loved to read, so they let me read. Even at church. Oh, at the appropriate times I'd stand and kneel and put my hands together, of course, but during the entire sermon I would read a book while my grandparents pretended not to notice. The other parishioners noticed, though, and one Sunday as we were leaving church one of the deacons approached my grandfather about it on the steps. Some consider it disrespectful, the man said, and my grandfather, who was such a recessive man, didn't hesitate a fraction of a second. He said, 'I suppose before talking to me, you discussed this with Reverend Steele?' The man nodded, and my grandfather said, 'Then please ask Reverend Steele which he prefers, my grandson and his book with us in our pew next Sunday, or my wife and me respectfully finding another house of worship.'" Judith's father stared into the fire a few seconds. "It was at that point I realized my grandfather was fond of me, too."

It was quiet, then Judith said, "What did Reverend Steele do?"

Her father shrugged. This wasn't what he wanted to talk about. "He wrote a note of genteel capitulation. *You, your grandson, and his books are all welcome,* et cetera."

He fell silent and kept looking at the fire, and much later in her life Judith would come to believe that he'd provided this anecdote as a gloss for his own way of parenting, and it would help her understand his general pattern of nonintervention and make all the more perplexing the single significant occasion when he had acted otherwise. That night, though, it was quiet for a time, until the burning logs suddenly shifted. Her father rose from his side of the desk.

"Ice cream?" he said.

Their favorite was black walnut topped with a chocolate sauce he made with his own proportions of cocoa, sugar, butter, and heavy cream.

———

One Saturday afternoon in early December Judith grew tired of waiting for her father—he'd gone to campus for unspecified reasons—so she took the book she was reading and walked down to the Dairy Queen, where Deena worked. She turned the corner onto King Street and was walking midblock when she became aware of a vehicle lagging just behind her. It was an orange newer-model pickup truck with yellow flames painted along the side of its hood and some kind of fancy chrome wheels. As the truck drew even with her, the driver leaned toward the open passenger-side window and looked at her. He wore a white cowboy hat, and his face was round and pink. When Judith set her chin and turned her head pointedly away, the truck crept alongside for another twenty yards or so, then shot ahead, wheels squealing, and at the corner turned out of view.

At the Dairy Queen, the owner, Mr. Edmundson, was doing the cooking, which meant no obvious monkey business, so Judith stood before the ORDER HERE sign and said to Deena, "One hamburger, well done, no mustard, extra tomatoes please, a small order of fries, unsalted, and a lemon Coke with three ice cubes."

Under her breath Deena said, "Up yours with mustard, Judith."

Judith stared at the elasticized plastic stretched tight over Deena's red hair and said in a sweet voice, "Love your headgear, Deena."

At the Coke machine, shielded from Mr. Edmundson's view, Deena pretended to spit into Judith's cup before filling it. "You did say a lemon Coke, didn't you?"

Judith laughed, which she'd always understood to be one of the critical things a friend should be able to make you do, but there was more to this friendship than that. Though she'd lived here all her life, Deena Schmidt, like Judith, preferred looking in from the fringes. Deena had taken the Dairy Queen job because it allowed her to earn pocket money while keeping tabs on the social ebb and flow—the unions and, more interesting, the partings. Most local girls wanted to be homemakers, stewardesses, or nurses, but Deena wanted to be a divorce attorney, because, she said, "there'll never be a shortage of irreconcilable differences." Deena had been pleased when Judith began referring to the Rufus Sage cheerleaders as the Sage Hens. (In honor of the fur trapper for whom the town was named, they worked out a pump, thrust, and kick routine for "Rufus, Rufus, he's our man, if he can't kill it, no one can!") Though she wouldn't have said so out loud, Judith believed Deena was the only girl in school smart enough to envy her.

This afternoon Judith took her hamburger and lemon Coke to a corner table, where she ate and read *This Side of Paradise* (the world of Princeton it portrayed was both incomprehensible and fascinating to Judith, and she liked Amory Blaine for the calculated way he tried to direct his trajectory upward). She was nibbling fries and Amory Blaine was screaming down the highway among a carload of boisterous schoolboys off for a wintry seaside weekend when Deena abruptly sat down at the table. She had a damp rag in her hand, but she'd taken off her plastic hat and was shaking out her long red hair.

Judith looked around and said, "Where'd Mr. Ed go?"

"He's in the boys' room taking advantage of himself." Deena grinned, and the yellow in her eyes glinted. "Guess you didn't see Melinda Payne come in." Melinda Payne was a six-foot-tall bank clerk who always wore twin sets that showed to advantage breasts that Deena enjoyed describing as *Tetonic*. "Mr. Ed always heads for the john after a visit from the Tetons."

Judith made a private resolution never to eat food Mr. Edmundson had touched or even been in the close vicinity of. She mentioned the pink-faced man in the orange pickup with flames.

"Sounds like Boss Krauss," Deena said. "He's a total troglodyte." This being Deena's new word. "What was he doing?"

"Staring."

"That's him. First he stares and drools, then after a few rounds of that, he tries to strike up a conversation."

Judith said that sounded like something to look forward to. They were quiet a second or two, during which time Deena's expression turned sly.

"So do you want to see Patrick Guest?"

"What?"

"Do you want to see Patrick Guest? It's not that tough a question."

Judith honestly didn't know. She liked writing Patrick Guest short silly notes, and she liked getting his odd notes in return, but he hadn't responded at all to her last two cards. "See him where? Is he in Rufus Sage?"

He wasn't, but Deena said that her two uncles were driving down to look at somebody's ranching operation near Woolcott, and they could drop them at Patrick's for a visit. This was the next day. There were more specifics, and though Judith nodded and said, "Okay," she couldn't bring herself to think it sounded like fun.

"You'll call him first, so he'll know we're coming?" she said.

Deena's eyes brightened. "What's the matter with a pop-in? Afraid we'll meet his new girlfriend?"

"Promise, or I'm not going," Judith said.

Deena promised, and was talking about how weird her uncles were when she abruptly stopped, and Judith followed her gaze to Mr. Edmundson returning from the bathroom. Deena was pulling her plastic hair cap on as Mr. Edmundson came through the door, but he didn't look at the girls. He just slipped behind the counter and went to work scraping the grill.

—ᴍ—

Melvin and Mickey Eleson were Deena's uncles on her mother's side, but they seemed to Judith as unlike Deena's mother as two humans could be. For one thing, Deena's mother rarely spoke, whereas the uncles hardly stopped. They were also cheerful. They picked up Deena and Judith two hours before dawn, and though Judith could hardly function at that hour, the uncles, sitting up front in clean snap-button shirts and sweat-stained cowboy hats, seemed to think it was the top of the morning. They talked, laughed, and bickered without restraint. The passenger-side uncle offered the girls brownies he'd made himself and poured black coffee into Styrofoam cups that to Judith's eye appeared to have been used before. The back seat of the Riviera was roomy, and Judith had almost dozed off when Deena made the mistake of asking her uncles just what kind of operation they were going downstate to see.

"You tell her," the driving uncle said, and the other uncle said, "Well, it's a fool's errand and that's why we have the job."

The uncles, it turned out, had gotten wind of some kind of

mysterious high-yield ranching operation from a man who'd stopped at Daylight Donuts on his way east a week before. When the uncles had told the man they were cattle ranchers, the man said he'd run cattle for years, too, until he got a little smarter. He pulled a card from his wallet that said, *Fritz C. Hoffman, Stock Consultant,* along with a telephone number with a 237 area code. At the bottom, in smaller letters, it said, *Legitimate Inquiries Only.* "Fritz is who you want to talk to," the man said, "but do us both a favor and keep it to yourselves." He smiled. "It's just one pie. We don't need smaller slices." The uncles watched the man drive away from Daylight Donuts in a late-model Coupe de Ville. When they'd called the number on the card, the man who answered acknowledged that he was Fritz C. Hoffman, but in terms of his ranching operation he wasn't forthcoming. Finally he said, "Look, fellas, if I was to tell you what we're doing down here, you wouldn't hardly believe it. The only way is to see it for yourself."

The uncles made a show of not expecting much from the trip, but Judith had the feeling the jokes about how they'd soon be driving Coupe de Villes and spending winters in Key West seemed to have something very much like real hope buried in the middle of them.

Shortly after dawn the geography grew flat and the uncles fell quiet. Judith drifted to sleep and didn't awaken until the driving uncle said, "Okay, gals, this is your stop," and the other uncle said, "Last call for all sleeping beauties."

Judith peered out at a row of small, untended houses. A squat stucco building of faint blotchy blue had the address 242 hand-painted on the door. "Is this Adams?" Judith said, because honestly, she didn't see how it could be.

"Unless it changed names midblock," the driving uncle said. The other uncle said there was a little restaurant a few blocks down where Adams hit the main drag, such as it was. "Country

Kettle or Country Kitchen or Country something. We'll meet you there at one o'clock."

The girls got out and stood in the sudden cold watching the car drive away. From the passenger window, one uncle extended his cowboy hat and gave it a sweeping wave, and then the old green Riviera turned the corner and was out of view.

Judith and Deena looked at the dingy blue house, looked at each other, and began moving toward the door.

"I feel like I need a little prep time," Judith said. All of her parts felt frozen, including her hair, and she felt strangely irritated. She wanted to say, *Whose idea was this, anyhow?*

There was a TV going in the house, some kind of sporting event, and Deena knocked twice before a boy who didn't quite look like Patrick Guest opened the door.

"Patrick?" Deena said.

The boy nodded.

After a full second passed, Deena said, "It's me. Deena. Deena Schmidt."

The boy stared blankly.

Judith thought she was having some kind of out-of-body experience.

Deena was actually pointing at her. "And Judith Toomey. We were in the neighborhood."

"Hi," Judith said. It was clear Deena had not called in advance, as promised.

The boy who shifted his bewildered gaze to Judith seemed no closer than a distant cousin to Patrick Guest. He'd lost his forward-leaning look, and beneath some kind of flesh-colored dermatology paste his face was alive with a secreting acne that made him hard to look at. He knew this, too—she could see it in the way his eyes slid downward from hers.

"I liked getting your letters," Judith said, but he didn't look up.

A woman's voice from within the house said, "Patrick?"

He turned, and there was Delia Guest, looking like her own ghost. Her skin was waxy, and her hair hung in strings. She blinked in the sunlight, took the girls in, then stepped back.

"These are girls from Rufus Sage," Patrick said in a flat voice. "Deena Schmidt and Judith Toomey. They were just in the neighborhood."

"I'm Deena," Deena said. "She's Judith."

A horrible silence followed, and Judith heard herself say, "I've never been to Woolcott before."

Deena gave her a look, and there they all were, Patrick in the doorway, his mother behind him, and Deena and Judith outside in the bitter cold realizing that if anybody were going to invite them in, it would have happened by now.

Finally Patrick's mother said in a small voice, "How is your father?"

Judith didn't realize Delia Guest was talking to her until Deena turned toward her. "Oh. He's fine," Judith said. "I'll tell him you asked."

Delia Guest took this in and said, "Did he know you were coming here?"

Judith shook her head, which was the truth. When she'd told her father about the excursion with Deena and her uncles, she'd left out the part about visiting Patrick Guest.

Her nose was running in the cold. She said to Patrick, "Where's Petey and your little dog?"

Patrick's eyes were open, but he wasn't looking at anything. He said, "That dog died." Then: "Petey's with some church people. They're pretty nice."

Judith didn't know what to say next. Nobody did.

Deena said, "Well, we have to go now."

Judith looked at her.

Deena said, "My two uncles are waiting for us up at the restaurant."

Judith was nodding now, and Deena said, "We just wanted to say hello."

"Okay," said Patrick Guest, and both he and his mother seemed to recede without taking actual steps.

The girls walked deliberately to the street, but a few houses away, before in fact they could be sure they were out of view, they began to run, and laughter began to spill out of them, spontaneous, inexplicable, up-from-the-belly laughter that bordered on hysterical, and when it began to abate, they rekindled it by repeating some line or other from their visit ("I've never been to Woolcott before" was the most dependable, but "We were just in the neighborhood" and "That dog died" also now seemed hilarious).

At the Country Kitchen, they ate tall stacks of buttermilk pancakes, greedily, silently, and then they settled into drinking watery hot chocolate and reading *This Side of Paradise* (Judith tore her copy in two so Deena could read the first half while she read the second). But once, when Judith glanced over her book, Deena was looking back at her.

She said, "What happened to them, do you think?"

Judith said she didn't know. "It's like they've been living without natural light," she said, and fell silent. Really, she couldn't bear thinking about it.

A little before 1 P.M., the uncles arrived in a broad mood. "So how was it?" Deena asked, and one uncle said, "Well, when we got there, this old boy Fritz says, 'Okay, fellas, I have one word for you and the word is ... *exotics*.'" When this uncle grinned, Judith saw for the first time the friendly gap between his front teeth. "He showed us emus and ostriches," the other uncle said, "and he's talking a mile a minute about high protein and low maintenance, and when he was about out of gas he turned around and he was beaming like a new daddy and he says, 'You know what I really like about these birds? They are completely *flightless*.'" The uncles were having a good time. "We could've got us little cards that said *Eleson Brothers, Purveyors of Flightless Bird Meat*," at which even Judith had to laugh.

—⁓—

That night, back at home, Judith and her father cooked up a supper of scrambled eggs, sausage, and spinach as a way of putting to use the seven-grain bread he'd baked that day while she was away. Judith uncapped a jar of orange marmalade and said, "Deena and I saw Patrick Guest today in Woolcott."

Her father seemed to hesitate a half-second before he slid eggs from the tilted skillet. "Did I know you were going to Woolcott?"

"No, I said I was going with Deena's uncles to a place near Fenton, and it turns out Fenton is near Woolcott." She took a quick bite and plunged ahead. "Anyhow, he looked awful. Like an actual zombie." She watched her father. "And so did Mrs. Guest."

Her father took in Judith's gaze and said, "Ah."

"She asked about you," Judith said.

Her father's eyes broke from Judith's. He chewed several mixed bites of spinach and egg without speaking. Then he said, "I suspect you're jumping to conclusions, Judith."

"So why don't you straighten me out?"

He pointedly kept eating. So did she. *Because it isn't your business.* She could hear the words as if he'd spoken them. Silence filled the room. He reached for a piece of toasted bread. His method was to puddle the marmalade on his dish, then slide a small amount on the edge of each bite of toast. He said that something seemed off with the bread—he wondered if the yeast had expired. He forked another sausage link from the serving dish.

But eventually his expression softened, he sighed audibly, and he said, "Look, sweetheart, Delia Guest and I met a few times for coffee here in town. Her life has not been easy—her father died when she was six or seven, and then she was thirty-seven years old, widowed twice, and losing her farm. She saw me, correctly, as a safe commodity. Our friendship was based on circumstance and proximity. I was her stranger on a train. Then she moved away and that was that."

"And that was that."

"Yes." He let his eyes fall evenly on Judith. "That was that."

So although he had, as she thought of it, thrown her a couple of table scraps, he'd ended where he'd started, with the position that none of this was really any of her business. Which meant that in regard to Delia Guest, if that *hadn't* been that, if there *had* been some kind of strange romance (*strange* because any romance between her father and someone other than her mother would be strange), well, then, that wasn't Judith's concern. But it was her concern. She couldn't help it, it just was.

She found she couldn't swallow the food she'd just chewed.

"Are you all right, sweetheart?" her father said.

She drank some water, nodded, and drank some more water.

Her father sat back in his chair. Probably he had some sense of her disturbance and gloom and saw the usefulness of distraction. In any case, he said, "You know, Delia Guest was born in that farmhouse we visited. Her actual Christian name is Cordelia, after Lear's good daughter." His voice was soft now, and thoughtful. "That's something, isn't it? A man and wife in a Nebraska farmhouse in 1933 giving their baby girl the name of Lear's good daughter."

Judith thought this sounded like too much credit. "Maybe they just got Cordelia from some let's-name-the-baby book," she said.

He ignored this. "Delia's father didn't live long enough to rage

125

on the heath." A small smile. "He died as abruptly as her husbands did—a hunting accident, though he hadn't been hunting. He'd just been a man in a brown hat on the upper contours of a field. She was six or seven—that's how early her bad luck began. What she remembers is how she was mad at him as he'd gotten ready to go off into the fields that morning and when he'd said his left cheek needed a mouse kiss and she was the only mouse he had, she'd snubbed him fiercely—she actually remembers setting her chin, crossing her arms, and turning her back—and then of course she'd changed her mind and run out, but by then he was gone."

"Oh," Judith said in a fallen voice, and when she heard how schoolgirlish she sounded, it brought her quickly back. She stiffened her voice and said, "Well, that's just a prime example of . . ." but quit because she wasn't sure what exactly it might be a prime example of.

That night, when she lay in bed thinking about herself and Patrick Guest and her father and Delia Guest and Delia Guest's father, it all wound up in a muddling confusion, and she finally gave up, and the thought she was left with, the thought she would remember, was this: *What if, in the end, we are all just flightless birds?*

7

In the days after discovering—or not discovering—Malcolm's infidelity, Judith found herself taking stock. In the past, she had occasionally speculated that a mistress for Malcolm might be more a good thing than a bad one—that it might allow her to sleep when she felt sleepy, might allow the less frequent occasions for sex to feel less dutiful, might even allow her to receive with secret pleasure the expensive little offerings of a penitent spouse—but she now realized that these idle thoughts needed considerable refinement. The existence of the mistress needed to be so abstract as to be credibly deniable, for one thing, and for another—or was this just a variation of the same idea?—the other woman needed to be someone of whom Judith had no image whatever (Francine Metcalf's white Rubenesque body poised in a casually sensual attitude on a hotel bed had turned out to be a difficult picture to dispel).

During other rough patches in her life—when her awkwardness with motherhood troubled her, or when Malcolm went through a period of distraction—Judith had always burrowed into her work, but that couldn't hold her now. Her mind wandered in the editing room, she lost her decisiveness, and many of her cuts were made just to end her exasperation. More than once Lucy Meynke had fallen overtly silent over her choices. Twice Mick

Hooper had to push back other sessions—looping the actors, sound spotting, mixing, coloring, titling—because Judith had missed her deadline.

Outside of work, Judith began doing things she had never imagined she might do. She checked Malcolm's shirts for Francine Metcalf's scent (having determined, by means of a casual drop-in at the bank, that it was jasmine-based), and she went through the American Express statement for unusual charges for food or lodging (even while knowing perfectly well that Malcolm would certainly have used cash). But in the end these searches and inquiries told her nothing.

Judith had heard of women fighting for their mates, using their charms and wiles to reel the wayward hubby back, but she was in no shape for it. The thought of Malcolm having casual sex with someone else was bad enough, but worse yet was the possibility that it wasn't casual at all. The thought of Malcolm routinely sharing intimate and important conversations with Francine Metcalf caused her to feel logy, dull, almost benumbed. The life she'd thought of as handsome and heavy-timbered now seem to tremble under her every step. She began having headaches, and the bad ones really were bad—she would have to see a doctor about them. They started with a black dot in her right eye, a growing dot set against a jagged edge of light, after which it began to bear into all the brain's tenderest spots, until nausea unfolded and overtook her and nothing seemed more attractive than a cool dark place to lie down in.

Even without the headaches, she found herself craving stillness. She stopped reading *Variety* and the *L.A. Times,* she stopped turning on music in the car, she turned off her cell phone. One night after work, she took a meandering route home, then parked across the street, sat in the car, and stared at her house long enough to imagine that it might be someone else's.

When Malcolm remarked one morning that Judith was look-ing tired, she said, "That would be because I *am* tired. I can't sleep. The show we're on isn't done and they've already brought in the next one to cut." She was aware that he'd heard this kind of complaint before, but then, although it wasn't true, she added another. "You've begun snoring," she said.

"Pardon?" Malcolm looked bewildered.

"You snore," she said.

"I snore?"

She nodded. "Unless someone else was in bed with me last night." She could hardly believe it—she was lifting her chin in mock thought. "But no, it was just you."

Her surprise at saying this caused her to laugh at a strange high pitch, and though he gave a small reflexive laugh, he was clearly hurt. When, later, on her way to work, she replayed the scene, she wished she could give it a hard edit. Why had she said what she said? What in the world was she doing? Malcolm was civilized, Malcolm was goodhearted, Malcolm provided. She reached for her cell phone, cupped it in the call position. Possibly, too—she lowered the phone—Malcolm fornicated five times a week with Francine Metcalf.

At a stoplight, through the closed windows of her Audi, Judith heard the pounding bass beat of rap music. It came from a tricked-out red Honda beside her. The music was so loud the car seemed to pulsate, but in the passenger's seat a pretty Hispanic girl, her face rigid with makeup, sat motionless, looking at noth-ing with blank eyes. Beyond her, the driver, a huge man with a goatee and slicked-back hair, sat in much the same ceramic atti-tude. Judith supposed that two blocks back they might've been laughing like maniacs, but she doubted it.

What she didn't doubt was that there was more going on within these two than she could ever guess, and probably more than they could guess either—that under our skin run whole streams of feelings and inclinations so slithery they are only rarely and uncertainly grasped.

There had been fog this morning in L.A., and on her way out to the car Judith had stopped between the house and the garage to look at the intricate dewy web of the large, brown, hairy-legged spider that waited at the edge in such perfect stillness that it seemed to Judith like indifference (a hypothesis she disproved by gently touching the web; the spider scampered toward her finger with alarming speed). She recalled the several times she'd encouraged Malcolm to take Francine Metcalf to dinner before one of the evening bank meetings, and she remembered how airily she'd told Malcolm, when declining to accompany him to some bankers' convention in New Orleans or Kona—the timing was always horrible in terms of her own work, and really, however good the nanny might be, they were both uncomfortable being away at the same time—that at least he could rehash the meetings with Francine at the end of the day, and what was up with offering those particular temptations? What kind of traps do we set without even knowing we're setting them, and, more to the point, what appetites crave the meal such traps might provide? She had no idea. No earthly idea.

The moment the light changed, the throbbing red Honda shot ahead. Judith eased forward, used her blinker, and moved into a slower lane. If Malcolm and Francine Metcalf were in fact an item, it might at least in part be due to her own orchestration. That was the possibility at hand. But why? To slash what picture, disturb what calm pond? Gain what leverage, give her what rights?

Over the next four or five blocks, as the Audi lurched along with the other traffic, Judith found herself formulating the notion that whether it was Los Angeles or Kyoto or Constantinople, the love between a man and a woman (and probably between a man and a man or a woman and a woman, too—why should they be excused?) had at the controls something thuggish. And this was not the last sobering thought she had before turning into the studio parking lot. The last was that, at least in regard to the state of marriage and the means by which its weaknesses might be described, she was becoming more and more like her mother.

When she walked into the cutting room, Judith was surprised to find Lucy sitting in the straight-backed chair Judith thought of as her own. On the monitor in front of her was the image of the Ben character about to shoot a basketball at night on a semi-lighted court, a frame Judith had never before seen.

"What's this?" Judith asked.

"New scene," Lucy said. "Pottle and Hooper ordered it because they hate the episode as is." She was rising from the chair so Judith could take her place. "They called me last night," she said. "They tried to call you on your cell but couldn't get through. I tried, too. Cell and landline."

"My cell was dead. As for the home phone, think Milla in full networking mode." Judith eased into the seat, strangely warm, and said, "Okay, what've you got so far?"

It was a long day, and a long week. They worked harder and fell further behind. Once—this had never happened before—she exchanged petty objections with Lucy Meynke. Friday night Judith, who should have worked late, instead left the studio early to buy fresh tomatoes, onions, and eggplant for ratatouille, then, having prepared it, sat at the table waiting for Malcolm. Camille and Sonya ate without expression or comment. Judith poured herself a third glass of wine and began to eat by herself, masking her irritation with careful unhurried bites, and why was she so irritated anyhow? Thirty minutes late—now thirty-five—wasn't that flagrant, was it? The work was whittling away at her, that was part of it, but it was also true that she kept noticing strangers doing overtly indiscreet things: sitting close to one another in parked cars in broad daylight, or, as happened this afternoon in a far corner of the Vons' parking lot, a middle-aged man leaning into a car to give the woman behind the wheel a lingering kiss before slipping into his own car, parked nearby. Judith had begun walking toward the market's front doors, but as the couple drove off in different directions, the woman passed close enough that the radiance in her face couldn't be mistaken. Judith tried to watch these little episodes with the distanced interest of a movie-goer and to restrict her thoughts along the bland lines of *Such is the human condition,* but all that notwithstanding, the moment Malcolm presented himself tonight in the dining room, she rose from the table and began cleaning up. He made apologies—they'd had a security malfunction at one of the branches just as he was leaving—but she didn't respond, nor did she offer to heat the rata-touille on his plate. She put her wedding ring in the tiny crackleware saucer she kept on the windowsill for that purpose and began rinsing dishes. Camille and Sonya helped just long enough to say they had, then slid off to their rooms at opposite ends of the house.

"The pugilists retire to their corners," Malcolm observed after they'd departed, a remark Judith pretended not to hear. Malcolm didn't seem to mind. He rose and took the day's mail to the table to sort through while he ate.

A few days ago, Judith, Lucy, and another editor had run into Tom Bergin's for a salad, and two tables beyond them, a man eating with his wife pulled out a book to read while his wife looked here and there with a chipper expression, as if this was exactly what she'd hoped for, to come out in public with a man who would rather read a book than talk to her. Lucy said, "If I had me a gun, I'd lend it to that woman." Judith laughed, and the other editor asked on whom the woman should use it, herself or the hubby. "First shoot the husband," Lucy said, "then assess your position."

Malcolm said, "Have you seen this Visa bill?"

Judith hadn't, but nearly had. Malcolm always handled the bills, but tonight, while heating water for pasta, she'd considered steaming open the Visa statement to check for incriminating charges. "No," she said. "Why? Should I look at it?"

"Sitting down, is my suggestion." Then he remarked favorably on the cold ratatouille. "Is that rosemary in there?"

"Basil." Her voice was sullen. She wondered what, culinarily, was the equivalent of tone deafness.

He was looking at her thoughtfully, which also irritated her.

She said, "Tonight, in the Laurel Canyon Vons, I had three different employees ask if I had found everything I wanted. Three. And they were all grinning like idiots. I thought I was in the Magic Kingdom or something." That Malcolm seemed amused by this only deepened her annoyance. "Three times. I was minding my own business, but three times. I should've said, *Solitude. On what aisle will I find solitude?*" Malcolm's smile, calm, knowing—it was driving her crazy. "What?" she said.

He kept his benevolent expression and gave his shoulders the subtlest shrug. "Do you think *miffy* is a word?"

Almost luxuriantly, something dark and venomous unfolded within Judith. She said, "What is that supposed to mean?"

Malcolm tried to keep the tone airy. "I suppose it would mean prone toward miffedness."

"A synonym of *pissy,* you might say."

"I guess so." He looked away, inhaled, exhaled. He was tired. A fight was not what he was spoiling for.

"Then why not just say *pissy?*"

"You've got me there," he said. "As a small nod to civility?"

Judith felt a little of the sourness drain from her mood, but only a little.

After a few silent seconds, Malcolm tried a change of subjects. "I'm taking Sonya and Milla to the Getty tomorrow morning," he said. "Something about a world-cultures assignment for Milla, and Sonya has never seen it." He gave Judith a hopeful look. "Care to join us? We could go to Modo Mio afterward for lunch."

An olive branch—she liked the restaurant's cozy atmosphere and salmon penne—so two Judiths fought for a moment, the one who wouldn't mind pretending all was well and by doing so perhaps in fact make it so, and the one who wanted to hold open her grudge-keeping options. She said, "Tempting, but no."

"No?"

"We're moving the bird's-eye maple tomorrow. I rented a storage unit."

He took this in. "We could stay and help."

"You could, but you shouldn't. It's all lined up with a guy from work who has a truck and can use the extra money."

Malcolm had finished the ratatouille but was running a scrap of bread through the sauce. "Should I feel unwanted or merely unneeded?"

"How about excused without prejudice or something like that?"

"Okay," Malcolm said, "but only on condition you and I have dinner next Saturday night at the new Italian place on Melrose with the chef from Valentino." He smiled his thin urbane smile. "The kind of place you might wear the little black dress the girls and I will acquire for you after lunch tomorrow."

She said, "Are you feeling contrite about something?"

He shook his head, and his expression—was it truly surprise or

134

simply meant to suggest it?—dissolved into amusement. "I'm not," he said. "But perhaps that's just a failure of self-awareness." Then he smiled at her, a warm, authentic, enfolding smile, and asked if she was still a flawless size six.

8

The first Christmas with her father in Nebraska was, in Judith's opinion, almost perfect: they cooked and consumed a delicious meal, he told her a story she'd never heard, and then they went for a walk.

It had snowed the night before, a dry, clean, piling snow, and when she'd come up from the basement in the morning, the streets hadn't been plowed, so the whiteness was unbroken and all the roofs and trees and fences were plump with snow. Judith and her father shoveled the front walk while the beef roasted (the accompaniments were to be twice-baked potatoes, peas with pearl onions, and curried fruit). Judith set out her grandparents' good china and silverware, and before her father brought out the serving dishes, she lighted candles and looked at the stemmed glass of red wine he poured for her, though she barely sipped from it. For dessert they had strawberry ice cream with slivered almonds, and he brewed them coffee. It was all serene and beautiful and orderly. They washed and dried the china and set the silverware into the slots of its velvet-lined box, then he laid a fire in the front room, where they unwrapped their presents. He'd bought her a Victorian punch-paper sampler in an old red frame. The sampler said:

LOST,

YESTERDAY,

SOMEWHERE BETWEEN SUNRISE AND SUNSET,

TWO GOLDEN HOURS,

EACH SET WITH SIXTY DIAMOND MINUTES.

NO REWARD IS OFFERED,

FOR THEY ARE GONE FOREVER.

—HORACE MANN.

He'd found it in an antiques store in Hemingford, a transaction he recalled wryly. "Before taking my money, the saleswoman said, 'Isn't it precious?'"

"Horace did lay it on pretty thick," Judith said, "but I still love it."

"Yeah. I did, too."

Her mother had sent an equally odd gift, an ancient handsome barometer whose brass arrow pointed to a section marked *Change*. Her father opened the present she'd bought for him—a bottle of Glenmorangie single-malt scotch—and seemed shocked into stillness. "How . . . ?"

"I knew you liked scotch, so I read up on it."

"No, but . . . logistically . . . how?"

"Mom did the actual ordering," Judith said, and felt a pang at the completeness of her own contentment. "I should call her," she said, and her father nodded distractedly while heading to the kitchen for a glass.

But when Judith went to the hall phone and dialed the number in Vermont, a man answered in an odd, not-quite British accent. "Greetings and goodwill to all," he said.

"Jonathan?" The tall man with the arm gestures and the Buffalo Bill jacket.

"Hello, love," he said, still using the half-baked accent. "I'll get your mum. She's been hoping you'd ring."

When he put the phone down, Judith could hear significant background commotion: loud voices, laughter, even some singing. She'd nearly given up on her mother's answering when finally she did. "Hi, sweetie," she said. "Merry Christmas."

Judith said, "Why is Jonathan talking like that?"

"Oh, sweetie, it's so quiet here without you and I was dreading Christmas and Jonathan saved the day by having everyone here for a traditional English Christmas. We're having duck and a roasted pear and Amaretto trifle and ever so many yummy things. Oh, and crackers! You know, those wrapped cardboard tubes that go pop? We have a gazillion of those!"

After a second or two, Judith said, "And that's why he's talking with that absurd accent?"

Her mother's laugh was merry. "It *is* absurd, isn't it, but it's been terrific for cheering me up." Silence lengthened, and finally her mother said, "So what do you think of the antique barometer?"

By the time Judith went back to the living room, her father had poured a small amount of scotch into two cut-glass tumblers and was waiting in his red floral chair.

"May we always have a clean shirt and a dollar in our pocket," he said, and they gently clicked glasses.

Judith sipped and nearly spit hers back in the glass. "Oh, my God!" she said. "How can anything that vile cost that much?"

Her father wore an expression of utter contentment. "Silk made fluid," he said.

She handed hers over. "Then please finish mine."

He took her glass and said, "And how is your mother?"

"She said she'd been depressed, so she invited some people over for dinner," Judith said. "Also, it turns out the barometer she gave me always says *Change.* That's why she liked it."

"Ah," her father said. "The unappeasable barometer. No matter how much we change, it asks for more."

Judith, who already viewed the gift warily, now wondered how to get rid of it. Set it out in the alley on top of the trash, maybe, and let some rummager haul the curse away. (She didn't. She stored it in the back of her closet, and years later, after her father's funeral, she discovered it hanging in his office at the college.)

Her father was regarding his tumbler of scotch, swirling the liquor gently, watching it coat the crystal. He said he had the feeling that going back to the cheap stuff was going to be a humbling experience. Then he said, "These are the same glasses my father drank bourbon from."

"Your father?"

"Is that what I said? I meant my grandfather." He thought about it. "He also had a cut-glass decanter he poured it from, but that's gone now."

Judith looked again at the barometer. Then, without giving it much thought, she said, "Didn't you ever wonder who your father was?"

He stared at her. "I know who he was. Who said I didn't?"

"Mom. She said your mother never married and would never say who your father was. Plus you never mentioned him."

Her father sipped his scotch and gazed into the fire. She waited until she couldn't wait any longer.

"So who was your father, then?"

The embers shifted and glowed orange, and he rose to feed the fire two more logs. From his armchair, he watched the flame spread and said, "Today my mother would be called a single mom, but in those days she was an unwed mother." He sipped his scotch and kept talking. He and his mother had lived in San Francisco from the time he was born until she died, when he was twelve. He believed his mother had gone to San Francisco because it was a more openhearted town than most when it came to misfits like herself. She'd found work with a legal publisher named

Bancroft-Whitney. His mother adhered to routine, a practice (he smiled when he said this) she'd passed on to her son. After school, he spent afternoons at the home of Henry Salvatori, a schoolmate whose mother made cocoa and cinnamon toast and would let them lie under the dining room table reading comic books (his favorite was a supernatural crime fighter known as Doctor Occult). Sunday afternoons he and his mother walked to the Cliff House, where his mother would have a Remus fizz, her one weekly self-indulgence, and he would have a Coke float. On cold or wet days they'd step down from the Cliff House to the Musée Mécanique, where he would stand a little back from the machines and wait for someone to put a nickel in the slot and bring the mechanical characters to life (his favorite was Susie the Can-Can Dancer). On pleasant days they would walk to the park. His mother would sit on a bench and read the *Examiner,* or gaze over it at him, or sometimes close her eyes and tilt her head back to receive the mild warmth of the sun. He assumed his mother to be happy, but later, looking back, he thought she was only as happy as a person waiting for the next phase of her life might be.

On the afternoon of his mother's death, he was called into the school office, where Mrs. Tompkins, the principal, explained that his mother had become ill at work and been taken to the hospital. *She'll be all right, though?* he asked, and Mrs. Tompkins said she truly hoped so. But Mrs. Tompkins didn't look herself—her face wasn't right—and she explained that he would spend the night with Henry Salvatori. Instead he stayed two. Henry didn't look at him differently, but Mrs. Salvatori did. So did the teachers at school.

On the third day he was called out of the classroom and found his grandparents waiting for him in the hallway. He had never seen his grandparents outside Nebraska, and their appearance in San Francisco frightened him. They were like Mrs. Tompkins and the other adults—they didn't look like themselves. They walked him outside. They sat alone near the flagpole—whenever he later heard the lazy resonant clinking of a rope against a metal flagpole he would recall this scene—and his grandfather explained that his mother had died when a blood vessel in her brain burst. He would go with them to Nebraska. His grandmother said they'd packed most of his things, but they wanted him to be sure they hadn't left anything important behind.

When he walked into the flat with his grandparents, it was no longer the place in which he'd lived with his mother. The furniture and carpets were gone. His grandparents' whispers sounded loud in the bare rooms. He went through a cardboard box filled with his discarded possessions and pulled out a few things to take along—a folded picture of Whirlaway from *Life,* three Doctor Occult comic books, and a Cub Scout buckle he'd found and kept even though he'd never been a Cub Scout. He went into his mother's room. There was nothing there. He took a deep breath, but it didn't smell like his mother's room anymore. He opened the door to the small walk-in closet. It was empty, too, but her smell was still there. He closed the door behind him. He stayed there, breathing in his mother's smell. He heard the tapping of his grandparents' shoes on the bare floor and stood perfectly still. They called his name and he held his breath. Finally the door opened. His grandfather looked in at him. "We need to go now, Howard," he said in a low voice, and Howard allowed himself to be led away.

On the train his grandparents gave him the window seat, so he could watch the countryside and then, at night, the lights. From time to time he would see a light in a distant farmhouse window, and once he saw a small campfire and wondered if there were still cowboys or Indians or hobos who slept out on the open plains. His grandfather was the first to fall asleep in the reclining seats.

His grandmother knitted in dim light. Finally Howard closed his eyes. Sometime during the night he dreamed he was in his room in San Francisco and his mother had come, as she came every night before she went to bed, and pulled his covers to his chin and said, *Another good day, kiddo.* He began to awaken then, and in those transient slippery moments between sleeping and waking, he felt the closeness to his mother he had for the past few days been craving. He opened his eyes. Evidently he'd been speaking or making sounds, because his grandparents were looking at him in the darkness.

He said, "She's here, isn't she?"

His grandmother seemed frozen by these words. She didn't move and didn't speak. His grandfather leaned forward. "Yes. That's right. We're taking her home, too. We've got a plot for her in the churchyard."

Judith's father rose, punched the fire with a new log before laying it into the orange coals, then reseated himself and said, "I haven't forgotten your question, if that's what you're thinking."

"I wasn't thinking anything," Judith said.

He finished his scotch and kept the glass in his hand. He said there were a surprising number of people at the funeral, most of them friends of his grandparents, but some of them had known his mother as a little girl. Two of them told him his mother had been sharp as a tack. If she'd been a man, one of them said, she would've been a doctor or a lawyer. The casket was open. He went up when no one was there. He touched her skin, but it had lost its softness. She felt like a doll of herself. He went out and sat under the porch of the funeral home, where he wouldn't be seen. Men came out from time to time, and one of them said to another that he was surprised that Mert Feister had showed up, and the other man gave a small laugh and wondered aloud whether Mert's wife had given him permission.

A few days later, Howard took the funeral register into the kitchen, where his grandmother was ironing. He read a couple of names—Alvin Lemon, Bob Brubaker—and asked who they were. She told him. Then he read *Mert Feister* and asked who he was, and his grandmother just said, *Oh, he runs the Western Wear in town.* He said he'd heard a man at the funeral say that it was funny Mert Feister would come. His grandmother sprinkled water on the shirt she was ironing. She had a pop bottle fitted with a corked sprinkler cap. He asked why it would be funny that Mert Feister would come.

His grandmother was being careful, he could tell, and finally she said, well, Mert Feister had been a sweetheart of his mother's for a while. Then Mert Feister had fallen for Dory Atkins, who, his grandmother said, had had her cap set for him since grammar school. His grandmother didn't think Howard's mother minded the loss much, to be truthful, but Dory Atkins never let Mert Feister say a word to Howard's mother ever after. She guessed that Dory was now thinking there was no point in fretting over a dead woman—a foolish idea, in his grandmother's opinion.

He asked if his mother had ever had any other sweethearts, and after a moment's hesitation, his grandmother said in a decisive tone that no, she had not.

The following day, Howard walked up to Feister's Western Wear. Mert and Dory Feister were both there. She quickly came down the aisle and said, "Let me know if you need help," and otherwise they didn't say another word to him. He went back several more afternoons, and even began saving for a long-sleeved green shirt he saw there. On his fifth or sixth visit, Dory Feister came up to him and asked what he was there for. Her tone wasn't friendly. *To see if the green shirt is still here,* he said. She asked which green shirt, and when he showed her, she pulled it from the stack and handed it to him. "Here," she said. "Take it, it's yours, but for God's sake leave us alone."

Judith's father turned the tumbler in his hand. "I did leave them alone, of course."

"So he was your . . ." Her voice trailed away.

"Putative father," her father said. A dry smile. "Though even at that age I had some sense that a man wasn't much of a father if all he was willing to give to the enterprise was a small donation of personal lust."

The fire needed another log, but her father didn't add it. He turned to Judith and said, "Shall we go for a walk?" and they did walk, heading no place in particular, just moving from one wide white street to another, warm within their heavy coats, not talking, listening to the clean squeak of their boots in the snow. They walked and walked. A few children were out playing, but no one else was out walking, or driving either. Judith and her father began walking down the center of the deserted streets. Eventually their route took them down Main Street, past all the shops closed for the holiday—Myers Drugs, Marian's Mademoiselle Shop, Love's Jewelers. Midblock, her father drew up and pointed a finger at a thrift shop on the west side of the street. "There," he said. "That's where Mert and Dory Feister had their Western Wear before they moved to Arizona."

It was still and quiet. They were surrounded by snow, but it was not snowing. "It was only a couple of years ago that they sold. I looked into when they put it up for sale. It was exactly ten days after my hiring by the college was announced in the local paper." He smiled. "Though for the record, Dory Feister cited their declining health as the reason for the move."

In a moment she and her father would again be walking, and they would again hear the clean squeak of their boots, but now, stopped in the center of Main Street, it was deeply quiet, and for that long moment Judith had the sensation of standing within an unshaken snow globe. For the rest of her life, whenever in some thrift shop or somebody's home she would come upon a broken snow globe, one where the snowflakes no longer swirled, she would be reminded of these moments standing in the stillness, staring at the thrift shop, and holding her father's hand. For it was true: she hardly knew when she had taken it, but she was holding her father's hand.

—⁓—

The weeks passed. In February, for her sixteenth birthday, Judith's father drove her to the National Guard Armory to take her driving test, which, because of her summer's practice on county roads, she passed without difficulty. He also gave her an electric blanket, which she pretended to like even though she was sure the looping white cords would ruin the look of her bed. Her mother sent her a beautiful suede miniskirt that Judith liked but wasn't about to wear to school. (She couldn't bear the idea of kneeling in front of the assistant principal to see whether it would touch the floor, as required.) Judith knew how much she ought to miss her mother and was sometimes able to create a mood from which letters persuasive in this regard could be written, but as the year wore on, communication between her and her mother became less frequent, and letters to Patrick Guest had stopped altogether. (After the misbegotten visit, she sent several bland letters, and the last one had been returned stamped *Addressee Moved No Forwarding Address*.)

Judith's favorite night of the week remained Wednesday, when she and her father still went to the movies, her father leaving the theater without comment after *What's Up, Doc?* and *The Hot Rock*, but saying after *The Last Picture Show* or *Fat City* that their "admissions hadn't been wasted."

"I get it now," Judith said when her father declared himself a satisfied customer after viewing *McCabe & Mrs. Miller.* "If we come out of a movie feeling good, we've been hoodwinked, but if we come out feeling like shooting ourselves, we got our money's worth."

Her father issued one of his puffing laughs and said that probably wasn't a bad rule of thumb. It was March, dark and steely cold. Judith had hated the movie's ending—Warren Beatty nattily dressed in black, dying in the snow, while Julie Christie lay dreamy-eyed in an opium den—but that little muddy godforsaken town with its frozen rain and gray skies and buildings of raw lumber had made a captive of her, and stepping from the theater into the bitter cold of her own world offered no particular relief. Her head throbbed, and as she and her father walked the five blocks home with their collars turned up and chins tucked into their scarves, she took real comfort in the fact that, before leaving for the movie, she'd remembered to go downstairs to her maple bed and dial her new electric blanket to its warmest setting.

—*m*—

In late April winter finally abated, and in mid-May school recessed for the summer holiday. Since February, Judith had planned to spend the first two weeks of vacation with her mother in Vermont, but a few days before she was to depart, her mother telephoned. "I need to talk to you about something," she said.

Judith felt herself settle into the cold metal chair of distrust. "About what?"

"Something tricky."

Judith was sure she heard her mother taking a deep breath.

"Okay," her mother said, "here's the thing. I was doing something a few minutes ago that made me ashamed of myself and then I thought, *No, I'm not going to do this. I'm going to call Judith and be out in the open.*"

Judith said nothing.

Her mother said, "I don't know why this is so hard, I really don't." She paused. "It's just the kind of thing that comes up all the time at my CR classes, how through our own complicity we strengthen the chains that bind us."

Judith didn't know what CR classes were, and wasn't about to ask. She said, "Mom, if you don't say what you called to say, I'm going to scream."

"Okay, okay." Another audible sigh. "The thing is, with you gone, I needed someone to help me with the cooking and cleaning and expenses and things, so I asked a friend to come live here." This last, critical information came out quickly, without much volume.

Cruelly Judith said, "So this girlfriend is using my room now, is that it?"

"Well, that's the thing, sweetie. It's not a girlfriend. It's a friend who is a man."

Later in life, Judith and her mother would recount this conversation with amusement, in particular the friend-who-is-a-man line, but within its living moment, Judith stiffened into a cold rigidity. "Is this that Jonathan guy?"

Her mother hesitated. "I know Jonathan didn't make a good first impression on you, but—"

"And he's using my room, is that it?" Judith said, though she knew he wasn't, not when he could ... But she didn't want to complete the thought.

Judith's mother slid away from the question. "I'd decided he would have to leave during your visit, and I was cleaning out his clothes and things in order to pretend he isn't living here, and I suddenly decided it wasn't fair to him and it wasn't really fair to me or to you either, and that's when I picked up the phone and called you."

"Why wouldn't it be fair to me?"

Her mother faltered. "Well, for you to be here sensing that something is wrong without knowing quite what."

Suddenly Judith didn't feel like arguing. Her feelings were bruised. There was a reordering going on here, and she'd just been bumped down a notch. She fell silent, and so did her mother, but not, Judith knew, because she was badly hurt. She was just waiting on the formality of a verdict, which was forgone. The visit was spoiled. This, after all, was the point of the phone call, wasn't it? To spoil the visit, to call it off? If Buffalo Bill was in the house with them, Judith's only pleasure would be in turning the two weeks sour; and if he wasn't there, his absence would be a fact her mother would begrudge in spite of better intentions. Either way, they'd both be counting the days until Judith returned to Nebraska, so why go to begin with?

"Maybe I'll come at Christmas instead," Judith said, and her mother rattled off a long sentence that began with "Oh, sweetie, I wish you'd reconsider," and ended with "so I don't know, maybe you're right, Christmas might be better."

Judith found her father in his little backyard garden, pulling weeds among a line of inch-high plants she thought might be cucumbers. He was wearing boots, denim pants, and a faded long-sleeved blue cotton shirt, a getup that might've had its dashing dad aspect except for the conical straw hat he wore on his head. Judith called it his coolie hat.

"Mom's shacking up with some hippie buffoon," she announced when she drew near. Her father didn't respond, so she said, "Did you know that?"

He tipped the conical hat slightly back to look at Judith. "I knew she had a male friend living with her, yes. She called to ask what to do with my clothes because she wanted to clear out half the closet."

"He'll need more than half," Judith said.

Her father chortled at this, but didn't comment.

Judith said, "The worst of it is, he's such a buffoon he doesn't even know he's a buffoon."

Her father let this pass, and she said, "Does this mean you and Mom are getting a divorce?"

A tired look crossed her father's face. "I don't know, peapod. Maybe. I suspect it'll be more your mother's decision than mine. I myself wouldn't rush into anything. I told her that if permitted, marriage can be a surprisingly elastic institution."

"What did she say?"

He made a soft unhappy laugh. "She said that sounded like something a polygamist would say."

Judith didn't laugh, or even smile. He was always using a wry remark for a magic wand, waving away something important, but not this time; she wouldn't let him. She stood and waited and made him feel her eyes on him. He took a deep breath and looked away. Finally—he still wasn't looking at her—he said, "What you should understand is that this isn't your mother's fault, Judith. I made every attempt to—" He suddenly stopped. It was as if he had just heard himself: *I made every attempt.* He turned and let his eyes fall on her. "Look, Judith, I tried to be the husband your mother needed, but . . . I just wasn't very good at it." He seemed on the verge of saying more, but didn't. He tugged his hat forward so his eyes were again shaded. He returned to his gardening.

Judith stood where she was, but she felt small and defeated. Her father was weeding his garden. Her mother was living with a fool. And Vermont, the Vermont that Judith had once believed indestructible and then at least mendable, well, it was gone now, and as much as she wanted to blame the loss on some moron named Jonathan, she knew it was something murkier than that.

She watched her father pull a snail from a leaf, roll it onto the grass, and step on it. She expected a crunch, but so soft was the shell and the ground that there was no sound at all.

⁓

When she'd signed up for the AP tests in the spring, Mr. Flood, Judith's school counselor, had advised her to start "beefing up her résumé." What résumé? Judith had thought, but within a week's time she'd volunteered as a candy striper at the hospital for the summer, and when the Vermont trip fell through, she reported early. She liked the uniform—a pink-and-white seersucker tunic that tied on each side over white jeans and blouse—but she didn't get to do anything but sit at a desk in the lobby and tell people which room their sick relative was in and, on rare, seminauseating occasions, deliver transparent bags of deep red blood to the lab.

She also volunteered at the college library shelving books, which was more to her liking. The library was quiet, air-conditioned, and odorless, and with the campus all but deserted, there weren't many books to shelve. Often she could sit and read or simply daydream. One day, standing in an aisle near a third-story window, she watched a couple of people passing below—a student with a dog trotting beside him, a long-haired girl in a green peasant dress—and then, a moment after spotting someone wearing a conical straw hat just like her father's, she realized that it *was* her father, probably on his way to the pool, which gave her a subtle jolt. Last summer they would've been walking this path together. He passed beneath a shade tree, then stopped and looked back: the girl in the green peasant dress must've called out, because she'd changed course and was now catching up to him.

When she drew close, she spoke to him, he listened, then glanced at his watch, said something, and they parted. It was brief—probably he'd referred her to his office hours—but there was something about the self-aware way the girl had stood before him that was disquieting to Judith, and she was glad when they broke off and moved in opposite directions.

If Judith's first summer in Nebraska had belonged to her and her father, and if the third would belong to her and Willy Blunt, then the second belonged by default to Deena. True, Judith's father went out of his way to plan outings with her whenever their schedules allowed it—an occasional farm auction, a swim at War Memorial Pool, a drive over to Fort Robinson, where the local troupe staged nightly melodramas—but most of Judith's unscheduled hours were spent palling around with Deena, talking over the counter at Dairy Queen, walking up to the pool, anchoring themselves in a corner booth at Pizza Hut, where a boy named Calvin Haden heavily discounted their pizza slices and let them, as he put it, gas up for free on Mr. Pibb.

Of this generally languorous summer, there was one occurrence that Judith found especially disquieting. It was mid-August, and the afternoon had turned close and cloudy. Judith had agreed to walk with her father up to War Memorial Pool, but a problem had arisen soon after their arrival. She'd worn her sunflower yellow swimming suit under shorts and a cotton top, but when she took off her outer clothes she noticed a dark spot on the front of the bikini bottoms—not a big spot and not a blood spot, though she feared it might be mistaken for that. She went quickly into the pool in hopes the water or chlorine might help, but when the suit began to dry, the spot seemed if anything more prominent. Judith pulled on her shorts and top and told her father she felt like taking a walk.

He looked up from the book he was annotating in the margins.

"Do you want company?" he said, but he wasn't putting his pencil away—he was putting a point on it with a little dime-store sharpener.

"No, I'm just suddenly hungry."

He said there was food at the commons if she didn't want to walk all the way home. Did she need money?

Judith shook her head and set off.

She bought a tuna salad sandwich and a can of V8 from a vending machine at the commons and walked south. It was still hot and close, but the clouds had broken and a breeze had begun to stir, so she kept walking. Beyond the fringes of campus, she veered from the faint path that led to Initial Hill (where small boulders, spray-painted white, formed the letters *RS*) and found a flat rock in the shade of a pined knoll. She opened her V8 and used it to wash down each bite of the tuna sandwich. She tucked the wrapper into the empty can and felt suddenly, overwhelmingly sleepy. The mild breeze felt cool on her damp skin and made a low flutish sound as it moved through the pines. She rolled her towel onto the ground, stretched herself out, folded her hands on her stomach, closed her eyes, and almost at once felt the first pleasantly hallucinatory yieldings of sleep.

Sometime later she awakened with a start. The angle of the sun had changed—the shadows felt longer. The wind moving through the trees still made its hollow sound, but there was something else. Noises carried from somewhere nearby, human noises, the kind that came from the back of the mouth, where sounds formed from discomfort or struggle, and Judith wondered if someone was sick, or being hurt. She crept toward an outcropping of round gray rocks, then eased forward to peer through them.

Before her lay a shady place even more removed from activity than her own. The sounds were coming both from a girl, whose face Judith could see but didn't recognize, and a large boy, whose face was turned away. His body was flabby and white—Judith guessed this was what a naked football lineman must look like—and dark hair was visible on his back and buttocks. Judith had never seen anyone having sex before, but it was clear that sex was what these two people were having now, though what it really looked like was a pummeling. The girl's eyes were squeezed closed and her face was clamped into an expression of endurance or possibly pain. Several times the huge boy withdrew his organ completely before a new thrust into the girl, at which moment he and the girl released their unsettling grunts.

"They weren't what you'd call quiet," Judith said to Deena when she told her about it later. They were sitting on a picnic table at a remote end of the city park, secluded enough that Deena could smoke her Tareytons without being seen and Judith could talk about seeing two people having sex without being overheard.

Deena said, "What did you do?"

Judith thought about what she'd done. She'd watched while the huge boy gradually converted his violent thrusting to something gentler, circular in motion, and surprisingly graceful, given the enormity of his buttocks. The girl had begun to murmur and moan, and Judith had become aware again of the flutish wind through the pines. But Judith didn't know how to talk about any of that. "I ducked behind the rocks," she said. "Then I called out, 'Amory, over here, you have to see this!' like I was talking to somebody, and then the noises stopped and I skedaddled."

Deena said, "God, Judith."

The truth was, there was nothing odder about the whole experience than her evolving reaction to it. Initially she'd been revolted, but gradually that impression had given way to something vaguer, less unpleasant, harder to explain. With Deena, she stuck to the first impression because it was easier to make amusing. "It was like those gruesome wrecks they show at safety assemblies," she said, "the ones that make you think you should never get into a car ever again."

Deena seemed disappointed. "But weren't they having fun?"

"Not as we know it."

After a second or two, Deena said, "Well, that's just it. It's not fun as we know it, because we haven't done it. It's like us saying frogs' legs or mountain oysters are gross without even tasting them."

Judith said that didn't seem untrue to her, but it also didn't seem like much of an argument for trying frogs' legs or mountain oysters. "Tell you what," she said. "You try all the weird dishes, and you can fill me in on your research."

"That a dare?"

Judith laughed. "No, it is not." Then: "Know in what way I am exactly like a redneck boy?"

Deena said she didn't, and Judith said, "I've got no use for a pregnant girlfriend."

This drew a snorting laugh from Deena. "Who said anything about getting preggers?" She lighted a fresh cigarette. "So, could you see his thingamajig?"

Judith said it was big and pink and purple and wet.

"Purple?" Deena said.

"Well, purplish."

"Still and all. God is supposed to be almighty. Why would he go with purplish?"

Judith said there was no reasonable way to answer that question.

Deena expelled a long stream of smoke. "So do you think that's what love boils down to—a guy getting a girl to the point where she actually wants to let the purplish thingamajig in?"

What Judith thought was that this sentiment was too cynical

even for her, who prided herself on her cynicism. She said, "That wouldn't be much to look forward to, would it?" and Deena, after some seconds and without much conviction, said no, she supposed it wouldn't.

—ɯɯ—

Two days after the start of her senior year, Judith was called to the office of Mr. Flood, the school counselor, a stout, dapper man with florid cheeks and heavily pomaded red hair. Judith had been in Mr. Flood's office three times the year before, most recently to talk about "beefing up her résumé." She couldn't remember the point of the other two occasions; she'd spent most of the five-minute sessions ignoring the drone of Mr. Flood's voice while wondering at the height and stiffness of his hair. Today, however, the counselor became animated the instant Judith appeared at his door. Instead of merely nodding at the chair opposite his desk, he rose and pulled it out for her. He said he was delighted to see her. Something was obviously up.

"Your AP scores," he said once they were both settled. "They've come in."

"Are they okay?"

Mr. Flood had hazel eyes that were at the moment shining bright. "They are to *okay*," he said, "what Mount Rushmore is to *minute*."

"That seems good," Judith said.

She could see that Mr. Flood wondered why she wasn't more excited. She wondered herself, and guessed it was because she wasn't really surprised. She'd expected to do well on the tests, and she had done well. It was all part of the plan. While Mr. Flood bent his head to thumb further through her file, Judith stared into the deep grooves his comb had cut into the red stiff hair. The teeth of the comb, she decided, had to be really large and widely spaced.

"So," Mr. Flood said, raising his eyes to Judith, "what colleges are we thinking of applying to?"

This was a question Judith could easily have answered—she'd spent hours of her idle summer time formulating lists of colleges to which she might apply, ranging from Major Reaches (Princeton, where Amory Blaine had gone) to Slam Dunks (Sage State, where Deena planned to go)—but to Mr. Flood she said, "I have no idea."

Mr. Flood leaned forward on his desktop, fixed his eyes on Judith's, and told her that although he had been the school counselor for seventeen years, he'd never had one of his students admitted to one of the really top-notch schools—the Stanfords, Harvards, or Yales. He kept his gaze on Judith. "Until now, I've never had the right candidate."

At which point Judith grasped that the real news here was that she now had an ally in this process.

"Well," she said, "what do you think we should do next?"

Mr. Flood smiled. As it happened, he had a plan, and it was already in motion.

"I've taken the liberty of signing you up for the SATs next month," he said, "and I've gotten approval for your enrollment in two classes at the college."

What? Judith thought, and Mr. Flood, looking down at his file, said, "Calculus and American literature to 1945." He smiled up at Judith. "Tuesday and Thursday afternoons. It's up to you, of course, but I've got the go-ahead from both your father and Admissions."

"My father?"

Mr. Flood nodded. "I also talked to him about the schools you might apply to." A brimming smile. "He takes a real interest in you. He's the one, for example, who mentioned Stanford." Mr. Flood chattered on. He talked about how they could use his seven-step plan for writing a "knock-their-socks-off" essay and which teachers should be asked for letters of recommendation and what kinds of points those letters should make. Her head was swimming.

When she got back to class, Deena leaned over and whispered, "What did Floodcakes want?" and Judith, sensing that she might already be inches past a fork in diverging paths, shrugged and said, "Nothing."

"Nothing?" Deena whispered.

Judith, while checking on the teacher, who was intently watching several students diagram sentences on the blackboard, composed a small lie. "My father enrolled me in classes at the college two afternoons a week"—she squinched her nose to signal her annoyance—"and it looks like I can't get out of it."

And so the school year proceeded, with the private Judith quietly making preparations for a departure the public Judith never discussed with either her father, because he himself never raised the subject, or Deena, because she was afraid it would cause her to retreat protectively, which Judith didn't want, not as long as she was stuck here herself. The coursework at the college was manageable and even occasionally interesting, and she liked drifting onto campus and into the role of college student. She looked forward to one aspect of the arrangement especially. On Thursdays she had a standing date to meet her father for lunch at the faculty dining room, where she ordered either the Cobb or the Waldorf salad and sat with Professor Toomey more as an adult than as a daughter. "You know," he told her once, "the other day one of my elderly colleagues wanted to know more about, and I quote, 'the enchanting creature with whom I was dining last Thursday.'" Her father smiled. "When I told the old fool the enchanting creature was in fact my daughter, his predatory enthusiasm waned."

Judith, who wondered how foolish and old an old fool had to be in order to find her enchanting, asked who the old fool was.

"Eldon Markham. He's on wife number four. Every ten years or so, he takes a new twenty-year-old bride. I suppose to an old fool a series of young wives can seem a bolstering course." Her father's expression turned wry. "Though I *have* noticed that Eldon's present bride does quite a lot of looking about."

This wasn't the only time her father hinted at a world bigger and more pungent than that of fatherhood and scholarship. During another of their lunches, he remarked that he'd just received the most astonishing question from a student during that morning's office hour. "We'd made an appointment. He'd said he had questions about *Othello*. But the first thing he said when he came into my office was, 'Dr. Toomey, I need to know what to do to get somewhere with the girls here.'"

Her father released one of his low puffing laughs and sat back, as if that were the whole story.

"What did you tell him?" Judith said.

"I said that being a valiant example of negritude worked for Othello." Again he laughed and seemed done.

"What did you really tell him?"

Her father seemed amused in Judith's interest. "What would you have told him?"

She had no idea. "He didn't ask me."

A small shrug from her father. "I told him if he'd only check the nameplate on the door, he'd see that the name was Howard Toomey and not Abigail Van Buren."

Judith said that sounded pretty brutal.

"Yes, well, I presented it as a little joke, so that was how he had to take it. In any case, what followed was a perfectly banal but congenial discussion of *Othello*."

Judith and her father ate for a minute or so in silence. Then Judith said, "Why do you think he came to you for advice about girls?"

Her father had ordered pork chops and sauerkraut. He popped the last bite of chop into his mouth and said, "I have no idea."

Another silence. Then Judith said, "What would you have told him if you absolutely had to tell him something?"

"Had to? Why in the world would I have to?"

Judith borrowed from Deena's Book of Horrible Consequences. "To keep God from splitting my skull with a lightning bolt sometime in the next ten minutes."

"Ah, well, in that case." He pushed away his plate and sipped from his coffee. "I guess for starters I might've suggested being a good listener. And not losing track of one's backbone." A slight smile formed on his lips. "A fellow wouldn't want the girl who would want a spineless man."

"And vice versa," Judith said quickly, and was relieved that after looking over its logic, she believed what she'd said. Evidently her father did, too, because he gave a small nod and said, "Yes, and vice versa."

The weeks slipped by. Mr. Flood arranged for letters of recommendation from the college library, the Rufus Sage Hospital, and one of her high school teachers (he gave them each what he called "a model letter for their reference and convenience"), and after several revisions she finished her college-entrance essay without any help whatsoever. She recounted the story of her father falling in love with her mother during the blinking realization that a book might be both an escape hatch from the ordinary and a door into the extraordinary, and concluded that she'd received from both parents—she knew she was laying it on thick here— "not only a love of literature, but also the gift of curiosity."

She'd planned on showing the finished essay to her father, but when the time came, she didn't. She didn't know why. Somewhere along the line, the process of her application to colleges had become the Unspoken Subject. Her father, probably following the model of his grandparents, didn't ask questions, and although Judith had loved talking about college the year before, when the event seemed distant, she'd become less interested in discussing it as the days brought its reality closer. The truth was, something about going off to college caused a disquiet within her, and the feeling had arisen full-force the morning she was driving down Highway 385, away from Rufus Sage, to take her SATs. Some part of her didn't want to go away to college, and why that was she couldn't guess. Leaving Rufus Sage wasn't a problem. Leaving Deena behind wasn't an insurmountable problem. Starting a new life wasn't a problem. Just the opposite. It was what she wanted. And yet.

In November, Judith's mother called to say she was going to Paris for Christmas. "I'm going with this brilliant French lit guy at the U who has an apartment in the seventh arrondissement," she said. Her mother gave the French word the full treatment, and Judith considered asking if she had just coughed up phlegm, but said nothing.

Jonathan, it turned out, was going, too, and Judith knew there was no possible answer to any question she might ask about this arrangement that she would want to hear. So she mentioned the fact that she'd been applying to colleges.

Twelve hundred miles away in Vermont, her mother seemed to be covering the phone and yelling, "Come on in!" Then, into the phone, she said, "You're already applying to colleges?" in a tone suggesting that Judith was jumping the gun by a year or two.

"Jesuit schools mostly," Judith said.

Her mother seemed again to have covered the phone and was talking to someone there in the house. When she came back on, she said, "I'm really happy for you, Judy, how everything's coming together." She wanted to hear more, every little detail, but she had company. Could she call back a little later?

And so the winter passed. The metal fire escape that had lain beside the county courthouse since October was finally attached to the courthouse itself, construction of a new Safeway on Morehead and Third Streets was ceremoniously commenced (to compete, the old Jack & Jill immediately started a policy of doubling its issue of S&H green stamps), wheat rose above four dollars a bushel, and, to Judith's mild satisfaction, Ironside, McGarrett, and Columbo kept cracking their cases. Judith's SAT scores were good, but not as good as her APs had been, and her applications to several upper-tier eastern schools were rejected, though she was wait-listed by one, as well as by Stanford, her Major Stretch school on the West Coast. Although Mr. Flood's attention flagged somewhat after the Ivy League rejections, he still warned against "senioritis," so as the months slipped by, Judith kept up with her schoolwork, spent odd leisure hours in the company of Deena (more) or her father (less), read novels, and tinkered with the plans she'd made for herself. She had by this time determined that she would marry someone with a quiet sense of humor, a respectable profession, and—she knew this one might be trouble—a bearing that suggested savoir faire (a term she'd lifted from Amory Blaine) without junking the backbone. She herself would have a career. For a long time she'd thought it would be in the law or higher education or possibly business, something anyhow that would require a briefcase, but lately she'd begun reading about the various people involved in the behind-the-scenes production of television and movies. She and her husband would not have children, perhaps because of some physiological shortcoming (preferably his, so that she might appear at once forgiving of him and forbearing of life's little reversals). They would live in a large house with cheerful wallpaper, high ceilings, walk-in closets, and at least one secret passageway.

This was the general framework, anyhow. Then, in the spring, the UPS man delivered a small, bare-root citrus tree to her father's door, and shortly thereafter, on the first Saturday in May, Judith's father sent her off to buy a large terra-cotta pot to put it in.

9

It took two trips in Señor Rocha's truck to haul Judith's old furniture to Red Roof Mini-Storage. Besides the bedroom set that had been sitting by the pool, Judith had decided to take a few odd things of her father's, as well as the old Persian carpet she'd had in her basement room as a girl, and which, since her father's death, had been rolled and stored in the ceiling joists of the garage.

"No problem," Señor Rocha said when he eyed the extra furniture and cartons.

He'd brought along a nephew named Raul, evidently just up from Mexico, because whenever spoken to, Raul would smile broadly and slide his eyes toward his uncle. Judith had never recovered the Red Roof key from Shutters; the hotel hadn't called, and she couldn't muster the will to pursue it. She'd told Señor Rocha that she'd lost the key, and he brought with him a long-handled pair of bolt cutters that snipped the padlock shackle without much effort. After removing the lock, he regarded it for a second or two. "Very cheap," he said, coming down hard on *cheap,* and drew from his jacket pocket a used lock, heavier than the other and recently oiled. He inserted its key and the shackle sprang neatly free. "Much better," he said.

Judith took the first lock into her hand and looked at it. When she swung the severed U-shaped shackle away, the action seemed strangely familiar, as if it might have come from a not-quite-remembered dream. She'd thought she would throw the lock away—it was useless, after all—but she didn't. She dropped it into her shoulder bag.

Within the storage room, Judith and the two men rolled out the pad and the Persian carpet first, then Judith helped with the drawers and lamps while Señor Rocha and Raul moved the heavier objects. After the quagmire that editing had become, it felt good to have work requiring little beyond physical effort. "Anywhere's fine," Judith would say to the men, and then add, "How about right there?"

As they neared completion, Señor Rocha said, "There's enough room left to live in."

"Oh, I'll fill it up," Judith said. "I have more stuff to bring later." This was a lie she didn't want to linger over. Even with the maple bed disassembled, the arrangement of the furniture had begun to suggest her bygone room in Rufus Sage.

She walked up to the vending machines near the office and returned with three Diet Cokes and two bags of potato chips (Judith, a little worried about the whole flawless-size-six thing, decided to forgo the chips). Señor Rocha and his nephew squatted in the shade with their backs against the cinder-block wall. They ate and drank and talked in low, genial-sounding Spanish while Judith stood looking out over the nearby buildings, feeling the same cool breeze that had swept through her on her first visit here.

"Good place for houses," Señor Rocha said, turning slightly to face the breeze. "Free air conditioning."

Judith laughed, and Raul gave his wide smile of incomprehension. He and his uncle went back to Spanish. Judith leaned against the wall. Hers was an end unit that faced east from a slight knoll, and it overlooked stucco buildings, chain-linked storage yards, and a huge, expansive structure, roofed but unsided, where triangular wooden braces were assembled. A large and weathered sign said JAKLOPS TRUSSES. The busyness was the perfect distance away—the whine of the saws was faint, and Judith couldn't see the faces of the workmen, though every now and then a shouted, or even sung, word or two of Spanish carried on the breeze, along with (or did she just imagine it?) the faint odor of cut wood. For the first time since that afternoon at Shutters, she felt pleasantly transported beyond the borders of her own life.

Judith turned and said, "I have a question for you, Sergio."

Señor Rocha said nothing, but shifted his old buried eyes.

"I have a friend," Judith said. "How hard would it be for her to get a Social Security card?"

Sergio Rocha made an exaggerated frown that was the facial equivalent of a shrug. "Easy," he said.

"How much would it cost?"

Another facial shrug, this time with a smiling component. "Very cheap." Again his *cheap* was emphatic. "Fifty bucks," he said. "Maybe less." His eyes were calm, and Judith had the sudden idea that his eyes did the listening. He said, "What is the name of this person who needs the Social?"

Judith printed the name on a piece of paper and gave it to him.

Three days later, she found a sealed envelope lying on the cutting room table when she entered. It was labeled *Mrs. Judith*. She opened it, reached in, and—this had the effect of a magic trick—pulled out a Social Security card for Edith W. Winks.

—⁂—

That night Judith again slept poorly and awakened early. On her way to work, she stopped at a Postal Annex and found that when it came to establishing an address for Edie Winks, she had her choice of Hollywood, Beverly Hills, or Toluca Lake. She chose

Toluca Lake, to keep things simple, and a day or two later, at Kinko's, she had a small photo taken against a solid background while she was wearing a black sweater and long dangly earrings, and another taken with a white top and different earrings, also dangly. Then she used these photos to order identification cards for Edie Winks from two Internet companies, each card to be mailed to Edie Winks at her Toluca Lake address. What she was doing, exactly, Judith wasn't sure. A kind of experiment, she supposed. A diversion. An alternative form of travel. The life of Edie Winks as an exotic destination, a small Caribbean island surrounded by turquoise water, a single red umbrella on a white beach, beyond phones, beyond televisions, beyond work and husbands and husbands' assistants, beyond speech, in fact, except—Judith smiled—perhaps a word in the morning with the cook and the gardener, who, come to think of it, were handsome and solicitous men with skin the color of caramel.

And then there was Judith's actual work, which each day stretched longer and longer even as the editing fell further and further behind. She hated her cuts, she hated the actors, she hated the show, she hated the fact that she had to work weekends (especially when Lucy was making an early Friday getaway for a reunion in Montecito with old college chums). Malcolm had in fact bought the black dress in a size six and made dinner reservations, but when Saturday night came, Judith begged off. She had a headache, she said, not one of the bad ones like she'd been getting, but a headache all the same.

Malcolm said he understood; a rain check was perfectly fine. He made them pork, pickle, and cheese sandwiches on a yummy ciabatta bread—nicely adaptive behavior, in Judith's opinion—but then he turned on a meaningless preseason football game and she went upstairs to watch *Treasure of the Sierra Madre* on DVD.

She awakened early Sunday morning and left a note saying she was going to the studio and would be back in an hour or two, but the editing quickly ran aground. She became stuck in a series of frames that ran too long but when made shorter bounced off the screen. It would give her a headache—already she felt the first hint of the aura, the tiny pinpoint of pain in her right eye. No, the best thing was to leave, grab something to eat, and come back to it later, but when she got to the parking lot, she sat with the engine running and the transmission locked in park. Oh, for God's sake, she thought finally, and did what she wanted to do. She drove to Red Roof and signed in as Edie Winks.

She swung the padlock open and raised the door on 17C. Everything was as she, Señor Rocha, and his nephew had left it, and she went right to work. She slipped the bird's-eye maple side-rails into the headboard, then the footboard. She set the support slats into their notches. It felt good, completing one little task after another. *She* felt good. The beginnings of the headache started to recede. The east-facing storage room had the dim cool-ness of a basement; in spite of the summer heat, she hardly sweated as she dragged over the box spring and mattress. She found sheets and tugged smooth the Young Man's Fancy quilt. She set up a floor lamp and plugged it into the unit's one electrical outlet. She stacked the sections of her glass-fronted bookcase and had the idea of filling them with favorite books, arranging them by author or perhaps in the order she meant to reread them, but she felt suddenly and overwhelmingly . . . what? Not tired so much as satisfied, and newly comfortable. Like a cat in winter who'd found the sunroom. She rolled the door down, wondered vaguely about asphyxiation, raised it a few inches from the floor, turned off the lamp. She plumped the pillow. She lay on the bed, held the quilt close to her nose, and took in its ancient scent. She fell deeply asleep.

When she awakened, she supposed her nap had been relatively

short—she felt cleansed and refreshed, with none of the logy internal dishevelment she associated with longer naps. Yet when she raised the door of the storage unit, she was surprised to look east and see Jaklops Trusses already in shadow, and by the time she crossed town and turned her Audi into the driveway, it was fully dark. Inside, Malcolm and Camille were eating In-and-Out hamburgers in the den and watching *The Princess Bride,* a movie they'd watched together so many times that most of their enjoyment now lay in reciting the lines a half-second before the actors did. They barely looked up when Judith entered, although Malcolm did ask how the work had gone.

"Okay," Judith said.

On the screen, Andre the Giant was carrying Wallace Shawn, Mandy Patinkin, and the princess bride up the Cliff of Insanity.

Malcolm said, "We bought you a hamburger and a strawberry shake—it's on the counter."

Judith was standing over the kitchen sink eating her hamburger when Camille and Malcolm recited loudly, and as one, "Hello, my name is Inigo Montoya. You killed my father. Prepare to die."

Edith Winks's sham identification cards—one from Sutton University in England, the other from the state of Oregon—looked surprisingly authentic. With these, plus her new address and Social Security card, all tucked into an old purse, Judith walked into an independent bank not far from the studio with the idea of opening a checking account. She had prepared a story about using cash all of her life and finally growing tired of it, and how she'd liked this bank when she'd come in with her friend, but none of that was necessary. The girl in New Accounts simply asked how much money she would like to deposit, and Judith counted out five hundred dollars. She explained that she didn't want to give her work number and she was switching cell phones. "No problem," the girl said, typing something into the computer. "We'll just need your new number as soon as you get it." There was an uneasy moment when the girl asked for a picture ID and Judith explained that she didn't drive and she'd never bothered with anything else, but oh, she did have her ID from studying abroad—would that help? While the girl was looking at the card from Sutton University, Judith said, "It's part of the University of Nottingham," and the girl said, "Like the sheriff?"

"I've also got the state ID card they gave me when I was working in Oregon," Judith said, but the girl, after glancing at it, waved it off. "It's okay," she said. "If we don't have all the right stuff, I can personally attest." Judith watched her making a notation on the form, and then she passed Judith the signature card. When the girl asked if she would also like to apply for a MasterCard, Judith considered it for a moment or two before saying yes. According to the application, Edith W. Winks was unmarried, self-employed, and three years younger than Judith.

Malcolm and Judith's bedroom was capacious enough for one alcove of it to be given over to a private study with bookcases, armchair, and small desk. This was where Malcolm was sitting Tuesday night when his cell phone rang. Judith was at the opposite end of the room, in the walk-in closet, looking for a nightgown light enough to be comfortable but prim enough to be discouraging, should Malcolm have any ideas. She stilled herself to listen but could not make out his words. Then he rang off and was calling to Judith that he had to run down to the bank to retrieve something from a secure computer; it shouldn't take long.

"I'll go with you," Judith said, to her own surprise. She popped her head out of the closet. "Would that be okay? I need to pick up a prescription and mail some letters."

"Of course," Malcolm said, but there was something fallen in his expression, she was almost sure of it. "If it's just mail and a pre-scription, I can handle it for you, no problem."

"I feel like going for a ride." She brightened her smile. "Throw in Baskin-Robbins, and maybe Milla will come, too."

Malcolm shrugged.

Judith went to Camille's room and threw in Baskin-Robbins, but Camille demurred. "Eeyew, *errands*," she said, squinching her nose. "Besides, I'm on a diet."

Malcolm was downstairs, getting his keys. Was there mur-muring? Was he making a quick phone call? The bastard.

"Ready!" Judith sang out as she went down the stairs, carrying her bag and her letters.

They were actually bill payments, including one written from Edith Winks's account for a charge on Edith Winks's card for a pair of stiletto heels at Neiman Marcus (Manolo Blahniks! She had never imagined buying Manolo Blahniks). The shoes were still wrapped in tissue within their box in the Red Roof storage unit. The prescription was for Imitrex, to relieve the cluster migraines she'd been getting recently, or at least that's what the doctor said they sounded like.

At the post office drive-through, she handed the envelopes to Malcolm, who slipped them into the mail drop without even glancing at them.

Judith closed her eyes for a moment and saw the black dot behind her eyelid, growing slowly within a fuzzy edge of light.

"Can we go by Rite Aid next?" she said as they were exiting from the parking lot, and Malcolm's right turn, instead of the left he'd intended, was abrupt. He said nothing, but she knew he liked running errands according to the most efficient route. He'd always loved playing Park & Shop with Camille. Zigzagging was discouraged. Backtracking, as they were doing now, was forbidden. He turned on the Dodgers game—since when did Malcolm care about the Dodgers?—and waited in the car while she went in to pick up her prescription.

When they reached the bank, Malcolm asked if she wanted to wait in the car or come in.

"Come in," Judith said. "I need to pop a pill."

He seemed slightly surprised. "You didn't say you had a headache."

"You didn't ask."

He entered a code and used two keys to get through the door. He flipped on lights, opened a wall-mounted metal box, and punched in another code. He gave her a chilled bottle of Evian water from a small refrigerator in the conference room and offered fruit or crackers, which she declined. She gulped the pill. "I'll just be a few minutes," he said, and headed for his office, the only one in the building that was enclosed.

Judith said, "I'll just nose around out here for money to steal."

Malcolm gave a small laugh and advised her not to do it when the security cameras were pointed her way.

Judith drifted. She liked the quiet tidiness of an empty bank. It smelled clean, faintly woodsy—one of those Mrs. Meyer's cleaning products was her bet. Already the calendar on the check-writing counter had been turned to Wednesday's date. Next to the counter, a stand-alone cardboard cutout said, *Your Business Is Our Business.* Her head was throbbing now. Why for Christ's sake pay fifteen dollars for a pill if it took six hours to work? It should just say it on the cover—overpriced *and* slow-acting! For a second or two, she closed her eyes and touched her fingertips to her eyelids.

She seated herself at the nearest desk and stared for some moments at a photograph of a twentysomething woman and two grammar-school boys before realizing that the pictured woman was a younger version of Francine Metcalf. Judith was sitting at Miss Metcalf's desk. She froze for a moment, started to bolt up, then checked herself. She glanced toward Malcolm's office; he'd left the door open, but she couldn't see him. She leaned back and eased open the desk's top drawer. Everything was neat. Coiled stamps, blue pens with blue pens, black with black, several sizes of Post-it notes, sorted gradations of clips, separate packages of bright self-stick arrows saying *Sign Here* and *Notarize* and *Initial,* and there, just beyond the edge of the wooden organizer, as startling as a small live reptile, lay the Red Roof keys. Judith stared at them. She told herself she shouldn't be bothered. Malcolm had freely told her that Miss Metcalf might use the room, and she *had* used the room, and while using the room had evidently found the keys and taken them with her, probably with good intentions. What was so terrible about that? But what was so innocent about it, either? Why not turn them in? Or give them to Malcolm? Judith touched the keys, picked them up, turned them over in her hand. *Red Roof. Your Safe Under the Red Roof.* And then, in smaller letters, *Postage Prepaid. Mail to Red Roof Storage.*

Judith looked up at the security camera. For a moment it seemed pointed right at her; then it continued its slow scanning arc.

"Two-minute warning!" Malcolm called out from his office.

Judith sat very still. Her skull was filling with thickening fluid. The pill—was it the pill?—was making her feel funny. She wanted the keys; the keys were hers, useless, but hers. She watched the security camera slowly swing back, forth, back again. She turned around. There was another camera there, too.

A scraping sound from Malcolm's office. He was getting up, coming out.

Think.

She couldn't think.

She set the keys back in their exact place inside Miss Metcalf's drawer. Then—why she thought of this she had no idea—she reached into her handbag and, down at the cluttered bottom of things, found the lock with the cut shackle. She pushed it into the deepest corner of Miss Metcalf's drawer and slid the drawer closed. At Malcolm's approach, she swiveled the chair around and stood. She nodded at the photograph on the desk. "Who're the boys?" she said. To her surprise, her voice sounded normal.

Malcolm regarded the photograph. "Miss Metcalf's nephews. A long time ago. I think they're both in college now." He had a folder under his arm. "Ready?"

As they crossed the parking lot, Judith's purse felt lighter.

"How's your head?" Malcolm said.

"Better," Judith said, and it was. Her headache was lifting, rising, leaving in its place a feeling deeply serene. "Imitrex," she said, forgetting her earlier resentment of the product. "One small step forward for mankind."

Malcolm laughed courteously and started the Jaguar, its motor a solid thrum. Judith closed her eyes. The car was moving, reverse, then forward, going somewhere. Home. Going home. Where was the receipt, the one written to Edie Winks for 17C? Where had that gone? And that nosy freaking camera. She should've winked. Should've put the broken lock into the drawer, slid it closed, looked up smiling at that camera, and winked.

10

Judith's father had ordered the dwarf lime tree from Four Winds Nursery in California with the intention of sheltering the tree in the sunroom during the winter months and wheeling it every spring into the backyard, where its fruit could be picked for use in the gin and tonics that were his preferred summer drink. All the plan lacked was a terra-cotta pot to put the tree in and a castered dolly to make it movable.

Judith was privately skeptical of the project—who, she wanted to know, grew citrus in Nebraska?—but happy to be set loose in the Bonneville for any errand, even a foolish one, if it afforded her the pleasure of being out on her own, sunglasses on and windows down. Her route, then, was unsurprisingly roundabout, and took her first by the brick buildings of the state college and then up and down Main Street before heading west to Gibson's Building Supply.

In the store's garden department, she slid a heavy pot from the shelf to a flatbed cart she'd shoved alongside it, then set the castered dolly inside the pot. She paid with the twenty-dollar bill her father had given her and folded the change to separate it in her wallet from the three one-dollar bills that were her own. She wheeled the cart down the sloping parking lot to the Bonneville, which is where things began to go wrong.

The pot was heavy. To lift it, she needed to stabilize the cart with her foot, but when she did that, she couldn't lift the pot.

An orange pickup—the one with flames and fancy chrome wheels she'd seen before in town—pulled into the lot and parked a few spaces down. There were two men in the cab. The pink-faced driver wore a cowboy hat; his taller passenger wore a seed cap. She'd forgotten what Deena said the driver's name was, but she remembered her calling him a troglodyte.

Judith steadied her cart against the Bonneville's bumper, leaned over, and rolled the pot to the edge of the cart's flat bed. Then— there was nothing else to do—she squatted, wrapped her arms around the clay pot, and jerked it up.

The cart slid free and, as she watched, began coasting down-hill.

Judith banged the pot back down and ran to catch up to the cart before it crashed into the front end of somebody's new Oldsmobile. The temperature was only in the low seventies, but she was sweating. She was also peevish. She rolled the cart to an enclosure marked *Cart Corral* and shoved it roughly inside.

When she turned around, the pink-faced man was standing next to her father's car. Out of his truck, he was stout and bowlegged. "Looks like you're in need of a little help," he called out.

He wore a royal blue snap-button shirt, and his cowboy hat was clean and white. His hands and face were mottled pink, as if, Judith thought, he'd been left too long in boiling water.

When she drew close, he said, "Are you a damsel in distress?" and added a puggish grin.

"Not really," Judith said and glanced over at the man's orange pickup. His passenger was still in the cab, his head tipped far back as he drank the last from a can.

"Where to?" the pinkish man said, drawing Judith's attention back. "Into the trunk?" He'd bent to pick up the pot. Up close, his cheeks were crazed with fine blue veins.

"I can get it," Judith said with as much chill as she could manage.

"It's no trouble, miss. It'll just take a minute and the clock ain't runnin'."

Judith had no idea what this meant and wasn't going to ask. She put her hand on the pot. "No, I'll get it. Next time you might not be here."

The man stepped back, shrugging amiably. "Well, you got a point there, to be truthful. You oughtn't to shoot what you can't carry out."

Judith was wearing the short suede skirt her mother had given her and suddenly wished she wasn't. She was also wearing an oversized nubby sweater that she tugged down before she squatted, hugged the pot, and, careful not to express even a minimal grunt, lifted it to the lip of the trunk, then skidded it in.

"Kudos," the pinkish man said.

The other man stepped out of the orange truck then and set his empty beer can in the back, adding to a collection of discards. Judith didn't look at him but was aware of him circling the truck and unhurriedly pulling a clean dress shirt over a sleeveless undershirt. It created the impression of someone late for an appointment he wasn't sure he wanted to keep.

She tried not to bend very much forward as she tossed a blanket over the pot and more or less secured the trunk with twine. When she straightened and turned, both men stood watching. The second man was tall, with a loose smile that seemed authentically friendly, but still, he stood with his hands in his back pockets, as unhelpful as the pink man. Judith hadn't wanted their assistance, but their standing and watching and doing nothing whatsoever was annoying, too.

She said, "Maybe for your next highlight, you buckaroos will want to go over to the Safeway and watch a produce truck unload."

The pink man's face stiffened, but the other man let out a soft laugh of amusement. He seemed familiar in a slippery kind of way, and she looked at him longer than she meant to. She started slightly when the pink man said, "We've met before, haven't we?"

Judith turned back to him. "Who?"

The man seemed to be trying to make his puggish grin less unpleasant. "You and me."

"I don't think so," Judith said coolly, and the pinkish man's eyes were suddenly smaller. The two men had formed a kind of enclosure around Judith, and with just the slightest shift from the pinkish man, the enclosure had tightened. Beyond them, the lot was deserted.

"I've got to go now," she said.

The pinkish man kept his tiny eyes on her and didn't move. Then the taller one in his easy voice said, "Boss Krauss, we're impeding the lady's progress. You can see she's got places to go and people to see."

Judith turned sharply toward the man. She *had* heard that voice before, she was pretty sure of it. Where was what she couldn't remember.

The pinkish man didn't move, but the other man stepped back, giving Judith a gap to step through. In passing him by, she smelled the slightly sour odor of beer and, just beyond that, the smells of sawdust and sweat, which were not unpleasant.

As she moved toward her car door, the pinkish man said, "I know where I saw you now."

Judith made the mistake of glancing back. "It was in a dream," the man said, and the truculent grin was back. "A real randy one."

He turned then and moved off toward Gibson's in quick short-legged strides that accentuated the bow of his legs. Judith slid into the car and was starting the engine when the tall man materialized alongside and with a little twirling motion asked her to roll down her window.

Don't, Judith thought, and then she did, halfway.

"Funny thing is," he said, bending toward her, "you and I *have* met."

"What would make that funny?" Judith said.

For just an instant the man's face went blank. "Funny odd," he said. "Not funny ha-ha."

Judith gave him no encouragement.

"We met at the Guest place. You and your father were buying a washing machine. I was roofing the barn."

So that's where it was. Except he'd had a beard then. But those were the pale blue-gray eyes, all right.

The man eased his voice down to a gentler level. "I said you were dangerous. *Muy peligrosa.* Maybe you don't remember it. "

Judith, perversely, said she didn't. "Why? Should I have?"

His answer surprised her. "Well, I remember you clear as day, and when you remember somebody clear as day, you just suppose they remember you in turn." He let his smile rest on her a second. "But I guess how often we're wrong is one of the things that makes this a funny old world." He looked at her. "Funny odd, not funny ha-ha."

These words had a softening effect on Judith, and without something sharp for retort, she found she had nothing to say at all. The only thing she could think of was that he looked better without a beard, and she wasn't going to say that.

He'd been leaning forward but now straightened to full height and looked off. He let a truck pass on the highway, and, still looking away, he said, "Now here almost two years have passed and"—he turned toward her—"you don't seem one iota less dangerous to me."

His gray-blue eyes settled into her, and with a shock of recognition she realized this was how he'd looked at her in the dream when he'd stood above her bed watching her sleep, and later—years later, in fact—looking back on it all, she wondered if this wasn't part of their particular compact, his ability to awaken in her the reckless girl he alone imagined her to be. A girl she hadn't thought existed.

"I've got to go now," she said.

She touched the accelerator, the car began to move, and with a flick of his finger he slightly tipped back the sweat-stained bill of his seed cap, so that as she drove away she could see a little more of his open, amused face.

—⟋⟍—

From Gibson's, Judith drove around for a while trying to settle her nerves, then headed for the Dairy Queen, where Deena waved her into the back, behind the service counter. She wasn't wearing her plastic shower hat or latex gloves. "Guess Mr. Ed's not here," Judith said. He rarely was anymore. His interest had shifted to another Dairy Queen he'd opened sixty miles away, where, he'd told Deena, "the leash needed shortening," though what actually drove him to the other stand, in Deena's opinion, was the fact that when he'd finally worked up the courage to ask Melinda Payne for an after-work cup of coffee, the Amazonic bank teller had brusquely declined and thereafter avoided the premises. "He thinks if he turns himself into a big hamburger magnate, it'll change her tune," Deena said.

Judith thought that if that strategy hadn't panned out for Gatsby or Heathcliff, it probably wasn't going to pan out for Mr. Ed, but she didn't say so. She noticed that Deena had undone the top two buttons of her Dairy Queen shirt, a tactic that, from the right angle, revealed what appeared to be real cleavage, and for the second or third time in less than a month Judith wondered whether Deena had put on an actual inch or two or just begun wearing push-up bras. She scooped a bag of French fries from under the heat lamp and sat on one of the prep counters.

"Slow today," Deena said. Then: "So who died?"

"What?"

"You look like somebody just died."

"Oh." She looked at the French fry in her hand, then at Deena. "I think I just got hit on by a grown man."

Deena said, "That's happened a couple of times to me. It wasn't that bad really. They were train guys."

The Southern Pacific had a switching yard in Grand Lake, sixty miles south.

Judith said, "'*He don't, she don't, it don't*,'" her code phrase for those local choices she saw as doomed, which was just about all of them.

Deena touched a wetted finger to the top of the big metal salt-shaker, then set the salted finger to her tongue. "Yeah, I guess."

Judith gazed out at her Bonneville with the terra-cotta pot sticking from the open trunk. "There were two guys, actually. One was that guy in the orange pickup with flames I told you about. His skin looks boiled pink, and he's got a little potbelly and little bowed legs." She nipped the end of a fry and chewed thoughtfully. "His attentions weren't that flattering."

"No, I don't suppose," Deena said. She absently licked her finger to lift more salt from the shaker and Judith said, "That's not hygienic."

"You think?" Deena said, and did it again, which made Judith laugh in spite of herself. They were both quiet a few seconds before Deena said, "Who was the other one?"

"What?"

"You said there were two guys. Who was the other one?"

Judith didn't know what to answer. Patrick Guest had once told her the roofer's name, but she couldn't remember it. All she could really tell Deena was that he had pale blue-gray eyes and he'd had a full beard the first time she'd seen him but now he didn't, which didn't help much by way of identification.

"But he was cute, though?" Deena said.

Judith said she guessed he was, in his own way, and Deena was working on a translation of this observation when Doris Cantwell came in. Doris was a regular. Deena said under her breath to Judith, "She's thinking she'd like a Dilly Bar," and moved to the service window.

Doris Cantwell, middle-aged, a routine fifteen or twenty pounds overweight, studied the posted offerings for a full minute and then said, "I'm thinking I'd like a Dilly Bar."

On her way home, Judith detoured by Gibson's, but the orange pickup was gone.

—⁓—

Although Judith had been accepted by the state university in Lincoln, she'd still heard nothing from the two more distinguished colleges that had not quite accepted or rejected her. "Wait-list situations," Mr. Flood told her, "are always iffy. The news can come anytime right up to September." It was only May, but still, upon returning home from school each day, Judith quickly sorted through the mail that lay scattered on the wood floor under the front-door mail slot. When there was nothing from the colleges, she sometimes got down on all fours to look under the library table, where a few weeks before a Nebraska Public Power bill had managed an improbable slide. Then, getting back up, dusting her knees, she didn't know what to make of herself. Why did she worry so much about colleges she wasn't certain she wanted to attend? Once, in Vermont, three different girls had told Judith that a boy named Lonnie Hazelwood was going to ask her to the Harvest Ball. She wasn't sure she wanted to go to the Harvest Ball, let alone with Lonnie Hazelwood, but every day that passed without his asking made her think she might really want to go with him after all. When he finally asked her, mumblingly, two days before the dance, without looking her in the eye, she had felt a kind of triumphant relief, then said she was sorry, but she'd already made other plans.

Following her final examinations in calculus and modern American literature, neither of which had proven difficult for her, Judith joined her father for a final lunch at the faculty club. Even before they ordered, her father presented her with a graduation present, a used hardbound copy of *The Portrait of a Lady* with tissue paper protecting the frontispiece illustration. He had inscribed it, *To Judith, upon her graduation, with much love from her father.* When she looked up from it, he said, "You'll need to tell me what you think of Miss Isabel Archer, as well as her suitors."

She turned the book to look at it from different angles. "It's so beautiful."

"But it won't be yours . . ." he said, and didn't have to finish the sentence. She knew how it ended: *until you write in its margins.* Her father felt a book hadn't been read if it hadn't been underlined and annotated.

There were only a few scattered diners—most of the faculty had already left for the summer—and the clinks of silverware and china seemed to echo in the room. The waiters and waitresses had little to do. Their own server, a thin girl with long white-blond hair, was at their table every few seconds to check dishes and replenish liquids. After the girl topped off their water, there was a slight lull and Judith said, "Maybe I'll just go to college here next year. At Rufus State."

Her father, idly freeing last bits of roasted chicken from the bone, looked up and regarded her for a second or two. Then he said, "Did you go home to check the mail before coming up here to eat with me today?"

The question surprised her. She flushed slightly and admitted she had.

"To check for a letter from one of the schools?"

She nodded. She should never have left the mail in a neat pile on the library table every day—that was how he knew.

"And?"

"There was nothing there."

"But you walked eight blocks out of your way to check in hopes there would be some word from one of the schools to which you've applied?"

She nodded again.

He said nothing but signaled for the waitress, who was upon them at once. He ordered a dish of chocolate ice cream for Judith and coffee for them both. "With cream," the waitress said, more a statement than a question, and Judith's father nodded. The girl's hair was the blond of cornsilk, and almost as fine. As she walked away, Judith had to keep herself from staring at it.

"Okay, Judith," her father said, "let's start with the facts. Where did you apply and what have you heard?"

So the unasked question had been finally asked, and the wall was down. Her answer was brief but complete: three rejections at upper-tier eastern schools, two wait-lists at Major Stretch schools, which were the ones she kept hoping to hear from, and the one acceptance at the U in Lincoln. "And if I'm staying in Nebraska, I'd rather stay here with you."

This was a surprise: she'd meant only to say she'd rather stay here in Rufus Sage.

"I think you're underestimating Lincoln," he said. "They have good people there. And after a year or two, if you're dead set on another school, you can transfer."

"I can transfer from here, too. And it'd be lots cheaper. The other schools, the ones where I really want to go—they all cost a fortune."

Something stiffened in her father, and she knew she'd made a mistake. "Money isn't the issue," he said. "We'll find the money."

This—and she felt it in her bones at this moment—was how her father had staked such a claim on her. He was the one who took care of her and loved her and yet helped her to do what she wanted to do and go where she wanted to go—all of those things, and all at once.

The blond waitress appeared with the check, which her father signed without scrutiny. "And a bit more coffee, please, if you don't mind." The waitress didn't mind at all. She brought it quickly and said, "Anything else, Dr. Toomey?"

Judith's father shook his head distractedly, and at the exact moment that it registered with Judith that the waitress was disappointed, had been hoping for something more, her father said, "But you've been very helpful, Zondra."

A faint pretty pinkness bloomed on the waitress's cheeks, and after she left, Judith said, "Her name is *Zondra?* With a *Z?*"

He nodded. "Zondra Evans. She's been in a couple of my classes."

Zondra Evans stood at the service area along the wall, adding water to two glasses of ice. Judith was trying to remember whether her eyes were blue—she didn't think so, which meant the whole blond thing might be store-bought—when her father said, "And Stanford's one of the wait-lists?"

"Mmm. But Mr. Flood told me not to get my hopes up there in particular."

"Why was that?"

Judith shrugged. If Mr. Flood had said, she couldn't remember.

Her father brought his fingertips together and was pressing them against his lips. Perhaps half a minute passed. Then the cage broke apart and he said he was going to tell her a story.

Judith had the sudden impulse to flee. "What kind of story?" she said. "Is it going to be about fledglings needing to leave the nest?"

He seemed amused. "Why? Is that the kind of story the situation requires?"

"No."

"Then I'll proceed as planned." He stirred cream into his coffee. "I was thinking of the house your mother and I had on Madison Street when you were born. There was a sewing room that your mother turned into a nursery. She painted everything a beautiful pale pink with mint-green trim—everything, even the crib and an old chest of drawers that was in there."

His gaze drifted, and he settled into his memories. "One day a month or so before your first birthday, I was the only one in the house with you. You were crawling then, and pulling yourself up, but not walking. You'd already had your nap, you were whumping your playthings around in the nursery, making happy little sounds while I worked at my desk, and then after a time I became suddenly aware of the quiet. A deep, strange, frightening quiet. I almost ran to the nursery. And there you were, sitting atop the chest of drawers. How had you gotten there? You'd pulled out the drawers, one a little less far than the one before, so you could use them as steps on your way up. When you looked at me from your perch, you were the purest essence of happiness. You had a pair of my rolled socks in your hands and happily waved them at me.

I can tell you this much: you were absolutely enchanted with your own powers." He issued a small laugh. "They were red-and-green argyle socks. *Are,* I should say, because I still have them. They're too ugly to wear, and I can't throw them away."

Judith had heard the story before, with slight variations, but she saw no need to say so, or to mention that it was a fledgling-needing-to-leave-the-nest story after all, because it was really, wasn't it? Her father looked out one of the large windows that gave onto mown lawn and leafy trees. Judith regarded the soupy remains of chocolate ice cream in her dish. She wanted to spoon it out but didn't want to risk the clicking sound.

"That moment of deep, strange, frightening quiet ..." her father said, but didn't finish the thought. Then he said, "You know, this is not where I wanted to come. I came here because it was the best I could do."

This was both a surprise to Judith and a hard idea to grasp. "What was wrong with Middlebury?" she said.

"Other than the fact that they weren't going to offer me tenure?"

Another surprise. "How'd you know that?"

"Dale Irwin was on the tenure committee. He was kind enough to give me a heads-up." Dale Irwin of the traveling-to-Florida-and-getting-in-a-car-wreck Irwins.

"Why?"

Her father's face twisted into a mild grimace. "So I could look for a job before tenure denial was part of my official record. The problem was, it was already there between the lines. Interviewers would say, 'Do you expect to be offered tenure at Middlebury?' and I would say, 'Yes, I'd expect that,' and the interviewer would say, 'Then why are you choosing to leave?'" Her father smiled. "Oh, it's fine. It's all fine. It takes no more than a single gin and tonic to see it as a not unhappy ending." He started to raise his coffee cup but set it back on its saucer. "I interviewed at a half-dozen places before interviewing here. When they asked me why I wanted to come to Rufus Sage, I said it was because it felt like coming home. As I heard myself saying the words, I realized not only that they were true, but that rattling within their truth was the admission that I was giving up on some wider ambitions." Again he smiled. "What's interesting is that it turned out to be strangely disencumbering. My life here is simpler and better proportioned." He paused. "This morning I was thinking of how people complain repeatedly about the pinched nature of the small town, how no tic or foible goes unnoticed and all the rest, but do you know what interests me? The fact that in a town like this, you have only to walk a mile or two out and you will have slipped into a vast landscape that is, when it comes to you, entirely indifferent."

Judith didn't expect him to stop talking then, but he did, and she sat wondering what these anecdotes might be circling around or wandering toward. Was he arguing for staying home or going to Lincoln or holding out for the wait-list schools or just learning better wilderness skills?

She hoped he would say more, but he didn't. He sat looking at her, or really, as it felt to Judith, looking *into* her, then he reached across the table, touched a finger to her hand, and said, "Shall we go?"

—◊—

At the high school there was little to do but check in books and feel time stretched long by empty waiting. Restrictions loosened, especially for graduating seniors, and during one idle, midperiod stroll through the corridors, Judith passed the trophy cases in the foyer and saw something that drew her attention.

It was a picture of the man she'd seen in the parking lot, the tall one who'd roofed Patrick Guest's barn, only the man was younger in the photograph, a boy, his skin almost as white as the basketball uniform he was wearing. An inscription read, *Willy Blunt, Second Team All-Conference.*

That was the name, all right, the one Patrick Guest had told her. Willy Blunt.

Judith stared again at the photograph. He *was* handsome, sort of, if you looked at him just right, but there was something else. His manner of standing didn't suggest arrogance or even pride, and the way he was smiling made it seem as if he were amused at his predicament, standing there holding a basketball and smiling at a photographer while wearing a uniform that resembled underwear. And then it occurred to her that this was also the way he'd been smiling in the parking lot at Gibson's, as if amused not just by her predicament but by his own, too, and that perhaps that was the way he got through his days, with amusement at the predicament that was everybody's life. This made her think of him differently, or perhaps just more intensely. As she stared at the photograph, notions that had nothing to do with past calculations and future plans slid down to her heart, and lower, beginning at that precise moment the preparation for the extravagant reaction the touch of his hand to her flesh would one day cause.

—⁓—

Judith next laid eyes on Willy Blunt less than a week later. She and Deena were sitting in a booth at Pizza Hut. Opposite sat two schoolmates, Paul Railsback and Paul Wells, whom Deena referred to as "the Pauls." Paul Wells was Paul One; Paul Railsback was Paul Two.

At various times since spring break, Deena had caught each of the Pauls staring at her breasts, and she had been wondering which of them would make the better summer boyfriend.

"Neither," Judith told her, but when Deena's interest in the Pauls persisted, Judith suggested that they interview for the job. Deena had telephoned the boys and told them that she and Judith wanted them at the Pizza Hut on Tuesday afternoon so they, as she put it, could be questioned. "About what?" Paul One had asked. Paul Two wanted to know who was paying for the pizza.

The protocol was simple. Judith and Deena would read from a list of questions; the Pauls would respond in writing. The first question was, *If you were invisible for five minutes, how and where would you spend your time?* Both Pauls had worn nice shirts, and Judith was surprised at how entertaining it was to eat pizza, sip Mr. Pibb, and watch them write down their answers in pencil. They were on question four—*You're remaking the movie* Swamp Thing. *What Rufus Sage resident gets the starring role and what would you feed him?*—when the front door swung open and Willy Blunt walked in.

He wore old jeans and a white T-shirt, and he was alone. Judith watched him as he said something that made Calvin Haden, the single on-duty employee, laugh out loud, but she averted her eyes when he glanced her way. He took a seat against the wall with his back to the angling sun, so that from Judith's vantage point he was merely a silhouette. He turned over his paper placemat and hunched over it with a pen, as if writing something.

"You are a heron with a stomach full of partly digested frog parts," Deena was saying. "On whose head will you drop your load?"

The boys hooted and Deena said, "You should decide when, too. Like, just as your candidate has begun taking roll in gym class." This prompted more juvenile laughter, which was suddenly embarrassing to Judith. To check it, she said, "And supply one onomatopoetic word to describe the sound upon impact."

Pauls One and Two stared blankly.

At the table by the wall, Willy Blunt hunched over the place-mat with his pencil, raising his head only now and then for another bite of pizza or a gulp of beer. She thought he might be writing someone an important letter, or maybe just a whimsical one. Either way, to her surprise, she felt a faint twinge of jealousy.

The Pauls were on question seven—*Spell and define* spermatozoa—when Judith rose without a word and walked over to Willy Blunt's table. He had a cupped slice of pizza in one hand and a pencil in the other. As she drew close, he glanced up and his expression, surprisingly intense, broke into a smile.

"There she is," was all he said.

This wasn't much, but Judith felt sudden heat in her cheeks.

He said, "You got that big ol' flower pot home in one piece, I guess."

Judith had the feeling her cheeks were paralyzed; possibly her forehead also. She said, "I just wanted to thank you for that day at Gibson's."

He laughed, which had an easing effect on her. She heard him saying he didn't know he'd done anything worth thanking him for.

"You helped get me away from that pinkish friend of yours." To her relief, her voice sounded more or less normal.

He smiled and nodded. "Boss Krauss isn't exactly my pinkish friend. He's my pinkish employer—" Willy Blunt's blue-gray eyes brightened—"though one of these days that might change."

Judith said, "For a perfect stranger, he was pretty cheeky."

"Sometimes it works." The amused smile. "You'd probably be surprised."

"I guess I would be," she said, and dropped her eyes to the table. He was on the last piece of an individual Canadian-bacon-and-pineapple. His small pitcher of beer was nearly empty. And he hadn't been writing a letter on the back of the placemat at all—he'd been making small, precise drawings of insects.

He said, "The truth is, I was going to stop by your table if it ever thinned out over there."

This was interesting information, though she didn't want to show it.

He nodded to the red bench seat opposite. "You could sit down if you wanted to."

She made a show of thinking it over before sliding in. When she glanced at her own table, Deena was staring back with disbelief. Judith turned to Willy Blunt. "So what were you going to come over to my table for?"

"To apologize for the pinkish man who isn't exactly a friend."

A laugh slipped from Judith, an easy, normal laugh. She nodded at the placemat. "So I guess drawing insects is your idea of a good time."

His eyes took on a teasing aspect. "That and watching produce trucks unload."

Another laugh from Judith. She'd forgotten she'd said that to them. "So do you want to be an entomologist or something?"

He made a snorting kind of chuckle. "You mean a bug man? Naw. Not me. But that'd be something, wouldn't it, being a bug man?" He kept grinning. "I could write *Here comes the Bug Man* backward on the front of my truck, so you could read it in your rearview mirror when I'm breathing down your neck."

Judith wasn't sure whether she was being made fun of or not. "I was just trying to make conversation," she said. The same words, she suddenly realized, that Patrick Guest had once spoken to her.

Willy Blunt had a hard time letting go of his grin. "I know," he said. "It's just that . . . I don't know, being a bug man, it just hit my funny bone." His voice trailed off and he tried to achieve a more serious attitude. He nodded toward his drawing. "Those're just fishing flies. I'm just doodling." Amusement again rose in his eyes. "I'm known far and wide as a big ol' doodler."

The term seemed to hint vaguely at sexual innuendo, but Judith decided the best thing to do was play dumb. "What're fishing flies?" she said.

"Flies to fish with. I draw 'em, then I tie 'em, then I catch fish with 'em, or try to. I like to go up to the Madison in the fall."

She asked what that was like, and while he told her, she watched his face and let her mind wander.

He was talking about flies tied with deer hair when he broke off and said, "I think I'm boring you, which I'd rather not do."

"No, you're not," she said, but she didn't ask any more about fly fishing. She said, "I'd better get back to my table."

He nodded, but she didn't rise. "We're giving those boys a quiz."

He nodded again.

"What's onomatopoeia?" she said suddenly.

He didn't break his smile or his gaze. "Squish," he said. "Slurp. Zip." He gave the smallest waggle of his eyebrows. "I'm not sure about *unzip*."

Judith laughed in spite of herself. A second or two passed, and she thought he definitely looked better without a beard, softer, smoother, more—she actually thought this—kissable. She said, "You're Willy Blunt, aren't you?" and when surprise showed on his face, she said, "I saw your picture in the display case at the high school."

He nodded and squinted out the window. It was late afternoon. Dust motes floated yellow. Out of the blue, in a soft flutish voice, he said, "And you're Judith Toomey," then said it again: "Judith Toomey." A full second passed before he turned and let his eyes fall evenly on her. "When I found out your name and said it aloud, I thought it sounded like a little riddle floating inside a soap bubble." He seemed suddenly self-conscious. "I don't know why I thought that," he said, and when he issued a low self-derisive laugh, it blew a small hole in the shaft of yellow floating dust.

That he'd gone to the trouble of finding out her name was surprise enough, but his saying it out loud to himself, and listening to it as it hung in the air, and coming to his odd (but charming, really) conclusion about it—well, she hardly knew what to think, let alone say. She said, "I'm not that much of a riddle, to tell you the truth."

An easy silence fell over the table. His expression seemed genuinely sweet. He said that in his opinion almost everybody was a pretty good-sized riddle, and then, with his eyes on hers, and in a voice just above a whisper, he said, "What I'm really hoping for here is that you'll write down your telephone number for me."

Judith gave him what she hoped was a frisky look. "What for?"

He laughed. "Not real sure. Something, though."

"Tempting, but I don't know." She remembered the story of Harold Toomey, whose wife, Christianna, had wanted the bird's-eye maple furniture; how he had memorized the information before burning it. "Tell you what. I'll give you the number, but you have to remember it—you can't write it down."

"Ever? I can't write it down ever?"

"That's right."

He gave a small disconsolate shake of the head. "That's a little severe, isn't it?"

It *did* seem severe, now that he said so. Besides, she didn't really want him forgetting it. "Okay," she said. "Not here in the restaurant. You can't write it down here in the restaurant."

He closed his eyes while she recited the numbers, then repeated them aloud. All the exchanges in Rufus Sage were 432, she suddenly realized, so when it got right down to it, all he had to remember was the last four numbers. "Two seven three one," he said.

"That would be correct," Judith said. "What wouldn't be correct is three seven four one or one seven three two."

He grinned and said, "You're kind of a hot tamale, aren't you?"

Odd sensations were moving through Judith, sensations she both feared and couldn't get enough of, so that when Willy Blunt suddenly stood up, it seemed to her that something she'd been waiting for a long time, if not her whole life, having at last been delivered, was now being snatched away. She said, "Where are you going?"

He picked up his cap from the table, stood looking at her a long second, and then bent forward, within inches of her ear, so that when he spoke in a low voice, it had a feathery effect. "Nice talking to you, Judith Toomey," he said. Then, after settling his bill with Calvin Haden, he walked straight out of the restaurant to a faded red Chevrolet pickup in the parking lot. It was an old truck, and he opened it by reaching through the window to the inside latch.

Later, when she climbed into this truck for the first time, she would see that a tightened pair of vise grips served as the interior handle on the driver's-side door, and that written on the metal dashboard with the thick lead of a carpenter's pencil were the numbers 2731.

—⁓—

That evening, while Judith stood in the bathroom towel-drying her hair, the telephone rang. She could hear her father's footsteps in the hallway, then his deep hello. Beyond that, his words were indistinct, so Judith cracked the door an inch.

"Ah," she heard her father say, and then, "I see." His tone suggested the detachment Judith associated with calls from a college administrator, or from a problem student, so she was surprised when he said, "Well, thank you for that. I'll pass this on to Judith when I see her."

Judith gently closed the door and stood in the bathroom trying to sort it out. Out of the darkness, a mild breeze stirred the white cotton curtain that hung over the bathroom's open window. It might've been a girl on the phone, but no girls ever called her except Deena, and her father had a friendlier tone altogether with Deena.

Judith left her hair damp and pulled on her clothes. Her father sat on his side of the partners' desk, writing on a yellow tablet in the midst of stacked and opened books. She picked up her copy of *Portrait of a Lady* from the mantel, and when her father didn't look up, she flopped into the floral armchair, sideways, with her back against one arm and her legs hanging over the other. She opened her book, and with as much casualness as she could manage, she said, "So who called?"

He didn't need to look up—he'd already been watching her, and now his intense expression gave way to something milder. "It seems the romantic phase of your life has stolen up on us, Judith. I pray to God you've assembled the tools with which to defend yourself."

Judith, already agitated, felt as if she might explode. "Meaning?"

"Meaning that one Willy Blunt just called. He seems to have the idea of taking you to dinner."

In one instant Judith felt herself flush with a deep and penetrating pleasure, and in the next she felt the need to conceal it. She didn't turn in the chair, or rise from it. She just stared toward the window as if considering it.

Her father said, "Would you look forward to that?"

"I don't know," she said without turning.

She could feel her father studying her, but when he spoke, his voice, to her relief, was not the clamped voice he used when anxious or angry. "Well, either way," he said, "you should telephone him with your decision. His number is by the phone."

Judith stared off again and made herself count to a hundred, slowly.

Then she put her open book down on the seat of the armchair. She could hardly feel her legs as she walked to the telephone in the hallway. Her father had printed the number neatly on the back of an envelope.

When she dialed it, a man's voice immediately said, "Hello?"

"Hello," Judith said. "Is this Willy Blunt?"

And Willy Blunt in a loose voice said, "Not if you're the revenue man."

Judith had to laugh. "Do I sound like the revenue man?"

"That's what so devious about the revenue man," Willy Blunt said. "There's one that can supposedly make himself sound just like Princess Grace."

"Like Princess Grace?"

"Yeah, and another one can sound like Suzanne Pleshette. They use voice transmogrifiers and shit."

Judith's chuckle was cut short by a sudden thought. "You're not serious, are you?"

Willy rolled out a deep laugh. "Naw, not very. I was just filling in the space until you tell me whether or not you'll have dinner with me Friday night."

She felt a flush of expectant pleasure that she wanted to prolong. "Why would I want to?"

"Well, first of all, it would be just you and me, which I would personally look forward to. And second of all, I've got something planned the likes of which you've never seen."

"How do you know that?"

Again the easy laugh. "Just do, is all."

Judith was aware that her father could hear her if she talked loud enough, so she turned toward the wall and said in a lower voice, "Well, there are things I've never seen that I might never want to see."

"Yeah," he said. "But this isn't one of them."

It registered that he at least wasn't a user of *ain't*.

"So what is this thing the likes of which I've never seen?"

"Well, I can't tell you that."

"Why not?"

"It'd be like going to the end of the book to read the ending before you even started reading."

Judith said, "I do that all the time. It doesn't spoil a thing."

Another laugh came rolling out. "You really are a hot tamale, aren't you?" he said. "But that doesn't mean I'm giving away my surprise."

She pried further but got nowhere, and finally said, "How about a hint, then?"

"Wear Levi's and a jacket. Where we're dining's not dressy."

"I haven't even said I'm coming yet," she said, but she knew she wasn't fooling anybody.

"Five o'clock okay?" he said, and after making herself wait a second or two, Judith said, "I guess so, sure. But I'm on record that I don't like surprises."

"Duly noted." He waited a beat. "Did that surprise you?"

"What?"

"Me saying *duly noted*."

Judith had to admit it did, just a little.

"And you didn't like that little surprise?" he said.

After hanging up, Judith wanted to go right downstairs to her room and lie on the Young Man's Fancy quilt and think about the unimaginable thing that had just happened, but she knew that besides being ridiculous and girlish, it would give too much away, so she walked back to the front room, sprawled again across her father's floral armchair, and after opening her book fell to wondering what she would wear, and what he would wear, and what it would be like driving with him in his truck, and how close to him on the seat she should sit.

After a while, her father gave her a start by speaking. "When pretending to read," he said, "it's important to turn a page occasionally."

Judith felt her face go hot and without looking up turned a page.

11

Over the next few visits, Judith's storage unit evolved into a mock living space. She spread fabric over the stacked boxes that lined the walls, and she draped the cinder-block walls with it, too, the fabric in a rich red paisley pattern, so it seemed she'd not just recreated her old room but dropped it into a fairy tale, or a dream. She began going through her boxes of books, setting aside her favorites to arrange alphabetically by author in the tiered glass bookcase.

When she came upon *The Portrait of a Lady*, she began flipping through its pages, surprised by the number of comments she'd entered in the margins. Early on, next to the paragraph that cited Lord Warburton's annual income of one hundred thousand pounds, she'd written in pencil, *10 times more than Darcy!!!* and she remembered how she couldn't understand Isabel's refusal of the fabulous man's offer of marriage. Elizabeth Bennet had sought a husband, but on her own strict terms, whereas Isabel Archer started with the idea of not wanting any husband at all. At the top of a following page Judith had written, *Dad thinks Isabel afraid of being lost in Warburton's large life .... "folded into the batter."* But wasn't that what happened with the man she finally did marry, the one who was all taste and treachery? Judith thumbed to the back and found it so. Isabel's marriage to Osmond had been suffocating. When

Osmond remarked to Isabel, "We're as united, you know, as the candlestick and the snuffer," Judith had underlined the words and written in the margin, *Ha! Send this 1 to mom!*

Judith turned to the beginning of the book, read the first line, then read almost without looking up for the next two hours, and over the following days kept reading until it was done. The plot and structure were familiar to her, but its details came to her fresh, and from a different direction than she remembered. The story of Isabel Archer, the girl who was taken from her dark house in Albany and deposited in a grand English country house, now seemed a kind of social experiment to Judith. Isabel's aunt and, more especially, her cousin, Ralph, meant themselves to be benefactors. They were interested in her frisky spirit and wanted to see where it would take her. They watched her escape two respectable suitors in Lord Warburton and Caspar Goodwood, but then Isabel was trapped by her inability to judge the character of Gilbert Osmond, who was both discerning and cruel. For Judith, personal referents presented themselves at every turn. She had escaped Willy Blunt and Patrick Guest, but they were not Lord Warburton and Caspar Goodwood, just as Malcolm was not quite Gilbert Osmond; just as, even more certainly, Judith was not Isabel Archer. Still, when Isabel had again rebuffed the last late entreaties of Warburton and Goodwood and gone back to the Palazzo Roccanera, Osmond's house of darkness in Rome, Judith felt as if she'd just attended the funeral of someone strangely close to her.

That Saturday night, after several postponements, she and Malcolm finally went to dinner at an elegant restaurant in the canyon that seemed to them both the right kind of venue for the beaded black dress. Malcolm, who very often didn't drink at all, ordered a Glenmorangie neat. After the waiter retired, he said to Judith, "In remembrance of an afternoon spent with the bride in a beachfront room."

But Judith, resisting the sportive tone, eyed the entrees just served at an adjoining table and said, "We may need to drink just to distract ourselves from the peewee portions."

The beaded dress suited her and had drawn a certain amount of attention from the men in the room as she'd passed, but she hadn't felt the small ignition of feelings necessary to raise the evening to the level Malcolm clearly intended. Judith knew it was Saturday night—she could see it in the bright eyes of other diners—but it felt to her more like a Monday.

Malcolm worked hard at his end of the bargain, telling an amusing anecdote about a check-kiting alderman, explaining the significance of the bank's imminent acquisition of a four-branch bank in northern California, and finally giving his own indignant analysis of how gerrymandering had turned the primaries into the real elections and driven both parties to extremes, or something like that, after which it took Judith a moment to realize he'd stopped talking. Her mind had drifted to poor Isabel Archer. Why, in the end, hadn't she done something about Osmond? Had she acceded to her situation for no other reason than that she was responsible for it?

Malcolm said, "I believe I'll have another scotch."

Judith had barely touched her manhattan, a drink she'd always loved but which tonight seemed too sweet. She remembered suddenly the night in the empty bank. "'Your business is our business,'" she said. "Who came up with that?"

"Consultant. What's your verdict?"

She shrugged. "Guess it's better than 'Your business is none of our damn business,' which is what I might've suggested."

Malcolm murmured good-naturedly and said it was possible her temperament was not well suited to public relations. Then, after the first sip from his fresh drink, he said, "Something strange happened to Miss Metcalf."

Judith waited.

"She found a lock in her desk."

He said this casually and without studying her reaction. In fact, he seemed to be throwing it off as a kind of joke. He let his gaze drift to the steaming dinner plates passing by in the hands of two waiters.

"I don't get it," Judith said.

He turned back to her. "Nobody does. That's why it's strange. Usually if there's a transference, it's out. But this was *in*. Yet useless—a lock somebody had cut through and nobody has the keys to."

But Miss Metcalf does have the keys, Judith thought, to a lock that could no longer secure anything, which wasn't useless at all, if your taste ran toward metaphors.

"Maybe it was some kind of swap," she said. "Something in and something out."

Malcolm shook his head. "Nothing's missing. Miss Metcalf is sure of it. She thinks somebody put it there when she wasn't looking."

"As a kind of . . . what? Joke?"

He shrugged. "Very probably."

A second passed. "Why not check the security cameras?"

"We did, but she doesn't know when the lock was put there, and the video only goes back seventy-two hours before it tapes over itself."

Judith sipped her manhattan. "Did you tell her I'd been sitting at her desk?"

Malcolm looked puzzled, then shook his head. "I'd honestly forgotten, not that it matters. And practical joking doesn't seem your style, does it? Besides, that was ages ago. She found the lock yesterday."

He'd finished his drink—when had he managed that?—and

202

something about his body language suggested that he might order another. Where were their dinners, anyway?

"What are you going to do?" she said.

"Nothing *to* do. Well, that's not quite right. Ed and I brought in several old broken locks, and when she was gone on break, we tucked them into various corners of her desk."

"And?"

"She was not unamused."

"And jokes all around about you and Ed in Miss Metcalf's drawers?"

He laughed. "Sadly, no. It's the new day and age. No hands-in-Miss-So-and-So's-drawers jokes. Thank God, of course."

He did order a third drink, and when finally their dinners were served, Malcolm regarded his plate and told the waiter he should be forewarned, he might require seconds. The waiter gave a bland smile and receded.

They tried to eat slowly, but still, it didn't take long. When their plates had been cleared and they were waiting for coffee, Malcolm leaned forward and extended his hand across the table. Judith took it. "Just for the record," he said in a low tone, "you're still the fetchingest creature I've ever laid eyes on, and I love you madly."

She was glad he left it at that. Alcohol could make him harebrained. Once before, in a similarly expansive mood, he'd mentioned the sun, moon, and stars, which in her opinion was dangerously close to the Twelfth of Never. "I love you, too," she said, and, hearing how pro forma it sounded, wondered if she was falling out of love with him. Or even already had. She hoped not, but she didn't need her mother to tell her that hope wasn't much of a stopper against the seepage of love. Judith had once formulated her own aphorism for a successful marriage—it was one, she believed, where the whole was greater than the sum of its parts—

but after a moment or two of smug satisfaction, she had to ask who could be trusted to do the math. Who would protect against rampant number-fudging? Because who wouldn't compute that their one plus one equaled three? Or at least two point one?

Later that night, at home, when Malcolm moved to make love with her, Judith merely acceded. At some point in his ministrations (at what point exactly, she couldn't say; to be truthful, her mind had been elsewhere), Malcolm abruptly rolled away and sat at the edge of the bed.

"What?" she said.

"Nothing," he said. Peevishness was not his style, but he was peevish now. "I guess your boredom was infectious."

He slipped into his silk robe and left the room, which was not quite like putting on street clothes and leaving the house—a more credible threat, in Judith's opinion, what with Francine Metcalf either on call or not. Still, Judith knew Malcolm's sequestering himself elsewhere in the house while she lay waiting for him to come back to bed would drive her crazy. Probably he knew this, too, and this probability cost him sympathy. She began thinking of the stillness of her storage room, the unencumbering feelings and strange ideas that incubated within it. She wished suddenly she could get in her car and drive there, but the Red Roof had a policy. You could visit your belongings only between 7 A.M. and 9 P.M., which, in Judith's opinion, was not always time enough. She had never again seen the sloe-eyed youth who had shown her around on her first visit, but there was one unkempt attendant, the one she privately called the Merry Man, who just before closing time drove through with a boom box playing a muddy recording of the Moody Blues' "Go Now." (Once, in passing, he gave Judith a grin gaping with missing teeth and called, "You don't have to go home, lady, but you can't stay here!")

Judith rose, put on her robe, and found Malcolm downstairs, standing at the kitchen sink. The smell of barbecued chicken hung in the air. He'd bought it at Albertsons, and she wondered why they never barbecued chicken themselves anymore, along with asparagus and onions, the way they used to do in school, soon after they met.

"Kitchen open?" she said.

Malcolm turned. "It is. But I'm afraid we've just served the last of the wings."

She came close and stood beside him. The tiny crackleware saucer she normally kept on the windowsill lay now on the kitchen counter. Her rings were in it, which wasn't itself a sur-prise—she often left them there overnight—but what she couldn't remember was whether she'd worn them that day. She thought back to her hands at dinner, but could as easily see them without rings as with. She turned to Malcolm, who was intently staring out the window.

"Was I wearing my rings at dinner?"

He started slightly, as if brought back from intricate thoughts. "What?"

She repeated herself.

"What a strange question. Of course you were. I held your hand over dinner, don't you remember? I would definitely have noticed."

He was looking away again. From this—his words and his pro-tective tone—she knew she hadn't worn them. She wished she had. She would have to pay more attention.

Down the canyon, most of the houses were dark, and beyond them, in the farthest distance, long lines of freeway traffic stretched through the valley's darkened contours.

He said, "It's funny, watching all the red lights going willy-nilly one way and all the white lights going willy-nilly the other." She didn't speak, and after a while he said, "I remember reading some-where that the first thing you should do when you're uneasy about something important—the pattern of your life, the direction you're going, a problem you're trying to fight your way out of—the first thing you should do is just stop. Really stop. Become the rock in the stream." A small smile. "Either those people out there haven't heard this advice or they're feeling just dandy about them-selves."

Judith didn't speak. Stopping and taking stock seemed like per-fectly good advice—she was more or less doing this on a daily basis herself—but what worries or regrets had brought Malcolm's mind to the solution of stillness? Or could it just be the tempo-rary abasement of failed sex? She took Malcolm's hand. "I'm sorry about—"

But he cut her off in a decisive tone. "Don't be sorry about any-thing, Judith. You are the one person in the world who hasn't a single important thing to be sorry about."

Judith knew this wasn't true and considered saying so, but he would only disagree, and where would that lead them? To him arguing for the purity of her life and her arguing against it?

She moved toward the door. "Coming?" she said.

"I'll be right up," he said. "We're out of wings"—and though in the dimness she couldn't see the thin smile form on his lips, she knew that it had—"but we're not out of drumsticks."

She said, "We can try again upstairs."

"Can and shall," he said, "but not tonight, if you don't mind."

On her way back to her room, Judith looked in on Camille. The room was dark. She drew close to the high bed and looked at her daughter curled under the sheet, the duvet pushed aside. Of the memories of Camille's toddlerhood that Judith could recall with undiluted fondness, the one that stood out was lying in bed with her at the end of the day, Camille's head tucked into the crook of

Judith's outstretched arm and Judith feeling the girl's restive, contrarian spirit finally give way to sleep, her intense little body easing into something softer, looser, dearer. For a moment Judith considered crawling into the canopied bed, sliding her arm under Camille's head, letting her settle again into her motherly embrace, but the thought didn't hold. Very probably Camille wouldn't turn, nestling, to Judith. Very probably she would awaken, alarmed, then indignant, and loudly so. So Judith instead felt the edge of the step stool and knelt on its top step to lean close enough to kiss Camille's earlobe, which, she knew, had everything—the plumpness, the softness, the smoothness—that lips might expect from a baby.

But upon the kiss Camille stirred. "Theo?"

Is that what she said? *Theo?*

"What?" Judith whispered, but Camille was asleep again, slipping back into her dreams.

—⁂—

A few days later, Judith and Lucy Meynke went out for a quick meal after working through the lunch hour. Every day Judith came in a little earlier so that she could squeeze in a bit more reading and relaxation at the Red Roof after work, but no matter how early she came in, Lucy had arrived before her. Judith appreciated it—Lucy was making some nice cuts, solving some tricky problems—but Lucy's fuller assistance tampered with the editing room's balance of influences. Judith's comments and cuts were sometimes now met with silences that she sensed were judgmental. "What would you do?" Judith asked once, more accusatorily than she intended, and Lucy matter-of-factly said this and this and this, demonstrating each step and leaving the sequence both more fluid and clearer than Judith's cuts had, which only deepened Judith's diffidence. Only when she and Lucy were outside the editing room did their friendship revert to its former ease.

Today Judith ordered a Caesar salad, and then, as the waitress turned to go, she added a martini. "Sapphire, stirred, two olives."

Lucy broke a piece of bread. "Something up with you and Malcolm?"

Judith blinked with surprise. "This being the question because I order a real drink?"

"Normally you don't. Not at three in the afternoon, anyhow."

"Malcolm's fine," Judith said. "I'm fine."

"Except for the hellacious headaches," Lucy said.

"Yeah, well," Judith said, and was glad to see the martini arrive in a chilled clear hand-blown glass, its yawning lip edged in cobalt blue, a swank look that pleased Judith, and evidently Lucy, too, because she said to the waitress, "Okay, I better have one of those myself."

After Judith took her first burning-soothing sip, Lucy said, "How about Milla? All well in the City of Milla?"

Judith considered telling her about the Theo moment but decided to keep her concerns more general. "I could make the argument that she's the perfect teenager—decent social graces, good grades, college-bound friends, blah blah blah—but the truth is, I have no idea. Every now and then I recognize her as my daughter, but most of the time she feels like a casual acquaintance. She's still forming, and most of the forming these days occurs away from home." She remembered what her own father had said to her the night Willy Blunt first telephoned: that he hoped Judith had collected the tools to defend herself. "What's hard is butting out, letting them do it themselves."

Lucy said, "Camille's spunky. She's got backbone. I'd bet the house on her."

Lucy had expressed a similar sentiment more than once, not that Judith minded hearing it again, but it didn't keep her from saying, "Though what you have to bet is not a house but a condo," and Lucy let a laugh burst out. "God, Judith," she said, "you're not supposed to fact-check a fucking *compliment*."

They ate and drank and talked about almost everything, except work. At one point, Judith became aware of two things: the dim sound of someone's cell phone and Lucy's bemused stare.

"What?" Judith said.

"Your purse is ringing."

Of course. It was short repetitions of the opening notes of "Clair de Lune." Which became much louder as Judith pulled a slim silver phone from the bottom of her purse. On the readout it said *Unavailable,* but while Judith considered whether to answer the phone or not, it fell suddenly quiet.

"Sleek," Lucy said. "New?"

"It's Milla's," Judith lied with some smoothness. The alcohol helped in this regard. "She left it in my car, and I wanted to remember to take it into the house tonight, so I put it in my purse." She stopped then, wondering what unforeseeable ambush she might have just begun leading herself into, but Lucy, possibly because of her own martini, did not seem remotely suspicious.

"That says something about Milla right there," Lucy said. "How many kids would go public with a Debussy ringtone?"

"It's probably keyed to her piano teacher," Judith said, and dropped the phone back into her bag. It was ridiculous, really, a phone for Edie Winks, but there it was. From the beginning, the bank had wanted a telephone number, and every time she deposited cash, this requirement came up as some kind of tickler on the computer screen. So once she had her new bank MasterCard, Judith went to the Nextel store, selected the cheapest plan and most stylish phone, then dumped it into her purse, where until now it had lain forgotten. She would have to figure out how to get it into freaking vibrate mode.

After the plates were cleared, Judith slid one of the

pimiento-stuffed olives from its glass toothpick. A question poised within her for days calmly passed her lips: "Remember when you hired that private eye?"

Lucy said she did. "Though I think I referred to him as a private dick."

Judith ignored the ribald drift. "You thought he was good, though, right?"

Lucy nodded. "Also pricey." She grinned and gave Judith the mischievous look of a co-conspirator. "And why do you ask?"

"There's an old girlfriend in Nebraska I've lost track of."

Lucy kept grinning. "What's his name?"

"Whose?"

"The old girlfriend you've lost track of."

"You're horrible," Judith said. "I'm sure you've been told this before."

"But am I not right?"

Judith smiled and shrugged. "Half right. I was going to check two names, actually. A girl named Deena Schmidt and a boy named Patrick Guest." Judith was a little surprised at herself. Until she spoke Patrick Guest's name, she'd presumed she was going to tell the truth.

"Patrick Guest?" Lucy said. "Have we discussed a Patrick Guest?"

Judith didn't mind Lucy Meynke chasing after Patrick Guest. "He was just this sweet competent hopeful boy in Nebraska whose father had died in a horse accident and whose stepfather died in a farming accident and whose mother then lost the family farm."

Lucy said, "This is going to be hard to sell as a comedy."

"When I last saw Patrick Guest, he and his mother were living in a tiny dark house in a row of tiny dark houses. I just always wondered if he'd made an escape."

The women both leaned back in silence while the waitress took their plates. Then Lucy said, "And the girl?"

After Judith left Rufus Sage for college, she and Deena had written for a while, but Deena had been critical of both Judith's friendship with Malcolm and her abandonment of Willy, and the correspondence had dwindled and died. Judith had considered asking Deena to be a maid of honor at the wedding, but it didn't feel quite right to have the maid of honor disapproving of her marriage, and if she wasn't going to invite her as an honored guest, she knew she shouldn't invite her at all. When, nearly a year later, she wrote a letter describing her new life in California, it came back with the words *Please return to sender* written on the front in what Judith recognized as Deena's own hand. It had stung (Judith had wadded the letter and thrown it away), but now she wondered if she hadn't deserved it, if not inviting Deena to her wedding hadn't made the gesture of the returned letter seem to Deena like the least she could do.

"She was my best friend in high school," Judith said to Lucy, "and then over time we just lost touch."

"And you always wondered whether she bested you in love and marriage?"

Judith gave a mild laugh and signaled for the check. "Something like that."

Lucy volunteered that she'd found a couple of old high school friends through Switchboard.com. "Didn't cost a dime."

"Tried that," Judith said. "And some others, too. Including a search engine you pay for." It had been a nightmare. They'd wanted his birth date, which she wasn't absolutely sure of, and where he lived, which she didn't know.

"Gilbert J. Smith," Lucy said, scrolling down the contact numbers on her telephone, "is the private investigator's name."

As she read off the number, Judith jotted it down.

When they returned to the studio and walked chatting through the reception area, there was the usual collection of three or four people waiting in the armchairs, browsing through magazines or staring at their laptop computers.

"Judy, sweetie!" one of them said, and Judith turned.

It was her mother.

"Mom. Jesus. What are you doing here?"

Her mother stood and wrapped her arms around Judith, who wasn't sure what to do. Finally her mother broke her clasp and stepped back to give Judith a motherly appraisal. "You look a little pale," she said. "Have you been having enough sex?"

An actual guffaw burst from Lucy Meynke, and Judith had no choice but to join in the laughter.

"There," her mother said. "You look better with a little color in your cheeks."

As for her mother, she looked happy. "I'm off to Mexico," she said. "San Miguel de Allende." She sounded vaguely triumphant, though over what, Judith couldn't guess.

"San Miguel," Judith repeated.

"But first I'm here," her mother said. "It's a layover. We have seven hours."

"God, Mom." She lowered her voice. "I'm working here. On stuff that had to be done three days ago."

Her mother's smile didn't give an inch.

"Judith, sweetie, when was the last time you saw me? Shortly after your father's funeral, that's when, and the next time may be mine." She tilted her head ever so slightly. "We need to commune."

Lucy Meynke cleared her throat and said she could handle the changes they were on, no problem. And if need be, she could explain to Hooper and Pottle, also no problem.

"Who is this marvelous woman?" Judith's mother said.

Judith felt herself carried along in a current she knew she ought to resist. "Are you sure?" she said to Lucy.

"Sure I'm sure."

"There, then, it's settled," Judith's mother said. "But first things first. Take me someplace yummy. I could eat a horse."

———— ⅏ ————

They went to Tom Bergin's, where her mother ordered vegetarian lasagna and Chianti, and Judith, sensing danger and in need of bracing, ordered a manhattan. When the waitress brought the Chianti, Judith's mother nodded at the glass and said, "When that's down to the quarter mark, bring me another."

Judith's mother, it turned out, had been seeing a new therapist, a woman who among other notions believed in the liberating effect of brutal truths. Suppressed heartfelt ideas and opinions, the theory went, could only convert to internal toxins. The unfortunate effect of this therapy was that Judith's mother no longer kept much of anything to herself. When for example Judith brought up the subject of that awful vacation in Florida with the Irwins, her mother said a number of unsettling things.

She said, "That night at Lefevre's we were all drinking Cuba libres, and while Dale Irwin and I were dancing, your father and Vanessa Irwin had sex in one of the toilet stalls of the men's room."

And: "It wasn't just that he was unfaithful—that had happened before. And it wasn't just that he did it more or less in front of me—that had happened before, too, although I'd always pretended it hadn't. No, what distinguished this occasion was that he did it with the wife of a man who sat on his tenure committee." She laughed. "Lust might be forgivable. Stupidity is something else."

"He told me he wasn't getting tenure," Judith said, on her father's behalf, though it was true he'd never said why.

"Did he also tell you he was offered three jobs, none as good as he'd had but two better than the one he took?"

Judith shook her head.

Judith's mother snapped a stretching piece of mozzarella with her fork and said, "Two years later, when you were living with your father in Nebraska, Dale Irwin knocked on my door late one afternoon out of the blue. It was springtime—I remember lilacs. He'd been drinking and had this funny grin. I let him in." She chewed thoughtfully. "Sex that afternoon with Dale Irwin is still on my top ten list."

Judith looked around; there were no other customers in the room except a couple of men drinking beer at a far table. She said, "If this is your idea of communing, I just don't think I'm up to it."

"Listen to you," her mother said. "You sound just like your father."

Her mother looked good, Judith had to admit, with none of the coarsening and sagging you usually saw in women her age, or at least not much of it. Sun—she kept out of the sun. Well preserved, Malcolm had called her once, and it was true. But it had seemed true of Judith's father, too. He'd seemed so solid, boulderlike, maybe not impervious to erosion but close to it, and yet. She said, "One of the Rufus Sage policemen told me the heart attack occurred while he was sitting on the toilet."

Across the table, her mother took this in.

"Probably while straining at stools, the deputy said."

Her mother's expression didn't change. It went through Judith's mind that the philosophy of brutal truths might advocate such an advanced state of tolerance that even mild surprise was discouraged. Finally her mother said, "The only shame of that is its lack of dignity, which would've meant something to your father. More than it should have, in my opinion, which by the way he rarely asked for."

After the funeral they'd retreated to a restaurant in Rufus Sage called Herman the German's. Her mother had been more subdued then. She had ordered a salad that came so drenched with dressing she couldn't eat it, but she hadn't said a word. Judith, for unknown reasons, had ordered the buffalo burger. They had eaten alone. Judith had all but forbidden Malcolm from coming. He had just taken over a new bank—it was only his third week on the job—and Camille was in second grade, when she might as easily come home from school humiliated as happy. Those were the reasons given. "Stay and tend the home fires," Judith had said, but Malcolm had been torn. She was his wife, after all, and Howard Toomey was his wife's dead father. Once, while talking about arrangements on the telephone with her mother, Judith had mentioned the standoff.

"Put him on," her mother said, and after handing the phone over, Judith heard the timbre of her mother's voice and saw Malcolm break into a grin. "Well, that's one way of putting it, Kathleen. I'll keep it in mind."

"What's one way of putting it?" Judith asked when the conversation was over.

Malcolm made his wry smile. "Your mother said your father couldn't stand the sight of me when he was alive and probably wouldn't want me around when he was dead either."

"That's not true!" Judith said, though they both knew it was, more or less.

Judith recalled the episode for her mother now, and said, "It's possible you like your new therapist because she gives you permission to be as brash as you always wished you could be."

"And the problem with that would be?"

They ate and drank silently for a few seconds, then Judith's mother said, "In case you're interested, I talked Malcolm out of coming to the funeral because I knew you didn't want him to come."

"And why was that?"

"You tell me."

"Maybe I have no idea what you're talking about."

Her mother nodded and chewed. "What I remember is how during the service you kept brushing your hair back over one ear and glancing over your shoulder to see if someone had stepped in late."

Judith felt a tightening in her chest and waited for her mother to say whatever she would say next, which might be anything, but in fact was, "You thought Willy Blunt would show up, didn't you?"

Good God, Judith thought. Never in her entire life had she mentioned Willy Blunt's name to her mother. Judith looked at her for a long moment, then reached for her water glass and let a rounded ice cube slide into her mouth. Her father. He must've told her. Judith shrugged, made a strange-feeling smile, and came more or less clean. "It didn't seem impossible he might come to that funeral."

Her mother took this in. "And when he didn't," she said, "were you relieved or disappointed?"

"Relieved," Judith said.

Her mother produced a good-natured laugh. "I should give you the name of my therapist."

Her eyes drifted from Judith toward a cluster of commemorative cardboard shamrocks on the wall, but she wasn't really looking at them. "It was February, wasn't it? What I remember is all those pickups and big American cars. They all carried the grime of winter. So did the roads and the walks and the windows. But the people, I have to admit, the people were nice. All those students and former students coming up and telling nice little anecdotes." She turned back to Judith. "I know you think I'm silly with my homilies, but there is an Italian proverb I thought of that day. *It is the first shower that wets.*" She changed her voice from the reciting mode. "Your father was my first shower, I'll admit it. And this boy Willy Blunt, whom I never met and who your father thought was simple yet actually dangerous, and whose photograph I have never seen, was yours."

Judith thought of the picture of Willy hidden in her wallet, thought of bringing it out, showing it to her. She was at the fulcrum, sitting still, wondering in which direction she might lean, but just like that, the moment was gone.

At the far table, one of the beer-drinking men laughed and said, "You're kidding, right? That bum's hitting about a buck something with men on base."

"Ready?" her mother said.

—⚌—

Outside, in the parking lot, the sun had angled lower and the heat was beginning to recede. Judith's mother said, "We still have five hours. Take me someplace interesting."

Judith wheeled her Audi onto Fairfax and mentioned the usual places. The Farmers Market. Olvera Street. Little Tokyo. Third Street Promenade.

"I said someplace *interesting*, sweetie."

Judith drove vaguely on, and her mother looked out the window and talked. "You know, I used to think the only widows who stayed widows were the ones who didn't like sex in the first place, but what I've found out is there's plenty of high jinks available to widows. Probably more than to those who sign up for a second tour of duty."

Judith hoped her mother was finished with this particular topic, but she wasn't. She said, "Latin men especially seem to value the seasoned woman from north of the border."

Judith said, "Mom, nobody talks like that here."

"Maybe you should move."

"I'll tell you what," Judith said. "If you promise not to make one more remark that in any way alludes to your sex life, I'll take you somewhere I've never taken anyone else."

Her mother turned from the window. "Where?"

Judith wasn't sure what to say. She said, "A secret place."

"*Your* secret place?" Her eyes were just short of predatory.

Judith said yes, she guessed it was.

"Okay, then," her mother said, settling back. "Now we're getting somewhere."

—⁓—

Judith tilted the Red Roof clipboard away from her mother when she signed in as Edie Winks.

As they drove down a dirty alley between rows of unvaried cinder-block buildings, her mother said, "I'll never forget this."

Judith chuckled. She remembered the line. Long ago, when her mother was in a good mood, she sometimes used it on her father when they were in the midst of some lackluster outing.

Judith unlocked the door to 17C and rolled it up. She turned on the floor lamp with the paisley shade. Dim light shone on the bed, the quilt, the commode, all of it. Her mother laughed. "It's a diorama," she said. "Get a pink princess phone for the bedstand and it's a teenage girl's room, middle America, late twentieth century."

The words stung. It *was* a little conventional, *she'd* always been a little conventional; was that a crime? Was it any worse than a mother in gauzy tops and rainbow-hemmed bell-bottoms?

Her mother had stepped into the room now, was looking at the books arranged in the tiered glass cases, running her finger over the stitching on the Young Man's Fancy quilt. "So you come here and lie down and . . ."

"Read. And think. And rest."

After a few seconds of silence, her mother said, "Judy, sweetie, I think you're trying to run away from home but don't know how to do it."

Judith said she would certainly know how to do it if she wanted to do it, which she didn't.

Her mother listened to this and changed approach. "You said you come here to think. What do you think about?"

"Nothing in particular. Mostly I read. Sometimes I nap."

Judith's mother kept looking around, studying things, taking them in. It made Judith nervous. It put her in mind of the canny detectives in those crime comedies—Columbo, Barnaby Jones, that fussy crime writer Angela Lansbury played. *The lady novelist, I'm sure she'd not be missed*—what was that from? And why might she care? She'd drunk too much. She wondered if she was just beginning to get a headache.

Her mother said, "Howard told me about this furniture, how it had been handed down, how the two of you whipped it into shape, how you went all over the countryside until you found just the right quilt for it." Her eyes turned from the furnishings to Judith. "So what brings it here?"

Judith explained as best she could.

Her mother listened, then regarded the room for another second or two. "So," she said, "with whom have you united on this quaint bed?"

Judith felt the color rise in her cheeks. "God, Mom. Somebody should shoot that therapist of yours. Maybe, just to be ironical, use a gun with a silencer."

But her mother didn't forget the question, and she waited for the answer. Judith had always thought of Willy's role in the history of the bird's-eye maple furniture as a small secret compartment to open up and look at and think about from time to time, but she was suddenly aware of its accumulated weight, and of the attraction of setting it free.

She picked up her purse. From her wallet she took the small plastic sleeve that held back-to-back photographs of Camille. She slid them from the plastic case, peeled them apart, and handed her mother the picture of Willy. Her mother held the photograph under the floor lamp and studied it. Judith had taken it with her father's Leica and developed it herself. In it, Willy was stretched out on a picnic blanket wearing old boots, old denim pants, no belt, no shirt, no hat. He looked asleep except for his grip on a long-necked Schlitz. Judith's mother said, "Why, he's as yummy as Christ on the cross." Then, after watching Judith slip the picture back into its secret place, she added, "Poor Malcolm." Then: "Poor you. Poor me. Poor every last one of us."

She slipped off her shoes and lay down on the bed. "Come here," she said, extending an arm, and strange as it seemed, Judith tipped off her shoes, too, and lay down beside her, fitting her head into the crook of her mother's arm, which suddenly held her tighter and closer, and just like that, Judith was overcome, or undone, or whatever it was. It didn't matter—she'd begun to cry.

— ❦ —

A few days later, from her storage room, with her heart racing like a teenager's, Judith telephoned Gilbert J. Smith. She gave her name as Edith Winks and explained that she was trying to find several people so they could be notified of an upcoming high school reunion in Nebraska.

"Lot of trouble to get a couple of old school pals to a reunion," Gilbert J. Smith said. His voice on the phone was flat, with a faintly plaintive quality—Judith imagined eyes surrounded by squint lines, something in the Harry Dean Stanton mold.

"Yes," Judith said. "But there it is."

Gilbert J. Smith was quiet for a few seconds, which Judith presumed was meant as an opportunity for her to say more, but she didn't. Why she wanted to find somebody was her business, whereas finding that somebody was his.

He said, "And you tried Googling and all that?"

Judith had, and told him so.

"Well, I guess we can locate them all right," Gilbert J. Smith said finally. "What we'll need are the individuals' names, dates of birth if you've got them, last known address, any other specifics you might have. That and a seven-hundred-dollar deposit."

Judith gave him the names of Patrick Guest, Deena Schmidt, and William Blunt, along with what little else she knew about them. Deena's birthday, which she remembered, and Willy's, within a range of three days.

"No middle names or initials?" Gilbert J. Smith said.

Judith told him that Willy's middle initial was *C*.

"Know what it stands for?"

"No," Judith said. Willy would never tell her. To change the subject, she said, "So what does the *J* in your name stand for?"

"Jones," Gilbert J. Smith said. "My father's idea. My father seemed to think he had a sense of humor. Though I don't hear you laughing."

"It's kind of funny, though," Judith said. She'd been distracted. She was thinking of something else. "One other thing," she said. "If you find William Blunt, could you give him my telephone number?"

"Your name and telephone number? And nothing else? No message?"

"No. No message."

"Tell him Edith or Edie?"

"Edie."

"All right, then," Gilbert J. Smith said. "Just as soon as I receive your check . . ."

Immediately after concluding this conversation, Judith went to the checkbook that lay on top of the glass-fronted bookshelf. Edie Winks of Toluca Lake. She wrote out the check and stared at it. She almost had to laugh. Money going from a person who didn't exist to a private investigator she'd never met in order to find three people she hadn't seen in over twenty-five years.

Judith slid the check into an envelope, which she addressed and laid next to her keys, where it couldn't be forgotten. She'd left the studio abruptly after lunch—she'd told Hooper she was seeing a neurologist about her migraines—and now she needed to get back to work, but she was tired, suddenly overwhelmingly tired. A short nap would be good. She wouldn't sleep long, and she would awaken feeling better, more productive, brand-new almost. She removed her shoes. She turned off her phone. She stretched out on the bed and fell asleep.

Part Two

1

When, five minutes before the appointed hour on that first Friday night, Willy Blunt gave the Toomeys' door a short set of solid knocks, they not only could be heard in the basement, where Judith sat waiting, but also could be felt resonating through timbers and beams and concrete until finally they reached the bird's-eye maple bed on which she sat, or so it seemed to Judith. In any case, the knocking sounds indisputably registered on the delicate instruments of her nervous system, and as she stared up at the basement ceiling and traced her father's footsteps across the hardwood floor, a tiny bulb of sweat broke from one armpit and ran down her rib cage.

Judith had been ready for almost an hour. The only real decision had been what long-sleeved top to wear with her Levi's and Frye Boots. It was still May, and thinking of evening coolness, she'd decided finally on one of her father's chambray shirts, the pale blue one with the cotton worn soft, which she wore tails out. She'd given her long straight hair about a hundred strokes, and then a hundred more, before clipping it into something slightly prim so her father would see she wasn't trying to give anybody the wrong idea.

Overhead, the latchwork of the front door.

Judith slipped off the bed and tiptoed across the Persian

carpet toward the stairs. She'd agreed to give her father a few minutes alone with Willy Blunt before she came up, but she hadn't promised anything about eavesdropping. She crept to the head of the stairs and leaned close to the basement door, which she'd left ajar.

By this time the introductions were over, and to her horror her father was saying, "Well, Willy, why don't you just tell me something about yourself that you think it would be in your best interests for me to know."

Good God, Judith thought, but Willy Blunt's laugh didn't sound nervous. "Well," he said, "I give a day's work for a day's wage, and no complaining."

Her father said, "And what else?"

A second or two passed, and Willy Blunt said, "I take people at their word and expect they'll do the same with me."

That was pretty good, Judith thought, especially since he'd been blindsided by this whole let's-interview-the-suitor thing, but her father seemed to be reserving judgment.

"Ah," he said. "And is there anything else?"

"That's about it, really," Willy said. "I like doing finish carpentry because I'm good at it. Or maybe it's the other way around—I'm good at it because I like it. I like doing baseboard and wainscoting but what I like best is crown molding."

Why her father didn't say something civil then, Judith had no idea, but he didn't, and after a few seconds, Willy said, "So do you think Judith's ready yet?"

Her father said he would just go see, but he didn't. He said, "You know, once when I was a boy in San Francisco, there was a little dog in the park who started playing with me. I would chase him and then he would chase me. The game ended when I chased him beyond a hedge and into the street, where he was struck by a car and killed."

After a second or two, Willy said, "Now there's a story for you."

"It is," her father said. "It really is. Now then, why don't I just go check on Judith."

"God, Dad!" Judith hissed when he opened the door and came a few steps down the basement stairs. "Who made you district attorney? And what's with the Aesop's fable?"

"Ah," he said mildly. "You heard us chatting."

"You didn't tell me you were planning a *bushwhacking!* Why didn't you just shoot him when he came through the door?"

When she saw that he was swallowing a laugh, she stormed past him up the stairs. She found Willy Blunt standing in the front room staring out the front window with his seed cap in his hand, and she had to admit, he didn't look especially perturbed. He was wearing a blue-and-black plaid flannel shirt and he stood loose-shouldered at the window, looking out and whistling to himself. The melody was dimly familiar, but she couldn't name it.

"Hi," she said.

Willy Blunt ceased his whistling and turned. "*Whoa*," he drawled. "Stop the presses."

She laughed. "What's that supposed to mean?"

The blue-and-black flannel shirt had a soft look, and he was wearing it over a clean white T-shirt. "No idea," he said. "Just came into my head and I let 'er fly."

She laughed again, and after a few last exchanges with her father that Willy handled as best as he could—*Good to meet you, Mr. Toomey. Oh, yeah, we can be back by then*—the door was closing behind them and Judith and Willy Blunt were out of the house, strolling down the walk toward his truck, small weights lifting from Judith's body with every step she took. It seemed almost dreamlike—she could hardly remember opening the door and sliding into the cab, and yet there she was.

The engine rumbled powerfully, but Willy merely eased the truck away from the curb. "The radio's on the blink," he said, and gave her a smile. "I can whistle, though, if things get dire."

"I like that shirt," Judith said.

"It's my lucky shirt." He grinned. "I haven't worn it in a while. When I was playing basketball at the high school, I used to wear it on important game days."

"And you always won?"

"Oh, hell no. I said lucky, not *miraculous*."

She began memorizing the details she meant to keep and never lose.

The funny mixed smells of sweat and sawdust.

The pair of vise grips on the driver's-side door where a handle should be.

The slow, easy smoothness of the truck's progress.

The numbers 2731 written in thick pencil on the metal dashboard.

"You wrote down my number *there?*"

He turned and said, "Yeah, well, I didn't have my steno pad handy."

The gray-blueness—or was it blue-grayness?—of his eyes.

After turning north on Main Street, Willy pulled the pickup into one of the diagonal slots in front of a bar called the Y Knot.

"We eating here?" Judith said, alarmed by the prospect.

"Naw. I'm just picking something up."

He jumped out of the truck but stopped on the sidewalk when he saw that she'd stayed put. "C'mon," he said. "It's not dangerous."

By the time Judith's eyes had adjusted to the dim light of the room, Willy was already at the bar, joking with a waitress he knew by name. "Whaddaya mean not ready, Lorraine?" he was saying. "I called it in about two days ago."

Judith turned her head and caught a thin balding man with a brushy mustache staring at her from a table by the wall. A dark form at his feet turned out to be a dog—it raised its head to lazily address the presence of a flea.

"Maybe you called one of our competitors by mistake," Lorraine said. "I hear you spread your business around." The waitress was somewhere past thirty, Judith guessed, and thick-waisted, but she had the kind of attitude and breasts that push-up bras were made for, and her presence made Judith feel strangely insignificant. Judith let her eyes drift past the woman to the sparkly waterfall of an illuminated Hamm's sign hanging on the back wall.

"What's your name, sugar?"

By the time Judith realized the question was for her, Willy had jumped in. "This is Judith Toomey," he said.

The waitress was smiling at Judith, but she was studying her, too. "Then this must be the lollapalooza you were talking about."

"The very one," Willy Blunt said, but in a distracted tone. He'd stood on the footrest of his bar stool and was leaning over the bar, craning to see behind. "So where's my damn package, Lorraine?"

Lorraine waited a beat before breaking her gaze from Judith and strolling past the black grill top and pyramid of soup cans to the end of the bar, where she slid a large brown paper bag from beneath the counter. She brought it back to Willy, who loosened the neat fold at the top and took a look inside. From the glass-faced refrigerator Lorraine took a six-pack of Budweisers and set it beside the sack.

"Why don't you just pay me later?" she said, and Willy shrugged and rolled a few toothpicks from a chrome dispenser. The waitress turned to Judith. "You be careful now," she said. "Willy only looks normal."

Willy shook his head as if in sorrowful disbelief. "Now what is the point of living a model life if all it brings you is ridicule?" he said, but before anybody could comment on his definition of a model life, he slid from the bar stool, picked up his parcels, and, motioning Judith ahead of him, made for the door.

Outside, Willy packed the beer into a cooler of ice he'd brought in the truck bed. Then they headed south through town, slowly, at what she and Deena, when they'd see boys cruising the streets like this, always called *prowling speed*. The surprise came when Willy hardly increased his speed as he turned west onto Highway 20, where the limit was 60. He slid a toothpick into his mouth. A couple of cars whooshed past.

"Lollapalooza?" Judith said as they passed the little airport outside of town. "That your term or that waitress woman's?"

"I might've used it," Willy said, "but not very often."

"What does it mean?"

"A lollapalooza?" He seemed as amused by this question as by everything else. "How about 'something or somebody worth paying attention to'?" He slid her a glance. "You, for example."

The remark sent pleasurable waves moving through her, and she gazed out at the passing green fields. Willy had been working a toothpick in the incisor region but pulled it out to say, "Want me to whistle?"

Judith laughed and said no, she didn't think so.

They crossed Deadhorse and Butte Creeks before he swung the pickup onto a dirt road running south and the ride lost its smoothness. She raised her voice a little to say, "So where're we going?"

He just smiled. "I think we talked about this. How it was going to be a surprise and all."

She recognized Crown and Crow Buttes, but she didn't know the rest. As they crested a small knoll, the fields and pastures stretched long and flat before finally giving way to timbered hills. The buttes above the hills stood in the late afternoon sun like monuments, black against a luminous blue sky.

"Pretty," she said, and after a second or two he said, "That's the truth."

They drew a mile or so closer to the hills and she said, "What did you think of that story my dad told you—the one about chasing the dog into the street?"

He shot her a quick sideways look. "How'd you know about that?"

She said it was an old house, with thin walls.

"Well," Willy said, "I think that story of your father's is what you'd call a cautionary tale. Only I think your dad thinks you're the puppy and I'm the chaser. He doesn't know who's the dangerous one here."

Judith felt a little thrill of pleasure at these words even while composing her denial of them. "Excuse me," she said, "but I think it was you asking me for my phone number, not the other way around."

He said, "That's because you probably didn't think I had a telephone."

"Maybe I thought you had a phone but couldn't remember your own number."

Willy let his laugh slide into a grin. "Now you be careful. It's not like you couldn't hurt my feelings with a thoughtless remark."

He had fun in his voice, and Judith could feel it, there was an easiness in the air.

A porcupine waddled across the road in front of them and Willy started talking about a dog he'd owned that wouldn't stay away from a particular porcupine that lived out behind some sheds on their place, and Judith's thoughts began to drift. She wondered where someone like Willy Blunt would learn a term like *cautionary tale,* and she remembered how Patrick Guest said that Willy Blunt had claimed to enjoy the *bountiful vista* from their barn roof. It was hard stacking up those terms with this boy.

"I know about six different fellas who have girlfriends just like that nasty old porcupine," Willy was saying, "but do you think they'd learn to stay away?"

To Judith's surprise, he seemed to be expecting an answer.

"I guess not," she said.

He nodded amiably. "You'd be guessing right."

For something to say, she asked what had become of the dog.

"Oh, his snout got a lot better after I shot that porcupine. I gave it to an Indian who wanted it. They use the quills for necklaces and shit, and I guess they eat porcupines, too, even old ones." He slid Judith a cunning glance. "How about you—would you eat a porcupine?"

Judith said eating a porcupine was a prime example of something she personally would never do in a million years.

Willy Blunt snorted. "You would, though, if you were hungry enough."

He turned the pickup briefly east, then south, then east again onto a road that narrowed and grew rockier and shadowy. Instead of dividing open pasture or farmland, it followed the course of a running creek and began to tunnel through box elder, cottonwood, and hackberry. Thickets of wild plum dotted the roadside ("Some's sweeter than others," Willy said). He stopped once and filled a plastic jug with water from a spring that seemed to issue from a mossy stone beside the road. A tin cup hung from a nearby branch, and after Willy used it for a drink, he filled it for Judith.

"Good water," he said.

It *was* good water, Judith had to admit. She held the cup under the spring and drank again.

Farther up the road, they hit the first of two post-and-barbed-wire gates, which Willy loosened and laid aside, replacing them again once they'd driven through. After the second gate, there was no road at all, and a lot of treefall and other debris.

"Willy?" she said, staring at terrain that to her looked impassable. It was the first time she'd called him by name.

"What?" He leaned over the steering wheel and gently accelerated.

"What if we get stuck out here?"

Willy kept the truck sliding and bumping around large rocks and fallen limbs, but he found time to cast her a quick sidelong grin. "Who said anything about getting stuck?"

It was remote up here, remoter than anyplace she and her father had ever ventured, but the truck kept bouncing, swerving, and surging forward. Then suddenly, up ahead and between trees, the ground appeared to give way completely and she yelled, *"Stop, Willy, stop!"* but he merely grinned and downshifted as the truck careered down a muddy bank and into a wide sandy creek, the rear end fishtailing this way and that before the pickup cocked sideways on the opposite bank and then finally grabbed and pulled forward to flatter ground.

"God," Judith said, and was surprised at how exhilarated she felt.

"Positraction," Willy said, as if he were speaking the name of a saint, or at least a beautiful woman, and when finally they came to a stop at the base of a wooded hill, Judith felt compelled to ask what in the world he was talking about.

"Positraction?" he said. "Why, positraction is the reason I bought this truck. They call it a limited-slip differential, but what it really is is a ticket to just about anywhere."

Judith stared at him sitting there beaming with satisfaction and said, "Well, I think what it got me is a ticket to the Twilight

Zone," and she was relieved when Willy gave the line a good-natured laugh.

As they stepped from the truck they were greeted with assorted bird cries, all shrill and alarmed-seeming, as if the intrusion of two humans were real news. Willy strapped on a backpack and carried the ice chest on his shoulder as he led the way up the incline and into the pines. The wind through the trees made a low flutish sound that fell just short of music, and the mat of needles beneath her feet was surprisingly soft and slippery.

"How you doing?" Willy asked every now and then, and Judith said "Fine," which was really all she could say, since he was carrying everything.

In about ten minutes' time they were overlooking a kind of encampment—a cleared space of ground among the pines and ash. As they descended, a fire pit came into view, and a couple of aluminum-and-canvas camp chairs that were showing their age. There was also a crude wide-plank table, with a plank bench on each side. The surfaces of both the table and the benches were clean. Kindling and small pieces of dry pine had already been laid in the rock fire pit.

"You've been up here recently, I guess," Judith said.

It didn't bother Willy to admit this. "Had to do a little housekeeping, is all. Didn't want you to find the place a mess." He set down the cooler and backpack and looked at her. "So tell me this, Judith Toomey. Is this your first first date?"

"No," Judith lied at once. "What made you think that?"

"Well, I knew it was our first date, yours and mine, which made it important—at least to me it did—but I had the feeling it might be your first first date, which might make it even more important, and I wanted it to be, you know, just real nice." His mouth again loosened into a friendly grin. "Like somebody gave a flying fuck."

He offered a bottle of beer to Judith, who thought she ought to refuse it but didn't. "To Judith Toomey and the big surprise," he said mildly, and gently clicked the neck of his bottle to hers.

He busied himself gathering firewood while she sat at the table and sipped her beer and took the place in—the tall ponderosas and the soft carpet of pine needles, the crickets and cicadas and birds and low hollow sound of the wind, which reminded her of that odd day up on Initial Hill. The birds seemed calmer now, as if the alarm had gone out of them and it was again business as usual. She liked it that Willy could identify the birdcalls, and she liked it that he knew the names of the butterflies—red admirals and painted ladies, mourning cloaks and yellow swallowtails.

"Soapweed," he said when she asked him what one yuccalike shrub was. "Cows love the stuff—blossoms, seedpods, roots, too, if they can get at them. They'll just about run from one bush to another when they're set loose in a pasture with 'em." He grinned at her. "It's about the only time a cow can make you laugh."

He pulled a red gingham cloth from his backpack and floated it over the plank table. Then he opened the bag of food. There were grilled sandwiches inside, pastrami and Swiss cheese on rye, and Judith never would have thought a grilled sandwich served cold could taste so good.

When she looked up from her food, Willy was regarding her. "I've seen rodeo boys eat daintier than that," he said. He tore the last sandwich in two and presented both portions. She took the bigger one, and he said, "I knew it."

The encampment was part of a large, beautiful, and, he said, agriculturally useless property owned by one of his mother's cousins. Willy harbored hopes of one day buying the land and building a cabin on it. While he and Judith finished off the last sandwich, he pointed to a draw where, with an earthen dam, a small lake might be formed. Judith could imagine it: the pine trees, the sky, the water, the birdcalls and flutish wind. "It'd be a beautiful place to swim," she said.

"Or to fish. I was thinking of stocking it with rainbows and bass."

Judith said, "Okay, I'll fish with you if you'll swim with me. 'Course, you'd have to teach me to fish."

He said, "Well then, that'd make us even."

"How's that?"

"You'd have to teach me to swim."

Judith came out with a real laugh. "You can't swim?"

He shrugged complacently.

The shadows of the trees and buttes had been stretching longer, and the light had all but drained from the sky. Willy put a match to the fire he'd already laid, and although the cool that came with the darkness had been refreshing at first, Judith was glad now for the heat.

He brought over the two old camp chairs and set them up near the fire in locations that seemed important to him. "That one's yours," he said, pointing.

They looked the same to Judith, so she said, "How come that one? Is it booby-trapped or something?"

"Why, yes, it is," he said. "What happens when you sit in that particular booby-trapped chair is that all your inhibitions explode and you start dancing naked around the fire."

She sat down in the chair and blinked at him. "Liar."

He shook his head and pretended mystification. "Well, that was how it worked last time."

For dessert, he'd brought graham crackers, chocolate bars, and marshmallows, and while the fire burned down, he whittled skewers from willow branches. Both he and Judith had the same marshmallow-roasting technique, patiently keeping the marshmallows close but not too close to the coals so they skinned a mellow brown before being sandwiched with chocolate and graham cracker. These, too, tasted so good that Judith wondered if she'd fallen under some kind of spell.

"Were those the surprise?" she said. "Because if they were, I'd be more than satisfied."

"Nope," he said. "That was just part of the dining package. Your big surprise is coming."

"Coming when, exactly?"

"In a little while, plus or minus."

For the next half-hour or so, they talked about anything that came to mind, just talking and listening and agreeing, always agreeing. Every now and then, Willy uncapped another bottle of beer or checked his pocket watch or fed wood to the fire.

"Pine's poor for heat," he said, "but it's unbeatable for popping and crackling."

When he went off to urinate or gather wood, he'd fall to whistling, and once while he was off, Judith put her head back, closed her eyes, and listened to the sounds of the wind and the fire and the crickets and the frogs and, just beyond those, the man-made whistling of a song she couldn't quite name. She was a long way from anyone, in a place where nobody could see what she did or what he might do, a fact that ought to have made her cautious or fearful but didn't. It made her feel a little excited.

When Willy came back, he sat forward in his chair and began to whittle a new skewer.

"For the next time you come?" she said.

He said, "To be truthful, I was thinking for the next time we come."

"You're already planning ahead."

"Oh, yeah. That's one of the things I do."

"Me, too." A silence stretched out, and then she said, "Once when I was talking to Patrick Guest, he said you kept working at their place for a while after doing that barn roof."

"I did, that's true."

"He told me you stayed out there and ate with them."

"That's right, too. My old man had thrown me out at the time—I can't remember what for." A smile formed on his lips. "Boarding with that family was a little different, though. They said they were vegetarians, so for meals we had corn and potatoes and beets, all stuff they grew there, but nothing else, not even chicken. So one day I asked the little one, Petey, how he liked being a vegetarian, and he said it was okay, he guessed, but he wasn't sure because he'd only been one for about two weeks." Willy laughed and nodded. "That woman made good rhubarb pie, though."

Judith said, "Patrick Guest said you didn't take money for that job."

"Maybe. I hardly remember."

"Patrick said you sat on the barn roof at night and threw your empty beer bottles down in the rhubarb."

"Sounds like Patrick did a lot of talking."

"He also said you called the view from the roof 'a bountiful vista.'"

"Really? I can't say I remember that."

"Patrick thought the view from the hayloft was just as good as from the roof and a lot easier to get to."

Willy said nothing to this.

Judith said, "So why didn't you just sit in the hayloft?"

"I don't know. Maybe the view from the roof was more inspiring."

"What's that supposed to mean?"

Willy grinned at her. "You want the truth here?"

Judith wasn't sure if she did or didn't. She nodded yes.

"Well, the barn roof was about eye level with Mrs. Guest's second-story bedroom."

Judith considered the words *Say no more,* but she said, "So?"

"So it was summer, and Mrs. Guest always took her bath at night down the hall, and when she got back to her room she'd turn on the light and sit up in bed reading and smoking. It was some distance, but it was still inspirational."

To her surprise, Judith laughed. "I guess it would be to a twelve-year-old."

"Yeah, well, we're not snakes. I've thought this many times. Adolescence is a skin we never quite shed. Maybe it's different for girls."

Judith wondered about that. She wondered about something else, too. "So that's all you did, just watch from afar?"

Willy seemed now to be picking his course. "Not exactly," he said. "One day I got up my courage and said to her, 'Mrs. Guest, one of these nights I could climb onto that little roof off your second story and come through your window, and if I did it would be the highlight of my life.'" He laughed a low laugh. "I gave her big eyes and a kind of hangdog look, thinking it would appeal to her maternal instincts, which I'm told sometimes works, but I can tell you it didn't with her. She looked at me and said, 'I keep a loaded gun in my room, and if you come near that window, I'll shoot you where it hurts.'" Willy let loose a massive rowdy laugh. "I said, 'Well, Mrs. Guest, that's about the most unfriendly invitation I ever received.'" Another good-sized laugh burst from him, and Judith laughed, too.

When they were both still, she said, "And that was that?"

A second passed. "Oh yeah, that was that. That very night she put a sheet up over her window, and it wasn't long after that that I was gone."

Judith considered telling Willy what had become of Mrs.

Guest, but the truth was, she didn't know what had become of her. She only knew she lost her farm and moved to a crappy little house in Woolcott and looked like a ghost one morning in December when Judith and Deena knocked on the door unexpectedly.

Willy whistled a few notes from his song, then broke off and checked his watch and the sky. "Okay," he said. "Time to get you ready."

He was holding a red bandanna at each end, twirling it into something vaguely ropey. "This goes over your eyes, but if you promise not to peek, I won't cinch it too tight."

Judith looked at the bandanna stretched between his hands. "You know, if something bad happens to me out here, my father will hunt you down and kill you."

"'Course he would," Willy said. "What father wouldn't?" He laid the bandanna over her eyes and tied it off. "That okay?"

She nodded.

"Okay, just sit back and relax."

Relaxing implied waiting, which alarmed her. "What do you mean, relax?"

"It'll be a minute or two. I'll tell you when."

He began again to whistle, and she said, "What is that song, anyhow?"

"Don't you like it?"

"I like it okay. It's just that I feel like I've heard it before but can't name it."

"Me either," he said. "It just always comes to me. It's one of my mother's old songs. Maybe sometime you can ask her."

"If I live to meet her."

"You're kind of funny," he said in an amiable voice.

He resumed whistling, and it soon seemed to Judith that she'd drifted just beyond herself and was hovering there listening to the

240

hollow wind in the trees, the hiss and crackle of the fire, the whistled song.

And then abruptly the whistling stopped and she couldn't hear Willy's breathing or feel his presence, and the other sounds that only moments ago had seemed comforting now seemed disquieting.

"Willy?"

He didn't answer.

"Willy?"

"Just a damn second," he said. "Okay, it's ready," he said, and the soft flannel of his shirt brushed her face as he unfastened the bandanna. She'd had her eyes closed behind the cloth, and opened them. He was pointing toward the two closest buttes, which were now silhouetted in blackest black against some new and grand source of light. It was a brilliant buttery yellow, and though it at first seemed stationary, it wasn't, for the light seemed to rise looming from the two buttes, and it gave them each the kind of aura that Judith associated with pictures of Jesus. But this soon changed, too. The illumination slid slowly upward, growing larger, wider, whiter, casting its dazzling light, becoming its entire self: a flush full moon, though, she had to admit it, this was not the moon as she had ever known it. It was a different moon. There was the low resonant wind through the trees, and the crack and pop of the fire, and there was this moon, free now of the buttes, hanging huge and luminous behind a slim filmy cloud. Judith took a deep breath so she could hold it all in.

"There," Willy Blunt said in a low voice. "That right there is the moon to watch."

Judith said, "If anybody painted that moon exactly as it is right now, right there, everybody would like it, but nobody would believe it. Not one person. They'd think you made it up."

In a low voice Willy said, "Maybe tomorrow we'll think we did, too."

She turned suddenly. "No," she said with vehemence, "we won't. Because you saw it and I saw it."

Willy was nodding and smiling. "'Course, one of us might wake up somewhere down the line and begin doubting what we saw."

Judith looked at him in the light of the moon and the fire. Then—and even during this moment it felt like something from a movie she'd seen or would like to see—she rose and swung a leg over his leg and settled into his lap so they sat face to face. "It's not going to be me," she said in a tight whisper. "It's not going to be me who doubts it."

What she had done and was doing was a surprise to herself, and his expression, too, seemed full of wonderment. He touched a single finger softly to her nose; then he touched her eyelids closed and began smoothing the soft round of his finger across her lips, and just like that she was kissing him, uncertainly at first, and then greedily, teeth clashing with teeth. When his free hand slid up toward her bra clasp, she arched her back to make it easier, and the instant the clasp fell free she felt herself breathe a different kind of air. He made a low murmuring sound and, leaning forward, began kissing her open neck while his hands cupped her breasts, lifting them a little, causing them, or so it seemed to her at that moment, to swell to new dimensions, and he began gently thumbing the nipples until she thought she might burst.

When the time came to leave, he was the one to dump ice and water onto the fire and shovel dirt over the embers. He gathered the empty beer bottles and their other trash into the ice chest. During this time Judith managed nothing more than standing, fastening her bra, and buttoning her shirt.

On the way home, once they'd bounced across the creek and rough terrain and were again on a graded road, she stared out at the moon, but it had already become the usual moon, distant, white, the one she'd known her entire life, until tonight. She turned and lay down with her head in Willy's lap. He drove slowly; she would find that he always drove slowly. Finally she said, "That *was* my first first date, just so you know. Also my first kiss."

He said, "Well, I hope you didn't find anything disappointing."

She laughed and burrowed her face into his flannel shirt, and then, to her surprise, she was crying.

"Hey, hey now, what's the matter? We didn't do anything you'd call extreme."

This was true. They'd both kept their hands above the waist.

"That isn't it," she said. "I just don't want it to end."

Willy Blunt combed his fingers through Judith's hair. A rock plinked against the undercarriage. When he spoke, his tone had lost its customary looseness. "I'm going to tell you something," he said. A second or two passed. Then: "The thing is, I think you're just a lot more interesting than any girl I've ever met."

She snuffled and lifted her head and dabbed a tissue at her nose.

"You do?"

"Yeah, I do."

"How come?"

He let out a low laugh, as if he hadn't expected that particular question. He glanced down at her, then back at the road. She had the impression he wasn't so much searching for an answer as waiting for it to come to him. Finally he said, "Sometimes that's a hard thing to put your finger on."

A few minutes later, Willy turned the Chevy truck from the graded road onto Highway 20. In the relative quiet, Judith said, "Will you come by tomorrow afternoon?" and he touched his finger to her nose and said why of course he would.

2

Willy Blunt dropped by early Saturday afternoon, and this time, when Judith led him into the backyard to say hello to her father, the conversation was uneventful. Judith pointed out the lime tree in its terra-cotta pot, and her father pointed out the blossoms that would turn to buds that would turn to limes. Willy stared at it for a moment and said, "Mr. Toomey, if you were to get one more of those little trees, it'd probably make you the biggest citrus grower in the state of Nebraska," which to Judith's relief earned him a small, puffing laugh from her father and, better yet, provided them an easy means of going back into the house.

While her father puttered in the garden, Judith sat at the kitchen table letting Willy teach her a card game called casino, until her father, stepping inside for iced tea, accepted Willy's invitation to join them, both of which—invitation and acceptance—Judith found irritating. Still, with her father there she learned the game, and took spiteful pleasure when the toothpicks they were playing for began to accumulate on her side of the table.

Around 3 P.M., Willy looked at his pocket watch and said he had to drive down south of town to see a farmer about a job. "Joe L. Minnert," Willy said. "He wants me to build a room on for him." Willy let his gaze move from Judith to her father. "Would the two of you want to ride along?"

Judith's father smiled—he seemed to appreciate Willy's ruse even while seeing through it—and said he was sorry, but he'd already made plans to go to campus this afternoon.

"Would it be okay if I go?" Judith asked.

"With me down to campus?" her father said mildly. "Of course, if you like."

"You know what I mean. With Willy."

Her father looked at Willy, then back at Judith. "I don't see why not."

It occurred to Judith that if her heart were hooked up to a monitor, a wild spike on the running graph paper would just have been observed.

The Minnert farmhouse was hidden behind a shelter belt of conifers planted along Dead Horse Road, and when Willy parked in front of the house alongside an open orange Jeep, a large woman at once stepped out the front door and stood looking at them. An even larger man soon appeared behind her. Judith supposed these were Mr. and Mrs. Minnert. They just stood silently, as if their mere presence were acknowledgment enough of Willy's arrival.

"I'm the carpenter," Willy said as he and Judith approached.

"Who's she?" the woman said, nodding at Judith.

"A friend of mine." Willy smiled one of his genial smiles.

The large man and woman stared. The man's face was stone, and the woman's was expressionless, too, but there was something wrong with her face. One side seemed to have drooped from its natural place; a terrible sag under that eye exposed wet red tissue.

Joe L. Minnert turned and took his great mass into the house.

His wife started to do the same, but stopped and turned back. "Well, c'mon," she said.

Judith followed Willy into the house, which was dark and held a smell that went well beyond the fustiness she'd occasionally noticed in farmhouses. She imagined decaying meat she couldn't see, and what she couldn't see was almost everything. The heavy shades that covered the windows left the room so dim that she extended her hand to Willy's shoulder as they advanced.

Finally a hall light was switched on by the large woman, who had somehow gotten behind Judith.

"There," Joe L. Minnert said, pointing toward a blank wall at the end of a hallway. "That's where my office goes."

"He calls it *his* office," Mrs. Minnert said in a low voice, and Judith wondered who she was talking to.

The big farmer produced a piece of lined yellow paper containing a drawing of a room. Willy looked at it a few seconds, then began talking about what was and wasn't a bearing wall and finally got to suggesting what types of windows and doors they might like, to which Joe L. Minnert said, "We ain't building the Taj Mahal."

A hard laugh erupted from Mrs. Minnert. In the confined space the meaty smell had grown stronger, and Judith felt a faint wave of nausea. When Mrs. Minnert crowded forward to assert the need for a lock on the new office door, Judith said, "I think I'll wait outside."

Willy smiled at her and said that'd be fine, this wouldn't take too long.

Judith turned, and Mrs. Minnert stepped back so she could pass by. She hurried through the front room toward the light of the mud porch and threw open the door. Outside, she stood and drank in the air.

The yard was weedy and unfenced, but an old wooden chair and side table stood under a hackberry tree among scattered deadfall. Judith went over and sat in the chair. The shade was a comfort. She closed her eyes and listened to the buzz of insects, and she had just begun to feel more or less normal when the snap of a branch gave her a start. She opened her eyes and saw Mrs. Minnert staring at her from a near distance. The woman tried to smile, which only accentuated the division in her face—while one side of the mouth turned up, the other seemed to slide down. "Want a washcloth?" she said.

"No," Judith said. "I'm better now. I think I must've eaten something bad or something."

"You didn't eat it here," Mrs. Minnert said. She drew a bit closer, not too close but close enough that she seemed to bring with her the faint smell of meat. She said, "Are you a nice girl?"

"Yes," Judith said. "Yes, I am."

The woman stared at her keenly. "You sure?"

"Yes," Judith said. "I'm sure."

"The girly-girl is sure," Mrs. Minnert said, and stood motionless with a slight forward lean as if clamped onto this thought. Then an abrupt unhappy laugh flew from her mouth. "Are you sure-sure, or just pretty sure?"

Judith squared her shoulders for some kind of answer, but she didn't have to speak. Mrs. Minnert suddenly said, "We have no issue." The right side of her face drew into a grimace while the other drooped like warm wax. "We had us one, but he died when he was two."

Judith tried to make a nod of the kind she would make if this were a normal conversation. Then it was quiet except for the pulsing chorus of cicadas, and Judith heard herself say, "What's that smell inside the house?"

"What smell?" Mrs. Minnert said, brought back. The suspicion in her face formed in two unaligned columns.

"I don't know," Judith said. "I just thought there was a smell."

"There's no smell." Then: "It could be a vermin. He baits for vermin."

Judith said nothing to this. By vermin, she supposed the woman meant rodents, but it wasn't rodents—she remembered the rat-and-mouse smell of the lean-to when she and her father had pulled out the bird's-eye maple, and this was different.

Mrs. Minnert shuffled closer, and the odor—it *was* meaty in nature, Judith felt sure of it—grew more potent. The woman glanced behind her and lowered her voice. "He said it was *his* office your lover boy's going to build, but it's not." The woman's good eye was gleaming, and the one with the moist pink sag beneath it had brightened, too. "He done something. He thought I wouldn't see, but I did. So now I'm getting my room." She looked as if she might laugh, and if she did, it would be something out of a bad horror movie, only it wouldn't be a bad horror movie, it would be real life. But she didn't laugh. She said, "It's my *lookout* room."

"It's your *lookout* room?" Judith said.

Mrs. Minnert seemed pleased by the question. She leaned close to Judith. "That's right," she said. "If you come into it, well, *look out!*" This time she did laugh, a deep guttural laugh, the joy overflowing her disjointed face, the fetid meaty smell blooming and wrapping Judith close. Mrs. Minnert drew an inch nearer. "And you tell your lover boy it's got to have a lock on the door, a real stout lock that only I have the key to."

"Water," Judith said, to get the woman away from her. "A glass of water."

At this moment a screen door slammed, and the woman stiffened and leaned away.

Willy and Joe L. Minnert were coming down the wooden steps into the yard, looking like two normal people. Willy was folding a sheet of paper, sliding it into his pocket, saying to Mr. Minnert that once he had a wood and hardware list together, he could get him a firm price, and the massive farmer was nodding blandly and sticking his hands into the deep pockets of his coveralls. "You'll be glad to know I'm a pay-as-you-go man," he said.

"I'll have some numbers in a day or two," Willy said.

Joe L. Minnert looked directly at Willy. "That'll be fine," he said. "And no need for a fancy contract. I prefer a man's handshake to a fancy contract any day of the week."

Mrs. Minnert turned to Judith and talked in a low, squeezed voice. "You tell your lover boy," she said. "You tell him about the stout lock and how it's me gets the key."

Judith, nodding, trying to hold herself together, walked toward Willy and Mr. Minnert, who were now talking about the orange Jeep parked out front. "I like all the flat stuff," Willy was saying. "Flat hood, flat fenders."

Joe L. Minnert nodded, but his stonelike expression didn't change.

"I drive it," Mrs. Minnert said, coming up. "It can go anywhere. They drove one right up the steps of the capitol building with the president in it."

Without looking at her, the big farmer said, "It wasn't the president."

"You drive it?" Willy said to Mrs. Minnert. There was surprise in his voice.

Mrs. Minnert nodded with satisfaction. "He bought it for me."

Mr. Minnert still didn't look at his wife, and Judith wondered if he ever did. "It's a M38," he said to Willy. "I got it off a widow woman. That's a Ramsey winch in the back, but the woman didn't even know it."

Mrs. Minnert sidled close to Judith and whispered that she could take her for a ride in the Jeep sometime if she wanted.

Judith felt herself nodding her head.

Willy had just asked a question about the Jeep's black-out lights when Judith said, "We've got to go, Willy. I don't feel well."

She guessed she didn't look that great either, because the moment Willy glanced at her, he hurried her to the truck, called to Mr. Minnert that he'd have prices by Tuesday, and put the truck in gear.

"You okay?" he said once they were moving, and she nodded but couldn't speak. She still felt nauseated. When she leaned her head out her window, he said, "Tell me if we need to stop."

Judith kept her mouth closed.

After a few minutes she began to feel more settled. She tried experimentally to breathe fully in, out, then in again. "I'm okay now," she said. "I'm feeling better."

"You sure?"

"Yeah, I am."

Willy's face relaxed to a smile. "Well, I'm happy to hear it," he said, "because pretty soon here I was going to try to kiss you, which is a little harder to look forward to after a girl's been chucking it up."

Judith managed a small laugh.

"So what hit you?" Willy said.

"That smell," she said. "Like old meat. I thought it was the house, but it was coming from inside her. That old woman. She should be billed with Vincent Price."

A chuckle. "Yeah, well, old Mrs. Minnert, she's a few fractions off in the upper story."

Judith asked what that was supposed to mean.

"She's half crazy. Minnert had her committed about five years ago, but then her sister got her out and brought her back to the Minnert place, and that's how it is. Nobody hardly sees her. I had no idea she could drive." He thought of something else. "A long time ago they were high school sweethearts. He's a year older. He took her to his prom one year and to hers the next. My mother remembers it because she wore the same yellow polka-dotted dress both times."

Judith said, "Are you really going to work for them?"

"Sure I will, if we can agree on a price. I can do it on weekends."

Judith was quiet. So was he. Then he said, "I don't want to work for Boss Krauss the rest of my life, you know."

He didn't say any more. He just kept driving slowly, looking serious, and then after a while his expression broke and he began to whistle. Judith watched him a little while, then leaned toward him and said in a voice barely louder than a whisper, "Where?"

"Where what?"

"Where were you going to try to kiss me?"

A smile stretched across Willy's face. "On the lips, unless you had other ideas."

"Very funny. I mean where were you going to take me to try to kiss me?"

"Oh, that." He peered forward. "Don't you worry about that. I know a shady grove."

"He knows a shady grove," Judith repeated in a mild voice.

Willy turned the truck east onto a smaller dirt road that before long led to a gate with a sign reading end of public use area. He got out and opened the gate and motioned Judith to pull the truck through, which she did uncertainly. After he secured the gate behind them, she started to slide back to the passenger's side, but he opened that door and got in. "You drive," he said, and she did, as slow or slower than Willy but with greater concentration because encroaching trees, shrubs, and rocks made the going tricky. She felt Willy's eyes on her, and when she flicked him a look he was grinning.

"What?"

"Nothing much," he said, moving close on the seat. "You just keep two hands on the wheel and we'll be fine."

He smoothed a hand under her chin and down her neck, several times, slowly, back and forth, sending what felt like little electrical charges to all the important areas, and then, gently—it reminded her of nibbling—his fingers began to work at the buttons of her shirt. She brushed him away several times, but without the kind of real seriousness she knew she should be using, and she soon felt the shirt front fall away and then he had one hand gentle on her breast and the other hand sliding up her bare back, and when the front wheel caught a rock and spun the steering wheel through her loosened hands, she said, "Oh!"

The truck rolled softly into an embankment. In her movie, she thought many years later, there would not be a sound.

For a moment everything was still, and then Willy burst out laughing, a full-throttle, up-from-the-stomach laugh, and Judith, who'd already formed in her mind a sharp sentence about how this would never have happened if he hadn't kept pestering her, felt as if a plug had been pulled, and laughter poured out.

When finally they grew quiet, Judith stared at the soft wall of dirt into which she'd driven the truck. "Now what?" she said, and as she turned to Willy, his easy smile tightened into something serious, and as he leaned forward, Judith seemed to feel his lips even before they touched hers.

—◊—

These, then, were the beginnings of what Judith later thought of as the Summer of Willy Blunt. All at once her life of latency and quiescence had turned metamorphic. She seemed to live differently within her own body, and if, standing in front of the mirror after a shower, she still couldn't quite come to regard herself as beautiful, she did find fewer shortcomings than before. She began to think less vaguely of the sexual act, began to think of how easy and, well, *fun* it might be with Willy, but then her heart would sink with the thought of carrying such a secret into the kitchen where her father sat reading the morning paper. For reasons she couldn't explain, she routinely tamped down her enthusiasm for Willy in the proximity of her father. She found it easiest to pass on conversations and anecdotes that played into her father's initial impression of him as the amusable roofer. How, for example, Willy believed in extraterrestrials ("Why not? If God or whatever can create a zillion creatures here, why not one or two creatures somewhere else?") and didn't believe in pennies ("If I run for president, that's my platform. No pennies. Also no Styrofoam peanuts. And no chihuahuas either. I have no use for small furless dogs.") When she heard Willy say such things, she saved them for her father, who always responded with an appreciative chuckle or nod. What these anecdotes were meant to tell him was that Willy, if not quite simple, was close to it, and someone close to simple could not sustain Judith's interest and was therefore harmless. And harmless, Judith intuited, was how her father needed to think of Willy.

"When are you and Willy going to fool around with a capital *F?*" Deena asked one morning on the telephone.

"Who's saying I'm going to?"

"Who's saying you're not?"

"I'm not saying anything."

"But you'll tell me when you do?"

Judith sat on the floor in the hallway with her back against the wall. It was late morning, drowsy and warm. By the time she'd gotten up, her father had departed in the Bonneville. The note on the kitchen table merely said, *Errands in Grand Lake. Back later on. Love, Dad.*

"You'll know after it happens, if it ever does." The truth was, she was having quite a bit of fun with Willy without actually having sex, and she wasn't sure why it couldn't just stay that way.

"How *long* after it happens?" Deena said. "Because I don't want to hear about it five days later or something. I want a fresh report."

From Judith's first date with Willy, Deena had probed for details about their goings-on. Her particular specialty was asking what things were like. What was it like to be out driving with him? What was it like to kiss him? What was it like to have his hand there?

"God," she said when Judith had told her how smoothly he'd undone the clasp on her bra, "the only way Paul Two's going to get to my boobs is if I undress myself."

Following the interview at Pizza Hut, Deena had chosen Paul Two, but she was already thinking of changing to Paul One instead. "Let me count the ways Paul Two appalls," she said after their first Saturday night at the Starlight Drive-in. "He kisses badly, he for some reason wants to lick my ears, and his hands are always cold. Last night they were also sticky. It was like being with a clumsy fifty-fifty bar."

Judith said, "You didn't count. You said you were going to count the ways he appalls."

"It was three. I figured you could count that high yourself, being such a math whiz and all."

Judith didn't respond to this. A fly buzzed in the hallway. Judith reached for one of her father's *New Yorker*s and rolled it into a swatter.

Deena said, "I knew a girl over in Harrison who thought she was in big love, but she was diehard RC and afraid of going to hell, so before she went anywhere with her boyfriend she smeared anchovy paste on the crotch of her undies because however carried away she got, she knew she wouldn't want him to think her private parts smelled like fish."

"How'd that work out for her?"

"Not that great. She got pregnant and the boyfriend dumped her. But I hear now he always orders his pizzas with anchovies."

Judith snorted and told Deena she was a really horrible person.

"Maybe," Deena said. "But it's a true story, except maybe for the pizza part."

The fly lighted on the lip of the front-door window, just above the mail slot. This past week her East Coast wait-list school had formally turned her down, which left only Stanford, where her chances were beyond remote (Mr. Flood had learned that they never went past the first name or two on their waiting list). She'd told Willy about the rejection, told him it was her last real chance for one of the schools she'd thought she actually wanted to attend, but that the surprise was she didn't much mind the rejection after all. Willy listened while she jabbered about Princeton and Stanford and Amory Blaine and Viennese waltzes and big-game bonfires and how, really, all those things had seemed to matter a lot more to her before she met him than they did now. She went on a little more and when finally she was done, he said, "So you'll go to the college here?" Either here or the U in Lincoln, she told him. "I missed the fee deadline at the U, but Mr. Flood wrote a letter and got me an extension," she said. "Till when?" he asked, and she told him: sometime in mid-July. Willy nodded neutrally.

The fly landed on the floor close by and then, as Judith slowly raised her rolled magazine overhead, buzzed away.

Deena said, "Guess Willy's working?"

Judith gave a murmur that meant yes. He was out at the Minnert place. The concrete foundation for the new room had already been poured, and the stud walls raised and joined by rafters, if she remembered it right. Saturdays Willy worked there all day, but he quit at two on Sundays and came directly to Judith's house, carrying with him those commingled smells of sweat and sawdust and beer she remembered from the meeting in the Gibson's parking lot. They would usually go first thing to a private lake south of town, where Willy stripped to his boxer shorts and without a word walked slowly out into the water until only his head wasn't submerged, at which point he gave his head a deliberate dip before rotating slowly and walking back out, a procedure he called the White Man's Ancestral Bathing Ritual or, once, when it applied, the White Man's Harvesting of the Leeches. On one of these occasions, Judith said, "You know, the white man doesn't have to be shy on my account," and without embarrassment he'd hung his boxer shorts from a tree limb before walking in. "What was it like to see him naked?" Deena had later asked, and Judith, remembering the stringy moss attached to his torso as he rose from the water, said, "Like watching the appearance of primordial man."

"So," Judith said now into the telephone, "are you doing something with Paul Two this afternoon?" and when Deena said, "Oh God, no," Judith asked if she wanted to come with her and Willy. "We're going to the lake," she said. "I'm making sandwiches."

"What kind of sandwiches?"

"Extremely droll. Are you in or not?"

"You sure Willy won't mind?"

"Sure I'm sure." Willy craved Judith's company, she knew this as a fact, just as she craved his, but beyond that he wasn't picky about things, and he wouldn't mind Deena tagging along. It was also true that Deena had a shift at the Dairy Queen that night, so there wouldn't be any awkwardness about parting company when the afternoon was over and darkness was coming on.

When Willy pulled up to the house that Sunday afternoon, Judith and Deena were ready for him with a basket of sandwiches.

Willy was in good spirits. He'd had a friend helping him that morning, and they'd gotten the room entirely sheeted.

"Whatever that means," Judith said. She sat in the middle of the truck cab, which meant straddling the gearshift. Both she and Deena were wearing T-shirts and shorts over their swimsuits.

"Means I'm that much closer to payday," Willy said. The arrangement, as Willy explained it, was that Minnert would pay for materials as they went, then pay the accumulated labor charges when the job was finished. "And at the rate we're going, we're going to make a nice little chunk of change," Willy said, shifting easily from third gear to fourth, the graze of his knuckles along her inner thigh setting off a tingling that radiated pell-mell in all directions.

He drove right past their customary turnoff, and Judith gave him a look.

"I was thinking about a different swimming hole today," Willy said. He shot both riders a mischievous look. "Long as you girls are game."

Judith mentioned that Deena needed to be at work by five.

"Or?" Willy asked.

"Or Mr. Ed has a cow," Deena said.

Willy laughed and fell to whistling his signature tune.

"I know that song," Deena said. Then, less brightly, "Except I can't remember what it's called."

Judith said that meant she could join the club.

After a few seconds, Willy said, "Guy at work's got a Blaupunkt radiocassette he'll give me for forty bucks, and I'm going to do it." He slid out a grin. "My whistling's something special, I'll grant you, but sometimes I need a little break."

Eventually they turned onto a dirt lane, drove past a farmhouse, then went through a gate marked no trespassing and across an expanse of pasture until Willy found a gate to a dirt road that curved through elms and ash and willow to a full stream. The narrow road that followed the stream pitched the truck with its rocky shifts and angles, and the more Judith was jostled into Willy, the more she wished Deena wasn't along for the ride.

A rocky precipice rose in front of them, with a thin spill of water dropping like a plumb line from its edge. Willy pulled the truck into a space where past parking had more or less subdued the brush. They followed a narrow footpath toward the splash of water and before long found themselves in a wide sandy area split by the shallow stream. Farther on, a cluster of boulders surrounded a pool of water fed by the overhead spill.

"There you go," Willy said.

"How'd you find this place?" Judith asked. The number of private picnic spots he could locate had become a strange source of fascination to her—it was as if he were some kind of oddball geographer whose specialties were shade, water, and seclusion.

Willy shrugged. "Me and my buddies used to fish here before Weck bought the place."

He'd brought his cooler. He cracked an Old Milwaukee, then took off his hat, shirt, and boots. Before removing his pants, he looked at Deena and said, "You may need to avert your eyes if you're squeamish." He flicked a grin toward Judith. "I know that's what Judith usually does."

The pool was steep-sided and Willy, wearing his boxer shorts, kept a hand on a willow branch while ducking into the water. Judith turned to Deena and said, "My hero can't swim."

Deena laughed but couldn't pull her eyes from the spectacle of Willy's trepidant bathing. "You can't swim?" she said. "How could you live this long and not learn to swim?"

Willy looked at her mildly. "Not hard if you set your mind to it."

Deena laughed again, and Judith said, "His fear of submersion is what you'd call morbid."

Willy gave her an amused look. "If you're such a swimmer, why aren't you in here?"

"Waiting to see if you come out spotted with leeches and blood."

"I'll go in," Deena said, and stood to unbutton her shirt. The emerald green bikini she was wearing beneath her clothes was either unusually skimpy or—and this was Judith's opinion—a full size too small. One thing was certain: Deena's breasts had been through a raucous growth spurt.

Willy said, "That suit could cause respiratory problems."

"For her or for you?" Judith said, laughing. Then, to Deena, "That new?"

"Bought it last year," Deena said. "Just never had the nerve to wear it."

Judith thought of asking where she'd gone to acquire the nerve to wear it now, but didn't. She said it looked great on her, because she had to admit, it really did. She turned to Willy and said, "Doesn't it look great?"

"It does, yeah. In fact, I think you'd have to call it eye-popping."

For some reason this didn't displease Judith. She merely laughed and cuffed her hand into the water to give Willy a mock-punitive splash while Deena slipped into the water.

After swimming, they sat on flat rocks eating their ham-and-cheese sandwiches and barbecued chips and drinking the beer that Willy pulled from his cooler of ice. Deena, who tended to burn, retreated into the shade, but not so far away that she couldn't see and be seen.

Willy said, "When the Pinneys owned this place, they had a sign up at the front gate that said, *Hunt and fish all you damn please, and when the bell rings, come to dinner.*" He sipped from his beer. "Old Ralph Pinney was my kind of people."

This reminded Judith of Isabel Archer's cousin Ralph, and for no particular reason she said, "The heroine in this book I'm reading? She says she doesn't want a lot of money, just enough to satisfy her imagination."

"Well, sure," Willy said. "But what you got to know is the nature of the imagination. I mean, what if you imagine a new wardrobe every fall and spring?" and Deena said, "As opposed, say, to imagining a new hunting rifle every deer season?" and Willy said, "Well, that's not quite fair, because whereas you can eat a venison steak, you can't eat silk or wool unless you're a moth, which none of us is"—a conversation Judith found more entertaining than could be easily explained.

She went to sip from her bottle of beer and was surprised to find it empty. Willy snapped the cap off another, handed it to her, and began looking for smooth stones to skip on the water. By this time, Judith felt there had been three Judiths on the picnic, each succeeding the other. The first was the Judith who craved Willy's touch. The second was the one who resented Deena's company. And the third one, the one she was now, was the Judith who imagined that the ground on which she lay was very slowly breathing in and breathing out.

When Deena raised her head into the dappled sunlight to take the band off her ponytail and shake out her red hair, Judith said, "Your hair in that light looks like something somebody should paint." She swung round toward Willy, who was turning a stone in his hand. "Doesn't she, Willy? Doesn't she look like she should be painted? I mean, if you were a painter, wouldn't you want to paint her just like that?"

Willy regarded Deena for a few seconds. "Problem is, I can't paint a lick. If I painted her, it wouldn't come out pretty at all. What you really need is somebody who'd do her justice."

"What I'm looking for, then," Deena said, "is a rugged rodeo boy with an easel in the back of his pickup."

"And a big ol' wad of money to support your imagination," Willy said. He skipped one last stone, then came over, stretched out, and laid his head in Judith's lap. She smoothed a finger over his forehead and he closed his eyes. Within a minute he would be asleep. Judith found it endearing. It suggested a satisfaction with his place in the world that she found appealing, and very possibly envied.

Shortly before five, when Willy pulled into the Dairy Queen parking lot, Deena was still in her suit beneath her shirt and shorts. "Big fun," she said as she slid out. "Thanks for the invite. I'd ask you in for a discount burger, but—" She nodded toward Mr. Edmundson's Cutlass parked a few slots down.

When Judith and Willy were on the road again, heading toward the town of Gordon, where Willy knew a grandmother who made and sold chiles rellenos every Sunday, Judith said, "Well, that was fun."

Willy seemed to have nodded, but maybe not.

"Didn't you think?"

"It *was* fun, yeah." Then, grinning: "As long as you're in view, it's a bountiful vista."

"Deena was kind of a bountiful vista, too."

Willy's murmur seemed ambiguous.

"There something wrong, Willy?"

He didn't speak.

"Something about Deena?" she said.

They were driving east on Highway 20. At a one-building rendering house just beyond Goodnight, Judith saw a man standing by a dump truck and then averted her eyes when she realized that what was sliding from the lifted bed was a stiffened horse carcass. This was something Willy would normally have commented on, but he didn't today. Neither did Judith. Finally he said, "One time I was playing cards with some fellas, and I don't remember the circumstances, but a man named Toby ended a story by saying, 'What is it about a kicked dog that makes you want to kick it?' This fella was a grand old storyteller and also a prince of a guy, but there was something about the remark so cruel and yet probably true that it took a second or two before everybody at the table could give it a big laugh, and then they did, myself included."

He fell silent.

"The point here being?" Judith said, and when he didn't answer, she said, "Are you saying Deena's like a kicked dog?"

"I'm saying she looks fine on the outside, but inside is somebody who's going to need a man a lot more than he's going to need her."

There was more. She could feel it. "So?"

"So with somebody like that you either feel sorry for them or you despise them, unless you happen to be so weak-kneed you need her more than she needs you, and then she'll despise *you* and go find somebody on the side to let you know it. All in all, it borders on misbegotten."

Misbegotten? Where did he get these words? She said, "Is that why you said if you painted her, she wouldn't turn out pretty?"

"I'd been thinking some of this stuff, it's true. But it's also true I can't paint a lick. In grammar school, I once painted a silage bin and my teacher said it was a very nice teapot but I ought to go ahead and put the spout on it, which I did."

He began softly to whistle. The highway slid through the tip of Rushville—grain elevators, municipal park with pool, Co-op service station—before again splitting farmland and pasture. Going 45, as Willy was, this took about a minute, which was how long it took for Judith to feel the full weight of the insult paid to her friend. Deena was smart, Deena was funny, and Deena was the one who saw the world more like Judith did than anyone else at Rufus Sage High. For that last reason alone, Judith didn't believe that Deena was facing the kind of future Willy had outlined, but even if she did believe it, she wouldn't want it foretold.

"Take me home," she said.

Willy stopped whistling and looked at her. She stared forward, but she could feel him trying to gauge the strength of her anger.

"Take me home," she said again.

At the first farm road, Willy turned the truck around. When they passed by the rendering plant, the dump truck was gone, and so was the man, and so was the dead horse. The next miles passed in swollen silence. Just west of Goodnight, Willy said, "I guess we're having an argument, but I'm not sure what it's about."

When Judith didn't comment, he said, "I guess it has to do with the stuff I said about Deena."

He pulled up in front of her house, and Judith got out without a word. She didn't look back before closing the front door behind her, though she knew he hadn't yet pulled away. When he did go—she was watching from behind the curtains—he went slowly. At the corner, the truck turned out of sight.

The house was quiet, emphatically empty.

God, she thought. Comparing Deena to a kicked dog. What kind of mind could ever find its way to a thought like that?

Downstairs in her bedroom, she found the unsigned letter confirming her intention to enroll at the university in Lincoln. She took out a blue pen and signed the letter with a flourish, then addressed an envelope and applied a stamp. The impulse flagged then—there was no hurry, after all; she had until mid-July to decide—so she slid the unsealed envelope back into the drawer of her nightstand. She went upstairs and looked out. It wasn't even dark yet, and she didn't feel like sitting at home. She telephoned the Dairy Queen and asked Deena to call her back as soon as Mr. Ed wasn't there.

"Not here now," Deena said. "Where're you?"

"Home. Willy's gone. We had an argument."

"You and . . . ? What about?"

"I'll be there in five minutes. I'll tell you then," she said, but by the time she'd walked five blocks past neighbors trimming hedges and moving lawn sprinklers and kids playing catch and croquet, and then crossed the highway to the Dairy Queen, her mood had softened. She heard herself tell Deena that the argument was over a song.

"Which one?" Deena said.

"'Horse with No Name.' He kept whistling it, and finally I asked him not to, and he said, 'You don't like that song?' and I said, 'Worse than that. I hate it, because it's silly and pretentious,' and he said, 'So only somebody silly and pretentious would like it?' and there we were." The truth was, they'd had a joking conversation along these very lines. The surprise was how easy it was to make it sound like an argument.

"'*Cause there ain't no one for to give you no pain,*'" Deena sang, and Judith joined her when she went into the la-la-la's. She was beginning to feel a little better again, her faith restored in Deena, and for that matter in herself.

Deena brought her a cheeseburger, extra onions, plenty of relish and ketchup, the way she liked it. "It's a pretty stupid song," Deena said, "but it's also a pretty stupid thing to have an argument about. Shouldn't you better call him?"

Judith took a bite of the cheeseburger—she hadn't realized how hungry she was—and said, "Maybe. I don't know."

It turned eight as Judith was walking home, something she knew because she heard the *Bonanza* theme song from the open windows of three houses straight. They'd ditched the old theme song—a mistake in Judith's opinion, not that she'd ever cared for the show. The men all wore the same clothes in every episode, for one thing, and for another thing, any woman dumb enough to fall for one of the Cartwrights was destined for a tragic death before the hour was up. But Willy. Willy had liked the show until Dan Blocker died. "They replaced Hoss," Willy had told her, "but Hoss wasn't replaceable."

When she arrived home, she went straight to the telephone and dialed the number for Willy's parents, something she'd never done before.

His mother answered.

"Mrs. Blunt? This is Judith Toomey."

"Oh, yes," Willy's mother said. She had a gentle voice, but there was a knowingness folded into it, too, a pleasant knowingness, as if she'd not only heard of Judith but heard nice things.

"I was wondering if Willy is there."

"Oh," said Mrs. Blunt. "Is something wrong?"

"Not really. I didn't feel well and he took me home. I just wanted to let him know I'm feeling a lot better now. I guess he's not there."

"No, not yet."

"Well, could you have him call me if he gets in before nine?" Her father wasn't home yet, but he might soon be, and he had a strict rule about calls after nine.

Mrs. Blunt said she would. "And if he's later, I'll leave him a note saying you're feeling better now and to call you in the morning."

By nine, Judith's anxiousness had escalated. She turned on a *Mission: Impossible* rerun but couldn't keep her mind on it. She went downstairs to bed, tried to read a little, then turned off the light. She dozed, waking every half-hour or so. Around midnight, headlights swept by the basement windows and the door to the

Bonneville slammed. There were footsteps overhead, and then the door to the basement eased open.

"Hi, Dad," she called.

"Hi, sweetheart," he said from the landing. "Good day?"

"Pretty good. I'm sleepy, though."

"Sweet dreams, then," he said, and quietly closed the door behind him.

She couldn't go back to sleep. She lay under the sheet thinking feverish thoughts about Willy and where he might be and what things he might be doing and who he might be doing them with and how stupid and unfair it was that she wasn't the one with him doing those things, whatever they were. Her thoughts pinballed from image to image until finally—1:25, according to her Westclox electric—she sat up and turned on the lamp with the vague idea that illumination might dispel her chaotic thoughts. It did. Almost at once she heard a tapping sound. She sat perfectly still, listening, and the sound came again. *Tap, tap, tap.* She slipped from the bed and tiptoed toward the window.

"Judith?"

"Willy?"

He was lying on his stomach with his head lowered slightly into the window well, smiling down from an odd angle, as if he were peering into a cave. She unlatched the window and pushed it open.

"I missed you," she whispered.

"'Course you did," he said in a low voice. "I missed you, too."

"I'm sorry about ..."

"Oh, that's all right. I shouldn't've said what I said about her future being ..."

"Misbegotten," Judith said.

He gave a little chuckle. "Yeah, that. In fact, the more I thought about it, the more I thought I was probably wrong.

267

Anyhow, anytime you want to bring Deena along, it'll be okay by me."

"And you won't feel sorry for her or despise her?"

Another quiet laugh. "I told you I've begun to think I was wrong about that, and anyhow, she's your pal, and I know how to play nice."

The window could be opened only a few inches; it was fastened by small chains at each side. "Wait there," she said.

She put on her summer robe, the green seersucker, and crept up the concrete stairs that led to the side yard. The only problem was the door. It creaked when she opened it, creaked when she set it closed behind her. Outside, she stood not breathing, listening for sounds from her father's bedroom, directly overhead, but there was nothing.

She slipped around the house and found Willy sitting at the edge of the window well with his back to her. The sky was clear and there was enough moonlight to cast shadows. *"Willy,"* she whispered, and when he turned, she retreated toward the garage and motioned him to follow.

"Shhh," she said when he drew close, "my father . . ." and she was pointing to his upper-floor bedroom when Willy tugged free the sash that held her robe closed and, pulling her to him, began to kiss her, and what started at the mouth spread through the body, an effusion of feeling coursing through her like warm liquid. When he pressed her against the smooth, cool contour of the Bonneville, she tilted her chin to give him her open neck to kiss, and what followed was one surprise feeding another, up to and including her fumbling urgently at his belt buckle, which was when his whole body suddenly froze.

"What?" she said. She wondered if she'd done something wrong. Broken something, possibly.

"Look."

The way he said it alarmed her.

She followed his gaze to the lighted upstairs windows of the house. In one of them the profile of her father could be seen, standing in his loose pajamas, staring out. Not at them, maybe, but still, staring out.

"How long has the light been on?"

"Just saw it," Willy whispered.

They stood together, perfectly still, looking at the lighted window, and then, before their eyes, the silhouetted figure of her father turned, vanished for a moment, then passed before the more easterly window.

"He's going to the bathroom," Judith said, pushing Willy away. Already she was pulling her robe tight around her. "I've got to go."

And she went. She didn't regret leaving. She had to leave. She had to open the creaky door to the basement the moment she heard the flush of the toilet upstairs, because after that she could slip down to her room and into bed without a sound, which she did. Then she lay in bed telling herself that she'd had a narrow miss, that they'd been lucky, that her father had merely been awakened in the night by the need to pee, and had, half awake, glanced out at the yard and evening sky before going to the bathroom. That was what had happened. She had been lucky. She was grateful. Yet when she closed her eyes, feelings of gratitude gave way to images of Willy, romantic yet specific images that slipped her back to the kindled feelings of a few minutes before.

Sweet dreams. That was what he'd whispered just before she slipped away.

The next morning, when she came up the basement steps for breakfast, her father was standing at the toaster whistling an unlikely tune.

"'Benny and the Jets'?" she said.

He turned, startled. "Oh," he said. "I heard that song yesterday

269

and I can't get it out of my head." He smiled at her. He appeared complacent, or at least more complacent than a man harboring suspicions about his daughter's carryings-on seemed likely to be. "So," he said, setting the toast, butter, and marmalade on the table. "Sleep well?"

3

The following Sunday, Judith went to Willy's parents' house for dinner. The Blunt place was just north of town, with a sign at the highway that said F.L. BLUNT and below that, NO SALESMEN ALLOWED THIS MEANS YOU.

Technically Willy lived with his parents, but more and more in the past year or so the house had become merely the place he returned to late at night and departed from early in the morning. He rarely ate meals there, which made this afternoon something of an occasion, and Judith was feeling a little pressure. Willy had bought the used Blaupunkt from the man at work, and it was tuned now to KOMA in Oklahoma City. "All the Way from Memphis" was playing, a song Judith liked, but she hardly heard it.

"Know what I'm hoping for?" Willy said out of the blue.

"Me making a good impression?"

"Pot roast." He glanced at her. "My mother's pot roast is outstanding."

As the truck rattled across a cattle guard, the kind of house you often saw on farms came into view, white, two-storied, mansard-roofed, with a wire fence around it. A barn, corn cribs, and silage bins formed a broad arc on its north side. What was notable was the absence of clutter and rusted implements.

"My mother," Willy said when Judith mentioned the tidiness. "She likes it neat. Frank couldn't give a shit."

"Frank?"

"The old man."

The house was neat, too, surprisingly free of the common knickknacks, with an enormous braided rug covering more than half of the living room's clean wooden floor. Nobody seemed to be on the premises, though the smells that poured from the kitchen—it *was* pot roast, Judith thought, and possibly a pie or some other kind of baked goods—made it clear that somebody wasn't far off. While Willy went upstairs for something, Judith examined a row of metal-framed family photographs that lined the mantel over the fireplace. One particularly drew her attention; she took a step forward and leaned close to it. It was of Willy, fourteen or so, not quite formed, grinning happily and hoisting to shoulder height a string of good-sized brown and rainbow trout, a lean tall boy with the kind of apple-red cheeks, big ears, blue eyes, and open wholesomeness that Judith associated with Norman Rockwell; a boy who, she would think many years later, again regarding this very photograph, seemed as far from the darker fates as a boy could possibly be.

"That was taken one summer up on the Madison River," someone said from across the room. A woman's voice.

Judith, turning, blushing, wondering how silly and smitten she must have looked studying the old picture of Willy and wondering, too, how Willy's mother—because this had to be Willy's mother, didn't it?—could've stolen in without her knowing it, said, "He just looks so *young*."

The woman smiled. The gentle smile was Willy's smile, and her gray-blue eyes were his eyes. Her hair, brown but graying, was just-brushed. "Ten years ago," she said, "but it seems like the day before yesterday." She was still smiling. "You must be Judith."

"And I guess you're Mrs. Blunt."

"Just Ella, if you don't mind."

Judith said she didn't mind at all. Already she had it in mind that Willy's eyes would age and soften as handsomely as his mother's had.

The thumping of boots on the stairs preceded Willy's appearance through a near doorway, smiling, disheveled, brimming with goodwill. It seemed to Judith that he was as comfortable in this house as he was in his own skin, and it made her wonder why he'd want to leave it.

"So where's the old man?" he said.

"In the corn, I imagine. But he'll be in. He's got both the Whiting boys helping him today."

Willy grinned. "Always told him it would take two to replace me," he said, then went outside to wash up.

Before a silence could develop, Judith remarked on the room-sized rag rug.

"It was easy braiding," Willy's mother said. "I'd just lay it over my lap and do a little every night while we were watching TV." When she wasn't smiling she seemed on the verge of it—something else she might have given Willy. "Cotton like this is easy. I knew a woman, though, who did a rug bigger than this out of old denim." Mrs. Blunt did smile now. "That rug was something. If you hadn't known the woman, you'd have thought it impossible, but she was not a quitter. Her name was Frances Moore."

Not a name Judith knew. Through the window, she could see Willy, who'd stripped to the waist and was giving himself a good going-over with soap and water. She had never seen a pornographic movie, but she had the feeling that if they made one for girls, this is how it might begin. Willy's mother glanced to see what she was looking at, and Judith felt her skin again begin to flush.

"He was always a clean boy," she said, and Judith, afraid that Willy's mother was on to her, tried to think what to say next, but she didn't have to speak because Mrs. Blunt said, "Willy paid you quite a compliment."

"He did?"

Mrs. Blunt nodded and looked at her directly. "He said you're smarter and prettier than all his other girlfriends put together."

This time the blushing was more pleasurable. "I don't know about any of that," she said.

Mrs. Blunt held her gaze on Judith for another second, then broke off. "Want to help me get the fixings into serving bowls?"

Outside, Willy was joined by two boys who looked roughly her own age and who came at him with a swatting of hats that quickly triggered the kind of male horseplay that Judith thought she would never in ten lifetimes understand. Following the boys by a few seconds was an older man, tall and thin and stiff-jointed, and when he said something—Judith couldn't hear what—the horseplay ceased. The man glanced then toward the window, and Judith quickly looked away.

"That Willy's dad?" she said, and Willy's mother, glancing out, said, "Oh, yeah, that's Frank."

The pot roast was tender enough to part with a fork, and it came with peas, mashed potatoes and gravy, a green-bean-and-bacon casserole, and a carrot-and-raisin salad. Willy and Judith sat on one side of the table, the two Whiting boys on the other, and Willy's parents sat at either end. Willy's mother kept looking for plates in need of filling, but his father hardly spoke—he'd managed only a nod when he and Judith were introduced—and he was soon lost in the steady consumption of the meal in front of him. The Whiting brothers didn't seem used to female company, and more than once Judith caught one or both of them staring at her.

"Okay, boys," Willy said finally, "she's nothing more than a pretty girl. If you speak to her, I'm sure she'll speak right back." Which of course only subdued them further, and a few minutes later Willy with exaggerated geniality said, "Well, if you're going to stare at her like a couple of retardates, for God's sake stop your drooling," at which point his father abruptly laid his napkin beside his plate and rose from his chair.

"Thank you, Ella," he murmured from his end of the table to hers, then passed both Judith and Willy a solemn look before turning to go. The Whiting brothers bolted the last of their food and followed, with Willy's mother hurrying out shortly thereafter with three pieces of mincemeat pie snugged onto a foil-covered paper plate, and as quickly as that, Willy and Judith were alone at the table.

"What just happened?" Judith said.

"Frank got annoyed. It doesn't take much."

For a few seconds, they simply sat. Then Judith said, "I don't think he likes me."

"Got nothing at all to do with you. It's just that the old man wants me to farm." Willy gave a slow shake of his head. "I think he thinks his last best hope is that a farmgirl will catch my eye and lure me back to the land."

To Judith, this sounded an awful lot like another way of saying that not only didn't his father like her, but he never would, which seemed deeply unfair, because she knew for a fact he hadn't gotten so much as a glimpse into her. Whereas she was pretty sure Willy's mother in just a few seconds had seen quite a lot of her, and still seemed open to approval.

Then, to her surprise, she heard herself say that she didn't think living on a farm would be so horrible.

Willy gave her a long stare that might or might not have been deadpan. "Well, that goes down in the book as the first truly misguided thing I've ever heard you say." Then, breaking a smile: "Though I don't suppose it'll be the last."

This brought Judith back. "Well," she said, "if I *do* settle on a farm, I'll put up a sign that says NO CARPENTERS ALLOWED THIS MEANS YOU. Then what would you do?"

Willy scratched his neck. "Well, I could shoot myself, of course," he said. "Or I could go find me a girl who appreciates a good carpenter. Or I might just tear the sign down and come on in." He gave her a look. "Which one do you think I ought to do?"

While he grinned at her, the mud porch's screen door slammed, and Willy's mother entered the room.

"Okay, now—you kids want dessert?" she said.

Her voice was gently businesslike, as if nothing unusual had occurred with her husband, and perhaps it hadn't.

Judith helped with the dishes, then walked into the yard with Mrs. Blunt while Willy went out to the barn to do something his father had asked him to do—fix a crack on a cultivator, she thought he said. Before departing, Willy turned his seed cap backward and put on a strange pair of dark glasses with leather blinders on each side. "How do I look?"

"Like a psychopath. What are those things?"

"Welding goggles. And I'm glad you like them."

After he went off, Judith followed his mother beyond the yard gate, where they were immediately joined by two lambs, who trailed right at Mrs. Blunt's heels as she escorted Judith out to see the sheep. "These're Somersets," the older woman said. "I'm the one who got us into sheep, but the price of wool is just pitiful"— she pronounced it *pity-full*—"so now we're going with the meat breeds."

"Is that a llama?" Judith said, pointing toward a tall-necked animal some distance away.

Willy's mother nodded. "His name's Eldon. He's supposed to

keep the coyotes off, and he does when he feels like it. We team him with a Kangal Dog named Turk. Turk's work ethic isn't so hot either. Some people use donkeys, but Frank won't have a donkey. He thinks mules are smart, but he can't stand a donkey."

There was a lull, and Judith leaned down to pet one of the lambs at the woman's feet.

"Ex-bum," Willy's mother said, regarding the lamb. "Two months ago, she couldn't stand up. The other bums were walking all over her, so I put her in her own private stall. We give the bums milk replacement, that's standard procedure, but after a week went by and this bum didn't get up, Frank said, 'That's it, I'm going to have to put her down.' But he got busy with something else and didn't do it that day, and the next day at dinner he says, 'Remember that little bum I was going to put down? Well, this morning I go into her stall and there she is, standing up tall as you please.'" Willy's mother picked up the lamb and let it nestle its pink nose in her arms. "He was as glad as I was. Frank can be a big softie—he just doesn't give you many chances to see it."

When Judith repeated this conversation as she and Willy were driving away a half-hour later, he let out a little snort. "I guess a porcupine's soft at the center, too, but finding it out firsthand can be more trouble than it's worth. I know Frank Blunt and I can tell you that most of the time he's one prickly individual. And I can also tell you that at least some of his happiness over that lamb came from knowing it wasn't going to die before getting to market. That lamb won't live to be eight months old."

They fell quiet, except for the radio—Rod Stewart, "Maggie May," playing low. They were driving into town, toward the high school basketball courts. Willy had told his mother they were going to shoot some baskets, which was true enough, but afterward they were planning to head for one of Willy's remote

locations to picnic. Mrs. Blunt had sent along roast beef sandwiches, mincemeat pie, and a thermos of lemonade, after which
they might play casino or just go right straight to kissing. Plenty,
in short, to look forward to. Still, Judith came back to the thought
of that pink-nosed lamb snugged in Mrs. Blunt's arms.

"So how come you don't want to live there?"

"On the farm, you mean?"

She nodded.

Willy stared down the dirt road. "I guess I always had a hunch
I didn't want to farm, but I didn't know it for sure until one
summer when first it wouldn't rain at all and then one day we got
hailed, and I mean *hailed*, the royal treatment. Farmers half a mile
east got nothing, no damage at all, but our crop was totally wiped
out. So the old man took me fishing. It was my mother's idea, and
I still wonder how she got him to do it, but she did. I was eleven
or twelve and we loaded everything into our old green DeSoto
and drove off to the Madison and fished for a week. You know, by
the end of the first day there, my father seemed happier than I'd
ever seen him. I mean ever. And me, too. At night at this fish
camp there was a big communal campfire, and my father, who
was always a teetotaler, would have one or two beers and talk it
up with some of the other men. One night one of them asked
him what he did back home and he said, 'Well, I'm a farmer, but
our only crop this year was hailstones,' and there was just a second
when nobody knew what to do, but then he broke into the
biggest laugh I ever heard come out of him—it was like passing
a kidney stone or something—and then everybody else was laughing, too." Willy paused. "The camp had a smoker to smoke the
fish and we had a Dutch oven to bake our biscuits, and I don't
know, it was like I saw for the first time that life didn't have to be
so hard. Then we came back to the farm and his face went
wooden again, and that's the face you see now just about every

minute of the week." Willy gave a small laugh. "I remember I started praying for another hail. Didn't happen, I'm happy to say, but what did happen was my deciding I wasn't going to do it the way my father did."

By this time, they'd wheeled off Main toward the high school. "Okay," he said, "I told you a story. Now you have to tell me one."

Judith felt the sudden panic she sometimes felt when people started telling jokes and everyone was expected to take a turn. "I will," she said. "Soon as I think of the right one."

They parked and headed toward the courts. As he walked, Willy spun the basketball on the tip of his crooked index finger. "It should have a happy ending," he said, "like mine did," and he gave the side of the ball a series of quick tangential taps to keep it twirling.

4

One morning Judith climbed the stairs to her father's bathroom in search of a new tube of toothpaste and found herself staring at something threadlike, almost white, that was stuck to the green tile surrounding the bathtub. She peeled it away, ran her tweezed fingers to its ends, and pulled it straight. It was a shoulder-length strand of white-blond hair. It was not her father's hair, or the hair of Mrs. Hill, who cleaned every other week, or the hair of anyone else she knew, but a few hours later, in the library, as she was red-stamping *Discard* onto the squeezed-firm pages of a cartful of books, her wandering thoughts fell on the waitress at the faculty club: Zondra with a *Z*. Of course, she thought, it had to be her—who else could it be? And when Judith followed this revelation through a sequence of images that ended with her craggy-faced father leaning forward to kiss the pale girl with the smooth translucent skin, she had to give her head a quick shake to dispel the picture. But her more settled reaction, like her reaction to her rejection by Princeton, like her reaction to the boy and girl coupling on Initial Hill, was not what she expected.

That afternoon, when her father was in the shower and his wallet lay on the dresser, Judith stole in and removed from it the small card where, in the tiniest handwriting, he recorded all the telephone numbers important to him. At the very edge of the card she found it: *Z 2323344*. Judith didn't recognize the exchange, but after her father departed, she dialed the operator and was told that the 232 exchange was Grand Lake, and would she like to be connected? *No, thank you,* Judith said, and set the phone down. Grand Lake was a railroad town about sixty miles south of Rufus Sage. Judith thought of her father, jaunty and soapy clean, gliding south on Highway 385, listening to *The Magic Flute* or *La Bohème*—a thought that gently seemed to release her, as if from a clenched hand slowly opened. What she was feeling was relief. There was no other word for it. If her father was happy, well, then, she could be happy. Though what exactly she meant here by happiness she wasn't quite willing to admit.

A few days later, Judith and Willy were picnicking in a clearing in the timberland north of Goodnight. They'd finished their sandwiches and begun drinking lemonade mixed with cherry vodka. It was private here, and the late sun was mild. They'd spread a blanket and opened the nearest door of Willy's truck so they could hear the radio. Judith had rolled her pant legs up and tied her shirt in rabbit ears so her stomach was exposed. Willy was unwrapping tinfoil from a small packet of elk jerky just arrived from a friend in Wyoming.

"Okay, I've got one," Judith said.

"One what?" he said.

"A story. Remember you said I had to tell you one."

Willy took off his shirt and rolled it into a pillow, then bit off a piece of jerky. "That's right," he said. "One with a happy ending."

She told him the story of the bird's-eye maple, how her great-grandfather Harry Toomey had remembered the details of the furniture, "*without* writing it down on his dashboard," and had not only purchased it but put the bedroom set in place without his wife knowing about it.

When she was finished, Willy stared up at the blue-white sky and said, "I like that story."

"Me, too," Judith said. The theme of exceeded expectations fit her mood.

Willy stood up and went to the truck, where he'd left the tin-foiled package of jerky lying on a fender. He tore off another piece and said, "And you've got that furniture in your room now?"

"Mmm."

Even while chewing he had a funny look on his face. "Why?" she said. "What are you thinking?"

What he said he'd been thinking was how, on account of the unusual privacy here, she might want to sun in her underwear. Judith didn't believe this was what he'd actually been thinking, but Willy stuck to his story and pressed his case for shedding her clothes.

"Why not?" he said. "That's the motto where I come from."

Judith said where he came from sounded like a dubious place.

He grinned. "I mean, who'd see you but me and the magpies and maybe a stray heifer?"

The Judith of a year before, or even of a month before, would've clamped tight against this wobbly line of reasoning, but this Judith didn't. This Judith felt an unfurling disposition to indulge him.

"Only humans who'd come here are hunters," Willy said, "and this is definitely not hunting season."

"We're humans who aren't hunters and we're here," Judith said, but she was already undoing the top button on her shirt.

Willy fell quiet.

"American Pie" came on the radio.

Judith was wearing white underwear from J. C. Penney, thin and minimal but nothing fancy. Still, closing her eyes and stretching out in them here in this remote clearing made her whole body feel lazy; the mild sun seemed to flow through her limbs. Even with closed eyes, she knew he was looking at her, could feel the slow travel of his eyes, could feel the places they rested. The song went pleasantly on, and Judith thought, *This must be the eight-minute version.* She felt a subtle sensation of buoyancy, as if she lay on a carpet magically suspended the barest inch above the earth's surface.

It wasn't until that evening that she could identify this as the moment that a decision was made, but still, this was the moment. She slowly blinked open her eyes and turned on her side, which she knew would have a plumpening effect on her breasts. While he looked at her, she took another slow sip of lemonade.

Willy said, *"Muy peligrosa."*

Her sense of waiting for what came next was so keen she couldn't speak. She wanted to say, *How come I'm down here and you're up there?* but after the slightest parting of the lips she got no further. He'd eased next to her and his lips touched her neck and she felt every part of her body rise to meet him. He was wearing clean, creased Levi's, and their kisses turned fierce—their open teeth pressed together and she was overtaken by the same bodily greed she'd felt in the garage when backed against the Bonneville, the same bodily greed that, no matter how many subsequent times with Willy she might feel it, would always surprise her. But what surprised her now was that when she began to roll off her briefs, everything else stopped.

She blinked open her eyes. "What're you doing?"

He said, "I didn't come prepared for this."

It took a moment for this to sink in. "It's all right, it doesn't matter," she said, and leaned forward, closing her eyes so he might kiss her again, and he did kiss her, but lightly, not as before.

She opened her eyes, a first strange hint of resentment rising within her. "What?"

He was just looking at her with his gray-blue eyes. Don McLean had stopped singing. An announcer was reminding them that prices for twelve different models of Case farm tractors would never be lower. Willy was running his hand slowly between her breasts down to a point just short of where she wanted him to go, and where she was pretty sure he wanted to go, too. She stared down below his belt and said, "Your little *compadre* doesn't seem to want to wait."

Willy said, "Well, if I let him make all the big decisions, my life would be a turmoil."

Judith turned away from him in high annoyance, which only seemed to amuse him. In a mild voice he said, "And just so you know, he doesn't really like to be referred to as little."

Judith didn't really care what his little *compadre* did or didn't like. "Will you hand me my underwear, please?" she said in her coldest voice.

He ran a finger smoothly along her spine. "You know I wasn't saying we had to stop entirely."

And from as little as this—a few words spoken in a genial tone, a soft touch on her bare skin—she was drawn back.

So they didn't stop completely. They both waited and didn't wait. They had fun, as Willy put it, making do. Fooling around with a lowercase *f*, Judith called it when relating the episode to Deena.

Of the remainder of the afternoon, Judith would remember only a few details. A game of naked casino, the gradual darkening and massing of clouds, dim thunder, the thick gray sky revealed by sheet lightning, the first fat drops of rain. "Quinn the Eskimo" playing on the Blaupunkt on the way home and Willy saying casually, "You know, when you told me the story of the bird's-eye maple, I was thinking maybe that would be the right place for"—here he'd given a waggish grin—"doing the actual deal."

So that was what he'd been thinking. Willy leaned forward on the steering wheel. The rain sheeted off the windshield and the lightning spread in a wide wondrous arc before them. He'd been right not to do it that afternoon, Judith could see that. The one thing they couldn't be forgiven—*he* particularly couldn't be forgiven, he being the older and more responsible party—would be her winding up pregnant, and besides, once she'd settled down enough to think about it, she didn't mind Willy's new idea. She kind of liked it, in fact. They would become a secret footnote in the family furniture history.

5

The following week, Judith was working one afternoon in the 700s aisle of the library, reshelving travel, geography, and history books. It was a Thursday; the building was all but deserted. A few minutes before, beyond view of her supervisor, Mrs. Humphrey, she'd browsed *Mexico on $5 a Day* and fantasized of driving south to El Paso with Willy, so when the actual Willy appeared suddenly before her, it gave her a start. He was stifling a grin.

"Don't smile," he said.

"Why not?"

"Well, there's someplace I need to take you right now, but if you smile it might queer the deal."

Right now? Judith's eyes drifted at once toward the circulation desk, where Mrs. Humphrey sat regarding them.

"I already cleared it with her," Willy said.

"With Mrs. Humphrey? What did you tell her?"

"That somebody ran over your dog but didn't quite kill it."

"I don't have a dog."

"His name is Chance. And at this very moment you're real worried he's not going to make it."

Judith stared blankly at him for another moment or two, then made a gasping sound and let her body collapse slightly. She leaned against Willy for a comforting hug. Mrs. Humphrey, she noticed, had stepped from behind the counter and was coming their way—to offer solace was Judith's guess—and she threw some dry snuffling into the performance, but Mrs. Humphrey, moving briskly by, said, "Let's not overdo it."

As they hurried down the long run of stairs to the entrance, Judith felt obliged to keep an expression of intent worry, but once they were outside and around the corner, she burst into laughter. "Not only are you a big barefaced liar, but Humphrey *knows* you're a big barefaced liar."

Willy was radiant with pleasure. "The reason that lady chose to believe me is because she knows how pitiful little you get done in an afternoon anyway."

Judith said a fat lot he knew.

"Ha. I watched you a full minute and you didn't do a thing but stand there reading in a book."

Judith felt giddy with the suddenness of being here with Willy, walking beside him, where she wanted to be, instead of in the library, where life stood still. She tried to describe the feeling to Willy, and this was when, nodding, he said, "Well, there's no joy like the truant's joy." It was all part of his larger notion that life didn't have to be as worn-down and reined in as people might have you believe; that in general, we all deserve a little more than we ordinarily think.

She said, "So where's the somewhere you just have to take me?"

Willy grinned. "Your dad's gone. Won't be back for hours."

Judith stared at him. "How exactly do you know that?"

Willy said he had his sources.

One Judith wondered if his sources were all that reliable. Another Judith, the Judith who called the shots, was alive with excitement. "Drop me off in front of the house," she said, "then park a couple blocks away and come through the gate off the alley. I'll leave the side door to the basement open."

And so he had dropped her off and she had hurried downstairs and brushed her teeth and waited. At first she'd waited on top of the Young Man's Fancy quilt wearing all her clothes, then she'd stood and taken most of them off and laid back down, and then she'd taken them all off and slipped under the quilt. She closed her eyes. She placed her hand to her heart to feel what a heart that seemed about to explode felt like. Eventually she heard the turn of the door handle, the prolonged creak of the door, the boots on the concrete steps. She didn't open her eyes. She waited to smell the mix of sweat and sawdust and alcohol, certainly alcohol, because what else could have taken him so long to park and walk a mere two blocks? When she couldn't identify the smell on his breath, she asked him.

"Whiskey," he said, pulling a flask from his pocket. "Want a snort?"

Prior to this afternoon, and many times afterward, Judith had read or heard of the difficulties of inaugural sex, all of which remained a minor mystery to her. It wasn't easy, she supposed, but it wasn't terribly difficult, either. It felt more like a series of pleasant variations rather than a single event. Willy was unhurried, which helped, and he slipped a dark towel under her in case there might be blood, which helped, and he used a prophylactic that was nothing if not slippery, which helped, and once they'd gotten down to the actual matter of admission, which did in fact feel intrusive, he suggested she *push,* an idea she found both silly and alarming but which, when she tried it, helped quite a bit. Thereafter it was . . . well, *fun.*

When they were done, Willy said, "Sound to the deaf, sight for the blind," and Judith laughed from a combination of happiness and relief not only that it had gone as well as it had, but also that she wasn't now overcome with remorse. Just the opposite, in fact. She said, "I hope there's more where that came from."

He said, "Oh, I imagine there's more all right."

They lay with the quilt at their feet and just two shafts of late light from the basement windows intruding into the room's dimness. She had one hand tucked under his leg, the other over her head, where her fingers ran idly along the curves of the maple headboard. Willy turned on his side, propped his head with his hand, and regarded her for some little while before he said in a quiet voice, "Well, there's no going back now."

He lay back then into one of the slanting shafts of light, so that when he began softly to whistle the melody he'd learned from his mother, dust motes stirred and glimmered before him and presented a moment that, when she thought of it many years later, might seem enchanted.

—⁓—

Willy picked up Judith every afternoon after work, and while their outings didn't adhere to a regular course—they might put in stops at the Dairy Queen or the bowling alley or the stock car races at the fairgrounds—their evenings almost always ended someplace out-of-doors where they could have some privacy. And then there were the Thursday afternoons, which began to be spent in Judith's room. Willy managed the time off by starting work at sunup and forgoing a break for eating so he could log his eight hours by 1:30, and Mrs. Humphrey reworked Judith's schedule to free her Thursday afternoons (for which favor Judith took the librarian regular gifts of challah and homegrown tomatoes). Judith always asked Willy if he knew for certain that her father was gone for the day, and Willy always said he was, though how he knew this he wouldn't tell, and where her father went he claimed not to know. But the pattern became reliable. He was gone in the afternoon and didn't come home until after dark. Off to some assignation with Zondra with a *Z*, Judith presumed, not that she

289

needed the details. Her father was gone. That was all that mattered.

"Thursday afternoon's turned into Saturday night," Willy said one Thursday, downstairs, lying on the cool bare sheets after sex. "It's Thursdays I count the days to."

"Me, too," Judith said, though when she thought about it, fooling around here, in her room, in the old bed with the Young Man's Fancy quilt folded down, really felt more like a Sunday afternoon in the kind of life where the domestic side of things didn't dull the romantic element. This was just the sort of thing that Willy could make you believe in—that you could be wicked and still be . . . well, *good*.

The days slid by. Judith and Willy fell into the lazy rhythm of their secret life, carried along by the presumption that all the foreseeable tomorrows would be more or less like the day before them. Years later, most of these days blended into a benign general remembrance, but there were other important days Judith could recall with distinctness, and there was another category, too—brief, disconnected interludes that settled themselves into her memory.

There was the day Judith and Willy and Deena were out driving and stopped at the old white country church that stood at the corner of two graded dirt roads, Eleson and Bethel. Deena and Judith cupped their hands around their faces and peeked through the windows at the dark pews and wood-burning stove. Willy wandered out beyond the privies to the fenced and neatly tended cemetery, and while he walked from headstone to headstone, Deena stepped back from the window and announced, "This is where I'm going to be married." Judith, going for a joke, said, "Would this be to Paul One, Two, or Three?" (Deena was fresh off switching to Paul One when bad-kissing, button-fumbling Paul Two had gone away for a week to attend something called Fossil

Camp.) Deena laughed and said at the rate she was going, it might have to be Paul Nine or Ten, and Willy, ambling up, said, "Paul Nine or Ten what?" but Deena flushed slightly and fell silent, a surprise to Judith, who said, "This is where Deena wants to get married someday," and Willy, after nodding approvingly, turned to Judith and said, "And how about you, Judy? You want to marry some unlucky jasper here?" which drew a strange collaborative laughter that allowed them all to glide over this subject and on to other things.

And there was the sticky, overcast afternoon when she and Willy challenged a couple of high school boys to a game of half-court basketball, and when Willy kept drawing the boys' attention and then feeding her the ball for easy shots, the boys were forced to guard her and while doing so kept putting their hands on her just as they might if she were a boy, but she wasn't a boy, and she knew it and they knew it, and afterward everybody's face was glowing when they shook hands, even the two boys who had lost to a team with a girl on it, and then when she and Willy got to the place where they were picnicking, the smell of their sweat and the slickness of their skin and who knew what else all added to the frankness of her needs.

There was also the day at the creek on the Weck place when Judith, treading water, tried to lure Willy into the pond for a swimming lesson, which he refused by saying, "What if I drown?" and she said, "You're not going to drown, you big landlubber," and they went back and forth like that until she said, "What if I were drowning and you needed to save me?" and he said simply, "Well, then I'd jump in."

—⁂—

One weekday morning when Judith wasn't working, Willy stopped by to ask her if she wanted to ride with him up to Hot

Springs, South Dakota, where Boss Krauss was sending him to pick up a set of blueprints and to buy a nail gun while he was at it. Deena and Paul One happened to be there, too, when Willy dropped by, and he at once included them in his invitation.

"It'll be good," Willy said. "You can bring your suits and go to the plunge while I run my errand." He turned a grin to Paul Wells. "I guess you've seen Deena in her green swimming suit?"

The boy looked at his shoes and murmured that no, he never had.

Judith guessed Paul Wells would probably one day be handsome, but that day was a ways off. The sleeves of his too-short T-shirt rode high on his arms, and Judith remembered his acned back from track season. These considerations, along with the roo do, were more than his angular cheekbones and doe-brown eyes could overcome.

"Well, you're in for a treat, then, because that suit's what you'd call token," Willy said, which made Deena blush a little and Paul Wells more.

Judith looked at Willy and said, "Twenty-four going on twelve."

They dispersed for suits and gear—Willy said he needed to pick up a few things—then reconvened at Judith's. On the way up to Hot Springs, they all rode in the cab, Willy at the wheel, Judith in the middle between Willy and Paul One, with Deena turned sideways on Paul's lap with her back against the door and her legs stretched over Judith's lap and into Willy's, a configuration producing just enough discomfort and physical intimacy to enliven the camaraderie. Paul One, at the bottom of it all, got a good laugh when he asked at what point he'd be allowed to breathe, and so did Deena when she said, "When we're good and ready."

They had cheeseburgers at the Hardee's on 385, then Willy bought admission to the Evans Plunge for the others while he went off to pick up the blueprints and locate the nail gun he'd been sent to buy—not much of a task, since he found the exact Bostitch he was looking for on closeout at the first stop he made. He then stopped at a drugstore to pick up a present for Judith before finding a friendly little place on River Street where he could pass a couple of hours before picking up the swimmers at the appointed time. By then, everyone was in good spirits—the swimmers from their long spiraling slides into the warm spring-fed pool, Willy from his slow, uninterrupted consumption of draft beer.

"I see nobody drowned his- or herself," he said by way of greeting.

An easy benignity was in operation here. Judith had taken hold of Willy's hand, and Deena even had an arm slung casually over Paul Wells's shoulder.

"And nobody popped out of her bathing costume?" Willy said, which prompted complicit laughter. It turned out that when Paul One had executed a particularly reckless headfirst slide, it had sent his suit to his ankles.

"Well, that sounds bawdy," Willy said, and Judith laughed and leaned into him like a cat might, she was so happy.

Deena said, "We caught sight of his thingie."

Willy said, "Trolling, that's called in some circles, though not mine," and Deena said that she personally would need a more tantalizing lure than that, and then laughed in a boisterous enough way that Paul had to try to laugh, too, but couldn't, not quite, and Willy said, "Well, there's a fish for every lure and a lure for every fish."

Judith appreciated the kindness of the remark—she saw he was trying to give poor Paul a hand up—but that didn't keep her from saying, "But there isn't a fish for every lure, though, is there?"

Willy stared at her for a long second, then said, "Anybody hungry but me?"

He'd gotten a recommendation for an Italian restaurant, and on the short ride over, the talk dwelled on the smell coming off the blueprints Willy had set into the gun rack at the back of the cab. "Ammonia," he explained. "Top-notch for clearing the sinuses." At the restaurant, they all ordered spaghetti but Judith, who tried the gnocchi with sage, then had to pretend she was glad she did. Willy in his broad mood seemed intent on keeping things lively. Before their food arrived, he showed off his skill in walking a quarter over his knuckles, then asked for Deena's class ring, pretended to swallow it, showed his open palms, and pulled the ring out of the pocket that lay close to Judith's left breast. "That your ring or Deena's?" he said and prodded her into demonstrating that it was too small for her index finger (and middle finger, too, although it did fit her ring finger). And when, over their meal, talk turned to the plunge—the number of people swimming, the new slides installed at the deep end, and the number of weird bathing suits on display—Willy twirled his spaghetti and told them the Sioux and Cheyenne had once fought over the hot springs, because both tribes knew that if soaking in the warm waters couldn't cure your winter ailments, it could at least make you forget them for a while.

Paul One said, "I heard that a dumb-as-dirt Indian sold the springs to a white man for a horse worth less than thirty dollars," at which point Judith, who'd spent parts of the afternoon feeling sorry for Paul One, decided it wasn't worth it. She was glad when Willy said, "I don't know. I never heard it told that way."

"Yeah," Paul One said, sopping meat sauce from his plate with a piece of garlic bread. "Couple people told me."

To change the subject, Judith looked at Willy and said, "Okay, so what's your middle name again?" A question she liked to ask because he would never answer it. Except now he did.

"Charlemagne," he said.

"What?" She knew it started with a *C*.

"Charlemagne."

"It isn't!" Judith said, and he blinked and said, deadpan, "That's right. It isn't." He turned to Deena. "I've told Judith a hundred times that the only person who'll get the exact nature of my middle name will be my blushing bride."

Deena said, "You'd think that alone would have her proposing," and Willy, nodding, said, "You would, wouldn't you?"

Judith said she proposed they pay the bill.

Willy drained the last of his Budweiser, grabbed the check, and pushed his truck key across the table to Paul One, who looked confused. "Drive slow and don't get us killed," Willy said.

Judith said she could drive.

Willy turned to her, smiling. "No, you can't. You got to keep me company in the back."

She didn't follow. "You mean the back of the truck?"

He did, and it turned out the idea wasn't impromptu. Beneath a tied tarp, he'd stashed two old patio cushions and two canvas-backed sleeping bags that had been zipped together into one. "In case we get cold," Willy said, and she could feel his sly ideas moving through her. It was dark by now, with a coolness coming off the river. They snuggled into the sleeping bag, and there she soon was, lying within the drone of the moving truck, feeling the quickening pulse of her own body, Willy unfastening things. Then, abruptly, the truck began to decelerate.

They both froze for a moment, then sat up and peered into the cab, where Deena was turned toward the rear window yelling something, they couldn't tell what, while Paul Wells eased the truck onto the dirt shoulder. The instant the wheels stopped turning, Deena jumped out of the cab and said, "The smell from those blueprints, it's getting in my eyes and nose and I'm getting a terrible headache."

Paul One, standing now on the other side of the truck bed, said he didn't think it was so bad.

Judith was suddenly wishing her bra wasn't unhooked. Willy said, "Well, why don't you just hand me the blueprints, Paul, and I'll put them back here with us where they won't be a bother to anybody?"

But Deena was shaking her head before he'd even finished the thought. "That chemical smell's already everywhere in the cab. It's *permeated*."

"We put the windows down and I told her we could open the wind wings," Paul Wells said, and Deena said, "*You* open the wind wings, Paul. I'm riding back here."

There was a long still moment before Willy said, "Sure, you can do that. And I'll just ride up front to make sure those blueprints don't knock Paul out cold."

And so the rearrangement was made. When Willy created a slight diversion by jumping out of the truck bed and poking his head into the cab to take a few exaggerated sniffs, Judith secured her bra, which Paul One seemed not to notice but Deena surely did.

"Jeez," she said as she swung a leg into the back of the truck, "he didn't waste any time, did he?"

Judith didn't respond. It seemed to her that the new configuration of people and places had managed to disappoint just about everybody, and who was to blame for that except Deena? She moved over grudgingly as her friend slipped into the bag.

"Sorry," Deena said. "It's just that I thought those chemicals might get into my lungs and brain and stuff."

The truck slowly accelerated from the dirt shoulder onto the smooth pavement.

"Really," Deena said. "I'm sorry. I guess I should've just stuck my head out the window or something."

After a few seconds, with the rush of the wind accruing, Judith said, "It's okay."

"What?" Deena said, loudly.

Judith turned and drew her mouth close to Deena's ear. "It's okay," she said again.

She laid her head back and opened her eyes to the deep dome of black night and white stars. It was nearly as strange and wondrous to Judith as the moon over the buttes, and it *did* seem okay that she was back here and Willy was up there. It wasn't like he was going one direction while she went another. They were together, going the same way, at the same speed, and to Judith there seemed enough time for everything. After a few minutes, she turned again to Deena's ear. "What day of the month is it?"

"July seventeenth," Deena said.

Which meant that the extended deadline for the U was three days past. So she'd be going to Sage State. Which seemed exactly as it should be.

"Why?" Deena said.

"No reason," Judith said. "I just wondered."

6

Given its throbbing element, it would later seem odd to Judith that what she remembered as the essence of the Summer of Willy Blunt was its illusion of safe haven and suspension of time. If Rufus Sage was a small world, then she and Willy lived in a small world within a small world, tucked away from all other influences. It wasn't so much that the outside world didn't exist, but that it rarely intruded. Late one afternoon, an hour or two before sunset, Judith sat leaning against a tree at the edge of a remote clearing with the sunlight slipping to a softer angle. She was reading *Washington Square*. Ten yards away, facing the open grass, Willy was tossing himself rocks to hit with an old Louisville Slugger he'd pulled from the back of the truck; the occasional *thunk* would jump from the relative silence. He would lob a rock into the air, swat it into an upward arc, watch to see where it might come down, then begin looking around for another rock of swattable size, a four-step process Judith thought could be most charitably described as harebrained. During one of these searches, he said, "They've got a James Bond double bill playing at the Starlight." He picked up and examined a rock. "*Diamonds Are Forever* is one of them. I don't remember the other."

Judith turned a page of her book. She and Willy had already fooled around. Judith could never read beforehand—the words kept sliding by without meaning—but afterward it was different. Because she'd liked *The Portrait of a Lady,* her father had brought home a nice secondhand copy of *Washington Square* he'd found at a used bookstore in Rapid City. He left the book waiting for her on the kitchen table, carefully wrapped in yellow paper, so carefully she wondered who'd done it. Her father had not only inscribed it—*For Judith, with a kiss on each ear, from your father*—but also attached a note saying, *Parental Warning: Beware Dr. Sloper.* It hadn't taken long for Judith to see why. Dr. Sloper's daughter, Catherine, was a little plain and a little dull, but her father's disappointment in these weaknesses deepened the daughter's awareness of them and converted them to shackles. (More than once, Judith wondered if her father had given her the book to help her appreciate the lightness of his own parental hand.)

She looked up from the book and said to Willy, "For guys, James Bond has got the cars, the gadgets, and the cleavage galore. But really, for girls, there's not much beyond Sean Connery and that great accent."

Willy turned a deadpan look to Judith. "They got girls in those movies?"

Judith shook her head and went back to reading. Catherine's Aunt Lavinia was busy greasing the skids for the caddish Morris Townsend, which was so annoying and yet believable that Judith thought she might explode.

Willy said, "You hear that Max Jackson and Vernon Topp sold two pounds of homegrown marijuana to undercover cops?"

Judith kept reading.

More or less to himself, Willy said, "Talk about shit for brains."

Thunk, pause, and then Willy said, "Guess you know that Sean Connery's real first name is Thomas? And just for the record, Gary Cooper was no Gary. He was a Frank."

She looked up from her book. Willy wasn't wearing a shirt,

and he seemed in the late light almost luminous, as if there were a filament gently glowing just below the skin. She wished she had a camera; she didn't have one picture of him, or of themselves, for that matter. She folded the book over her finger and said, "I didn't say I wouldn't go. I just said they're made mostly for guys."

The truth was, she liked going to almost any movie. If she couldn't get caught up in the story, she'd just sit back and try to figure out how they'd actually made the thing, and where it had all gone wrong.

Thunk.

For a moment he stood as still and smooth as a statue as he watched the arc of the swatted rock. When he reached for another, a small rock, almost a pebble, there wasn't even the slightest bunching in his stomach, and not for the first time she wondered how he could eat so much and stay so thin. She said, "Here's one. If you were an actor and had to take a stage name, what would it be?"

These were the kinds of idle questions Willy always threw himself into. "What kind of actor?" he said. "Action hero, or what?"

He then hit the pebble: *tink.* It didn't go far.

"Romantic lead," Judith said.

Over the next half-minute, Willy produced the names Thaddeus Lightfoot, Jack Oaks, and James Montague, at which point Judith burst out laughing. "Those are horrible!" she said.

Willy said he thought they were pretty good if a person would only give them half a chance. "'Course, if you want more of a sidekick type, I'd go with Mumbles McKunkle."

Judith laughed again. "Mumbles *McKunkle?*"

Willy nodded. "That's right. Mumbles would do a lot of cranky comic grumbling. Like Walter Brennan in *Rio Bravo.*"

He then laid the bat over his shoulder and stared grinning at Judith until finally she said, "What?"

"You're dying for me to ask what your stage name would be, aren't you? But I'm not going to, not after you making fun of Thaddeus Lightfoot and them."

"Edith Winks," Judith said, but then, having heard it, she changed it to Edie.

"Edie Minx?" Willy said. "With an *x* on the end? Well, shoot, I guess I'd buy a ticket to a movie with Edie Minx in it. In fact, I think I might already have seen her in a certain kind of movie."

"*Winks,* you moron. Edie Winks."

"Twinks. Edie Twinks?"

Judith said it was times like this that made her see that growing old with Willy would be a trial.

Willy said, "Oh, I think what you'd find is that I'd just get more wondrous with time."

He took a bottle of beer from the cooler and came over to sit on the blanket. He sipped beer and looked off. "I like it here," he said.

"You like it everywhere."

He nodded. "That's true. I mostly do." He leaned a little closer. "I like that perfume smell, too."

It was something called Charlie, which Willy had bought for her that day they'd gone to the plunge in Hot Springs. The girl at the drugstore told him it was the coming thing, and Judith had to admit it wasn't so bad. "I like it, too," she said. "It's a little bit sassy, don't you think?"

Willy nodded. A magpie screeched, then it was quiet again, and he said in a casual tone, "I was thinking you and me might drive down to Denver the Saturday after next."

This was news. They'd gone to Hot Springs, and one day they'd driven up to see Wind Cave, but Denver was a more exotic destination. Denver was a five-hour drive. "And do what?"

"Buy you dinner someplace fancy."

"Really?"

He nodded. He'd gone to the library and in the Denver directory found a restaurant where Teddy Roosevelt had once eaten and where from the roof you could see both the railyards and the downtown skyline. They could leave before dawn and eat dinner around one. That way, they might have a little time to do some shopping beforehand at one of the big department stores.

"What sort of shopping?" Judith wanted to know.

"Oh, maybe get you a new dress and shoes and all that kind of stuff. To wear to this Buckhorn place when we eat." He smiled and didn't try to hide his pleasure in all his planning.

Judith had to admit the whole idea was pretty exciting. "So how're we going to pay for this big adventure?"

"Well, I'm about done with Minnert's room, so he'll be paying me. I'm going to buy some tools, but there'll be money left over, too."

"And we'll be going and coming back all in the same day, right?" She was thinking of her father and what he might say.

"Sure," Willy said. "And I already made the reservations, so don't start fretting about that." He slid out a grin. "I told them it was your birthday. That way we get the free dessert."

"Not to mention the horrible singing," Judith said.

He stretched and yawned and snugged his head into her lap, preparing for a little nap. Judith looked up from her book when she heard the gentle call of a mourning dove. *Oo wah hoo, oo oo.* And then again: *Oo wah hoo, oo oo.* The light was soft and dappled. She ran a hand over Willy's chest and let it rest there, receiving the rhythms of his slowing breath. She was purely happy. She knew it then, within the moment, rather than sometime later, which was when she usually recognized her brushes with happiness.

7

On a Wednesday afternoon in late July, Willy applied the final coat of paint to the Minnerts' new room, then folded up his tarp and hauled away his tools. Minnert himself was away, so Willy gave the deadbolt keys to Mrs. Minnert, who clasped her hand tightly around them and kept nodding as Willy explained that he'd been paid for all the materials, so all that was left was payment for the labor, and he'd be back Sunday afternoon with the final bill. Judith accepted his invitation to tag along, and when they arrived, it was clear they were expected.

The big farmer sat in an old chair under the hackberry tree, seed cap tipped back, boots off, a blue enamelware cup in his hand. A hatless man sat alongside, a small man with a sharply pointed chin. This, along with his skittery eyes, gave him an almost feral quality. Though it was hot, he wore an unlined denim coat stained with several colors of paint, chiefly yellow and red. As Willy stepped from the truck, this man drank quickly from his own blue cup and set it back down on the stool they were using as a makeshift table. Possibly Willy had seen it sooner, but it was only then that Judith noticed the handgun lying on the stool.

Mrs. Minnert sat on the wooden steps of the mud porch, hunched forward, her housedress pulled over her widely parted knees. Half her face seemed expectant; the other half sagged. She said, "He brought his girly-girl with him."

Willy seemed to take this as a joke. He smiled at the woman, then turned to Mr. Minnert and said politely, "I've come so we could settle our account."

"It's settled," Minnert said. He set his cup down next to the gun, then leaned back. "I paid as I went." He folded his hands over his ample stomach, *like Farmer Buddha,* Judith would think later, but not right now. Right now, she just wanted to leave. She saw at once that nothing good could come from this visit.

Willy returned to the truck and came back with a file folder in his hands. "These're—"

"What those are don't concern me at all," Minnert said.

The small man shifted in his chair. Judith had the clear idea that this was what he had come for, but what his role might be, she had no idea.

Willy seemed about to speak, but stopped. He looked at the open folder in his hands, then closed it and looked at Minnert. "We had an agreement. We shook hands on it. You pay the materials up front and—"

"That's right," Minnert said. "You did the work right along and I paid right along. I'm a pay-as-you-go man." He took the time to inhale and exhale deeply, as if thinking. "Now it's true, I took a little risk letting an unlicensed fella like you do the work without a contract, but that's all behind us. The work was slow but it finally got done and you've been paid on time and in full."

A still moment passed before Minnert casually reached toward the stool. He took the blue cup, sipped from it, set it back beside the gun. He knitted his hands behind his head and stretched his stocking feet out from his chair. Judith looked at the feet in their worn gray socks—Minnert seemed actually to be wriggling his toes.

The small man was less sanguine. He'd tipped his chair back and jammed his hands into his jacket pockets. And whereas Mr. Minnert was actually smiling, this man could only try.

Willy said, "I generally go through my life trying to do right by the next guy, but . . ."

He stopped, and when Judith turned toward him, it gave her a start. He looked as if he didn't know what to say next. She had the feeling he hadn't expected Minnert to be drinking and hadn't expected a gun on the stool and hadn't expected a little feral man to be sitting next to the gun on the stool. He'd just been Willy, who expected the best of people.

"But?" Minnert said. He was completely composed; he'd again folded his hands over the dome of his stomach. When Willy didn't answer, he said, "You said you try to do the right thing with people *but.*" He smiled. "But what?"

"But what!" Mrs. Minnert said in a squawky voice, and this seemed to break Minnert's spell somehow. Willy glanced at Mrs. Minnert, then returned his gaze to the farmer. He said, "But in this case, I'd have to say that you're not much more than an asshole dressed up like a fat man."

The words shocked Judith and everyone else, too. All at once Mrs. Minnert let loose a splintery laugh and Joe L. Minnert stiffened and the little skittery feral-looking man pulling a gun from his left pocket snapped off a shot that puffed into the dead grass some distance from Willy—a mistake, possibly, a nervous impulse of the finger, but the shot seemed to please the man, and settle him. His smile now seemed authentic.

Mrs. Minnert's laughter rose in pitch.

Willy took a step forward, and Judith grabbed his arm. "Let's go, Willy," she said. "Please, let's just go," and to her relief he did stop his forward lean, and when she pulled at his arm, she could tell she'd turned his thinking. He took a step back.

Mrs. Minnert broke her laughter long enough to say, "Lover boy takes orders from the girly-girl!"

Judith was tugging at his arm, and finally he let himself be pulled toward the truck, but slowly, as if leaving weren't what he really wanted to do. Judith released his arm and hurried around to her side, just wanting to get away from this place and these people but expecting something—what, exactly, she didn't know, but something, and she was right.

As Willy reached through the window for the vise-grip handle, a single shot thupped into the side of the truck bed.

Willy's whole body froze.

"Forget it, Willy. Let's just go," Judith said, but Willy stepped back from the door and walked the few feet required to inspect the hole in the metal. Then he turned around to regard Minnert and his crony, the little one smirking and Minnert staring out from behind his placid smile, and still looking at them evenly, Willy said, "What's funny is you'd think all assholes would look pretty much the same, but just look at the two of you."

Mrs. Minnert let out another crackling laugh, and Judith in a hissing voice said, "Willy, c'mon!"

She cranked the vise grips and pushed the door open.

He got in, and to her complete surprise they drove away unimpeded.

When they were beyond what she supposed was firing range, she said, "Those are horrible, horrible people."

Willy didn't speak. He drove and stared forward and worked his jaw. This was something new. Judith had never seen him stew, could not in fact have imagined it. His first words came thirty minutes later, when he said, "That little guy was left-handed."

An odd remark, but at least it was speech. Judith said, "Who *was* he, anyway?"

Willy shook his head. "No idea. Not from around here, I know that." They drove a while more and he said, "Minnert did the same thing to Nick Packer on the gun cabinet Nick built him. And when the Porterfields got killed in a car wreck, Minnert bought the property off their eighteen-year-old-daughter for a fourth what it was worth, then turned around and sold off all the hilly crap to some out-of-state hunting group for what he'd paid for the whole place, and although he didn't broadcast it, he didn't mind letting it drop that he'd gotten himself a farm for free."

I told you so came to mind as something to say, but what Judith said was, "When did you learn all that?"

Willy didn't answer her question but instead seemed to answer some other question, one he was asking himself. He said, "But that man gave his word. We shook on it."

Three days later, while the Minnerts had gone to Thermopolis, Wyoming, to pick up a grain cart, Willy and a group of men— all of Boss Krauss's crew, as well as the Whiting brothers and a few others—drove out to the Minnert place to take apart the room Willy had built. Willy provided crowbars, sledgehammers, and beer for the occasion. By the time Judith arrived after her library shift, there was nothing left but the floor joists, and they were going fast. The men's high spirits derived from more than just the stimulus of work and beer; they seemed to take pleasure in justice quick and rough. The demolition debris was sorted according to material, into separate piles of trim boards, plywood, sheetrock, and framing lumber, all of it broken and ragged, nails sticking out everywhere. An overhead light fixture lay in a wild nest of electrical wire.

"What're you going to do with all that stuff?" Judith asked, and Willy said, "Leave it. Those are Minnert's materials. That's what he paid for, on time and in full."

They could've left the place in worse shape. They cobbled together plywood to cover the door opening and picked up their trash before heading for their trucks and cars. Willy and Judith were the ones to take the last look back, and she said, "So. Are you happy?"

He stared at the sight and shook his head. "Had nothing to do with happiness," he said.

———∿∿∿———

Shortly after noon the next day, the Rufus Sage chief of police showed up at Boss Krauss's job site east of town. Willy saw him driving up but pretended not to. Ted Seers was an ex-Marine who'd played fullback at a small college, one of those solid, compact body types that sports commentators often liken to bowling balls. His voice was unvaryingly low, flat, almost uninflected. He parked his cruiser, strolled over, and after waiting for the hammers and saws to quiet, he said, "This thing out at the Minnert place yesterday. Anybody know anything about that?"

Nobody said a word. Chief Seers in his low-voltage manner scanned the blank faces and began to nod to himself. "No, I didn't think so." He caught Willy's eye and motioned him over with a minimal tilt of the chin. Seers looked unperturbed, but Willy knew Chief Seers *always* looked unperturbed and that didn't keep him from being a severe ball-buster when it came to criminal behavior. He said, "How about you, Willy? What do you know about these shenanigans?"

Willy thought about it a second or two and said, "All I know is that Minnert's handshake isn't worth shit."

Again the chief was nodding. He looked at Willy, at the other men, then back to Willy. "Yeah, well, I had to ask." He looked away. He didn't seem unhappy. He said, "I told Minnert I'd have to ask a lot of folks, there being so many he's treated poorly over the years." And then Seers was straightening his back, sighing, letting Willy know he was done. "Okay, then," he said. "You get back to me if you hear anything I ought to know." As he walked back toward his cruiser, he nodded at Boss Krauss and said, "I pick up a nail out here in one of my all-seasons, I'll have to send you a bill," to which Boss Krauss put up a big laugh to show he was taking it for the joke he hoped it was.

"And you think that's that?" Judith asked that night.

"I do, yeah. I don't think Minnert really wanted that room in the first place. I think it was her who wanted it. It's possible it all worked out more or less to Minnert's satisfaction."

"Except for the public humiliation."

He was turning the truck into the parking lot. "That's why he went to Seers, which got him nowhere, and what's he going to do beyond that?"

Something, Judith thought. Because people like Minnert are built to do something. And for the next week or so, she had the occasional feeling she was being watched, observed, studied even, but when she turned to confirm the suspicion, there was never anyone there. She told Willy about this phenomenon one evening as they were heading up to Hilltop Lanes to eat pizza, shoot pool, and maybe watch a little of the women's bowling league before finding someplace to be alone.

"'*Course* you never see anybody," Willy said. "It's because you're not being followed by a run-of-the-mill secret agent man. You're being followed by an *invisible* secret agent man." He ran out a broad smile. "Those invisible ones can be *vexatious*."

"*You* can be vexatious," Judith said. "Fairly often, in fact."

As Willy wheeled the pickup right onto Tenth, she played her ace in the hole. She told him how that very morning she'd seen the Minnerts in town, Mrs. Minnert at the wheel of the orange Jeep, with Joe L. Minnert slouched in the passenger's seat, slowly scanning this way and that.

"No lie?" Willy said. "She was in town and driving?"

Judith nodded. "And what do you think they were looking for?"

Willy, turning the truck into the bowling alley lot, offered a grin. "Their missing room?"

Judith didn't laugh. "They were looking for you, you idiot. That's what I think."

Willy shrugged. "Not like I'm that hard to find."

That was true, she had to admit. Besides, by this time he'd parked the truck and was leaning over and brushing back her hair so he could give her neck a nibbling kiss.

8

When Judith tore off the July page of the Alcorn Insurance calendar, it reminded her of those sequences in black-and-white movies meant to indicate the passage of time, the wind blowing free one month after another, and it gave her a wistful turn. July was gone, summer would soon end, and things would change. Classes were to begin at Sage State before the end of the month, and to Judith's surprise, Willy had himself inquired about admission. He figured he could work weekends and holidays, live at home, and take at least twelve units of coursework.

"Why?" Judith asked. She supposed she should like the idea, but she didn't, not really. It wasn't what she'd planned on.

Willy shrugged. "Lots of reasons. Not freezing my butt off working construction in the winter would be one. Another is, my mother thinks I should do prelaw." Then: "'Course, my father thinks I should take ag classes." Then: "They said they'd pay for my books and all that stuff."

Which meant he'd discussed this with them and more than once, from the sound of it. "And this is because you want to become a lawyer or a farmer?"

"Well, not just a farmer. I was thinking farm management, working for one of these big outfits that are buying things up. Some of those boys make a pretty nice living."

They were on their way to the timberlands, to a place Judith had named the Thickety Hill, where they liked to picnic and where Willy could shoot tin cans with the .22 rifle he'd brought along for the job. Judith observed him as he drove—he was in his maroon snap-button shirt, whistling softly, as if he didn't have a care in the world. She couldn't imagine him as a lawyer and she couldn't imagine him as a corporate farmer. He'd made buildings out of matchsticks as a boy, progressively elaborate buildings, and after that he'd built a whole fort out of whittled willow branches. If he wasn't born to build things, she didn't know who was.

"So you're doing this for me, then?"

"No," he said. "Well, yes and no. I mean, being with you makes me think about the bigger picture, and then the other thing was you saying you didn't think a farming life would be that bad."

First of all, Judith had said this while under the influence of a pleasant afternoon in the company of Willy's mother. And second of all, the idea of walking around campus thinking that at any moment she might turn a corner and find Willy carrying books and pretending to be a student seemed odd. More than odd. It seemed slightly creepy, as if he would be there to keep an eye on her or something.

"I talked to the basketball coach," Willy said. "I could probably play on the team. Maybe not start, but coach said he'd give me some good minutes if I got in shape. I'd be what's called a walk-on. That'd put me in line for scholarship money after the first year."

They'd gotten into the pines now, and the road had narrowed to a single track, rutted and rocky. From time to time the steering wheel jerked in Willy's hands, and she shifted a little away from him so he had some room. Gradually the tall pines increased their encroachment from both sides.

After a while she said, "And you want to do that? Play basketball again?"

"I think so, yeah. I used to like it." He seemed to be trying to figure it out. "Going back to it sounds like fun but doesn't seem quite real. Kind of like going back to an old girlfriend or something." Then, realizing what he'd just said, he added, "Not that going back to old girlfriends sounds like fun."

They fell silent then, and when they reached their clearing, Judith put out the blanket and food while Willy popped open a bottle of beer and canvassed for cans to shoot. On such occasions in the past, the sexual impulse was generally so compelling there would be nothing else they could do first, but today their conversation in the truck had left them in their own separate spheres of private thought. It didn't surprise Judith when, even before finishing his sandwich, Willy stood to begin his target shooting. He'd only found a couple of rusty cans plus the two Budweiser bottles he himself had emptied. He set them all on a log that lay perhaps fifty yards off against a hilly backdrop.

"Want first shot?" he said, but she declined and pulled from her bag a library copy of *Things Fall Apart,* which she'd been meaning to get to all summer long; it was the first book on the Sage State freshman reading list. She'd finished *Washington Square* the night before, and regretted parting from it. Plain Catherine Sloper's reward for being wrong about the caddish Morris Townsend was a strange combination of spinsterhood and dignity, not a happy ending exactly, but better than her father's. For correctly expecting too little from his daughter and even less from her suitor, the good doctor seemed only to grow smaller and bitterer until at last he was dead, and Judith was glad of it. (When she'd mentioned this to her father at the breakfast table that morning, he'd only said, "James was interested in Puritan angularity," which was not much help, as far as Judith was concerned.) What struck

Judith was how the doctor, who was the book's most dominant force, could seem so cold and yet the book could seem so tender. She loved the final chapters, so much so that she'd reread them this morning, and wished she'd brought the book with her today so she might read them again.

Willy had finished another beer and mounted a scope to his rifle. He'd taken off his maroon shirt, which was an improvement, in Judith's opinion. The rifle was something called a Ruger 10/22, he'd told her, with a ten-shot magazine. He'd received the gun on his thirteenth birthday as a gift from his father. Judith had seen rifles that were pleasing to look upon and pleasing, she supposed, to hold, but this wasn't one of them—its stock seemed to have been made of hard black plastic. She watched as Willy raised the rifle, peered through the scope, squeezed the trigger, and then looked up at the shards the bottle had just become. He then in swift succession hit the two cans, missed once, and dropped the last bottle with his fifth shot.

"Aren't you the fancy shooter," Judith said.

He turned to her and said, "What's fun is to pop a watermelon with a fifty-caliber Barrett. You talk about things falling apart."

Judith, feeling herself tugged back toward him, feeling that he was becoming again what he always had been, said she could see how, for some types, that would be fun.

He nodded, evidently satisfied, then took his one empty and on the way out to the log drank another, so he'd have two to shoot, which he did, *tink tink,* and after grinning through Judith's jest that this wasn't so much target shooting as long-distance littering, he did it all over again, *tink tink,* thereby completing his full-tilt march back into Willyness. He then grabbed the first beer from a second six-pack and said, "Only got one round left. Saved it for the grand finale."

"And what would that be?"

"You pace off a hundred yards and put the bottle on your head."

"*I* do?"

"Yep."

Judith had to laugh. "That sounds like a prime example of something you might do in order to make the national news as the world's most moronic girlfriend killer."

"Whose girlfriend are you calling most moronic?" he said. Then: "So I guess that means you won't do it."

"That's right, Willykins."

He emptied the bottle, wiped his mouth with the back of his wrist. "Then how about you just hold it out in your hand like this?" he said, and demonstrated the position.

"Nope."

"You can hold it in your left hand, which is not even your writing hand, so even if something did go wrong, which it won't, you could still do all your homework."

Judith nodded. "And yet."

Willy chuckled and shook his head. He was definitely in high spirits. "Okay, then, I'll do it myself," he said, and without any hesitation whatsoever, he held the empty bottle by its neck at arm's length, aimed the rifle without quite shouldering it, and fired. The glass shattered and he stood holding the neck just as he had before the shot.

Judith said, "Well, that was something."

He seemed deeply pleased. "Wish I'd brought more ammo," he said.

Sometimes after a day with Willy, Judith would wonder how she could possibly have done or said some of the things she actually did and said. Now, for example, she said, "Well, since you are out of ammo, why don't you put that thing away and come over here? Because if you did, there isn't much I'd say no to."

He swung around, and almost at once his loose grin flattened into an expression she recognized as ardent. He clicked on the rifle's safety latch, then let his eyes run slowly up her leg. When his gaze reached her breasts and stopped, her eyelids drooped closed, and a feeling passed through her that she would for the rest of her life refer to whenever she heard or read the word *swoon*.

Afterward, Willy leaned back and said, "Sound to the deaf," and waited for her to say "Sight to the blind," which she did, and then they lay there awhile, letting their heartbeats slip back to their normal rates. Birds chattered and Judith's mind fell pleasantly blank. She couldn't have guessed how much time had passed before he said, "May fifth, May eighteenth, and June twenty-eighth."

She'd almost been drowsing. She opened her eyes. "What're those?"

"Willy Blunt's famous dates." He grinned. "All the dates important to me up to now."

"Okay, say them again."

He did. She had no idea what he was talking about. "What are those, anyhow?"

Willy gave a dry laugh. "Jesus, Judith Toomey!" he said. "You know what you just did? You just failed the Big Love Quiz."

He was laughing, but she sensed that just behind it was some actual sense of affront. She stretched out with her arms behind her head, which afforded a view she knew he liked. "Tell me, Willykins."

"Okay then," he said. "Saturday, May fifth—when you and I talked in Gibson's parking lot. Friday, May eighteenth—our first date and kiss. And Thursday, June twenty-eighth"—he grinned—"would be our first time on the maple bed." He went on to tell her what clothes she'd been wearing on each occasion (or which clothes, in the case of June twenty-eighth, she'd put on afterward). Judith was impressed.

"How do you remember all that stuff?" she said.

Willy shrugged. "Just do." They fell quiet. She closed her eyes. Even so, she could feel his gaze on her, and he said, "If you really want to know, I write it on the bottom of my sock drawer in my room. It's like a permanent record." A pause. "I thought those days deserved a permanent record."

She looked at him. "So are those the only dates written there, just the ones about you and me?" she said, and when he didn't answer at once, she said, "Ha! You wrote down dates for other girls!"

Willy drew himself up a little. "What I said was that the dates I gave you were Willy Blunt's most important dates. I didn't say they were the only ones."

Judith was amused. "Well, one of these days I might just have to go upstairs to your room and look at that sock drawer to see what kind of records you're keeping up there."

Willy began softly to whistle. Then, after a time, he said, "August thirteenth."

"You mean last year?"

"Nope. Coming."

Two weeks away. "August thirteenth," Judith said. "What's that?"

Willy smiled. "A Monday."

"No, really," she said.

"Full moon. Thought we'd go up to the camp and have an egg fry." He smiled. "Unless you have something else planned."

Judith, playing along, said she'd check her appointment book.

By the time they walked back to the truck, the light had softened and the shadows were stretching long. In the back of the truck, Willy moved a shovel and a Skilsaw to make room for the picnic hamper, then checked each of the tires, as was his custom. Judith closed her eyes for a moment to hear better the flutish sounds of the breeze, the calls of birds, the scrapings of crickets. Somewhere far away the sounds of a revving engine, a motorcycle, maybe, or a chain saw, and beyond that, the dim drone of a plane. Soundtrack for a dream, Judith thought.

"See something?" Willy said, which retrieved her.

"No," she said. "I'm just looking and listening." The faraway sound of the small engine had suddenly ceased. "Did you hear that before? A motorcycle or chain saw or something?"

He nodded. "Chain saw," he said.

Even the drone of the plane had now receded. The sounds were smaller and closer now, of birds and of insects. It made her think of that little encampment where he'd taken her to see the moon. She said, "I hope someday you make that camp you were talking about."

When Willy turned to her, his face caught the soft light and itself looked radiant. "Oh, I just might, if things go right."

They drove slowly out of the timber, across a stream, with glimpses down through the pines of the farmland below lying in neat blocks and squares of yellow and brown. Judith leaned against the door and extended her legs across Willy's lap. The warm air slid across her arms and into her clothes.

"We should call it Camp Blue Moon," she said. "I could make you a sign."

They fell into an easy silence. She liked Camp Blue Moon. They'd given names to other areas, too—the Thickety Hill, the Eighty-Acre Wood—but Camp Blue Moon sounded like something more enduring. She shifted position and put her head in his lap. He was whistling the song his mother liked and she was drowsing off when he suddenly braked to a stop.

She sat up and looked.

A hundred or so yards in front of them, a tree lay across the road, a ponderosa, with its green limbs stretching in all directions.

This didn't alarm Judith, but Willy's face did. It was set into something tense, and he threw the truck in reverse, the wheels spinning, making the turn in tight quarters.

By the fallen pine tree, a man peered out from the roadside bushes. She had no idea who. The man ducked back into the brush.

Willy's truck was not moving. The engine revved, but the tires spun sickeningly, going nowhere; then all at once—it seemed to Judith a small miracle—one of the tires found traction and the truck jerked forward. They were moving again, headed back toward the thicket from which they'd just come.

"What's happening?" Judith said. "What's wrong?"

Willy accelerated, and the engine seemed to explode. The whole chassis jumped and careened. The engine had always sounded big, but Willy had never used it. Now he was. She looked at him—his face was stony—then through the back window.

Nothing.

And then, from a copse of trees, a vehicle turned onto the road behind them. An open orange Jeep, driver and passenger, man and woman.

"It's the Minnerts," she said.

"Yeah," Willy said. The truck flew over the narrow road, scrabbling through a tight turn. As it bounced over one dry creek rut, Judith's head pressed through the cloth liner and thumped against the metal roof of the cab.

Judith looked back at the orange Jeep. "She's driving. He's got something." It looked like a rifle, but she didn't want to say so. She didn't want to believe it.

Willy slid the truck through a long turn.

"What do they want?" she said.

Willy was just opening his mouth when she heard a small

sound—*thip-thip*—and saw a hole appear at the top of the windshield. She looked back. There was a hole in the back window, too, a small clean hole with little crackling lines spreading from it.

"God *damn* it," Willy said.

Judith kept looking back. The orange Jeep, hidden for a moment, rose up over a hill. It was unquestionably a rifle. Minnert had it shouldered and aimed their way.

"Get down," Willy said through clenched teeth, and when she crouched low in the seat, he said, "Lower."

She squeezed to the floor. The truck kept tearing along. She was too scared to cry. She didn't know what to say or do, because there didn't seem anything to say or do, except what Willy was doing, which was to try to get away from these people. From the floorboard she heard metallic noises, *thup thup thup*. She hoped they were from rocks on the undercarriage. She made a quick set of calculations. They knew about the room and they had a rifle. So did Willy, but he had no ammunition. The truck was fast and had positraction, but it couldn't go anywhere the Jeep couldn't. So it was bad. It was bad and it was all because of Willy tearing the room down and thinking that would be that. She thought of her father. She wished she was with him. She felt like crying and she wished her father were here and she wished they hadn't gone someplace so far away from everything.

"Okay," Willy said in a tight voice. "Just up ahead here I'm going to stop, and when I do, you get out and beat it into the bushes and don't look back."

"What?" Judith said. She looked up at him from the floorboards. With one hand he was tugging free the snaps of his maroon shirt; she had no idea why.

"Just go ahead now," he said. "Get your hand on the door handle, and when I tell you to go, you just go ahead and go."

She could feel the truck sweeping uphill, then suddenly down—they'd crested a little ridge—and just then he hit the brakes hard and the truck fishtailed and skidded to a stop.

"Go!" he yelled.

She did. She threw open the door and rolled out and got up and at the same time crouching and running broke through the brush until she fell and hid.

The Jeep was coming. Judith could hear it coming. She raised her head just a little. There was Willy's red truck sideways in the road, and off behind it, hanging ragged in a bush, was Willy's shirt.

"Willy?" she called, but he didn't answer.

The Jeep flew over the ridge, and the moment Mrs. Minnert at the wheel saw Willy's truck, she began to brake, and Joe L. Minnert, half standing, looked over his rifle toward the shirt—in her movie this peering look of Minnert's would slow almost to stillness—and that was the way he was looking when Willy suddenly rose from his cover at the other side of the road, and holding a shovel stafflike in both hands, he turned his body in a quick compact punching motion, and with shocking abruptness the metal shovel head smashed into the side of Minnert's skull, and snapped it back.

Mrs. Minnert, flinching from the shovel, jerked the steering wheel left, and the Jeep crashed through the brush for a second or two and stopped.

Willy, still carrying his shovel, ran toward the Jeep and with one hand reached into it and dragged Minnert out. Minnert no longer had the rifle. He was clamping both hands to his bloody head as if trying to keep it from coming apart. Willy shoved him onto the ground and kicked him in the stomach and groin, then, stepping back and slipping his grip to the end of the handle, he swung the shovel in a long arc, coming down fully on Minnert's already bloody head. Judith, who had been running, slowed. Everything slowed. Minnert's big body was curling into itself. Willy was raising the shovel. Mrs. Minnert was crawling to the back of the Jeep, where the rifle lay. Judith needed to tell Willy this fact, but couldn't. Her lips parted. Nothing came out. *Willy,* she said, but it was just her lips—she had no voice.

Mrs. Minnert had the rifle now.

Willy stood beating Mr. Minnert. The farmer's big face, when Judith glimpsed it, looked like freshly skinned meat. Willy saw nothing. Willy's eyes were stones. He was living in some place where the only thing that mattered was killing this man. The sound of the gun was almost not a distraction to him. He just looked up from the farmer's moist red pulpy head and regarded Mrs. Minnert holding the rifle. She might have tried another shot then, might have in one quick instant proved him mortal, but his look paralyzed her, and before the next second passed he'd cracked the shovel handle across her hands and the gun was on the ground.

Willy picked up the rifle. Mrs. Minnert was holding her damaged hands in front of her, staring at them, her eyes wide with fear and confusion. Willy turned to Joe L. Minnert, who was still breathing, who in fact turned and tried to raise himself to his knees. Willy moved close and put the point of the barrel to Minnert's skull.

"Willy."

This time she said it. This time he heard.

She said it again. "Willy, don't."

He kept the rifle pointed there, but he had heard, and something in his shoulders loosened and he lifted the rifle away, but even then he was not done. He brought the butt end of the rifle across the back of Minnert's head so that he lay back down— dead, probably, was Judith's guess. Willy fired the rifle into the side of the Jeep until no more shots came out. Then he just stood breathing through his mouth.

Color returned. Sound returned. Birds, a cricket. Judith in a soft voice said, "Willy?"

"I'm done," he said, and set the rifle down.

Mrs. Minnert came over, sat on the ground, and got herself under her husband. His bloody head was in her lap. *She's caressing a dead man,* Judith thought, but then she saw blood bubbling at his nose and thought it possible she was wrong, that he was alive after all.

"You stay here," Judith said to Mrs. Minnert. "We'll go get help. We'll go get the doctor and the sheriff."

She didn't expect Mrs. Minnert to do anything other than what she'd been doing, which was holding the big bloody head in her lap and smoothing her thumb over the one ear that still had its skin. But Mrs. Minnert looked up, her face waxy and unaligned.

"We seen you," she said. "We seen what you did out there—"

Immediately Willy was standing over her, rigid again, fierce again, grabbing Mrs. Minnert's oily hair, leaning close to her ear, and saying through clenched teeth, "Your fucking husband tried to kill us and why I don't kill you right now and leave you for the dung beetles I do not know, so maybe you should just be real real quiet," and of course she was.

9

The consequences of the incident were not what Judith expected. After leaving the Minnerts, she and Willy drove back the way they had come. Willy had brought the chain saw he found lying upside-down in the brush near the Jeep. He intended to use it to cut the pine that lay across the road, but it turned out he didn't need it. He was able to grab the tip of the tree and drag it far enough to get by.

"What're we going to do?" Judith said once they were again moving south.

"Well, if we keep going straight, we hit Mexico," Willy said, but without any life in his voice. This wasn't the Willy she'd known, not quite. This was still something left over of the other Willy, the Willy with the shovel, the Willy who stood outside the boundaries she wanted all lives lived within, especially her own. With one tug, this new Willy had pulled taut the lazy line of their life.

"No, I mean really. What are we going to do?"

He looked at her. "We're going to send out an ambulance and we're going to go see Chief Seers and we're going to tell him what happened. How when Mr. and Mrs. Minnert tried to kill you and me, I tried to kill him."

After a second or two she said, "And might've succeeded."

He said nothing to this.

"That didn't seem to bother you."

"What was that, Judith?" A note of exasperation in his voice.

"How you were turning him into hamburger."

He opened his mouth to breathe in and breathe out. "We weren't playing for pennies out there, Judith. That man was pissed off. He was trying to kill us."

Willy steered the truck onto the highway, toward town.

"Maybe you shouldn't have pissed him off so much."

Willy veered onto the mowed shoulder and skidded the truck to a stop. She was suddenly afraid of what he might do next, but he didn't do anything for a few seconds. He just sat staring forward. Then he turned to her. "Look, Judith, I don't give a damn about those people, and the truth is, when he was shooting at us, I didn't give a damn about me. All I thought about was how that spineless son of a bitch might kill *you,* and I can't tell you how fucking mad that made me, that somebody so worthless and . . . puny as Joe L. Minnert might do something to you."

"Okay," Judith said, as much to get him to calm down and start driving again as anything else. "Okay, I get it. I do."

It took a while for Willy to pry his gaze from her, but finally he did. Finally he checked the side mirror and eased the truck back onto the highway. Judith was glad to be moving again. She felt as if she'd been on some long reckless vacation and was ready to go home.

In town, Chief Seers listened to their story without expression, writing a few things down in pencil on a sheet of paper but mostly doodling his way through an enlarging mass of geometric lines. He'd been eating supper at home when they'd called him out, but he didn't seem to mind. When Willy was finally done, he turned to Judith.

"Anything else?"

She shook her head. "Not really. Mr. Minnert shot at us while they were chasing us and then Mrs. Minnert shot at Willy when he had Mr. Minnert down on the ground."

Chief Seers looked at her. "When Willy was subduing Mr. Minnert."

Judith nodded. The chief stared at her and waited. By this time, Minnert had been taken by ambulance to the hospital. They knew what shape he was in. "Alive, more or less," was the way Seers had described him.

"Subdued him and then some, to be honest about it," Willy said, so she wouldn't have to. "I might've got carried away."

Chief Seers swung his gaze to Willy. "Carried away?"

Willy said, "Minnert bushwhacked us. Bushwhacked us and tried to kill us. That kind of set me off. Once I started beating on him, it was hard to stop."

Chief Seers watched him, waiting.

"He did stop, though," Judith said. "I said, 'Willy,' and he stopped." Though that was a little later, she realized. That was when he had the rifle at Minnert's head.

The chief offered a neutral nod and let a silence stretch out a few seconds before he said, "Truck outside?"

They went out and took some photographs of the bullet holes, which, it turned out, were seven in number.

Willy and Judith then signed a statement that, Judith thought later, contained most of the episode's facts but not quite all of its truths. The statement said that William Blunt and Judith Toomey were the subjects of a premeditated attack from a concealed location by Mr. and Mrs. Joe L. Minnert, and it identified the road and nearest mile marker of the attack. It said that the Chevrolet truck carrying Mr. Blunt and Miss Toomey was subsequently pursued by the Jeep driven by Mrs. Minnert. That Mr. Minnert fired a rifle at Mr. Blunt and Miss Toomey, seven or more shots hitting

Mr. Blunt's truck. That Mr. Blunt then stopped his truck and struck Mr. Minnert with a long-handled shovel, and while Mr. Blunt was subduing Mr. Minnert on the ground, Mrs. Minnert fired one shot at Mr. Blunt but missed. That Mr. Blunt disarmed Mrs. Minnert and discharged the rifle into the Jeep. That Mr. Blunt and Miss Toomey then left the scene to get medical help and report the incident to the police.

"Sound right?" Chief Seers said.

Judith and Willy both nodded, and Seers handed them the pen they used to sign.

By the time they walked out of the station, it was fully dark. Seers followed them into the street without speaking. Nor did he seem to mean to speak. He was just accompanying them in some way that to Judith didn't seem unfriendly, so she turned to him and said, "What's going to happen to us?"

Chief Seers straightened his back. "Not much, if the way you told it is the way it was. Joe L. Minnert isn't the kind of fella people rally around. Not what you'd call the golden rule type." The barest hint of a smile appeared on his lips. "If he doesn't make it, you might get a few thank-you notes."

It turned out that Joe L. Minnert did survive Willy's beating, but not by much. He was "neurologically compromised," according to the account in the *Rufus Sage Record*, whose reporter was quoting a doctor. Minnert had been charged with attempted murder, with Mrs. Minnert as an accessory, though neither, according to Chief Ted Seers, "was likely to stand trial, given the circumstances." The circumstances, citizens understood, had to do with Minnert's semivegetative state and the need of his slow-witted wife to attend him.

The larger problem was Judith's father. He was sitting in his armchair reading when she came in that night, and the moment he peered up over his glasses to say hello, his expression changed.

"What?" he said. "What's happened?" And she made a terrible mistake. She allowed herself to cry. She gave in to the luxury of it, the warmth and pleasure of it, the tears streaming, and her father standing, moving, taking her into his arms, holding her, the years falling away until she was twelve or eleven or ten again, whenever it had been before boys ogling your mother was something you ever thought about. "What, sweetheart?" he said in a gentle coaxing voice. "Tell me what happened."

She did tell him. She explained how horrible the Minnerts were, and how Mr. Minnert and his little left-handed crony had shot twice in Willy's direction when he'd gone to collect the money rightfully owed to him, and how Mr. Minnert had fired a lot more shots while he and his horrible wife were chasing them, and how Willy had tried to get Judith in a safe place when he stopped the truck, but as the succession of explanations and particulars came tumbling out, the events seemed ever more fantastic even to her own ear, and her father's physical attitude visibly stiffened.

Early the next morning he went down to the police station and came back with the news that Joe L. Minnert would live, and that without quite meaning to, Mrs. Minnert had corroborated Willy and Judith's version of events.

"That's good, right?" Judith said, but her father's eyes were dark.

"The Minnerts were after Willy," he said. "They believed he'd torn down the room he'd built for them."

He looked at her and waited.

"They didn't pay him, Dad. They had an agreement and Willy did the work, but Minnert didn't pay him."

"A written agreement?"

She looked down.

"They were after him," her father said, "but they were going to

329

get both of you, set fire to the truck and run it into the ravine. They'd been watching you for days, waiting for you to go someplace private with only one way out."

For a moment these words gripped Judith and held her still, but though the idea of her and Willy going someplace private hung there in full view, this wasn't the element that occupied her father. There was something else, something more important to him. "You were in harm's way, Judith." His voice was low and hard. "That boy put you in harm's way."

"That's not fair!" Judith said. "All he was worried about the whole time was me—I told you that already."

Her father spread his hands and touched them to one another. He was heading off into his own thoughts, she could see that, but before he went, he said, "This is Nebraska, Judith. You hit somebody below the belt, they're going to hit you back."

"But that's what horrid Mr. Minnert should've known!"

Her father had his caged fingers at his lips now, and when he glanced at Judith, it was as if from a great distance. "They both should have," he said.

Judith didn't know what to think. All she knew was that everything had changed. The color of the sky. The air she breathed. How her father's eyes fell on her. How her eyes fell on Willy. Everything.

A day went by, then another and another. One day, two hours into her shift at the library, Judith told Mrs. Humphrey she didn't feel well and would like to go to the infirmary, but instead she just walked home and, finding the house empty, went downstairs and without turning on a light or changing her clothes fell asleep.

Sometime later—how long, she had no idea—she was awakened by the sound of her father's voice. He was upstairs talking on the telephone in a voice that had a strange brittleness to it; it made him sound both worried and annoyed. Judith tiptoed up the basement stairs and positioned herself on the landing near the half-closed door. She could hear her father saying, "But you understand the importance of this, don't you, Rene?" Then, after a few seconds of silence, he said, "Swim? What's a goddamned *swim?*" and then, after another prolonged silence, her father in a tone of mild but unquestionable resignation said, "Okay, Rene. I understand. Just let me know." Judith heard him set the phone down, but she didn't hear him move, not until, from upstairs, she heard a girl's voice say, "You coming or not?"

Judith went back to her room in the basement and lay there in the dark for another hour or two. She could hear an opera she didn't recognize playing dimly from the uppermost rooms, and then the house was still for a time before she again heard footsteps and low, indistinguishable speech, her father's and the girl's. It gave Judith a turn when the door at the head of her stairs slowly opened and she heard her father say, "Not that way," and the door was pulled closed. Before long, Judith heard the doors to the Bonneville slam, heard the car roll down the driveway, heard its thrum recede down the street, but she lay still on the bed in the dim cool basement.

Who, she wondered, was the girl upstairs with her father? Was it Zondra with a *Z* or someone else, and which answer would be better? Neither, she decided. It didn't matter. She didn't care. And she didn't care who Rene was either, or what a swim might be other than something done in water. She fell back to sleep.

As the days went by, Judith kept expecting to feel herself again, and when she didn't, expectation became craving. She had always thought of herself and Willy as a kind of secret place, safe and exotic and intoxicating, but now it was a place she could no longer find. Some kind of geographical dislocation had occurred—she thought of that goofy musical, *Brigadoon,* where the village only appeared every eighty years or whatever it was before again vanishing into thin air. But Gene Kelly had somehow found a way back into the village, and Judith had not. She and Willy hardly talked. They hardly touched. He didn't whistle. She sensed he was always grappling with the episode with the Minnerts without ever quite understanding it. During one of their silences—they were sitting in the truck overlooking the White River—he said, almost to himself, "I don't know why I couldn't stop hitting him. That's the part I don't get." And then fell silent again.

One afternoon he went up to the hospital to see Joe L. Minnert, but the second he got to the room, Minnert became agitated and began making loud noises that weren't quite words, and then Mrs. Minnert came in and started screaming at Willy, all kinds of crazy things, and although he had gone to the hospital because he meant to say he was sorry about the way things had turned out, he found in those few moments that he wasn't sorry at all, that he in fact felt like strangling them both with the IV tubes that were dangling everywhere. "Guess that doesn't help much, does it?" he said to Judith when he finished the account of his visit.

"You can't help it, Willy," she said, and that much was irrefutably true. He couldn't help how he felt; nor could she. She had the horrible idea that all the fervent sensations she'd savored and clasped tight and believed in had somehow slipped free and vanished as irretrievably as a dream.

And then one morning snow fell. It started around dawn and wasn't much—it fluttered down and did little more than cover the ground, really—but it brought a welcome change. What had been dry and hard and dusty the day before was now soft and wet and white. Judith was staring out at it from the front room when Willy's truck, itself dusted white, pulled up in front of the house. They drove to the park and sat in the cab with the heater on, looking out and eating and drinking the maple bars and coffee he had picked up at Daylight Donuts.

Willy told her how a few years back there had been an August snowfall so severe that county plows were called out to clear the streets, and then he told her how one year they'd had at least a trace of snow in eleven of the year's twelve months, July being the only one absolutely snow-free from head to toe.

"Oh, that's a big fat lie," Judith said, and was slightly surprised to hear the hint of fun coming into her voice.

"Wanna bet?" Willy said. "Because I'm willing to, and you name the stakes." He grinned encouragement. "Go ahead. Take it to the limit."

She thought of betting him six kisses but couldn't quite do it. "No thanks," she said. "I'm not betting. Not when you know the answer and I don't."

"Maybe I'm a big fat bluffer," he said.

Judith said maybe he was and maybe he wasn't, and took a bite of her maple bar.

They had a few minutes before Judith needed to be at the library. Willy got out of the truck and walked backward through the snow to the middle of the playing field and then returned within the same footprints. He looked back at his work.

"That's quite an achievement," Judith said, which seemed to please Willy.

"I'll tell you what," he said. "Your average tracker will have no choice but to figure those prints for someone dropped straight from outer space."

Judith said, "That'd be pretty close to correct."

He laughed a full, easy laugh, and as he slipped back into the cab of the truck, Judith realized two things: first, that Willy had been trying hard to get them back into their secret place, and second, that she suddenly already was. It was as if a tenacious, low-grade headache had finally lifted. She felt normal. She felt herself. She leaned over and kissed him on the ear, and found she didn't want to stop there. Neither did Willy, but he kept his head about it.

"Whoa, Nellie," he said, leaning back and grinning. "This is a public park." His gray-blue eyes were alive, though. "Maybe I should pick you up just a little bit early tonight."

"Let's go to our place near the plunging pool." She smiled. "Pinney's Piney Pond." Where, she knew, it was particularly private, and there was more than one route out.

By noon the snow had all melted, but Judith's sense of well-being remained. After work, they drove to Pinney's pond, parked nearby, and fooled around in the cab of the truck. "Whew," he said when they were done. "I was beginning to think we'd forgotten how to do that." They ate the sandwiches she'd packed and he reminded her of their planned egg fry up by the buttes. She'd failed to remember it, not that she said so. Willy, after all, had once thought of it as one of his famous dates. They got out of the truck and went for a walk. Once they stopped to listen when they thought they heard a twig snap behind them, but it was nothing. He said, "What happened with the Minnerts—I guess you know I wouldn't let that happen again." He said some other things, and then he said, "My real miscalculation was in thinking all I had to worry about was me and Minnert, but that's not how it is anymore. What it is now is you and me." As they'd walked, their hands had come easily together.

10

The morning of Monday, August 13, broke dim and cool. From her basement window, Judith could see a wispy line of clouds hanging above the neighbors' green-shingled roof. She wore wool socks and a heavy robe while ironing the blue shirt of her father's she meant to wear to work, but by 9:30, the time she set off for the library, the day had grown warm enough for her to wear the smooth-pressed shirt with shorts and sandals.

There was no denying that her spirits were high. Over the past day or two she had achieved a pleasant equilibrium. She'd grown more accustomed to the idea of Willy's going back to school, and had even begun a quiet campaign to nudge him toward honing his basketball skills, because really, what would be so bad about sitting with Deena in a warm gym on a wintry night, rooting Willy and the home team on? And tonight she and Willy were going up to the camp for the full moon, and the night before, whispering in his ear, she'd asked him to bring the double canvas sleeping bag so they could snuggle inside it while the moon rose over the buttes. She also had the strange feeling that Willy had something up his sleeve. She'd mentioned this to Deena, who'd grinned and said she'd bet a dollar he was going to pop the question. The suggestion startled Judith, but it didn't exactly terrify her. Probably Willy wouldn't ask (it was too soon, she was too young, he wasn't ready, and so on), but it wouldn't be unpleasant if he did. She would say no, of course, not right now, but, really, why shouldn't she marry him? It was true she'd hatched the plan of trying to sneak into moviemaking sideways, quietly, almost before anyone realized she'd done it, but what were the chances of that? And besides, there had to be a career for her right here, or hereabouts, something requiring a plainer briefcase maybe, but a briefcase all the same.

Idle, meandering thoughts of this type carried Judith through the first few hours of her day at the library. Around 11:30, she was shelving books in the 800s and actually imagining a neat yellow-brick law office with *Blunt & Blunt* written in black-shadowed gilt lettering across the front window when Mrs. Humphrey appeared.

"Judith?" The look on Mrs. Humphrey's face was expectant; her face almost glowed. "You have a phone call. You can take it at my desk."

Dead. Someone has died. These were Judith's first thoughts, she had no idea why, but if she was right, she would never forgive Mrs. Humphrey her strange, luminous look. The librarian's phone was avocado green. The receiver lay beside its heavy base. Judith picked it up and said hello.

"Is this Judith Toomey?" A man's voice, and he didn't sound grave. He sounded, in fact, almost cheerful.

"Yes."

"This is Daniel Montgomery. I'm an associate in admissions at Stanford University." He paused, as if to let this information sink in. "I'm very pleased to inform you that you have been chosen for admission as an undergraduate this fall."

"Daniel Montgomery?" she said. She needed for him to go on, to convince her that this was real, and Daniel Montgomery did go on, giving her details, letting her know that a formal acceptance letter was being mailed to her home. When she set down the receiver, she turned to find Mrs. Humphrey hovering nearby.

"I've been admitted to Stanford," Judith said, and though Mrs. Humphrey took a step or two closer and said, "Congratulations," she didn't offer a hug or even a hand, but just stood there smiling. Finally she said, "You better call your father."

He answered on the first ring. He'd hoped this was what was in the air, he said. They'd called the house first and wouldn't say why, but he'd had his hunches. It was very good news, he said, but also as it should be. "You've earned this, Judith," he said. "You deserve it."

"Oh, Dad," she said, and began softly to cry. The depth of her happiness surprised her. She knew enrollment at Stanford meant leaving her father and Rufus Sage and Willy, if only for a while, but the truth was, whenever she'd thought about going off to a faraway school, she'd always been a little bit afraid of how she might feel if it ever actually came to pass, whether she'd feel—as she feared she would feel—like a family pet let loose in the wild. But now that it was here and had actually happened, the feeling was more like that of a colt released from its pen. Stanford wanted her. Stanford. She felt frisky and impatient and, to use one of her SAT vocabulary words, ebullient. She seemed to have asked something about Palo Alto, because her father was saying, "A town like that is made for a person like you."

She couldn't wait to tell Willy, or at least she thought she couldn't wait. Over the course of the afternoon she worked out a plan for managing it all—how she would write to him every day and how they would call every week and how she would come home every holiday, and how, really, this separation would only intensify everything she felt for him, and (this, too, had happily occurred to her) it would give the Minnerts a chance to die or move or at least fade far enough into public memory that they could not again encroach on the little world that was hers and Willy's. But when he arrived to pick her up that night wearing his blue-and-black plaid flannel shirt, the one he called his lucky shirt, it didn't seem like the right time.

They drove west on Highway 20, and though he was whistling, he seemed in an odd state of preoccupancy. "Something wrong?" she said, and he, as if surprised by the thought, turned and said, "Not a thing," and fell back into his soft whistling.

They turned off the highway toward the buttes, and soon turned again onto the shaded lane that tracked the creek and passed the spring where the tin cup hung from a branch overhanging the bank, the one from which she'd drunk on their first date, which now seemed a long time ago. When they reached the barbed-wire gates, Judith opened them for the truck to pass through and secured them again afterward. They bumped across the rough terrain and forded several creeks diminished to a trickle by the long days of summer.

They parked where they had parked before. Willy shouldered the ice chest, grabbed a deep black frying pan, and led the way. Judith was in charge of the double canvas sleeping bag, which was surprisingly heavy. She hugged it to her chest as they made their way up through the pines toward the encampment. When Judith spied the white full moon already hanging huge and blank in the white-blue sky, she felt a slight dent of disappointment. "Looks like that full moon of yours didn't wait for us to arrive."

Willy looked and nodded. "Still a full moon, though, and even your most basic full moon is nothing to sneeze at."

They traveled a little farther and Judith said, "So without a full moon to peek over the buttes, what're you going to do for a big surprise?"

Willy pretended amazement. He wasn't gasping. In fact, he

seemed not at all tired. "Here now," he said, "I thought it was your turn to spring the big surprise."

"I'll see what I can come up with," Judith said.

When they went over the ridge and down into the encampment, Judith stood catching her breath and looking at the draw that Willy meant one day to dam for a lake, and the already risen moon notwithstanding, she felt purely happy. There was the gentle fluting wind through the pines, and there were the clicks and calls of birds and insects, and there was Willy getting his fire going and uncapping each of them a cold bottle of beer, and there was the irrefutable fact that both Willy Blunt and Stanford University wanted her.

"What?" Willy said, and she shook her head, smiling. "I don't know." She made a vague wave of the hand. "This." Then, turning: "You."

He nodded and gave his loose smile. "That's what I'd say, too."

He'd brought a full pound of thick-sliced bacon to fry over the fire, and when that was done, he began breaking eggs into what looked like two inches of bacon grease. They plunged into the oil and floated back to the surface.

"How do you like 'em?" Willy said—a strange question in Judith's opinion, since the eggs were already poaching in grease.

"Hard, I guess," she said.

She'd never eaten six eggs at one sitting before, but she ate six on the evening of August 13, and might've eaten more if there had been any. Willy had brought some of his mother's buttermilk biscuits and chokecherry jelly to go with the bacon and eggs, and they didn't leave any of that uneaten either.

So this was how the evening eased toward its decisive moments: Willy and Judith ate and drank and fed the fire and let the mood turn soft and pliable. There was something afoot, Judith could feel it, if for no other reason than that Willy was holding off on the normal overtures, and so was she. She waited for him to say or do his surprising something, but when he didn't, she began to wonder if he, sensing something in *her*, was himself waiting. Finally a sentence formed in her head—*The strangest thing happened to me today*—but before she could speak, he said, "You know what's peculiar about that tree?" He was staring at a nearby pine.

"What?" she said.

"It's got a cork in it."

She saw nothing like a cork. "A cork?"

He nodded. "You can't see it from where you are. You'll have to get up."

She did, and approached warily—this had all the earmarks of a Willy-style practical joke. "Where?" she said, and as she moved to the side of the tree she saw it: an actual wide cork stopper wedged into a silver-dollar-sized hole. She looked back at Willy. His lips had stretched into a wide, brimming grin.

She said, "If I pull this cork out, is anything going to happen to hurt or humiliate me?"

"I hope not," he said.

She worked it free carefully, and there, inside the freshly cut hole, lay a small velvet pouch, and within the pouch was a silver band with a small diamond inset. She slipped it on, and thought at once of the day in Hot Springs when he'd made her try on Deena's class ring. The small diamond ring fit perfectly.

It was growing dusky, and Willy's eyes in the firelight seemed soft and possibly watery. In a voice with the slightest tremble to it, he said, "Before you came along, I told myself I had a life, but I didn't, not really, and now I do, and it's a life better than I ever dared to dream about, and I don't ever want to go back to the way it used to be ever again."

Even before he'd finished, Judith seemed to be floating toward him, feeling the glad release of tears, thinking anything was possible, everything in fact, and saying, "Oh yes, Willy, yes, the answer is yes, definitely yes," and then, "I do want to marry you, and I will marry you as soon as I'm back from college."

They'd been embracing, but his grip loosened.

"What do you mean?" he said.

In a rush, she told him everything: how she'd just that day been accepted, how it was a big honor, how she would write every day and they would talk every week and she'd come home every holiday.

She said, "We can get married in June when I'm eighteen."

And: "You could do a year at Sage State and then transfer to a school out there."

And: "They have all sorts of schools in that area."

"In California, you mean," he said. He was standing back now, looking at her in the dark.

"I like the ring," she said.

His gaze moved from her to the fire. "I'd wanted to get something fancier, but when Minnert didn't pay . . ." His voice trailed off.

"No, Willy, it's perfect," she said. "Everything's perfect."

He seemed to be nodding. She couldn't be sure.

They did make love that night, but something had slipped into it, something wistful, and when they were done, she laid her head on his outstretched arm and stared up at the night sky. The stars, so many and so white, seemed each to pulse with brightening light, and as the sky darkened, the bland moon grew prettier— it was circumscribed now by a broad band of white and a narrow outer band of yellow.

Three weeks later Judith would depart by train to Oakland, California, where she could board a bus for the short trip south to Palo Alto. Willy took her to the train station. In the predawn they sat together in his truck listening to KOMA from Oklahoma City at low volume, until after a time Judith thought she heard something and leaned forward to turn down the radio. She cocked her head and listened. There was no sound, but a barely discernible tremble could be felt rising from the earth.

"It's coming," she said.

Willy didn't speak or tighten his arm around her shoulder. Since the full moon at the encampment, he'd asked almost no questions and made no arguments; he'd merely fallen into a state of such subdued quiet that it had caused Judith to offer more and more avid lines of reassurance. When she did this, the peering-in quality of his eyes seemed especially keen.

All summer long they'd taken no photographs of themselves, but one afternoon this past week, with time running out, they finally had. She'd borrowed her father's Leica and developed the pictures herself. A few of them were surprisingly good—the late afternoon light had given a glow to their skin and faces. The one she liked of Willy, the one she'd trimmed and tucked into her wallet, pictured him with his shirt off, drowsing, one hand on a beer bottle. Of those he'd taken of her, she liked best the one of her standing on a tree limb in her shorts—her smile seemed natural, and the way she had turned seemed to add a fraction to her bust size. She remembered the photograph now, pulled it from her purse, and gave it to him. He looked at it and nodded.

"I've still got the ring," she said, and fingered the slender silver chain from which it hung. She softened her voice. "Beneath my sweater, close to the skin."

But she had said this before, more than once, and she worried that it was losing its flavor.

Willy glanced at the necklace and nodded.

The dim rhythm of the train was soon a heavy throb. Willy

slipped his arm from her shoulders and tried to make a smile before touching his index finger gently to her nose. Then he turned and took hold of the vise-gripped handle to his door. She stood by as he lifted her two suitcases from the bed of the truck. They moved to the platform and didn't try to speak over the noise of the braking train. After he set her bags just inside the train door, where they might easily be snatched back if she were to change her mind, Judith had a moment of indecision. She wished suddenly that there were two of her, one who could go off to college, one who could stay here with Willy Blunt. Perhaps it was more than just a moment. In any case, the whistle blew. The engine pounded and seemed to strain against the brake. She imagined the train actually beginning to move. She reached up and threw her arms around Willy's neck. Her kiss was so fierce it was almost a collision. The sound of the engine grew louder yet. Into his ear she shouted, "I love you to pieces"; then she broke away and stepped up the stairs into the train. When she looked back through the window, Willy Blunt was standing with his hands in his front pockets, as he'd stood that day she'd talked to him in the parking lot of Gibson's Building Supply, except then he'd been loose and shambly, and now he was wooden and still. Twenty-seven years would pass before she would lay eyes on him again.

Part Three

1

Upon opening her eyes in her storage room, Judith felt heavy, dull, disoriented. It was late afternoon; she'd fallen asleep, and what awakened her was the ringtone, the Debussy one. "Hello," she said, but it came out too loud. She was trying to sound wide awake. It was the middle of the afternoon, a workday. What if it was Lucy Meynke, or Hooper or Pottle?

"Edie?" A man's flat voice.

"Who?"

"Edie Winks."

Of course. Clair de Lune. The Edie Winks phone.

"Oh," Judith said. "I couldn't hear you. It's not the best connection."

"It's Gilbert Smith."

Judith didn't speak. Who was Gilbert Smith?

"Gilbert J. Smith. You hired me to—"

"Oh, right."

"I have the information you requested."

He has the information I requested. "Okay," she said.

"I thought we might meet to discuss it."

"Okay."

The detective suggested the next morning, at the Hamburger Hamlet on Hollywood Boulevard, say ten-thirty?

Which meant slipping away from work again or going in late again, both bad options. "I'm at work then," she said. "How about first thing tomorrow—sevenish? Or tomorrow night after six?"

Gilbert J. Smith said that wasn't possible tomorrow, but he could do either of those times on Friday if she liked.

This was Monday. Friday seemed like sometime next year.

"What do you do?" Gilbert J. Smith said softly, innocuously, but Judith ignored the question. "It's all right," she said. "I can work it out for tomorrow."

After hanging up, she sat on the side of the bed. It was late, almost 4:30. When had she fallen asleep? And how had she slept so long? She pulled her own phone from her purse, turned it on, checked missed calls. Lucy Meynke had called five times. Mick Hooper twice. Leo Pottle once. There was only one message, and it was from Lucy: "Bad news—Pottle took the next show from us. Do I sound hysterical? Because I *feel* hysterical. Where *are* you?"

What excuse had she given? A migraine specialist? A battery of tests? She couldn't remember. She called Lucy and said, "I had to take an Imitrex, but I'm better now. I'll be right there."

She returned to the studio—one of the other editors, passing in the corridor, averted her gaze—and found Lucy alone there, turning from the monitor at the sudden admission of outside light. "Oh," she said. "Thank God you're here." They stayed until after midnight, grindingly, painstakingly working their way through the cuts. When they'd gotten six minutes of film behind them, they felt good enough to go home. As they approached their cars in the empty parking lot, Judith said, "How about we work late tomorrow night, too?" She opened the Audi with the remote and added, "I've got an appointment at ten-thirty tomorrow morning, so I won't be in until eleven-thirty or so, but we can go gangbusters after that."

Lucy, at her car, turned as if in surprise, but Judith slipped at once into the Audi and turned the ignition key.

The next morning, she turned up a narrow ramp to the second and top floor of an old auto-service garage adjacent to Hollywood Boulevard. The garage was wood-framed, with glassed walls that from Judith's parking space gave onto Grauman's Chinese Theatre, where tourists already milled. The Hamburger Hamlet stood just across the street. It was 10:20. Judith was early. Gilbert J. Smith had said he'd sit toward the back of the restaurant and would be the one with a green loose-leaf notebook. He had asked what she would be wearing. "Black and white," she'd said, and that's what she showed up in: black ballet shoes, black pipestem pants, white boater top, and diamond stud earrings—no-nonsense Judith clothes.

She still harbored an image of Gilbert J. Smith as Harry Dean Stanton, but the man waving her over to his table was enormous, well past routine obesity, and his crew cut gave his large head an odd flatiron aspect. His polo shirt, pants, belt, and shoes were all black. (He looked, she would decide later, like someone who'd been a lineman for his high school football team, then done a stint in the Marines before turning to a life of eating, sleuthing, and listening to Johnny Cash.)

"Gilbert Smith?" she said, not that she needed to. The green notebook lay on the table before him, next to a neatly folded *Times* sports page. He'd pushed himself up to greet her, and he now breathed heavily through his mouth, as if the mere act of being upright were physically exhausting. "And you must be Edith Winks?" he said.

They both sat down. When he turned to catch the notice of the waitress, Judith scanned the restaurant (crowded, casual), then looked out through the window at the uneasy mix of dazed tourists and stony locals. "I haven't been on Hollywood Boulevard for years."

"I'm not often here myself," the detective said. "It's just that I had work nearby today." Now that he was seated, his eyes, deeply set in his fleshy face, were fixed on her as if from a duck blind.

A waitress appeared, a white woman, midthirties, hardened and bored. In the old days, this restaurant had hired only black men and women, a practice of which Judith approved, though she'd sometimes wondered how she would've felt had she been Vietnamese, say, or Guatemalan. In any case, the policy was gone, litigated to smithereens was Judith's bet. "Herbal tea," she said.

The waitress gave her a *That's it?* look and walked away without writing anything down. Her hawking a loogie into the hot tea was not out of the question.

Gilbert J. Smith said, "Winks is an interesting name. Is it English in origin?"

So. He was on to her. Which for some reason irritated her. "I think it derives from forty winks," she said, and the detective reacted with such a quick set of staccato laughs that Judith was aware of his flabby breasts jiggling beneath his tentlike polo shirt. Then he said genially, "Forty winks as in you dreamed it up?"

She could feel her skin pinkening. "My check's good, if that's what you're worried about."

The detective's face seemed to relax then, as if they'd now had some meeting of the minds. "I know that," he said, and this was his Harry Dean Stanton voice, the one she liked. "And you'd be surprised how little I worry about. I don't have a spouse, or kids, or a big bank account, and that's where you see the bulk of your real worrying." He seemed actually to be thinking about this. "I keep tropical fish, but you couldn't say I worry about them."

The sullen waitress brought Judith a small pot of hot water and a saucer containing two tea bags, Earl Grey and Orange Pekoe. The hot water wasn't hot at all, but it at least looked unadulterated. Besides, the mere process of slipping the tea bag from its jacket and dipping it into the tepid water was calming. She said, "So you seemed to be saying on the phone that you'd found my old friends."

Gilbert J. Smith opened the green notebook and flipped through a number of pages before clicking open the binder and slipping a single page free of the metal rings. He tipped the page toward him and began to summarize what he read. "Patrick Guest," he said. "Living in eastern Brazil. Has been for the past twelve years. Cattle operation, plus soybeans. Now developing a portion of property into a gated community of oceanview building lots with a website targeting rich Americanos."

Judith stared at him and said, "You're kidding."

Behind the heavy lids, Gilbert Smith's eyes rose. "The truth is, I used to do a little kidding, but I gave it up. It's not compatible with this line of work." He returned his attention to the page. "Mr. Guest is married to a Brazilian, the former Maria Madalena Abreu Silva, who has borne him four girls. All ems: Margarita, Monica, Miryam, and Mariana." He stopped then, turned the page facedown, and, as a little intermission, tore open a pink packet of sugar substitute and stirred it into his coffee.

Judith found the news she'd just received deeply pleasing. She liked thinking of Patrick Guest on a green ranch overlooking a foreign ocean, liked thinking of him spending his evenings with his Brazilian wife and daughters with names beginning with *m*. She imagined white cotton dresses and a white plaster house with dark heavy beams.

Gilbert J. Smith set down his coffee. "Now with William Blunt and Deena Schmidt," he said as he again scanned his sheet of paper, "we get a little lucky. They turn out to be a twofer. Seems they both live in Grand Lake, Nebraska." The sheet of paper dipped an inch and his hunter's eyes locked on to her. "In fact, they live at the same address."

"What?" Judith said, and wished she hadn't.

Gilbert J. Smith was slowly nodding to himself. "That's right. They were married"—his eyes drifted down the page—"on June 25, 1978."

One year to the day after she'd married Malcolm.

"Well, good for them," Judith said, trying to recover. "That's the most astonishing news."

Gilbert J. Smith regarded her blandly, then returned his gaze to the page. "He was a general contractor, built single-family houses primarily, but is now retired. She works in a doctor's office. Two sons, one in high school, one in the navy. House in Grand Lake free and clear. Same with a metes-and-bounds property in Rufus Sage, Nebraska. No criminal records, no judgments against them."

The detective read a little more to himself but evidently found nothing worth repeating. He slipped the sheet of paper into a folder. "The telephone number for Mr. and Mrs. Blunt is here, but under the circumstances, I took the liberty of not contacting Mr. Blunt to give him your contact information." He smiled. "I can still do that if you like."

Judith shook her head.

The detective slid the folder across the table. "You'll see that all I have for your *vaquero* is an address. And of course the website for the housing development."

Judith opened the folder to glance at the page—it was all neatly typed, and was followed by several pages of photographs. One was of a hundred or so Brahma bulls clustered sedately against the most brilliantly blue sky. Some of Patrick Guest's cattle, she supposed. She looked again at Gilbert J. Smith.

He said, "Satisfied, Mrs. Winks?"

She glanced down at her wedding ring—and wished she hadn't—then again raised her eyes to the detective. "I am," she said. "It all seems quite complete. What do I owe you?"

352

He shook his large head and gave a dismissive wave. "All covered by your check. No extras on this one."

As she stood to leave, Gilbert J. Smith handed Judith his business card. "In case you need anything further," he said, and out on the sidewalk, waiting for the stoplight, she casually dropped the card into a nearby trash can. Across the street, the crowd at Grauman's had thickened. A Darth Vader impersonator posed for a picture with two small boys. Another impersonator held his red furry Elmo head under his red furry arm and drank from a plastic water bottle. A low-slung car passed by with four low-slung Hispanic boys staring sullenly from various windows.

Deena had married Willy. Willy had married Deena.

It seemed like the biggest surprise in the world and yet, when she thought about it, not much of a surprise at all. All of Deena's prying questions when Judith and Willy had been together, all of the looks she'd thrown Willy's way. And the way Deena's letters suddenly stopped after Judith had broken off with Willy.

But it was good, she told herself. It was good, better than any other scenario she might've imagined. Willy hadn't just recovered, he'd recovered quickly. Now she could call and talk to Deena and find out how they both were, she and Willy, and their two sons.

Judith and Lucy stayed late that night and started early the next morning, but the work resisted, seconds of film grudgingly growing to one minute, then two, then three. By early evening they were too tired to think properly, and after declining Lucy's invitation for a quick bite at Tom Bergin's, Judith went to her storage unit, opened the folder given her by Gilbert J. Smith, and checked the time. Six forty-five. Seven forty-five in western Nebraska. Several times she gathered in three staggered breaths of air and slowly released them. She practiced saying hello, out loud, in a normal voice. Finally she tapped out the telephone number of Willy and Deena Blunt on her keypad, hit the send button, and then, upon hearing almost at once the brusque hello of a woman who must certainly be Deena, she hung up without a word.

The next night, when she reached a taped message in Deena's voice asking the caller to please leave a message, Judith hung up on that, too. But four or five days later someone who sounded quite a lot like Willy answered on the first ring. When Judith didn't speak, he repeated his hello.

"Willy?" she said.

"Warren."

"Warren?"

"Willy's son."

"Oh. Could I speak to Willy?"

"Not here."

"When would be a good time for me to reach him?"

"You mean at this number?"

"Yes."

"Never. He's never at this number."

"What number should I try, then?"

Away from the phone, Warren yelled, "I don't know! You come get it if it matters so much to you!" Then, back into the phone, he said, "When we want him to call us, we leave a message at this number."

He read it out.

She wrote it down.

"Okay?" he said. Warren was ready for this phone call to be over.

"Yes," Judith said. "Thanks very much."

Before hanging up, Warren said, "Don't say I didn't warn you," which made no sense whatsoever. Why shouldn't she say he hadn't warned her? Because he hadn't. He hadn't warned her about anything.

Had he?

No, he hadn't.

Judith called the number immediately, without thinking, and after three rings a voice said, "This is M. McKunkle. Please leave a message and I'll either call you back or not." A beep sounded and Judith hung up feeling quite stunned.

M. McKunkle. Mumbles McKunkle. The stage name he'd chosen that day for a comedic sidekick. So it was Willy, all right, though it didn't sound exactly like Willy, not anyhow the Willy she remembered, and would his using M. McKunkle just be some little private joke or some signal to her, Judith, should she ever call?

She took her three short breaths in, one slow extended breath out. Several times she did this. Then she redialed, waited for the beep, and said, "This is Judith Toomey Whitman and I'm trying to reach Willy Blunt." She gave her number, once, but slowly, so there would be no mistake, and hung up.

It was late afternoon. She'd gone into the studio early, before six, with the idea of doing a marathon day, but by midmorning she'd felt the aura coming on, and though the Imitrex she'd taken preempted the migraine, it had made her feel sluggish and nauseated. "Go home," Lucy had said to her, clearly preferring working alone to working with the Judith at hand. "Get better." And so Judith had come here, the one place where she might feel better. She braced her back with pillows, stretched her legs over the honeymoon-cottage quilt, and tried to read. She couldn't, of course. Her thoughts fled the page in all directions. That boy, Willy's boy, with Willy's inflections. Saying, *We leave a message at this number if we ever need to talk to him.* Why was that? And why was Willy never at home? Were they separated? Divorced? And why would Willy have a message like that? M. McKunkle. That was odd. But he couldn't really say *Mumbles McKunkle,* could he?

That would sound like … What? A rent-a-clown agency or something. Mumbles McKunkle. Every occasion. Mister Pottle-Wattles. Goosey-Lucy. Jemima Puddleduck.

At the first chords of "Clair de Lune," Judith nearly jumped. She stared at the slim ringing phone.

On the third ring she flipped it open and said, "Hello?"

"Edith Winks?" A woman's voice.

"Yes."

"It's Therese Aiken from Valley Oaks Bank. How are you?"

Judith said she was fine.

"Well, this is just a courtesy call to let you know your name just showed up on the overdraft list. A check for four hundred dollars came through and you're short. Not a lot, about fifty dollars. The overdraft's covered, but there'll be a fee unless you want to come in and make a deposit today."

"You call people to save them overdraft fees?"

"It's not required, but we try to as a courtesy."

"Why?"

"Why?"

"Yes. I mean, isn't that why they put those niggling little fees in place? So they can make a pile by collecting them all over the land?"

Therese Aiken, to Judith's surprise, issued a soft laugh. She also seemed to lower her voice slightly. "I can't comment on bank policy, but truthfully, the reason we call our customers is because our branch manager gets sick of people coming to her all p.o.'d about these 'niggling little fees.'"

Judith made a deposit at the bank (and ventured over to New Accounts to give a quick thank-you to Therese Aiken for the heads-up), then drove home. It was the first time in a week she'd been home before dark. It was also Wednesday, a fact of which she hadn't been particularly aware until she opened the door and walked into the sweetish scent of meat loaf. Sonya's note on the kitchen table said, *Mr and Mrs W, 2 dinners in fridge, S.* And so they were—two big plates covered with stretched Saran wrap, as if beamed there straight from Hutchinson, Kansas: meat loaf, baked potato, a mix of carrots and peas. By the time Judith took it steaming from the microwave, her mouth was actually watering. She grabbed a fork and began to eat standing up.

From the courtyard she'd been hearing the jangling sounds of girlish merriment, so she stood back from the kitchen window and looked out. There in the softening light of early evening three of Camille's friends were laughing at a fourth, a prankster named Torry McQuaid, who Judith knew was a Roberto Benigni fan and who now stood on the diving board pretending to sketch with her hands the trajectory of a preposterously difficult dive involving twists and, if Judith counted correctly, a triple reverse. This drew rowdy hoots from the girls—Lauren Hartman was one, Isabella somebody was one, and Judith didn't know the third. Fit girls in skimpy suits, with streaked hair and perfect teeth; girls who Judith would bet the house had snubbed the meat loaf completely. Except Lauren Hartman, of course. She would've tried some meat loaf and praised it as if she meant it. Lauren was so smart and so pretty and so kind that Judith's approval of the girl mingled with envy of her parents. Torry the Prankster slowly, reverently crossed herself and then, haw-hawing, cannonballed into the deep end, and a second or two thereafter she broke up through the water grinning, receiving her friends' derisive cackles as if they were tens straight across. And where was Milla, the hostess of this soiree? There, alone, away from the others, moving from the deep shade of the gazebo into the open doorway, phone to her ear, deep in conversation. The other girls shouted something to her—Judith couldn't hear what—but Camille looked up, squinched her nose, and merrily waved her middle finger at them all, which provoked further laughter from her friends.

Sonya sat by herself on the shady stoop of the guesthouse, the unwanted chaperone, the paid informant, watching while not watching, reading a book, wearing jeans and a dowdy brown T-shirt with some indecipherable inscription on its front. Here was a surprising fact: Sonya could dive. Judith had seen her one day standing still on the diving board in a surprisingly stylish black one-piece, looking straight ahead, waiting for some kind of internal composition to fall into place. Then, decisively, she stepped forward and bounded up from the springboard, her sleek tight body describing a graceful arc before the water's surface swallowed her in one quick gulp. Judith wished she would do it now, go put on that same slimming one-piece suit, walk before these girls to the diving board, and demonstrate how incomplete their imaginations regarding her might be.

Judith rinsed her plate—she'd eaten every bite and craved more—then pulled the Edie Winks phone from her purse, powered it up, and checked for messages. None. She felt strangely thwarted. She stared at the phone as if it were a magical box that contained important secrets but couldn't be opened. Finally she just switched it off and put it away. She removed her shoes, sorted the mail, and sat down with a Pottery Barn catalogue, pulled in by the beautiful bedding on the cover. She found herself regarding something the catalogue was calling a glass tealight holder. Monogrammable, it said. Was that a word? And why would people want their initials on a candleholder? Or—she flipped the page—on soap sets or bedsheets? To say, *Just so you know, these sheets are mine? Also the candleholders. But anything else you see, without my initials? Go ahead and take it. Feel free.* Really, she thought, dropping the catalogue into the recycling bag, too much is too much.

She opened the kitchen door to the courtyard and presented herself to the girls. Camille sat now in the middle of the others, turning over Tarot cards one by one.

"Milla?"

Camille turned a card and said something that provoked laughter.

"Have you heard from your father?"

Camille looked up and shook her head.

"He called," Sonya said from off to the side, closing her book over her finger. "He said he'd be home between eight and nine."

Judith took this in. "The meat loaf was scrumptious, Sonya. Everything a Wednesday ought to be."

Sonya smiled. "Glad somebody liked it besides Lauren."

So Judith had been right. The others had snubbed it. "Everything else okay?" she said.

"It's all good," Sonya said.

The girls had grown quiet. In a certain kind of movie, they would meet later to discuss ways of killing Sonya, or perhaps selected parents. "I'll be inside if you need me," Judith said, and some not quite audible response—"Fat chance," maybe?—provoked murmuring laughter at the fortune-telling table.

Judith bristled at the laughter and turned around. "Do I know you?" she said.

All four girls at the table turned to her with odd frozen expressions, but Judith looked only at the girl she hadn't recognized. It was Camille who figured this out by tracing Judith's gaze to the new girl. "God, Mom," she said. "It's Olive. You've only met her about a gazillion times."

Judith didn't remember meeting anyone named Olive, ever, but that didn't mean she wanted to argue it out in public, so without another word she went back inside, picked up the *New Yorker* that had come in the day's mail, and sat with it in her favorite armchair

359

near the front window. As the room dimmed, she looked out into the yard on the north side, where the impatiens still bloomed. And the hydrangeas, which Milla had helped her plant to earn money for a sock monkey. It seemed only a few months past, but—she was counting—it was eight years, or maybe nine. Milla had made a little bed for the sock monkey every night, and she set a separate place at the dinner table with the monkey in a little chair before it. The monkey's sole diet was grapes, and Judith and Malcolm would take turns diverting Milla while the other snitched a grape. Then Milla, playing along, would say, "Well! I see Socko ate another grape, or"—looking about with exaggerated suspicion—"*somebody* did." Darling precocious Milla, not so innocent even then. Still, it was during that time, when Milla lived for tea parties, stuffed animals, and picture books, that Judith's love for the girl could honestly have been called keen and pure. As soon as Milla found Judith sitting still, there she would be, a determined set to her face, presenting a copy of Babar or Curious George, Madeline or Amos and Boris, saying, "This one, please," and "Now this one," preferring Judith's reading voice to the nanny's or even Malcolm's. Judith had to smile. For that little girl, she would've given her life in a heartbeat.

"Mrs. Whitman?"

A dim presence on the other side of the dim room.

"Oh, hi, Sonya. You gave me a start. I was just . . ." Just what? *Regretting Milla's growing up? Wishing my high school lover would call? Wondering whether my husband is off humping his assistant?* She switched on the lamp, which changed the mood at once. She could see, for one thing, that the inscription on the front of Sonya's T-shirt said, *It's not about me.* Which meant what, exactly? What was it about, then? And Sonya was barefooted; that was how she'd stolen in so quietly.

"Sit, sit," Judith said, waving her toward the other armchair.

"This is such a nice room and nobody sits in it." Then, as Sonya seated herself, Judith said, "You know, I was thinking of you a while ago. Of how beautifully you dive. You did high school gymnastics, too, didn't you?"

Sonya nodded.

There was something else Judith sketchily remembered, some disappointment about cheerleading, but that couldn't lead anywhere good. "They're related, aren't they? Diving and gymnastics?"

"Diving and gymnastics related?" Sonya said, and Judith, wondering if somebody would just please shoot her, said yes, she bet they were.

A few uneasy moments passed before Judith thought to say, "This new girl, Olive—is she nice?"

"As nice as most of Milla's friends." Judith knew what this meant, and Sonya knew what Judith's next question would be so went ahead and answered it. "She's in AP classes and also on the tennis team. Number three on the varsity."

Judith nodded. It came to her suddenly just how much Sonya *knew*.

"By the way," Sonya said, "I don't think you've ever been introduced to Olive before."

Judith smiled and murmured, "So I'm not *completely* losing my marbles." She'd begun to wonder what business Sonya had come in to conduct. "So, Sonya, is everything okay?"

"Better than okay." She waited a moment. "I guess you know I got into GCC."

"GCC?"

"Glendale Community College. The nursing program."

"Oh, Sonya! That's just perfect. You'll make a wonderful nurse!" Clearly Judith should already have known about this, so she added, "I always thought so."

Sonya nodded. "I start next week but I just wanted to let you know I've got it worked out so I'm always home before Milla," she said, and there were more details, how many units she was taking, what classes she was looking forward to, the length of the commute—during which discussion Judith was thinking how predictable it was, Sonya's going from nanny to nurse, trading one form of subordination for another, though nursing paid real money, she supposed, and then Sonya was saying, "Well, anyhow, thank you again. Without you and Mr. Whitman, I could never have done this. I mean, the money you're lending me for the car and insurance and all."

They were lending her money for a car and insurance? Yes. They were. And here was Sonya, watching her, savoring the intimate release of her secret. "Really, Sonya," Judith said, employing a sedate tone as she scrambled to higher ground, "it's nothing. We'd always been looking for a way to help. I can't think of anyone more deserving."

Malcolm, due home between eight and nine, pulled into the driveway at 10:23. From their upstairs bedroom, she could hear the pinging sounds as he heated his meal in the microwave, then heated it some more. She could also hear him chatting it up with Milla and her girlfriends, who'd stayed to watch a movie, something with a lot of singing. Thirty minutes passed and he still didn't come to bed. Finally she went down. There was Malcolm in the front room, seated in the midst of the kids, a glass of red wine in his hand, his empty plate on the coffee table before him.

She'd recently had a dream in which Malcolm sat naked in a room full of Persian carpets, bright pillows, and other naked people, women primarily, and when she arrived fully clothed he talked to her as if nothing whatsoever were out of the ordinary. Now he looked her way, and at once his cheerful expression slackened. "Uh-oh. Headache?"

What? She looked sick to him? Miserable? Shrewish? "No, I

just couldn't sleep." She glanced at the wide, flat television. *Little Shop of Horrors,* with Steve Martin as a sadistic singing dentist. "I was wondering if you could just—"

"Sure, Mom," Camille said, preferring reduced volume to extended conversation with Judith.

Malcolm, rising, smiling, said, "And we might just close the door as well."

Upstairs, alone, Judith pulled the silver cell phone from the depths of her shoulder bag and again checked for a message that wasn't there. And during the night, when she awakened with Malcolm's dead weight against her, she took her bag into the bathroom, where the voice within Edie Winks's phone again informed her that she had no unheard messages.

At work the following afternoon, Judith was standing in the women's bathroom, waiting for the phone to power up, when Lucy walked in. "So there you are!" she said, and disappeared into a stall without another word. Lucy and Judith had spent most of the morning undoing edits Lucy had done on her own and then going with cuts that Judith admitted to herself, if not to Lucy, were inferior.

Three days passed without a return call from Willy, which only tightened the grip of her preoccupation. Why wouldn't he call? Why would he go to the trouble of putting on his answering machine a message customized specifically for her, then not call her back? Why in God's name would you bait for a particular fish and then, when it bites, just let it run off with miles of line? What if he'd never forgiven her? Loathed her? Couldn't believe after all these years she would have the nerve to disrupt his life? Judith was thinking thoughts like these one evening at the kitchen sink while pouring pasta into a colander when, from behind, Camille said, "What's with the slutty new phone?"

"What are you talking about?"

"The seriously slutty one at the bottom of your purse."

Judith, turning, seeing the Edith Winks phone in Camille's hand, forced a laugh. "I'll pass your verdict on to Leo Pottle. He provided the phone so the studio would be able to get hold of me. Though I may have to explain to him that *slutty*'s no pejorative among the thirteen-to-sixteen age group."

Camille had the phone open now and was punching buttons, looking at the screen, punching more buttons, making Judith really nervous. "For God's sake," she said, "put that back. It's not yours. It's not really even mine, and I don't want to screw it up." Her voice sounded strange to her. She remembered what she'd been preparing to do. She slid the pasta from colander to serving bowl.

Without looking up from the phone, Camille said, "Did you give Dad this number? So he can always get through to you, too? Because sometimes he can't."

"No, Milla, I didn't. It's the studio's phone. It's for them to get to me."

Camille kept playing with the phone, trying this and trying that. "So it's like seriously limited minutes?" she asked.

"Maybe. I didn't ask. Because I have no intention of making calls on it."

"Can you give the number to me? For emergencies and stuff?"

"No, Milla, I can't. For reasons I just explained."

Camille abruptly stopped tapping the function keys. Surprise registered on her face. She looked from the phone to Judith and back to the phone. "Well, somebody's been making calls," she said.

Judith had never really understood what it meant to feel clammy, but she understood it now. She needed to say or do something, but she couldn't. She just stood there.

Camille kept punching buttons and studying the phone.

"Camille, I mean it. Put the freaking phone back where you found it."

Camille looked up from the phone and produced a benign expression that Judith understood was designed for vexation. "God, Mom. It's not like I found a derringer in your purse or something."

"*My* purse," Judith said, but it was no use. Her authority had slipped away, and in some perverse squeeze-and-bulge transaction, Camille's had grown.

Camille smiled, shrugged, and, having won, held up her hands in mock surrender. She went off to put the phone back in Judith's purse. When she returned, she said, "Where's 308, anyhow?"

"What?"

"The 308 area code. That's what was dialed and I was wondering where it would be."

"I have no idea," Judith said, but, really, enough was enough, so she said, "Who, by the way, is Theo?"

"Theo? Well, there's a Theo Lane on the water polo team, if that's who you mean. He's Torry's go-to guy. At least he was."

"Until?"

"I don't really know." Camille's face was so placid and pretty and unruffled that it gave Judith a chill. She could almost guess what she was thinking. *Who, by the way, is Theo? How did we jump from a 308 area code to Theo?* Maybe not those exact words, but that would be the basic progression.

Usually when Camille returned to school, Judith's productivity improved, but this year, if anything, the opposite seemed true. When she wasn't at work, she tried to stay away from the storage room. She scheduled weekend outings with Malcolm and Camille—a drive to the beach, a visit to Huntington Gardens—but she was besieged by either headache or torpor. She fell asleep in the car during both outings.

Work incrementally worsened. One morning when she got to the studio, Lucy handed her a Post-it note that said, *Air date 12 days away, Judith, and line forming behind you. Where is the fucking show?!!!!* It wasn't signed. It didn't have to be. Everyone knew Pottle's left-leaning cursive.

"It was stuck to the middle of the monitor when I came in," Lucy said. She gave Judith a look of startling sincerity. "Do you think he's going to fire our asses?"

"I doubt it," Judith said, but the truth was, she was as uncertain about what Pottle might do as she was about the cuts she was making, as she was about the odd marital and parental thoughts she was having, as she was, in fact, about the entire termite-eaten life she was leading. Sunday, for the first time in years, she went to church, and felt as fraudulent there as she did at home and at work. She was sitting in the church parking lot wondering what to do next when her own cell phone rang. It was Malcolm calling to say he was taking Camille and some of her friends to a street festival in Santa Monica.

"If I understand correctly, someone's cousin is playing in a band called Snitch Is Rich," he said. "There will also be crap booth after crap booth." An old line of his. Then: "Would you like to join us?"

Judith declined, and added that she really needed to log some hours in the editing room. But she didn't drive to the studio. She drove to her storage room and plugged in the charger for her Edie Winks phone, which had gone dead. As soon as it had a partial charge, she checked for messages—none—then stretched out on the bed. She didn't even try to read. She folded her hands on her stomach and closed her eyes. She was dreaming—of what, she wouldn't remember—when the chords of Debussy began softly to sound.

Judith reached for her phone, flipped it open, and preposterously, recklessly, foolishly said, "Willy?"

After a long moment, a voice said, "Yeah. It's me."

It was his voice all right, slightly sagged with age. "Oh, Willy," Judith said in a tender fallen voice. "How are you?"

He was quiet for a few seconds. "I'm okay."

Something was happening. The room unhinged itself and, very slowly, began to revolve. She wanted to speak, but first she had to close her eyes.

Willy said, "I need you to do something for me, Judith."

Judith took three quick breaths in, expelled them, then eased open her eyes. To her relief, the room and everything in it was fixed, unmoving, normal-seeming again.

"Judith?"

"I'm sorry, Willy. What were you saying? You need me to do something?"

"Yeah, I do. I need you to come out here for me."

"What?"

"Yeah, I do. I need you to come see me."

"When?"

"Right away. I mean *right away.*"

Judith issued a small laugh. "You have no idea how impossible that is."

He didn't speak.

Judith said, "This really isn't a good time."

"It's the only time. Honest to God, Judy." His voice sounded faraway and small. "This is the only time."

2

Judith disliked telling lies as much as the next person, and yet here she was, telling lies right and left. Or rather, telling the same lie right and left. A friend of her mother's had called from Mexico. Her mother was in the hospital. She'd asked if Judith could fly down. "It sounds somewhere between urgent and life-threatening," Judith said to Lucy Meynke over the phone, "but I've got to go."

"Jesus, Judith. Hooper and Pottle'll go ape-shit. Have you talked to them yet?"

"No." She should have called them first, she knew that, and she made a sudden decision. "I'm writing Leo a note."

"Couldn't you send Malcolm or something?" Lucy said. "We're already behind on two shows and about to get a third, if they give it to us."

"I can't send Malcolm," Judith said. "And I can't not go."

The silence between them began to lengthen, and Lucy said, "Where do you fly into?"

This much Judith had prepared for. "León. Then a long taxi ride to San Miguel."

"God, Judith. This seems way beyond not good."

Malcolm was more understanding. It was no problem, he said. In fact, he could take a couple of days off and go along if she wanted him to. Leave Sonya in charge, she could handle it. When Judith said there was no need for that, he said okay then, but if Kathleen took a turn for the worse, Judith would call him, right? He could fly right down, no problem.

She mentioned that the cell phone probably wouldn't work in Mexico, but yes, she would definitely figure out a way to call if there was anything serious to report. They would go on the basis of no news is no news.

Alone in their room, she first took out the Briggs & Riley carry-on, which was best for flat packing, but decided finally on her leather shoulder bag, because it looked more casual and spur-of-the-moment, the kind of bag a person would throw things into if she was leaving in a hurry to see a sick parent.

Malcolm had ordered a service to take her to the airport, and the long black town car pulled quietly into the driveway several minutes early. From the entry, Malcolm gave the driver an acknowledging wave. The day was hot and brittle, the morning sun already harsh. Both Judith and Malcolm lingered back in the cooler shadows.

"I'm sorry this is all such a rush," Judith said. She glanced into the house, toward Camille's room, and felt a sudden rush of tenderness. She wished she could look at her and maybe take her hand while saying good-bye, but she was in school. So was Sonya, becoming a nurse. "You'll tell Milla how much I'll miss her, okay?"

"Sure." He gave her a small smile full of affection. "I'll also promise her you won't bring her a shellacked armadillo."

They'd done that once, coming back from Zihuatanejo. Camille, eleven or twelve at the time, had called it "a completely inappropriate present," and for a while it had taken its place on the rail of her balcony, where, especially at night and from a distance, it looked like a mammoth rat. Eventually one of Camille's girlfriends had cracked its shell by playing on it with drumsticks.

The driver, youngish, wearing a dark suit, courteously retrieved Judith's single bag and bore it toward the town car.

Malcolm turned to Judith. "Got everything? Watch, wallet, spectacles, and testicles?" Another old line of his.

"Three out of four," Judith said.

"Ticket?"

"Electronic."

"Passport?"

Passport? Why would she need a passport? Mexico. To go to Mexico. "Oh, my God. I can't believe it," she said. "I completely forgot it."

She glanced at the black car, engine idling, air conditioner running, but Malcolm strode back into the house and quickly returned, passport in hand. "You're in luck. Still current."

Judith tucked it into her purse and shook her head. She was sweating. "God," she said. "I'm so bad at this."

"Maybe," Malcolm said, leaning just slightly toward her, "but you're in the very high percentiles at everything else."

He seemed to expect something further, but the driver stood in the direct sun near the rear door of the car, taking in the view of the canyon, pretending patience. She couldn't wait. She had to go.

"I'll call when I can," she said, and she went. The driver, hearing footsteps, pulled open the wide rear door to receive her. It was cool inside, with a faint hint of lilac—it reminded her of the cooling room of that flower shop in Pasadena, Jacob Maarse, where they'd gone once to . . . but she couldn't remember why they'd gone there—and then the car began to roll smoothly forward and Judith suddenly understood that Malcolm had been wanting her to kiss him in the moment before she turned away, just lightly, on the cheek, but still a kiss, that was what he'd been waiting for, and she thought of that woman in Nebraska, Cordelia Guest, who as a small girl hadn't given her father his mouse kisses as he walked off to his last day of farming. Frantically she tried to find the button that would lower her window so she might at least blow him a small kiss, or wave good-bye, but by this time the car was turning onto the road and Malcolm was closing the front door of their house behind him.

3

In Los Angeles, the sullen heat had given the morning the clenching feel of summer, but six hours later, emerging from the doors of the small terminal building in Rapid City, Judith seemed to have stepped pleasantly into autumn. The yellowed leaves of the trees lining the grassy median, the vast blue-white sky, the faint sweet smell of cropland—all of it seemed consoling and hopeful. For a moment she could feel that some fantastic temporal elision had taken place, that this day followed by only a sunrise or two the morning twenty-seven years before when she had set out for Palo Alto and Willy Blunt had stood at the platform watching as the train strained forward and away. If Willy appeared before her now, smiling as he used to smile, the fastness of her embrace would be at least partly traced to this strange illusion of having reversed the irreversible.

But Willy did not step forward. No one did, other than the occasional traveler approaching from the parking lot. It made no sense, but she found herself scanning the scattered cars in the lot for Willy's faded red truck. She checked the exit before which she stood, and she checked her watch. She was where they had agreed to meet.

"Excuse me?"

She turned and saw a bearish man addressing a pretty young

woman in her early thirties. "You wouldn't be Judy, would you?"

The girl shook her head and moved purposefully away from the man, who stood watching her go.

Judith said to him, "Judy who?"

The man turned without surprise. "You Judy?" he said.

"Judy who?" Judith said again.

"Oh. Well, I don't know. My boss just asked me to pick up someone named Judy right here. From California. On Frontier Airlines."

"Judy or Judith?"

The man seemed confused. "Could've been Judith, I guess."

"Who's your boss?"

"Willy Blunt."

Judith glanced around. "And where is he?"

"He couldn't come." The man thought suddenly to remove his hat, which revealed a full head of closely cropped gray hair. "You wouldn't be her, would you?"

Judith couldn't help smiling. "Just exactly how did he describe this Judy or Judith, if you don't mind my asking?"

"He didn't, not really. That was the problem. He said she was fetching and that's all. Which you are, of course, if . . ." His voice trailed off and his face began to flush, which seemed to vex him further. "So are you her or not?"

Judith smiled professionally. "Yes. I'm Judith Whitman, and I've come to see Willy Blunt."

The man slapped on his hat and was already reaching for her leather bag. "Thisaway," he said, and headed toward the lot.

Judith thought the man would be easy to cartoon since he seemed composed of distinct shapes—big round head, broad sloping shoulders, large pear-shaped trunk. Bearish, really, a cartoon bear, ambling across the grassy median, ducking under a

373

limb of yellow leaves, carrying her soft leather bag into a mostly empty parking lot. He must have heard her following, or just presumed it, because he didn't look back until he'd reached a yellow sedan parked with its windows down and doors unlocked. The man swung Judith's satchel onto the back seat, then opened the passenger-side door for her. Judith looked at the front seat and at her bag in the back. "How do I know I'm not being abducted?" she said.

The man gave her a look of earnest confusion. "How do you know you're not being what, now?"

"You have the advantage of me. You know my name. What's yours?"

"Batch."

"Batch?"

He nodded. "Batch Batten."

"Well, Mr. Batten, tell me this. Why didn't Willy Blunt himself come?"

"He would've," the man said, and stopped as if this were a complete thought. He walked around the car, settled in behind the wheel, and started the engine. Judith actually considered writing down the car's license number, but then what? Give it along with a note to an employee inside the terminal? To be opened if ... if what? A man in California begins missing his wife who is in Mexico?

Judith slid into the car, and when Batch put on his seat belt, she did the same. The car was a Buick, and Judith had the sense it had just been to the car wash. Batch lifted open the console, where a half-dozen CDs stood on end in plastic slots.

"Your pick," he said.

There was a little of everything—Steve Earle, Lester Young, Johnny Mathis, Bruce Springsteen, Little Walter, and, preferring atmosphere to distraction, the one she selected, Vivaldi's *Four*

Seasons. A sticker on the case indicated it was the property of the Rufus Sage Public Library. By the time she adjusted the volume and fast-forwarded past the allegro of "Spring" to the slower second movement (which she loved), they were on the highway, traveling south. It was a quiet, smooth-riding car. The cornfields passed by, and so did fields where winter wheat had just begun tinting the brown earth green. *Glad,* she thought. *Glad I am here.* She turned to the bearish man beside her. A while ago she'd wondered if he might be taking her captive; now she felt he was helping her escape.

"So, Mr. Batten, are you a friend of Willy's?"

Batch nodded.

"But Willy's not feeling good today. Is that it?"

The man gave her a quick sidelong look. "Yeah. That's pretty much it."

"But he was feeling better yesterday?"

The man said he wouldn't say that.

"Last week? Was he feeling better last week?"

"You'll see when you get there."

These were curiously similar to Willy's own words when Judith had quizzed him about the urgency of her traveling out at short notice. *You'll understand when you get here.* Judith had said, "But what if I don't?" and Willy said simply, "You will, though."

"Where's *there?*" Judith said, and the man said, "What's that, now?"

"Where are we going?"

"Oh. Cabin of Willy's."

"Willy's got a cabin?"

Batch nodded.

"Where?"

"South of Rufus Sage."

"Does Willy still build houses?"

"Not so much anymore."

"So what does he do? With his time, I mean."

This time Batch gave Judith a look that was clearly discouraging. "You hungry?" he said.

She was, a little, she had to admit. On the plane she'd had nothing but tomato juice.

He reached behind the seat, pulled up a small red-and-white cooler, and set it on the console. "Help yourself," he said. "I already ate."

There was a sandwich—grilled pastrami and Swiss cheese on rye—along with a bottle of Budweiser packed in ice. After tasting the sandwich she said, "The Y Knot still in business?"

Batch nodded.

"And this came from there?"

This time he smiled as if he'd received a small compliment. "It sure did," he said.

By the time she'd finished the sandwich and the bottle of beer, Judith felt an even keener sense of well-being as she stared out at the countryside. Along this particular stretch of highway the earth looked dark and damp.

"Yeah," Batch said when Judith commented on this. "We got nothing at all in Rufus, but they got almost three inches up this way. I was listening to a couple of farmers talking there in the airport, and one of them says, 'Three inches is okay, but I'd lots rather had an inch a day for three days.'" Batch snorted through his nose. "Guess that's what makes us farmers."

"You're a farmer, then?"

"Was. I've worked for Willy over fifteen years now. You still worry about the weather in construction, but not near so much as farmers."

In an hour or so, the car reached Highway 20 and turned east toward Rufus Sage, and a pleasant curiosity began stirring in

Judith, so she was disappointed when Batch slowed at a county road and turned onto it, heading south, driving too fast for Judith's taste.

"I was hoping to take a quick look at town," she said. "Maybe pick up a couple of things." She wanted to see the downtown, and the Dairy Queen, and the park, and the house that had been her grandparents' and then her father's and now was hers. She hadn't seen any of it since her father's funeral.

Batch kept driving as if he hadn't heard her. It *was* drier here— the dust rose behind them—but the fields and farmhouses looked well tended, nicer than she remembered, in fact. Bethel Church appeared before them—the same graveyard, the same outhouses, the same neatly tended grass, the same beautiful gaunt white church, the place where Deena had wanted to be married, and perhaps had been.

"Could we stop a minute here?" Judith asked, but Batch didn't even begin to lift his foot from the accelerator. He said they were fighting time. He turned right, then left, around one farm or another, but their general bearing was south, toward the buttes. Presently they were driving along the remembered creek, through the remembered trees, past the remembered spring in the rocks, still running. The gates they used to open and close had all been swung open. A narrow graded road had more or less tamed the stretch where, years earlier, Willy had dodged trees and boulders and been so proud of his—the odd word suddenly popped into her head—*positraction*. Batch was finally driving slower now—he had no choice—and Judith lowered her window. The sound of the cicadas, the smell of the pines—it all caused a strange gathering of images and emotions within her. She would've liked to have walked. To get out and walk. They forded two more creeks, their streams down to a trickle, the rocks rattling under the tires. And then they splashed through one more slim creek and they were there, in that wide trampled space across the creek and at the base of the slope where they had stopped, she and Willy, that first night those many years before.

Batch Batten leaned back from the wheel and, turning to Judith, looked like a man who'd had worrisome work that now was done. "Willy said you'd know your way from here."

Judith looked up the hill and nodded. She got out of the car, lifted her bag from the back seat, and leaned into the passenger-side window.

"So are you coming back for me?"

Batch seemed perplexed by the question. "Why, sure."

"When?"

"Whenever you like, I guess."

"How do I get hold of you?"

"What?"

"How do I get hold of you? Do you have a cell phone?"

"Oh. No. Phones don't work up here at all. But Willy can get hold of me. He'll let me know."

"Okay," Judith said. She was beginning to feel a little funny about this whole enterprise. But before stepping away from the window she thanked Batch for driving her.

"Nothing to it," he said, and Judith stood back so he could make his three-point turn. Once reversed, he paused to lean out his window. "How long since you seen him?"

Judith told him.

"Okay, then," he said. "Be prepared." Then, eyes forward, he drove away.

Judith nudged the strap of her bag tighter to her neck so it bore more directly over her spine. She looked up at the hillside, listened to the low flutish sound of the wind. It wasn't cold or even cool yet, but it soon would be; she could feel it in the shadows. Prepared for what? she wondered. The pines began slowly to sway.

She wondered who, if anyone, might be watching her. Really, she thought, this would make a perfectly serviceable scene in your basic horror flick, but this wasn't a horror flick, was it? It was her movie. Real life. She began to walk.

The hill seemed longer than it had seemed in her memory, steeper, the soft covering of pine needles slicker underfoot. Once she slipped and broke her fall with her hand. Twice she stopped to regain her breath. Then something pleasant and reassuring: the breeze began to carry on it the smell of wood smoke and then, as she drew closer, the smell of cooking meat. She slowed as she approached the crest of the hill. Then, for no reason she understood, she crouched and eased forward so she could peer down unobserved.

What she saw was a surprise. Where there had once been nothing but a rough clearing there was now a sizable encampment containing several small, widely spaced log buildings with steeply pitched tin roofs. The grounds were raked and tidy. Smoke tailed up from a stone grill in the middle of the camp, and Judith's eyes followed a rock-lined path leading through the trees to a body of water where a red kayak and gray dinghy floated tethered to a wood dock. Mixed with the green pines were the yellowing leaves of cottonwoods and ash. The scene was almost unnatural in its perfection; it might be the cover of a catalogue trading in nostalgia and pricey Adirondack camp gear. But where was anybody? Where was Willy?

Judith knelt there in the pine needles, staring down. The smallest and most peripheral building was clearly an outhouse, and the largest seemed the most cabinlike—he could be in either one, she supposed. She waited. She crouched and listened to the birds and the insects and the low flutish wind, and she waited for something in the camp to move. Nothing did. The sun was lower. In half an hour, it would be dark.

Then, out of nowhere—it gave her a start—a voice called out: "Nobody's going to pounce you, if that's what you're worried about." It was Willy, it was unquestionably Willy, and she was happy to hear there was fun in his voice.

"Where are you?"

"Sitting down here watching you up there acting real odd."

His voice came from the direction of what might be a wood-shed. There, in its shadow, there might or might not be someone in dark clothing sitting in a chair.

"You coming down, then?" he said.

She picked up her bag, dusted off her pants, and started slowly down the slope. He must have sensed her uncertainty, for as she got a little nearer he stood and stepped into the dusky light. But this if anything increased her confusion. Willy had been lean; this man was bulky. He had been smooth and semi-handsome, and this man's face, what she could see of it, was coarsened and, a bad surprise, bloated looking. This man looked unwell, and *old*. But then as she drew close he tipped back the brim of his hat, and the smile that formed there made it Willy's face.

"Well, look at you," he said. He reached out a hand and touched her nose, softly, the way he used to do, and then she closed her eyes so he could touch her eyelids, first one, then the other. When she opened her eyes again, his smile was still brimming.

"So what did you do? Go out west and stop time? You look dangerous as you ever was."

She tried to think what to say about him. His skin seemed not only swollen but also to have taken a swarthy turn, as if from too much weather. "Yeah, well, you've got kind of a desperado look going there yourself."

His eyes slid away. When he wasn't smiling, he wasn't easy to look at. She turned and surveyed the camp, beautiful in the late slanting sunlight. "So you did it. Built the camp and filled the lake."

"Oh, yeah, I did it and then some," he said in a soft voice. He looked around, too, now. "Turns out I don't really like to lake-fish, so whenever I come up, I get to building something."

Judith kept scanning the property in wonderment. "Camp Blue Moon. I was going to make you a sign, I think."

She was suddenly aware of him standing there, looking at her, drinking her in. She turned to him and he made a smile and said, "You coming all this way . . ." His voice trailed off, but she knew what he meant. This was all as strange as strange could be.

Did she imagine that he leaned slightly toward her? It didn't matter. She stepped forward and he spread his arms and pulled her close and solid, and she felt suddenly different, better, much better in fact, because held close within his smoky smell, she could shut her eyes and imagine his forgiveness and listen to the hollow wind and smell the cookfire and slip back through the days and days and days.

Finally he relaxed his arms and released her. "Hungry?" he said.

"I wasn't until I smelled something cooking."

He moved his bulk toward the fire slowly, stiffly, as if bearing a weight just past his capacity. The rock fireplace stood at one end of a shaded retreat composed of a wooden framework and latticed roof, enclosed on three sides by stub walls of stone and mortar. Everything else was open. A small hammered copper bowl on the wooden picnic table was filled with wrapped peppermints. Above the fireplace proper was a grilling area, but the hinged grill had been lifted and secured so that two deep black cast-iron kettles could sit directly in the bed of coals. Hot briquettes had also been patterned on the kettle lids. Willy used long-handled tongs to set aside the coals from one of the lids, then lifted the lid with a doubled length of wire. An extravagant aroma of onions, beef, and tomatoes blossomed in the air.

"Good God," Judith said. "What is that? It smells fabulous." And then realized that *fabulous* didn't sound right here. She wouldn't use it again.

Willy murmured, "Chili," and set the lid back into place. Then he turned and was doing it again, drinking her in. "It is you," he said quietly, "and you are here."

Judith laughed. "It is, and I am."

A second or two passed, then she said, "This isn't the same plank table we used the first time I was here, is it?"

He shook his head. "That one gave out a long time ago. This is maybe the third one since then, but there's not much difference one to the other."

She looked around. "And what is this structure we're sitting in, anyhow? Is it a pergola or what? Or a summerhouse? In an Edith Wharton novel, it might be called a summerhouse."

Willy looked around at the enclosure as if to see whether Edith Wharton's ideas might alter his opinion of it, but they didn't seem to. "We never called it anything other than the plank-table area. If I sent the boys for something, I just said it's up to the plank table. It seemed simpler that way."

The sensibleness of this was unassailable, Judith had to admit, but, still, if it got into her movie, her character was going to call it the summerhouse.

Willy said, "We eat in five minutes." He pointed her toward a log building with a covered front porch and its own stone chimney. "That cabin's yours if you want to get comfortable."

The formality of this arrangement was fine by Judith—a relief, in fact. She'd wondered what Willy's expectations in this regard might be, and for that matter what her own expectations might be, especially in light of the Malcolm-and-Francine situation, whatever it was, but Willy's deterioration had been a shock, the changes in bones and tissue and muscle and blood so stark that it made the zealous physical element of their past seem almost preposterous, or unimaginable.

The cabin was a pleasant surprise. Every plane—floor, walls, and ceiling—was composed of wide pine boards, and the room's three windows were trimmed in a rich, high-sheen yellow. Nailed to the wall close to the door were a couple of coat hooks made from old horseshoes. Vintage suit quilts in browns and grays covered the metal bed. On a small wooden table, a red enamelware bowl sat alongside a white tin pitcher filled with water. A battery-operated lantern stood nearby. The top two drawers of a white chest had been emptied for her use, but Judith closed them and laid her leather bag on top of the chest. She was only staying a day or two. Why not just live out of her bag?

She brought out her cosmetics case, where she'd put the chargers for her phones, then, after looking around, put them away again. There was no electricity here. And—she checked—there was no signal for either phone anyway. She zipped the case closed and rooted through her soft leather bag for her sweater. Already it was turning cool.

When she came back out of the cabin, Willy sat by the fire sipping from a tin cup. On the plank table, he had moved aside the little bowl of wrapped peppermints and set out two plates, along with forks and knives, a loaf of bread, and two pie tins, one inverted and set on top of the other to form a closed container. There was also an iced drink in a red tin cup that matched Willy's.

"That's yours," he said, nodding toward it. "Thought you might like a little pick-me-up."

The idea of a predinner drink *was* appealing, and the iced

drink in its red cup stood there prettily, but when Judith took a sip, she gave an involuntary shudder. "Yikes," she said.

"Kind of stout?" Willy said.

"Would be an understatement. What is it?"

"Scotch and lime juice." He took an appraising sip of his own drink. "Not enough lime, maybe."

She took another sip, then set it back down. She looked at him and said, "So, Willy. How are you?"

He gave a dismissive kind of shrug. "I'm better here tonight than I was this morning," he said. Then he turned to his cooking duties in a manner clearly meant to abandon the subject. He sliced two slabs of bread from the loaf, one thicker than the other, and laid one on each of the plates. He took the plate with the thicker slice over to the black kettle, lifted the lid, and ladled chili generously onto the bread. He handed the plate to Judith and repeated the process for himself with the thinner slice, though he ladled less.

Judith looked at the generous portion he had given her and said, "Guess you remember my appetite in the great outdoors," and Willy, with something wry in his voice, said, "Oh, I remember, all right. "

When they were seated at the table, he uncovered the pie tin, which was filled with fresh sliced tomatoes. "They're late, but they're good," he said, and when she had taken some, he slid several slices off for himself.

They ate. Willy ate his tomatoes but took only an occasional bite of the cooked food. Mostly he sipped his drink and watched Judith eat. The chili, the bread, the fresh tomatoes—they were all delicious, and between bites Judith made a point of saying so.

Willy said he was happy she liked it. "Chili's kind of bland," he said. "I used to like it downright tangy, but not anymore."

"No, it's just right." She leaned back and looked around at the buildings in dark profile, the path parting the forest and giving a line of sight down to the water, already mirroring the half-moon.

"Tomorrow you'll have to show me the lake," she said.

"It's not real big," he said. "But it's big enough for my uses." He rose and took her empty plate. When he started to dish her out another portion, she said, "Just a little," and took another sip of her drink, better now, diluted a little by the melted ice. "How do you get ice up here?"

He set her plate down full. "Little propane fridge." He nodded toward another cabin. "That's where the kitchen is. But that's the only convenience. The stove's wood-burning and there's no running water."

There was a wooden cabinet snugged into a corner of the picnic structure. Willy pulled a bottle of scotch from it and made no attempt whatever to hide the size of the drink he poured himself. While he was doing this, he mentioned that he had installed a solar-heated shower. "A fella doesn't have to get too terrible rank," he said, "as long as the sun shines." He didn't go for ice. That's what made his drinking quiet. She took another bite of chili and said, "Who made the bread?"

"Oh, that would be my personal chef." He looked exaggeratedly around. "Now where'd he go off to?"

This pleased Judith. It was cornily funny in the way Willy had always been cornily funny. "So I guess the wood-burning stove's got an oven?"

It did, Willy said, but he made the bread right here in a Dutch oven. He nodded at the black kettle the chili had been cooking in.

"That's a Dutch oven?"

"Why, sure. What did you think it was?"

"I don't know—a black kettle, I guess. I've always heard of

Dutch ovens, but I never really knew what they were. I always imagined something with a front door on it."

This seemed to amuse Willy. He took one of the peppermints from the bowl on the table, tugged each end of its wrapper, watched it twirl open. "My father showed me how to cook with it a little bit that time we went up on the Madison River." He set the peppermint into his mouth. "You remember me telling you about that?"

Judith did.

"Well, my father told me that one summer when he was a boy during the thirties, when everybody's farms just about blew away, my grandfather stayed on the place to do what he could and my father and his mother went up into the Black Hills to live in a campground, and the only way they cooked was with their Dutch oven. My father told me that was the happiest time of his life, sleeping in a tent and fishing all day and cooking in a Dutch oven every night." Willy shook his head and made a small snorting laugh. "And then Frankie grew up and became Frank and strapped that fucking farm on his back."

So. The feud with his father still simmered. Somehow this was no surprise. "Is he still alive?"

"I guess. More or less."

Seconds built toward a minute, then Judith said, "You know, sometimes I would call your folks' number and not say anything but just listen to your mother say hello." She shook her head. "I don't know why I did it, so don't ask, but what got me was one night your father said hello and when I didn't say anything, he said, 'Willy, is that you?' and there was something terrible in his voice, like you'd gone missing and were presumed dead or something."

Even in the dim light Judith could see Willy's face close down. He gave a low, grudging laugh. "'Presumed dead' is a good way to put it. Presumed dead was kind of how Frank viewed me there for a long time." He sipped from his cup. "After you left, he wanted me to come back to the farm worse than ever. Then when I took up with Deena, he went to work on her, and let me tell you, he was a bulldog—he had Deena about half talked into it. And every time I went around there, he'd start up on it and wouldn't let go, so I stopped going around. Then my mother tried to patch things up and got him to say he wouldn't talk about it, but then I'd go around and after a little while he'd just turn stone quiet and in the silence it was like I could hear exactly what he was thinking, every argument he had ever made about this being the Blunt family farm and this being a Blunt's rightful place in the world and there being boys working night and day to get the kind of start that was being gift-wrapped for me, on and fucking on. So one Sunday we drove away from there and I said to Deena that she could do what she wanted, but I was giving my word I was never setting foot on that farm again."

The little breeze had quit, and the trees were quiet. Crickets chirped, and a low croaking of frogs carried up from the lake.

"And you didn't set foot again?"

He seemed surprised by the question. "Of course I did not." He sucked on the peppermint. "Oh, a few times I drove Deena and the boys up, but I didn't get out of the truck. I just let them out and went into town until it was time to pick them up again. While I sat waiting for Deena to get the boys and their stuff together, my mother would come out to the truck to talk to me through the window, but Frank just stayed back on the porch looking at me, so I stopped even doing that."

After a moment, Judith said, "God, Willy."

"Yeah, well. It couldn't hardly be helped." He sipped from his cup and said, "My mother was a sweetheart, though. She came down to Grand Lake and stayed with us from time to time, always making things easier for Deena and doing things with the boys. They made doughnuts pretty often, I remember." He began to unwrap another peppermint. "Those were good doughnuts. And summers she'd make peach ice cream. Anyway, she got cancer and that was that. Frank got pretty shaky for a while there. That was probably when you got him to answer the phone."

"And you still didn't go to the farm?"

Willy just stared off—his way, she understood, of saying no, he never did, he'd given his word. A silence stretched out and filled with the sounds of the night.

"Deena didn't try to talk you into it?"

"Oh, she did, sure, but Deena was never very good at talking me into things."

Another second or two passed.

"Not even marriage?"

A robust snorting laugh issued from Willy. "Well, you should know something. That was my misbegotten idea."

"And who set the date of the ceremony?"

"Oh, that was me, too. Deena knew what I was doing. She didn't care for it much, if I read her right."

Judith took this in. "And how is Deena?"

"All right, I think. Here lately we don't see a lot of each other, to tell you the truth. But she was a good mother to those boys. Lots better than I thought she'd be. I was okay with them, nothing great, but okay, especially after they could do a few things and before they thought they knew everything. Ages six to twelve, say. Those years were okay. We shot baskets and went fly fishing and I taught them some carpentry—not much, but a little. For a while there, we were pretty good together. It was a good diversion for me. Then they got into the teenage years. They began to look at me like I was a stranger, and pretty soon I was one. Maybe it's different with mothers and daughters."

"Not much," Judith said. "My mother told me once that parenting is just ten million baby steps toward estrangement."

Willy laughed at this. A silence followed, but it was an easier silence. After a time, he said, "Frank's been wheedling the boys to go up and work the farm, and they might just do it, though they don't say so to me." A pause. "They grew up and got slyer. When they were littler, they were just mean. I understood that better."

Willy rose, shoveled the coals into the fireplace, and added kindling, which quickly ignited. He then laid in larger pieces of split pine, and the flames soon took hold and spread. The wood crackled with such clarity it seemed artificially amplified. Pine wood. He'd said something about it back then. All talk but poor heat—something like that. Judith turned up the collar of her sweater, which was too light for the weather. She'd forgotten how the temperature could drop. She pulled her chair closer to the fire, as he had, so that now, when she stretched her legs, their feet lay within inches of one another.

"Okay," she said. "This is good." And it was. The warm stone fireplace, the chorus of crickets and frogs, the rising view of tall pines and stars pulsing in a black sky—it was elemental and good and it produced in Judith a kind of buoyant calmness. As another silence stretched pleasantly out, she said, "Melinda."

"What?"

"I just remembered the name of that statuesque bank clerk in town. Melinda something. Ed Edmundson would"—she thought of saying what he really did—"drool like a rabid dog whenever she came into the Dairy Queen."

"Melinda Payne," Willy said.

"Right. Deena used to say she had 3-D breasts because they looked like they'd poke your eyes out." Judith stared into the fire. "I always wondered if they were real."

A few seconds passed and Willy said, "They were, yeah."

"What?"

"They were the real thing, all right, if that's what you were wondering."

"And you know this how, exactly?"

"Just do." He sipped from his cup. "This was after you ceased and desisted, just in case you're wondering about that, too." Then: "There's lots of women who see somebody's heart run over by a truck and they think they can put it together again."

Judith decided to ignore the runover-heart metaphor and said laughingly, "Maybe that's just your way of explaining away the behavior of a wide-ranging fornicator."

Willy said maybe it was and maybe it wasn't.

After another little while he said, "She married Ed Edmundson, you know."

"What? She married Mr. Ed?"

"Yep. He became a Dairy Queen tycoon of some kind. Well, maybe not tycoon, but he had six or seven of them. That seemed to have some effect on her. I can't snigger at what he did. For a time there I worked like a dog, thinking if I could just make enough money ..." His voice trailed off.

A shifting of the fire, followed by some crackle and pop.

"I did make me a pot of money, but by the time I did ..."

Judith felt a terrible ambivalence about this topic. She didn't know what to say, or, if she tried, what tone to say it in. She said, "What?"

"I knew it didn't matter." Willy had a length of steel rebar he used to poke the fire, which he did now. Then he settled back again. "You know once when Deena and I were having a row, she said, 'So what would you do if you heard Judith got a divorce? Go out and get one, too?' and you know how in the heat of the moment you say the kind of true things you normally wouldn't, and I said, 'That's right, I would, by the next business day.'"

Judith waited.

"Deena laughed. I'll say this—you will never hear her laugh so hard as when it pops up from pure, one hundred percent scorn. She said that showed her exactly how stupid you had made me, because you would marry ten more bankers before you'd come back here and marry me." This time Willy was quiet a little longer before he spoke again. "You know what I did? I looked her right in the eye and said, 'That's not true.'" He drew in a deep raspy breath of air, then expelled it. "'Course, that was a long time ago."

Judith didn't say anything. What could she say? That she wouldn't have married ten bankers before coming back to him? That she would only have married two?

Willy said, "Deena used to say she saw the actual Judith and I only saw the dream one. I didn't believe that either." After another silence, he said, "I'll tell you the tipping point, if you want to hear it. One afternoon I was in a bar in Grand Lake. We'd been framing a house, but a big old lightning storm came through, so we packed it in. Everybody on my crew had places they wanted to go but me. So I was in this bar I knew. The Elkhorn. The storm had also stopped this fella who was on his Harley-Davidson, headed for Washington State, I think it was. Every now and then he'd go to the front window, look out at the lightning and rain, and come back to the bar muttering. Him and me got to talking, and before long I'm telling him all about you and how I was going to make all this money to win you back, and right then, hearing myself say it out loud, was when I knew it wouldn't make any difference at all." Willy breathed heavily in, and the rasp was there, Judith heard it clearly. "It turned out this fella had his own problems, beyond the weather. He was some sort of history buff, and he said that all his life he wanted to publish a book about . . . hell, I don't remember, cliff-dwelling Indians or something, and then when he finally did, he wondered what the fuss was all about. He said, 'You think you're going to be somebody else, but you're not. You're still just you.' He seemed pretty disappointed about it all. He said, 'So here I am sitting in a bar halfway between someplace I didn't want to be and someplace I don't want to go.'" Willy chuckled to himself. "That bird and me got to drinking pretty hard after that."

He rose to put a few more pieces of wood on the fire. He adjusted the cushion on his chair, sat back down, sipped from his cup. Judith waited. She had the feeling he wanted to say more. He wanted to speak. He'd been thinking about these things for twenty-seven years and now he wanted to speak. Pretty soon he said, "For a while there, I thought that you took my blood and left me a zombie, but it was different from that. It was more like you took away my *right now.* You gave me a past, and for a while, when I thought you might come to your senses and wander back, I had a kind of a future to think about, but the right now was gone, the right now was what you'd taken away." In the light of the fire he seemed to be smiling unhappily. "I substituted alcohol."

Blaming her for his drinking didn't seem quite fair, but the other business, the right-now business, made her too sad to want to refute it. She said, "We were so young, Willy."

"No, we weren't," he said with a sudden low vehemence. He gazed off toward the trees and the lake. "I wasn't, anyhow."

Perhaps a minute passed, and there was nothing but the sounds of the fire and the night. In a softer voice Willy said, "There's some way you can compute the temperature by the number of chirps a cricket makes in a minute, but I never can remember it."

Judith started to count but saw the hopelessness of it, so they both sat listening, and then Willy said, "Once my folks argued off and on almost all of one winter about whether you could predict the next year's rain from the size of a woolly worm in the fall. My mother kept politely saying you could, and Frank kept saying you couldn't. He said all a fat woolly worm could tell you was that there had been plenty of food for a woolly worm to get fat on. I wanted my mother to be right, but I knew she wasn't."

They kept talking and sitting, and Willy kept sipping his scotch and poking the fire and feeding in logs, until finally Judith could hardly hold her head up. She turned her watch to the fire-light. "It's past midnight, Willy."

"You should throw that thing away," he said.

"I'm turning in."

He kept looking at the fire as if his mind were still prowling and he hadn't quite said all he had to say, but she was too tired for it. She carried a flashlight down to the outhouse, which, to her surprise (and relief), smelled only of damp, freshly dug earth. As she walked back through the encampment, Willy emerged from her cabin carrying a lamp.

"Got the fire going for you," he said as their paths crossed. "Just to take the chill off. I meant to do it sooner."

She nodded and thanked him and said she was sure it would be fine.

"Holler if you need anything," he said, a sentence open to interpretation, so she laughed and said, "I will if I do, but I won't."

She was at her door when he called, "Sleep tight."

She looked back at him, reflected there in the firelight, and found to her surprise that already she was almost accustomed to his bulk and change. "Thanks," she said, "I think I will."

In the cabin, she found he'd hung an old Levi's jacket from one of the horseshoe hooks. The burning wood crackled nicely, and Judith again had the strange sense that everything here was slightly amplified, or was it that her ears were suddenly open to it all? She didn't know, and it didn't matter. All that mattered was that she had come, she was here, and she was glad she was. She undressed in the fitful light of the fire and slipped into bed. The sheets were flannel, freshly laundered, perhaps even new. She pulled them close, and for a pleasant few moments the plank floor and plank walls and plank ceiling allowed her to imagine that she lay within a beautiful toy box, and then, almost before she could have another thought, she had fallen to sleep.

When she abruptly awakened during the night, the fire was down to embers, the moon through the trees cast swaying shadows onto the cabin walls, and three simple chilling words, years and years in storage, were suddenly upon her: *There. It's done.*

There. It's done.

Simple and chilling and brutal.

But brutal had been the only way, hadn't it? She didn't know. It had seemed so. And yet.

Before she left for Stanford, she and Willy made arrangements to talk by telephone every Sunday night, and initially these calls, along with a regular exchange of letters and cards, afforded Judith a kind of loose, easy lifeline to that time and place that was theirs. But time passed. A metamorphosis had begun in Palo Alto, and the change came at Willy's expense. Judith loved going to foreign movies at the Varsity or the Park, and talking about books and movies in coffeehouses, and going to lectures in warm wood-paneled halls filled with clever kids and urbane adults. Occasionally, and without really intending it to happen, Judith would allow images of Willy to impose on these settings—of Willy plinking bottles with his rifle, of Willy pulling plywood fast to two-by-fours with bursts of a nail gun, even of Willy standing over Mr. Minnert with the shovel—and these juxtapositions unsettled her, and made her wonder how Willy might fit into the life she saw forming before her. It was not at all that simple, she would later

394

see, but at age eighteen, carried along on the currents of college life, it seemed that simple. The Sunday night conversations with Willy grew more labored, dutiful, irritating even. She felt more like talking to her friends or her roommate, a sweet and smoothly beautiful Chinese girl from Hawaii who spoke in a silky low register and seemed to subsist on little other than fresh carrots and oranges. The difference between conversations with Willy and conversations with her new friends was the difference between hiding and sharing, between crimping down and opening up. Still, through the winter term, Judith was in her room at seven o'clock every Sunday night to take Willy's call and her roommate would discreetly slip out until the call was over. Then one Sunday afternoon Malcolm Whitman and some friends stopped by to see if Judith and the roommate wanted to ride along to a blues club in Oakland. Judith presumed her exotic roommate had inspired the visit from these jocular, loose-jointed boys and so was surprised when they didn't retreat once the roommate demurred. The boys stayed on, cajoling her, talking up the band, the place, the barbecued ribs. "A *sterling* day for a drive," Malcolm added, and she smiled, not at the remark but at the sudden notion that these boys, in a different time and place, might have run in Amory Blaine's crowd. Malcolm stood to the side, a tall thin boy with long, beautifully groomed hair, regarding her intently. Judith remembered her scheduled telephone conversation with Willy and said she was sorry, she'd really like to go but she needed to be home early to study. Before this could become the moment in which the boys finally surrendered, Malcolm gently cleared his throat. He was driving, he said, and he was *officially* putting her in charge of departure time. When his friends murmured in protest, he grinned at them and said, "Oh, shush now."

All she could remember of the club was that it was dark and warm and throbbed with music. Eli's, it was called. Eli's something, with a mix that night of savvy-seeming black people and two or three tables of white college kids. She liked it there, especially after a while, once she'd begun to feel the repetitive pulse of the music encircle the room and pull it toward what she wanted to believe was a pleasant state of suspended differences. Judith's group drank draft beer and ate ribs and coleslaw. Malcolm was attentive to her. She had forgotten her watch, but every now and then—between songs, for example—she was suddenly aware that time was passing, lots of it. "Do you need to go?" Malcolm would ask, leaning close enough for his long hair to brush her bare arm. Yes, she did need to go, but what she said was, "Not yet." Finally she recognized that possibility had hardened to fact: she was staying. Until that moment she had drunk only one bottle of beer so that when she talked to Willy she would seem her normal somber Sunday-night self, but now she ordered another beer, and she remembered how, after quickly drinking half the bottle, she tilted her chair back so that the front legs lifted slightly from the floor.

It was nearly 2 A.M. when she returned to the dorm, and her roommate was asleep in her twin bed. The room smelled pleasantly of oranges. The phone had been unplugged. On a notepad beside the phone, her roommate had written:

> *Your friend Willy called 7 p.m.*
> " " *8* "
> " " *9* "
> " " *10* "
> *Disconnected phone after last call.*
> *(blotto-slurry)(him not me!!)*

And this was when, looking at the note from her roommate, Judith had thought, *There. It's done.* She had known Willy wouldn't call again, and wouldn't write again, and he hadn't.

Perhaps six weeks later, Judith had slipped from her neck the silver chain that held the ring, and then spent a long, teary Sunday afternoon writing a letter that tried, ineffectually she knew, to tell Willy how sorry she was. The next day she had put the letter and the ring into a padded envelope and sat on a bench near a mailbox for more than an hour before finally walking over and pushing the envelope inside.

Judith tilted her watch to catch the moonlight: 2:40. So she hadn't been asleep long. She rose from her bed—she felt the cabin's sharp chill—and stole to the window to peer out. Willy still sat near the plank table, cup in hand, staring into the fire.

4

The next morning Judith dressed quickly in the cold, pulled on the denim jacket hanging on the wall—the fit was fine—and found Willy already poking at the coals in the rock fireplace. The effect of the bright morning light on Willy's appearance was a shock. What had passed for swarthiness the night before now seemed more an odd, unnatural yellow-brown cast. For one preposterous moment she wondered if he'd applied Man Tan, or whatever the current version of Man Tan might be. But of course Willy would never do such a thing, so the odd color must have to do with whatever his unwellness was.

"So did you stay up all night or finally go to bed?" she said.

"How's that?"

"I woke up in the night, and when I looked out, you were still down here tending your fire. And now you're here again."

"Oh, I finally turned in." He shifted to face her directly. It was meant, she guessed, as a frank presentation, so she resisted averting her gaze. Besides everything else, the strange cast extended faintly even to his blue-gray eyes, which now seemed faded. "How about you?" he said. "How'd you sleep?"

"Fine. The bed's comfy, and it's such a beautiful room."

He was nodding, but she had the feeling his eyes were looking further, searching, though for what exactly, she couldn't say.

On the table he'd set out a slab of sliced bacon in brown butcher paper, a plastic bucket of eggs, and several more fat tomatoes. "I'll help," she said, "but first . . ." She pointed toward the outhouse.

When she returned, bacon was sizzling in a heavy black skillet, and the aroma was heavenly. She began slicing tomatoes. "So has that privy ever been used?" she said.

"The privy proper, yes, but that's a new location for it. Batch and a couple of boys dug the pit day before yesterday. In your honor, you could say." He nodded at something propped against a post she hadn't seen the night before: a shovel with a roll of toilet paper slid onto its short handle. "I prefer something a little more portable myself."

"Very deluxe," she said—one of Malcolm's phrases. She felt a slight pang that until this moment she hadn't thought of him since she'd arrived here.

Willy had percolated coffee and she poured herself a cup. "There's sugar and cream powder in that cupboard," he said, pointing toward the cabinet where he'd gone the night before to refill his cup. There, besides a small carton of sugar envelopes and another of powdered Coffeemate packets, Judith found two quarts of red-label Johnnie Walker, both full, and a quart of Gilbey's gin, half empty. At the table, she stirred a packet of creamer into her coffee and said, "So how does it work? Gin before noon and scotch after?"

"Something like that," Willy said. He cracked four eggs into the skillet and they began to sputter and bubble.

"Is that what's made you sick?"

He'd been patting the eggs with a spatula but stopped now to look at her looking at him. "You're not going to start in on me now, are you? Because it wouldn't be a good use of our time. I'm way past that."

He'd grilled bread in butter, and set a slice on her plate and one on his own, along with the fried eggs and several strips of crisp bacon. He broke off a small piece and began to chew. She couldn't shake the feeling that something was on his mind, some question to which he hoped to find the answer without asking for it.

"So it's going to get you?" she said.

He made a small smile. "Oh, yeah, it's going to get me all right." Then: "Look, Judith. My guess is, all of us find our own special ways to do ourselves in."

Judith didn't like the sound of that. "What about the old duffer who'll be a hundred and eleven this Tuesday? What's his weapon of choice?"

Willy sniggered. "Boredom, probably."

Okay, Judith thought, *I kept my mitts off for twenty-seven years, I can keep my mitts off now.* She listened to the soft sounds of the trees for a while, then she said, "When I woke up this morning, it took a second to remember where I was, and when I thought, *Oh, I'm at the camp with Willy,* my whole body seemed to relax at the thought of it." Then: "I think happiness is the hardest thing in the world to put your finger on, but for those few seconds, realizing where I was, I felt purely happy." Their eyes met and he began to nod a little, more at ease, and she thought that, for a second or two, anyway, she'd freed him from his other, more morbid thoughts or questions, whatever they were.

He said, "So are you going to eat what I cooked you or just look at it?"

She was surprised at how hungry she was. She ate intently, and finally, after sopping up egg yolk with the last of her bread, she looked up to find him regarding her with what appeared to be amusement.

"I don't always eat like that," she said.

"Well, if you did, and kept small as you are, people would talk."

She laughed. "About what?"

"Bargains with the devil, that kind of stuff." He finished what was in his cup and stretched his arms. "Want to take a stroll down to the pond?"

It was far more than a pond, Judith thought, if slightly less than a full-blown lake; the opposite shore seemed suitably distant. The dock, with a flat-bottomed dinghy tethered on one side and a sleek red kayak on the other, still lay in shade, as did a small cabin tucked perhaps twenty yards away among pines. Like all the other little log buildings in the compound, it was simple, unprepossessing, inviting. On its porch, oars and paddles protruded from the top of an old wood barrel. An array of safety vests hung from nails on the wall, most of them bright orange, two or three of them old and faded.

Judith, touching the fabric of one of the older vests, said, "What're these? Nautical artifacts?" and was sorry to hear herself sounding like Malcolm.

But Willy took no offense. "Oh, they're still functional in their own way. They still work well enough for my purposes, plus Deena thought they were decorative."

"I like them," Judith said. At this moment she decided that if the plank-table area was the summerhouse, then this was the boathouse. She stepped inside and found it as chilly as out-of-doors, and without much in the way of furnishings: a wood-burning stove, some shelves of books and board games, and a pine table and chairs that looked handmade. Nearly the whole of one wall was taken by a set of mullioned windows giving onto the lake. She said, "Well, if this isn't just about my favorite room in the whole world, I don't know what is."

Willy scanned the room, then rubbed his neck. "I don't know about that," he said, grinning, "but I can tell you that if you spend a cold winter's day in here with just a bottle for company, you can get a helluva lot of brooding done."

Judith drifted to the books—lots of titles by Louis L'Amour and Tom Clancy—and the stack of games. "Oh my God," she said, "you've got Pay Day!" She pulled it out from the others. "Let's build a fire and play Pay Day!"

"Why not?" Willy said, and though she expected him to, he didn't add that that was the motto where he came from. While Judith laid out the board, money, and cards, he adjusted the stove damper and began crumpling sheets of an old newspaper. He followed that with cardboard, dry twigs, and slightly larger pieces of wood, then lit a match to the paper and watched the fire work its way up from one element to the next. When he sat at the table to play, she saw that his enamelware cup had again been filled, though from what source, she couldn't say.

Still, he didn't guzzle his liquor. He took small, widely spaced sips, his own alternative, Judith thought, to an IV drip. He began to survey the Pay Day playing board; the days of a month were brightly blocked out with instructions like "Mail" and "Deal" and "Found a Buyer" on random squares. Finally he said, "So what does a fella have to do to win?"

"Have the most money," Judith said. "Be the biggest capitalist pig."

"All righty then," Willy said. "I can be every bit as piggish as the next fella."

Judith suggested a two-month round for starters, and though Willy had never played the game before, he seemed to find it amusing, the Deal cards in particular, a number of which had been customized by former players. "The Double-Dee Bra Shop," he announced after looking at one card. And then, smiling, upon completing his purchase: "It's not every day you get to buy your-self a bra shop."

"Guess your sons were the ones tampering with the cards."

Willy said it looked like their brand of humor, all right, and she remarked that the apple didn't fall far from the tree.

Pay Day was a game that Milla had received on her sixth or sev-enth birthday, and in addition to Sorry and Chinese checkers, it was one of the few tabletop activities that Judith, Malcolm, and Milla all enjoyed. Almost immediately Malcolm had recognized that all Deals—offers of something for sale—should be purchased early in the game, and over time Milla and Judith had learned to follow this strategy, too.

The stove warmed the room quickly, and Judith soon shrugged out of her jacket. "No need to stop there," Willy said.

"Think you'll be making randy remarks from your deathbed?" Judith asked, and Willy said he certainly hoped so. Judith's next roll landed her on Mail. "Maybe it's from Deena," she said.

Willy said, "Maybe it's from ... what's your hubby's name again?"

"Malcolm."

"Maybe it's from him, then."

"Nope," Judith said, reading the card. "It's from my semiliter-ate, make-believe son saying Camp Snakebit is g-r-a-t-e."

After the first game, which Judith won handily, Willy said, "Except for losing, I liked that game. 'Course, with you shedding clothes on the other side of the table, I'd probably like tiddly-winks."

Judith was enjoying herself. She felt good. She asked him if he wanted to play again but make it a three-month game this time.

"Why not?" He stretched lazily. "Only this time let's play for something."

"Like what?"

He leaned back and looked out at the water, glinting now in the midmorning sun. "If I win, I chuck your watch in the lake."

She glanced at her watch, a Cartier. "My watch cost a little something, Willy."

"But you don't know how much exactly."

"No."

"Because it was a gift."

"Yes."

"Tell you what, then," he said. "I won't chuck it in the drink. I'll just put it away for safekeeping."

She nodded, glad to have the subject of the watch behind her. "And if I win, you tell me a secret."

"What kind of secret?"

She smiled. "Up to you. But it better be good."

He shrugged and began shaking the die in his cupped hands. He seemed strangely complacent. Confident, even.

"Are you gaming me here, Willy? Are you some kind of Pay Day Zen master?"

"Until a half-hour ago, I'd never played Pay Day in my life," he said, which was no doubt true, but the game that followed proved him a quick learner. He no longer gambled. He no longer took the high-interest Pay Day loans. At the front end of the game he purchased every Deal available (including those for "Le French Tickler Shoppe," "Fred's Food Cuisine," and "Captain Caveman's Fossil Beds & Chairs"), and before the thirty-first day of the third month, which marked the end of the game, he'd found a buyer for them all. "Okay," he said, clearly enjoying himself. "I guess now we count up our cash and our savings, then subtract our loans." He gave her a smirky grin. "Not that I have any."

Judith didn't bother counting. She handed over the Cartier,

watched him slip it carelessly into his jacket pocket, and wondered if she'd ever see it again.

After their noon meal, they went out on the lake. Willy retrieved two of the newer life vests, gave one to Judith, and strapped on the other one.

"Guess you never got around to those swimming lessons, huh?" Judith said.

He inhaled to fasten the last snap. "No, I never did."

The bright orange of the vest made his skin seem even yellower. "I was going to give you swimming lessons," she said, "and you were going to teach me to fish."

"That's true. That was how it was going to be."

The water lapped against the dock; the boats rocked gently. Willy broke the silence by saying, "Let's take the kayak."

It was a perfect autumn day, cool in the shade, warm in the sun, which cast down on the lake from a southerly angle.

He sat in the back—"Beauty in the front, weight in the stern," he said—and held the dock to steady the kayak while Judith settled herself forward. The craft wasn't what she expected. It had low-slung seats, for one thing, and for another the forward seat was turned to face the rear. The arrangement seemed friendly but impractical. "How do we paddle?"

"Don't," Willy said.

"Then how do we go?"

He took hold of the lever in front of him, and—this could not have been more surprising—the slender boat gently reversed from the dock and then moved forward into open water. It was almost completely silent. They might've talked in a whisper.

"How do you do that?"

He nodded toward a wooden housing before him. "It's called a PowerYak. There's a little battery-powered motor under there." He scanned the small lake with evident satisfaction. "I used to like to paddle, but it got to be too much for me. I built a runabout with a little inboard motor, but the noise spoiled things. I like the quiet. So I built this."

"You built it?"

"Yeah. I built a bunch of little boats. The boys and me, mostly. We'd start one out in the garage in the winter, and when things warmed up in the spring, we'd put it in the water. We made a couple of one-man canoes, a sailboat, a drift boat. That dinghy back there at the dock. Once we made a little paddleboat for the two boys."

A different life, and peeking into it made her feel both better and worse, relief that he'd had it, regret that she hadn't. "Sounds like fun," she said.

He made a murmuring sound. "The boys don't come here anymore. Haven't since they got into their teens." He gazed off across the lake. "There were good periods there, though, with the boys. And with Deena, too, to be fair about it. But sometimes, I'll tell you. Last Christmas the boys wanted some fancy video thing—cost a small fortune—and Deena wanted an expresso maker, except she kept telling me it was *e*spresso, not *ex*presso, and it was not just any old expresso maker but an Italian one, and when I said, why in God's name would we want an Italian expresso maker, she looks at me and says, 'It doesn't just make espresso, Willy. You can make cappuccino, too. It comes with a *frother.*'" He shook his head. "I don't know a lot, but I know this much. The more fancy shit you put in your house, the weirder your life gets."

Judith laughed and suggested that Bartlett's would be all over that one.

Willy said, "'Course, it's true I brought home a lot of weird fancy power tools." He seemed to be considering this. "That was my profession, though. Deena wasn't starting up a damned doughnut shop or something."

406

"So what did you do?"

"About what?"

"The fancy video game and the espresso maker?"

"Oh. Gave them all something else. Coats from Cabela's. Nice ones. Pretty close to blizzard-proof." He emitted air that was half wheeze and half snigger. "Those coats weren't well received. Turned everybody quarrelsome, in fact. I had to go out and find a place to drink in peace."

Judith laughed at what was funny in this and discarded the implications of what was not. The kayak cut smoothly through the water. She closed her eyes and after a few seconds said, "We're like a swan gliding."

Perhaps a minute passed. Then from overhead came a sudden muffled shuffling, and Judith snapped open her eyes. Three descending ducks skidded onto the lake, tucked their wings, and settled into themselves. The water rippled, then resumed its calm. Nobody spoke, which added to the effect. She took off her life vest to use for a headrest, then leaned back, tilted her face to the sun, closed her eyes, and said, "Mmm." She could feel Willy looking at her, but it didn't bother her. It felt as pleasant as the pale sun. She kept her eyes closed and listened to the calming sound of the kayak moving through the water. The stillness was so deep and ongoing that when Willy finally spoke, it gave her a start.

"Want to make a stop?"

He was looking toward a small inlet and a second dock.

"Whose is that?" she said.

"Mine. Or really the boys'. They built it. They wanted their own private place."

As Willy guided the kayak to the dock, another small building came into view, one that at first seemed to be set back among the trees, and then she saw that it was actually up *in* a tree, a massive cottonwood, so it was a tree house, and a stylish one at that. On the dock, Willy knelt to secure the kayak to a cleat. She looked away while he pushed himself up onto his feet.

"The boys called this area Tennessee," he said. "I don't know why. They would just say, 'We're going to Tennessee,' and take some bologna sandwiches and get in their canoes and paddle over here."

Judith wandered up toward the cottonwood that supported the tree house. The path was overgrown, and though the tree house had been neglected, it seemed unusually attractive. The roof and sides were wood-shingled, and the window openings were cross-hatched with slender pieces of wood to suggest windowpanes. They'd cheated a little for support: a long post stilted down to the ground from one floating corner of the platform.

"How did they get up there?" Judith asked.

Willy had been following along, stopping every few paces to take a breath or two. He pointed a finger up at something in the tree. "See that? It's a rope ladder, but it's hooked over there to the opposite tree so you got to climb up there first and let it swing down. The boys said it was their way of keeping the Indians out." He smiled. "I went to the trouble of climbing up there one time. Turned out what they wanted to keep the Indians from seeing was their little stash of girlie magazines."

After they walked back to the dock, the rasp in Willy's breath seemed more pronounced, and Judith suggested they sit for a bit. There was one old wooden chair, which she declined and instead walked out onto the sunny dock, took off her shoes, and sat at the edge, dangling her feet in the cold water. Willy positioned his chair back in the shade, and she again closed her eyes and tilted her face to feel the warmth of the sun. Heliotropic. Malcolm had said once that Californians were heliotropic. This was soon after their move to L.A., and he'd meant it metaphorically, that they weren't just drawn to the sun (though of course many of them

408

were) but were more broadly drawn to money, glamour, fame—the limelight, in other words. She pulled the towel from the kayak, and then the life vest to use for a pillow. She floated the towel onto the dock and began rolling up her pant legs.

"Be easier to take them off, don't you think?"

She looked at him over there in the shadows. "There's a Willy-sized suggestion if I ever heard one."

"Just because it's my idea doesn't make it a bad one."

Judith gazed at the watery smoothness. She'd packed nice underwear, Bloomingdale's, not quite immodest. The ones Malcolm called slightly zesty.

"Nobody here but us chickens," Willy said.

Judith scanned the opposite shoreline. "This is a private lake, right? No hunters or fishermen?"

"Not a one."

She gave him an even look. "And you won't get any big ideas if I do?"

Willy gave this a quick, snorting laugh. "Particular medications I'm on, Judith, I'm just about past big ideas."

The truth was, she felt oddly at ease slipping her pants off, folding them neatly onto the dock.

"No need to stop there," he said, but she left her shirt on and stretched long on the dock, ankles crossed. She closed her eyes. He said nothing. Neither did she. She just lay feeling the sun touching her and listening to the slow, strangely vivid creak of the dock, the watery rocking of the kayak, the occasional cry of a bird, and she wondered what it meant that stripping her life down to as little as this could afford more contentment than anything more complicated ever would.

Without opening her eyes she said, "My father loved Indian summer. He always wanted me to see it. But the one year I was here at the right time, it didn't happen. There was no last burst of warmth and color. Summer ended, and presto, winter took hold."

After another little while Judith turned onto her side, looked at Willy there in the shadows, and said, "You didn't come to my father's funeral."

"No."

"I was hoping you would."

"I would've, I think. But I didn't know about it. We were living in Grand Lake by then. Those who knew about the funeral had no interest in my finding out about it."

His father, she supposed he meant. And maybe Deena herself, if she somehow heard of it. But it seemed like someone might have wanted him to know. "Your mother didn't tell you?"

He shook his head. "My mother liked you, Judith, but then . . ." He didn't finish the sentence. "She might've seemed like the forgiving type, but she wasn't really."

This time it was Judith who didn't speak.

After a second or two Willy said, "You know, for a while there after you left, your father acted kind of funny around me. I'd run into him somewhere in a store and he'd nod and say hello, but as soon as I'd turn away, he'd be gone. Then one night in a bar, same thing, I turned away and he disappeared, but a while later he walked back in and came over and said he needed to tell me something. He said he'd worked against me with you. That's what he said—he'd worked against me—and then he just stood there stiff and waiting, like I might want to hit him or something. But I told him it was okay and not exactly a surprise. I told him if I'd been in his shoes, I probably wouldn't have wanted you to marry me either. That interested him. He asked me why. I told him dim prospects and all. No, he said, that wasn't it. He thought my prospects were fine, all things considered. It was me putting you in danger. I laughed at that one. 'Hell,' I said, '*life* puts you in danger,' but there was no reason to argue the point. He thought what he thought." He paused. "I have to hand it to him, though, coming up to me and telling me the truth like that." Another pause. "'Course, if you'd cared enough about me, he could've talked himself blue and it wouldn't have mattered."

Judith sat up and stared across the water, thinking of telling the truth, and then she did. "It wasn't anything he said, Willy. It was what he did." She looked at him, his great unhealthy bulk, back in the shadows. "He got me into Stanford."

Real surprise registered in Willy's face. "You're shitting me."

Judith nodded her head. She understood. She wouldn't have believed it either. "It's true. You know how that motorcyclist came into the bar out of the rain and showed you something you hadn't managed to see for yourself? The same thing happened to me. Only my motorcyclist was a man named Rene. Rene Gassault."

She had gone to one of those little assembly rooms in one of the dorms for a poetry reading, the kind of thing she hardly ever went to, but her Hawaiian roommate was going and so there she was, waiting for the poet to arrive. When someone peeled her roommate away, Judith drifted to the refreshment table and was considering the cider and wine when a man materialized beside her, an older, slightly plump, but dapper man in a sport coat and tie, presenting himself as Rene Gassault and asking if she was Judith Toomey. Rene Gassault explained that he was a friend of her father's from the University of Chicago. Had her father ever told her about their nickel-limit poker games? And how was her father? And how was she fitting in here? *Fitting in,* those were his words, and she would never forget them: *How are you fitting in?* Half a minute later, someone called Rene Gassault away and Judith never laid eyes on him again. But his sudden appearance and the strange ballast of knowledge he seemed to carry disturbed her. In the midst of the poetry reading, Judith abruptly remembered the conversation she'd overheard from the basement door at home in Rufus Sage, her father talking excitedly to someone named Rene, whom Judith had presumed to be a woman, but now . . . Her thoughts were brought up by sudden clapping: the poem had ended. Before another could begin, she stood and made for the door. The poet made some remark; Judith didn't hear it but understood that it was about her departure, because members of the audience simultaneously laughed and turned their eyes toward her. A few days later at an interdorm mixer, she ran into a young woman who worked in Admissions. Judith guided the conversation to the woman's job—did she like it, were the people nice, was it stressful, that sort of thing. Then she asked what beyond the normal package of SATs, grades, and extracurricular stuff might get someone admitted. The woman shrugged. There were the athletes, of course. Then, after enumerating minorities and what she called "the bred-bys"—the children of famous people and big donors—she mentioned children of friends of important people. Judith asked if the woman knew Rene Gassault. Of course she did, the woman said, or knew *of* him. He was the vice provost, a very big wheel. The woman finished her glass of wine and was subtly scanning the room for conversations of greater interest when Judith asked if she had ever heard of the term *swim* in regard to applications. The woman laughed. Sure, she said. Swims were the poor saps on the waiting list. Why they were called swims, she couldn't say, but maybe—she laughed again—it was because they were swimming for their lives. Then the woman, waving at someone across the room, excused herself. On Judith's way out, a hand reached out for her arm. It was a dorm friend, asking if she was okay. Yes, Judith said, she just needed some air, and she felt a little all-overish. *All-overish*. A term she had heard in Nebraska and never imagined using herself. The dorm friend seemed befuddled, but Judith didn't stop. She kept going, out of the stifling room and into the night. She felt suddenly different, diminished, and she was as sure as sure could be that if people knew how she'd been admitted, it would change everything, plant uncertainties everywhere. She'd seen the very thing with black and Hispanic students after they'd fumbled a few questions from a professor. Why were they here? How had they gotten in? She never mentioned Rene Gassault to her father, never passed on his greetings and good wishes. She never told anyone about Rene Gassault's help, not her mother, not Malcolm, no one at all, until now, to Willy, who listened to the story and gave it a dismissive shrug.

"So what?" he said. "You graduated, didn't you? And you got okay grades, right?"

She nodded. In fact she'd done very well.

"So all it really tells us is how bad your dad wanted you out of my clutches."

"It was you, I guess, but it wasn't *just* you." She gave herself a second to try to get this right. "It was who he thought I wanted to be." The sun had moved. Its slanting light gave the water a soft glow and made it look welcoming and warm, though she knew it wasn't. She heard herself telling Willy about the story her father had told her, the one about her climbing the chest of drawers and waving the argyle socks around, and of how he himself had gone to Rufus Sage as a kind of tactical retreat, and then she told him about the night her father turned onto a dirt road, switched off the headlights, and drove her faster and faster through the black night. She stopped talking then. It seemed enough.

"He thought this was too small a box for you," Willy said finally in a soft voice, and something in Judith went out to him.

"I guess," she said. But then, so he would understand it hadn't all turned out as hoped, Judith began to fill in the details of her own recent circumstances: telling the boy at the mini-storage her name was Edie Winks, losing the key, going to the hotel room, seeing the woman who was her husband's assistant and a man who might or might not have been her husband, the headaches, the conversion of a storage room to a retreat resembling her basement bedroom in Rufus Sage. "Whew," she said when she was done. "I had no idea how strange all of that might sound."

After a time Willy said, "Well, it's all a kind of puzzle, isn't it? You start out with your own little set of pieces you're trying to fit together, then you get married and it's a lot more pieces, way more than double in my opinion, and next thing you have kids and all of a sudden there are too many pieces for the table, and more showing up every day." He gave a small dry laugh. "I suppose the Buddhists and them would say you just got to appreciate the ever-changing thinginess of the puzzle."

"They might," Judith said. But she didn't really like the idea of its all seeming unsolvable. It was why she liked editing, because sometimes in the cutting room things *did* fit together, and with enough good fits you had a whole that did whatever it was meant to do—affect, unsettle, entertain, inspire even. She told Willy this, and thought she'd done a perfectly good job of presenting it, but when she was done, he looked at her and said, "So you work in a dark room all day?"

She laughed. She'd never thought of it that way. "Not completely dark. But, yeah, pretty dark."

The shade had inched its way along the dock and now overtook her. For a minute or two, the sudden coolness felt good, but then quite suddenly it didn't. It felt cold. She glanced at her wrist and remembered she'd handed her watch over to Willy. But it didn't matter what time it was; it was cold and getting colder. She stood to pull on her pants.

"Well, now, that's a disappointment," Willy said in a mild

voice. But he stretched and looked about. "Time we headed back, though."

Judith said she was hungry.

"Well, there you are," Willy said. "And I've developed a thirst."

At the encampment, Willy poured her a small amount of scotch and a larger portion for himself, then began to count briquettes into the one-gallon can, open at the top and punched with triangular holes near the bottom, that he used to ignite them. When the little chimney began to smoke, he headed off toward the kitchen cabin and came back with a bag containing a can of tomato sauce, a box of cracker crumbs, an onion, some bell peppers, two eggs, and a package of ground venison. They worked together. Judith halved and hollowed the peppers. Willy diced the onion, then roughly measured the other ingredients into an old metal mixing bowl. He cracked the eggs into the mix, turned back the sleeves of his flannel shirt, and used his bare hands to knead the gooey mass, slick extrusions of meat sliding out between his knuckles, working the mixture toward something more or less uniform and smooth. After a minute or two of this he stopped abruptly and cocked his head. The gesture alarmed her—it reminded her of how once he'd stopped to listen to the distant high-pitched whine that would turn out to be Joe L. Minnert's chain saw.

"What?" she said.

"Oh," Willy said, as if caught at something. "I was just trying to think when the last time was my hands might've been clean."

Judith, relieved, gave this a small laugh. "You're a funny man," she said, and Willy, clearly pleased with himself, said, "I am, aren't I?" Then: "Just for the record, I washed up before I started. Used hot water from the shower tank. Kind of hot, anyhow. Fact, if you want to use it, now's a good time, while the water's still warmish."

Judith had finished her scotch and was in good spirits. "What? You don't think I'm looking my best?"

"Truth is, I think you're looking just a tad better than your best." He smiled. "'Course, my eyesight's not good and you're some distance away."

The shower was primitive but efficient. A stout overhead platform supported a black metal drum of water, canvas walls enclosed three sides, and a floor had been built of redwood slats spaced to drain. A corner shelf held new bottles of Prell shampoo and conditioner. Prell. When had she last used Prell? And Dove soap? There were hooks for hanging clothes, which she did quickly, and then she stepped through the open side. She pulled the metal chain hanging from the overhead valve and the water sprinkled through. She'd taken a deep breath but hadn't needed to. The water was surprisingly warm. It fell without much force, so washing and rinsing her hair took some time, but she didn't mind. It felt mildly exhilarating to have warm water running over her as she looked out at the lake in the last paling light. *Beyond the profane*—who said that, and what did it mean? Free. Freed. *Amo, amas, amat. Amamus, amatis, amant.* What in the world was she thinking? How far away could an inch of scotch take you?

She returned to the summerhouse wearing fresh clothes and a towel turbaned on her head and found Willy rolling dough on a board. "Use all the water?"

"I don't think so."

"You'd know."

"I liked it. Looking out at the lake like that."

He was using an empty soup can to cut circles from the dough. "Yeah," he said. "I've built some fancy showers for people, but that one right there is hard to beat."

They ate the bell peppers stuffed with venison and for dessert they spread butter and chokecherry jelly over hot biscuits.

"God," she said when it was over.

"See him, did you?" he said, and drew a small laugh from Judith.

After they'd washed the tin dishes and wiped the Dutch ovens, her hair was still damp, so they went up to her cabin and played casino in front of the fire. She hadn't played the game since that summer with Willy, but after a couple of hands she said it was all coming back to her.

"You're just talking rules of the game, right?" he said, arranging his handful of cards.

"What else might be coming back to me?"

He shrugged. "Just getting it straight is all."

It wasn't *all* coming back to her—there had been too much distance and decay for that—but it had been the voice and eyes and smile that had always supplied the potency of Willy's appeal, and whatever else had changed in him, the voice and eyes and smile had not.

While shuffling the cards between games, he said, "You know why you came here, Judith?"

She'd been entering their point totals on a pad of paper. "Very possibly to give you some instruction in casino. I'm ahead by thirteen."

He nodded mildly and kept shuffling cards. She felt her hair—almost dry—and stood close to the fire to brush it, tilting her head first one way, then the other, so it could hang straight. She felt rosy warm, as if clothes could ease off on their own. He sized and squared the deck of cards, sipped from his cup, and watched her.

"So I guess you do," she said.

"Do what?"

"Think you know why I came."

He issued a small husky laugh. "I do, yeah."

"So?"

"Oh, you came because you wondered."

She waited for the sentence to go further, but it didn't. "Wondered what?"

"I don't know," he said amiably. "Just wondered."

She decided two could play this game. "How about you?" she said. "You told me I had to come and come fast. What about that?"

"Same thing."

"Meaning?"

"I wondered, too." He smiled. "Only I probably wondered more."

She finished with her hair and he took up the cards. He dealt the next hand and while sorting it said, "So when do you have to go back?"

He could not have helped noticing her bag still filled with clothes on top of the empty dresser. "Not sure," she said. This was true; she wasn't. She tried to put some fun in her voice. "How long can you put me up?"

"Oh, a little while yet." He smiled. "Though this wouldn't be the place to winter over. One of these days the hot water will give out."

He looked at her and waited. The fire shifted. Then Judith heard herself speak words she couldn't remember ever before speaking. She said, "Let's just wait and see what happens."

This seemed to surprise Willy, too. "Okay," he said. "That's fine." Then: "Only thing is, you'll need to give me a two-day notice. I don't want to wake up one morning and find you waiting on the steps with your bag and ready to go."

"Okay." What she was actually committing to was three more days, which she knew should bother her, but it didn't. "Okay."

After he left, she laid her clothes in the top drawer of the dresser and pushed her empty bag under the bed. She slept well that night, and the following morning she awakened to the sound of something she hadn't heard since she'd come: Willy whistling. That old song, the one they couldn't identify that summer.

He stopped and turned when she approached. "Well, there you are. I was afraid you might miss breakfast altogether." He was in good spirits, and his physical attitude had loosened, too. He didn't look less unwell. He just looked more at ease, something that as the day slipped by Judith came to associate with the deal struck the night before. The certainty of a forty-eight-hour notice.

This morning he was pressing corned beef into oiled dessert molds.

"Know what song you were just whistling?" she said.

He nodded. He'd finished three molds and went on to the fourth. "Found it out one night in a bar a few years after you'd vamoosed."

"Me, too," she said. "Only not in a bar and I don't remember when."

Though she did, actually. She was whistling it one day in the kitchen and Malcolm not only told her its name but sang a few lines, not that she could remember them now. *There aren't any magic adjectives to tell you all you are . . . .* She couldn't remember what came after that. "So what are you making?" she said.

"Hash and eggs. The boys and I always liked it. Deena would take one look and start jabbering about cholesterol." He smiled. "Her working for a health professional had its ups and downs."

He broke eggs into each hash-lined mold and began setting them into the Dutch oven.

"Looks yummy," she said.

He nodded. "Only bad thing is you got to wait fifteen minutes to enjoy them."

Judith sipped her coffee and drew in a deep breath. Except for some birds chattering, there was only the low hollow sound of air moving through the trees. "I don't know," she said. "It's as if all of a sudden my ears have been cleaned out or something. I just hear everything really well. I breathe better, too." She smiled at him. "You might want to advertise Camp Blue Moon just for its decongestive properties."

"What about the fine dining and scintillating conversation?" Willy said.

"That, too, of course."

Willy's appetite was somewhat improved this morning: he ate one hash-and-egg bowl and part of a second. As they were cleaning up, he said in an offhand way, "I was thinking we might want to play that Pay Day game again. Maybe gin up the stakes a bit."

In the negotiations that followed, it was determined that Judith would again play for a secret from Willy, but not, Judith said, just any workaday secret; it needed to be something notable. And if he won, she would have "to go boating in less than her skivvies" (his condition), but not until (her condition) the temperature hit seventy-five.

Willy said seventy-five was kind of high. Seventy-two, he said, was plenty warm for skivvy-free boating.

They settled on seventy-four.

"What if it doesn't hit seventy-four at all?" Willy said, and Judith said that was the chance he'd have to take.

They played an extended six-month game of Pay Day, with lots of lead changes and casual cajoling, especially over her acquisition of "The Artificial Insemination Supply Warehouse," but in the end Willy narrowly won, which led to what Judith began to refer to as the Great Thermometer Watch. That afternoon, while Willy sat in a chair positioned nearby, the temperature pushed up to seventy-three, and when it fell back to seventy-two, he said, "You know, in most circles, you'd round seventy-three right up to seventy-four."

Judith said those were not the circles she traveled in, and she was now preparing to go out in the PowerYak fully clothed.

"Wouldn't have made the damned bet if I'd known you were going to split hairs," Willy said, affecting a sulk as he strapped on one of the old life vests.

Not far into the water, over in a marshy inlet, a doe raised its head to stare at them for a moment, then went lazily back to browsing.

"Scared her shitless, didn't we?" Willy said.

A few seconds passed, and Judith said she was glad the deer wasn't afraid of them. "Never did understand shooting them."

"Oh, I did a bunch of that, and then I just kind of gave it up. One of the things was the way a mule deer will take off when it's spooked, then when it gets a couple hundred yards away, it'll feel safe and stop and look back. That's when the big scopes and high-powered rifles get into the act. At some point it just didn't seem fair anymore."

They moved on through the water. "I went out hunting once with a guy using a bow and arrow, which I thought would be a little more sporting, only it wasn't like the bows you see in Robin Hood, it was one of these compound bows with cables and pulleys and stuff. Still, I thought it would be okay, but not till I'm out there does the guy say that what we're trying to do is get the front end of the deer from forty or fifty yards. I was surprised, killing a deer with an arrow at that distance, but no, he says, you don't kill it outright, you wait for it to bleed to death. Follow the trail of blood until it stops. I thought, *Now god damn, there's a way to spend the day.*"

"And?"

"What do you mean?"

"What did you and Burt Reynolds do then?"

"Oh. We parted company. Told him I had to see a man about

a dog. Later he came into the Eleventh Man down the road. 'Shoot you a deer?' I say, and he says, 'No. Get you a dog?' I laughed at that, and we began playing dice for beers, which is more my idea of fun."

Judith leaned back, tilting her head to the sunlight, breathing in, breathing out.

Later that afternoon, when Willy retired to his cabin for a nap, Judith went for a meandering walk. Outside the encampment, moving through the shadows on the soft litter of pine needles, she began to feel like she was in a dream. A distant ash tree shimmering yellow through the dark pines might pull her toward it. So might the cooing of a dove or the whisking of a small animal. Fairly often she drew herself still to look and listen, and once, where the cushion of pine needles was thick, she lay down, cradled her head in her locked hands, and stared up.

One day during her summer with Willy, they had driven up to Wind Cave and walked the path to its source, a rocky opening no more than two feet in diameter with cool air blowing out. The Lakota had at one time considered this opening the source of their life, the birth canal for the first of their people. Willy had said that that was not quite right, and Judith had laughed when he explained that the authentic true story was that the very first Indian came out of the opening, took one look at South Dakota, and went back down the rabbit hole. But the small rocky opening seemed no less mysterious to Judith than it must have seemed to the Native Americans. For her, it seemed to breathe, and she was unsurprised to learn that in fact the mouth of the cave sometimes blew air out and sometimes sucked it in, a phenomenon explained by some kind of difference in barometric pressure or something. It didn't matter. What mattered was the idea of the earth breathing, and lying here now, staring up through the slow sway of the trees, she could just feel the soft, slow breathing of the earth beneath her.

She rose and kept walking. Twice she came upon discarded pint bottles in the needles and leaves, the glass crusted and dirty, metal collars dulled with rust. These seemed mysterious artifacts of Willy's life without her, but when Judith crested a ridge and was presented with a sudden view of farms and barns and houses, she averted her eyes at once and retreated downslope to the safety and secrecy of the trees. She followed a deer trail around the lake, and then, approaching the boathouse from the rear side, she happened on another path curving away from the camp, a path that after some minutes of gradual ascent brought her to something odd: a crude pinewood flagpole equipped with pulleys and rope. Hanging from the top of the pole was a shabby green flag, pennant-shaped, like something used long ago to signal ship to ship. To the base of the flagpole someone had wired a rusted black mailbox, inside of which Judith found a frayed and faded red flag, also pennant-shaped. From the flagpole the descending trail widened beyond the need of foot traffic. One of those all-terrain vehicle things could traverse it easily, and Judith guessed a truck might, too, if driven with care. The lane curved down through trees and rock outcroppings to a small graded clearing, from which a rough road sloped down to the east. An easier way in, she thought, but not the one Batch had used to deliver her.

"Less picturesque," Willy said when she asked about it after returning to camp. He'd had his nap and was rolling out biscuit dough on a cutting board. "I thought you'd want to come the way we used to do."

"And the flagpole?"

"Boys built it." He shook his head. "One day they just got a notion and there was no stopping them. The older boy climbed up to the top of one of those ponderosas, bolted in a pulley, strung the rope through, then sawed off the limbs as he came down. It took a few days, but they'd hardly eat breakfast before heading out, they were so excited. It wasn't safe, but it was pretty ingenious."

He began cutting biscuits from the rolled dough with his tin can.

"And the mailbox at the bottom of the pole with a red pennant inside?"

Without the slightest hesitation Willy said, "Oh, when I need something, I just run up the red flag and leave a note at the bottom."

She stared at him. "And then the forest fairies take care of it sometime between midnight and sunrise?"

A small snorting laugh. "Something like that. Though I don't know ol' Batch would care to be called a forest fairy."

"That's some little system you've got going there."

"It is, isn't it?" He shrugged. "I could forage, I guess. And kill wildlife and shit. But I think I told you, I don't really have much stomach for killing things anymore, other than biting insects." A smile. "I said that, more or less, to Frank a few years back, and he looked at me and said, 'That ain't it. You're just lazy.'" Willy gave a wheezy laugh. "He might've been right." An envelope and a pencil lay on the table. Willy nodded toward it and said, "I've got a list going for this afternoon if you have any requests."

The list was written in block letters: 2 lbs grnd beef. Meds. Eggs from Mack. Tomatoes from MaryAnn. S-n-G.

"Meds?"

"Sure. The doctoring goes on. Till I shed the mortal coil, I'm a cash cow."

She wasn't sure how to respond to that, so she said, "And S-n-G?"

"Scotch and gin. Batch knows the brands." He smiled and nodded again at the list. "I'll add anything you want as long as it doesn't come from Saks Fifth Avenue."

Judith thought about asking him whether alcohol wasn't contraindicated with his medications, but what was the point, really? She looked at him and said, "I don't want anything that's not already here, Willy." She meant it as a compliment, and she could tell he took it as one. But then, while he was laying his biscuits in the Dutch oven, she said, "Could he get me a hat?" She was thinking of the sun on her face when they were out on the lake.

"Why, sure he can. And I'm sure it'll be stylish." Then: "How about laundry? I'm sending some of my dirty clothes on down."

This was a surprise. "Batch does laundry?"

"No, he doesn't. But he knows somebody who does."

Judith began to think what it would mean to have another four or five days' worth of clean clothes, and how she really shouldn't stay another four or five days, but what she said was, "Won't doing wash for me mean everybody in town knowing you're up here with someone whose underwear comes from Bloomingdale's?"

Willy shook his head. "Woman who washes them is an old Indian gal who's not talkative." He let his faded blue eyes settle on her and said gently, "So why don't you just set your stuff out on the porch there—would that be all right?"

She was surprised to feel her head subtly nodding. "All right."

The next morning Judith opened her cabin door and found her clothes laundered, ironed, and tightly folded within two tied plastic grocery bags. There was also a brand-new John Deere hat, pink twill with the leaping stag logo in white—a hat, she thought, clearly meant for the little woman in agriculture, though she had to admit, assessing herself in the cabin mirror, that it had a certain cachet. She liked it quite a lot.

"A lakeview cabin with laundry service, personal shopper, and self-propelled kayaks," Judith said when she joined Willy for breakfast. "Camp Blue Moon is moving up toward the top of my list of all-time favorite resorts."

Willy said he was happy to hear it.

She looked around, listened to the chatter of birds. Again the strange suggestion of amplification. "I hate to tell you how much you could rent this place out for," she said. "With a few more cabins, it would be the perfect place for reunions and weddings and retreats." Willy's eyes slid away, and she knew at once that she'd blundered, infringed somehow on the intentions of the place. "But that would ruin it, wouldn't it, strangers coming and going?"

He was nodding, accepting her surrender on this point. "I think it would, yeah." He let a few seconds pass. "But I'll tell you what. You'll get to decide."

She gave him a quizzical look.

"It's true," he said. "I die and you get it. That's the way it's going to be."

Judith felt a sense of encroachment, and alarm. "What about Deena and the boys?"

"Oh, Deena. She just wants shut of it. She called it an albatross, I think. Or maybe a white elephant. One of those, anyway. And the boys lost all interest in the place ages ago. Besides, I'm leaving them enough they can build ten camps like this if they want, and then they can bring in electricity and computers and jet-skis and all the other crap they seem to think a camp can't do without. Anyhow, they already know about this. If they were disappointed or surprised, they didn't show it."

"Why not surprised?"

He shrugged. "Oh, I don't know. I think from almost the beginning Deena knew I was building the camp with you in mind."

Judith wasn't sure what to think. That he would build this place and keep tinkering and tampering and fiddling with it, all with the idea that she might someday look upon it and grasp its

426

implications, whatever they might be, and then become its steward was as disturbing as it was flattering. It was true, she liked the way she felt here, the way she breathed and heard and saw, but she dreaded how it might feel without Willy's presence. What if Willy was giving her all the ingredients but the recipe was in his head? "I don't know, Willy. I like it here, but . . ." She let her voice trail away.

"Well, that's okay, Judy," he said. He was using his soft, tender voice. "When the time comes, you'll sort it out, one way or the other. You will. You'll see."

Judith nodded. He'd done it, and now he'd told her he'd done it, and that was that. She wished the matter were open to further discussion, but it wasn't.

Each day seemed to Judith as placid as the last; it was as if her own well-being and their common goodwill could alter the weather. Her thoughts were not quite as circumscribed as the encampment, but they were close to it. Whenever she thought of Malcolm or Milla or Leo Pottle, it caused a strange puncturing sensation, but during the day, at least, it took only a word from Willy, a bite of food, or the quick flight of a bird through the trees to dispatch all thoughts of Los Angeles. At night, lying in bed with her quilts pulled tight against the chill, the pangs were more piercing, and more than once she resolved to tell Willy the next morning that the time had come, she needed to go, but then the day broke and the urgency slid away. Really, she thought, nobody was worried. Probably they were all enjoying their vacation from her, especially from the Judith she had become before she left. And who besides Hooper and Pottle would really miss her? Milla had her friends and schoolwork, and Malcolm had . . . whatever and whomever he had. It was all okay. It was all fine, in fact. She was breathing in, breathing out, letting go, unfolding her fist into an open hand. Her mother would approve.

Still, she made a decision. She arranged for Batch to take her to the nearest public telephone—a booth behind a highway gas station in the little town of Crawford—where she called home. She'd planned the call for a time when nobody should be in the house but she was nevertheless relieved when nobody was. "Hi, it's me," she said into the answering machine and went on from there. She was fine, she said, but her mother was not. She'd written a few talking points on a card—*parasite, inflammatory bowel syndrome, fluid accumulation in her legs, Mexican doctor who's supposedly a gastroenterologist*—and when she was pretty sure that she had, as intended, made the situation seem like an impenetrable muddle, she took a deep breath and said, "Anyhow, the good news is she's probably going to be okay and her spirits are good but it looks like it's going to take a while to sort it all out." She covered the phone and to no one at all said loudly, "Okay! Okay!" then, back into the phone: "I've got to go, but don't worry about me. Calling from here is an unbelievable nightmare so I probably won't call again unless something goes terribly wrong. Miss you both, and kisses on the ears."

She'd thought she might do a little shopping in town, but found now that she didn't want to. She wanted to go straight back to the camp. Batch had picked her up below the pine flagpole, but she asked if he would drop her off on the other side, where he'd dropped her off the first time, where she and Willy always used to begin their climb.

"Why, sure," Batch said and they didn't speak another word until they'd forded the last creek and pulled into the trampled space at the base of the hill. She turned then and thanked him for the lift.

"Happy to do 'er," Batch said.

But she didn't open the door. She looked at Batch and said, "You're pretty loyal to Willy."

Batch shrugged.

"Why is that?"

Batch Batten looked stricken and confused, so she said, "Was it because he always trusted you?"

Relief flooded Batch's face; he was glad to have been supplied an answer that he saw at once was a good one. "Oh, yeah," he said, nodding and brightening. "He always did. Right from the start he always did. And good to me? You don't know the half of it."

Judith didn't find Willy in camp, and as she made her way down to the dock, she saw that the red kayak was gone. It took a few seconds to spot Willy floating in it on the opposite side of the lake. She thought of shouting out to him but instead closed her eyes and felt the subtle sway of the dock and listened to the sounds of the water and of the trees and of the birds and, finally, of the kayak's tiny engine coming her way.

She opened her eyes and was met with Willy's grin.

"What were you doing out there?" she said.

He shrugged. "Nothing. Waiting."

"I was going to do some shopping but found all I wanted to do was get back here."

"Well, there you go," he said.

Though later that night, over the fire, he mentioned that it had been his plan to wait out on the lake until she returned, however long that was.

"And if I didn't?" she said and wished at once she hadn't, but Willy took it in stride.

"Oh, I knew you would all right," he said, and then slid a little fun into his voice. "Me still having your fancy watch and all."

"That was the least of it," Judith said.

Willy remained quiet.

"You know that, right?"

"Oh, sure," he said. "I know that."

So a few days passed, and then a few more. Willy drank, not heavily but steadily, and when late in the afternoon the shadows stretched out and a chill stole over the camp, she joined him in a little scotch while they played cards or board games. His spirits were good and his physical condition seemed barely to change. He was unwell, that seemed certain, but he didn't seem in imminent peril. After the noon hour he would often go off to his cabin to rest or nap, and in these absences Judith would walk or read or shower or try something in the Dutch ovens, with mixed results (the baked squash was delicious; the apple cake couldn't be eaten). The weather held. Twice the sky thickened with clouds the color of blued metal, and one morning a cold blowing rain fell, and for the first time during daylight hours she began to think of leaving, but by midafternoon the sky cleared and the sun was warm enough to draw vapors from the wet dock, and before long she and Willy were raking up limbs and needles and talking about going out on the lake as if nothing had happened.

One chill sunny morning Willy was stirring the ashes with his length of rebar, turning up orange coals, while Judith ran a dry rag over the table and benches. She felt him watching her, and when she turned he looked at her a second longer before gazing off toward the lake. "Maybe we'll have Indian summer till spring," he said. Then, back at her: "I mean, it's nothing we wouldn't deserve."

In her movie, Judith thought, this would be the section with just wistful images of yellow and sepia leaves, pallid light and still water, no dialogue, none, just a muted soundtrack of Samuel Barber's *Adagio for Strings.*

She was almost embarrassed by the pure, low-grade pleasure she took in board games. They would talk and play, play and talk. Besides Pay Day, Othello was her favorite, notwithstanding the fact that Willy, upon winning, would recite with Zen-like calm the game's tagline: "A minute to learn, a lifetime to master."

One afternoon while they were playing Blokus in the dock house, Judith looked out toward the lake and saw something startling protrude from the water: a hoary head, almost beaked-looking, with a dark crescent shape following behind.

"Is that a turtle?" she said, pointing, and Willy abruptly pushed back from the table, took the rifle down from the wall, and hauled himself out to the front porch, where he steadied the barrel over his fist and against the porch post, sighted, and fired. The water plinked just behind the moving thing, which then dipped below the surface.

"*Fuck,*" Willy said through clenched teeth. He kept staring at the spot where the creature had submerged.

"So it was a turtle?" Judith asked.

"Snapping turtle." His eyes were still fixed on the lake. "This rifle's for shit. Sights right and I overcompensated. Which does piss me off."

"What's so bad about a snapping turtle?"

A slow blink. "Eats small fish."

But the fervency of his attempt to kill the turtle had been surprising to Judith, and once they'd settled back into their chairs and he'd snapped one of his geometric pieces into place, she said, "The other day you said you weren't that crazy about killing things other than fish and biting insects."

He nodded.

"Yet you seemed pretty excited about killing that turtle."

"Yeah, I should've added snapping turtles to the list."

"Why is that?"

He looked up from his cards, then out at the calm water. "Okay, it's kind of embarrassing, but here you go. As you're aware, I can't swim a lick, and it's not completely impossible I might

431

wind up in the bottom of that lake someday, which in itself doesn't bother me near as much as you'd think. What bothers me is the idea of that fucking turtle fucking feeding on me." His eyebrows lifted slightly, comically, but his tone was sober. "Ripping the skin from my soggy corpse and such."

A second passed and then a sudden laugh burst up from Judith. "You know who you are? You're Captain Hook, and that turtle"—she waved vaguely toward the lake—"is your crocodile!" She laughed, then made a series of tick-tocking sounds and laughed again.

"Laugh all you want," Willy said with a kind of comic passivity.

Judith said, "'Course, I guess that could make me Mr. Smee."

"Knock yourself out."

"Or *Mrs.* Smee!" This also struck her as hilarious. Willy stared at her while she fought to contain her laughter. Then, semicomposed, she said, "I ask you, what kind of woman would marry Mr. Smee?" Which set her off again.

Willy tilted his chin and sniffed exaggeratedly. "That's all right. You go right ahead and have your sport."

She could see that he extended this pose for her entertainment, but then slowly, unexpectedly, her amusement converted to a strange flooding affection. She reached across the table to touch his hand. "You're funny," she said, and the warmth that had suddenly spread through her didn't recede, it lay simmering within her, strange and profound, and when she awakened that night and looked out her window toward his cabin, she felt the kind of exciting, insistent pull she hadn't felt for years. She put the denim jacket on over her pajamas and walked down. Some nights he had a lantern on at all hours, but it was not on now. At the stoop she stood listening to his fitful snoring, which immediately ceased when she eased open the door latch. He didn't stir, though. There was moonlight in the room. He lay on his side, turned toward the wall. She took off her jacket and pulled back the heavy bed coverings. "It's me," she whispered. "I was cold." He didn't speak or turn, but when she curled in against him and wrapped her arm over his bulky body, he reached up and took her hand and held it there against his chest.

She'd pretended to herself that they could sleep like this, but they couldn't sleep.

"Warmer?" he said finally, in a whisper.

She murmured yes.

A few still seconds passed. Then, with the barest pressure, she touched his shoulder to turn him over, and she lay back and let him unfasten the pajamas. He didn't kiss her. She opened her eyes when he didn't kiss her. In the pale light his gaze upon her seemed rapt. He touched her eyelids closed and ran a finger gently along her neck. The effect was startlingly intense. He peeled back the covers, and when finally his hand grazed her stomach and moved slowly lower, she felt herself rising to meet it. She heard small murmuring sounds. They were coming from her. She began not to think.

"There," he said when she was done. "Sound to the deaf, sight to the blind."

She just lay there breathing.

"Almost too easy, wasn't it?" he said.

She felt suddenly greedy, or selfish. "What about you?"

A small raspy laugh. "Judy, sweetie, that was more fun than I've had in decades."

Judith said she doubted that.

Again he laughed. "Doubt all you want, but you'd be wrong."

He extended his arm; she laid her head on it, curled into his bulk, and fell quickly, deeply asleep. When she awakened, sun was streaming into the room and Willy was already up at the summerhouse tending the fire. She looked about. Willy's cabin was paneled with the same wide pine planks as hers, and trimmed in the same high-sheen yellow paint, but the similarities stopped there. The furnishings were mismatched, cobwebs spanned nearly every corner, and the dust on the floor was broken by paths linking the front door, the bed, and the chest of drawers topped by a framed mirror. A dozen or so plastic containers of prescribed medications stood in a cluster on top of the chest. Tucked into the edges of the mirror were two photographs.

Judith rose and walked over to the chest, meaning to look at the pictures, but her eyes were drawn to something behind the pill bottles. A small saucer held a dusty collection of coins, paper clips, rubberbands and—it jumped like a sudden close-up—the small diamond ring that she had returned to him years before. She lifted it and turned it in her hand and looked at it as she had by the campfire when it was first given to her. She pushed it easily onto her finger and then, a moment or two later, pulled it off again. She shined it on her sleeve—would he notice?—did she hope so?—and then set it back into the saucer with the coins and paper clips, but still, even with its new sheen, it was a dispiriting sight.

She leaned closer to the pictures wedged into the mirror frame. One was the photograph of fourteen- or fifteen-year-old Willy grinning into the camera with his apple-red cheeks and big ears while his raised hand held a long line of fish. The other was of Judith, in the soft light of earliest evening, standing on the low limb of a tree in her short, frayed shorts, heels together, turned just so, trying, she knew, to look saucy. But she'd failed, she saw that now. She looked as wholesome as he did, and just as unlikely a candidate for darker fates.

5

Was it the next day, or the next, or the day after that—Judith would not remember—that Willy told his secret? She had won it playing one of their games of casino, but he'd said he wasn't paying up on his bet until she made good on her R-rated kayaking, as he had come to refer to it. As far as Willy was concerned, the Great Thermometer Watch had yielded disappointing results. Twice the thermometer had climbed to seventy-three degrees before falling back, and Willy with broad equanimity said, "Well, that's okay. I just get to keep my little secret a little longer," which Judith could only pretend didn't vex her, so on this particular afternoon, slightly warmer than the preceding two or three, she made a show of checking the thermometer—it said seventy-two—and upon her return said, "Guess what?"

He looked at her. "What?"

"Thermometer says seventy-four."

A wide smile broke on his face. "Well, then, we better git after it before the temperature falls back half a degree and you welch on your bet."

She undressed before getting into the kayak and let Willy stash her clothes in a plastic bag. He strapped on one of the newer life vests and offered one to her, which she declined on the grounds of the weirdness of wearing a bright orange vest and nothing else.

"I think the Pooh-bear look can only look good on Pooh bears," she said, and Willy said, "If that."

She did, however, put on her sunglasses and pink John Deere hat.

Willy, after an appraising look, said, "My, my."

"First mosquito bite and the clothes go back on," Judith said once she'd settled in, but there were no mosquitoes, or other biting insects either. It was pleasant, in fact, once she got used to it, moving through the water without a sound, feeling the sun on her body. She'd had her eyes closed for a time when she opened them and found Willy smiling.

"What?"

"Oh, I don't know. Just admiring that fine pair of ... sunglasses."

Judith shook her head. "Welcome to Never Land. Where boys never grow up." She lay back and again closed her eyes. She didn't know how it might be with a man in his state, but she knew it didn't feel wrong to let him look at her. Though she wouldn't say it out loud for all sorts of reasons, it made her feel benevolent— generous, even.

They tied up at the dock near the tree house and snacked on crackers and salami. It reminded her of the picnics they'd had, the ones where he'd worn some clothes and she'd worn none, like that Manet painting, the one with the naked woman picnicking near a stream in the woods with the two dandyish men in black jackets, or a little like it, anyway, though Willy was far more attentive than those dandies in the painting, who seemed more interested in their discussion of politics or Plato or whatever it was they were chatting about than in the fact that a naked woman was within arm's reach. Whereas Willy watched her like there was no tomorrow and had no qualms about commenting on, as he called it one time, "the majestic nature of the scenery."

After eating, she stretched out in the mild sunshine of the dock, and she was just beginning to doze when Willy decided to pay up on his own bet. "You haven't seen me for twenty-seven years," he said, "but it hasn't been quite that long since I saw you."

Her eyes blinked open and she lifted her head. "What do you mean?"

"I went out there. That's my little secret. I went out there after you sent the ring back." He smiled and nodded and stared off across the lake. "I didn't know what else to do. So I got on a bus. A lot of buses, in fact. When I finally got there, I stayed in some little motel in Redwood City. I'd put a gun and a scope in my suitcase. I saw that everybody out there was carrying a backpack, so I bought one of those and put my scope and stuff in there, and took a bus to Palo Alto. I felt like a freak, to tell you the truth— I walked down that main drag there and felt everybody looking at me, my boots, my belt buckle, my hat—and that just kind of pissed me off, I don't know why, but it was like everyone there thought they were so hoity-toity. I had one of your letters and I went to the address on it, this big tall concrete-and-glass building with lots of kids coming and going, not just girls but boys, too. I didn't go in. I found a bench where I could sit and watch the entrance, but people kept looking at me, so I went and found a thrift shop and came back the next day wearing tennis shoes and an old Stanford sweatshirt that covered my belt, and carrying the backpack and a couple of books. I couldn't tell you what they were, but I just sat there pretending to read them and watching the comings and goings. I sat there all day and didn't see you, and then, you know, it was getting toward dusk and I saw three kids walking across a big lawn, and just the way the one in the middle walked, I knew it was you. There was a boy on one side, a tall boy with hair down to his shoulders and a tennis racket in his hand and a leather backpack slung over his shoulder, and on the other side was a pretty girl, Oriental-looking. You were talking a little bit to her, but most of your attention was on the boy, the skinny, prissy-looking one with the hair right out of a Breck commercial, and you were all in a world of your own, talking and laughing and walking right toward me, getting close enough that I could hear your actual laugh and your actual voice, and honest to God, all of a sudden I didn't know what to do. What I did was to pretend I was reading, and then, when you were just passing by, I looked up over my book, straight at you. And at almost the same time, you and the boy flicked about a half-glance right past me and kept on walking. I watched you. I thought it might dawn on you what you'd just seen, but you kept walking and talking and laughing, and then all three of you went into the building and the doors closed and that was it. There I was. I don't know, it was like I'd been shot in the head and couldn't think but couldn't die. I walked like a zombie all the way back to Redwood City and left the tennis shoes and sweatshirt and all that stuff in that shitty little motel room and went down to the Greyhound station. It took me three days to get home, and while I was staring out the bus window up in the mountains by Elko or Reno or one of those, I just kept trying to understand how quick you were able to fit into things there in that college town, and how I never could, not in a million years. I am a land animal. That was what I figured out. Only you were amphibious. You had more choices. You could've lived there or you could've lived here, but seeing you there with that Oriental girl and that boy with the Breck hair, I knew it wasn't likely you'd want to come back to live in Rufus Sage." He'd been staring across the lake as he talked, but now he turned to Judith with a wintry smile. "Not that I gave up hoping."

She didn't remember the day he'd just described. There were probably a dozen just like it, she and Crystal and Malcolm walking together toward the dorms. "I didn't see you, Willy. Believe me, if I'd seen you . . ."

He inhaled, exhaled, looked off. "Yeah, well." Then: "That boy. I suppose he was the one . . ."

He was. Probably he was. But she said, "I don't know—maybe, but really, it might've been anybody. The girl sounds like my roommate, Crystal, from Hawaii."

He nodded and looked away.

He'd had a gun. She couldn't get past that part, how some line of thinking would've taken him to laying a gun onto the folded clothes in his suitcase. She said, "Why would you bring a gun?"

But he shrugged as if this were normal, or perhaps merely incidental. "Well, you know, you get to feeling like I was feeling, you can start having some funny ideas."

"What kind of funny ideas?"

He rubbed his neck. "Okay, well, one that I had—and I know it will sound a little strange, maybe—but I was thinking I'd figure out what room was yours and then when nobody was there, I might plink the window."

"Plink the window? Why would you plink the window?"

"Well, I don't know for sure. To make you wonder, I guess."

To make her wonder what, she wanted to ask, but then she supposed that might've been the very point of the exercise. Just to make her look at the hole in the glass and in guessing how it got there force her mind off in every direction, including one that led to Willy.

The shadows had gained on her. "I'm getting cold," she said, and he said, "You can cover up, then. But I'm playing for those stakes again. Those are stakes worth playing for."

After she'd put on her clothes and was adjusting the collar of her sweater, she said, "Marrying Deena. If you had to do it all over again . . ."

He didn't answer right away, but then he said, "I would, yeah.

439

Those boys—honest to God, those boys got me through a lot of bad patches. And Deena, you couldn't say Deena didn't do her best."

He could be describing her own marriage, it seemed to Judith, or at least an aspect of it. There had been that one long stretch when Milla had loved her picture books and sock monkey and tea parties, and her face had so often beamed with happiness that it seemed the child's natural state, and Judith had been able to insulate herself from annoyance or discomfort simply by calling up the image of the small girl's radiance. And Malcolm—who could say Malcolm hadn't done his best? He, after all, had been asked into marriage by a woman who may or may not have loved him. Who had the complaint there?

As they were riding quietly across the lake, Willy laughed and said, "You know, one day we had a terrible hailstorm, and when I came home I saw the windblown hail had broken a window, and there was Deena in the living room, shoveling the hail back out the window with a flat shovel. She was working like a demon, so I got in to help, and then she just stops and breaks into the funniest grin. 'What?' I say and she says, 'Well, I'll bet this is a different kind of fun than Judith's having out there in California.' I don't know, we both found it funny, thinking of you while shoveling hail out of the living room window."

Judith said she was glad she could provide them comic relief. She hadn't stopped thinking of her marriage with Malcolm; she supposed that was why she'd asked Willy about his marriage to Deena in the first place. One seemed born of calculation, the other of revenge, and yet they had both taken on a life of their own. She said, "Malcolm and his assistant . . . It wasn't like I even knew anything for sure, but it didn't matter. Every time I really looked at him, he just looked strange to me. Like a replicant in one of those science fiction movies."

He seemed to be waiting for her to say more, but what she'd

said felt not only incomplete but disloyal, a kind of useless pandering to her audience, so she didn't say anything more. After a few seconds Willy said, "You know, for a while there we kept horses for the boys, and we had a mare that had broken down. Couldn't ride it, except maybe to walk it around the corral. You could feed it and brush it and water it was all. Sometimes I've thought that's what most marriages get to. A horse you still care a little bit about but cannot any longer ride."

It was a sad metaphor, Judith thought, one her mother would like, and to put further thoughts of Malcolm out of her mind she began talking about her. Her proverbs and grim marital aphorisms. And now her unrestrained truth-telling, filling Judith in on her sex life. "She's in Mexico now. I've been where she is, a beautiful colonial city called San Miguel de Allende. That's where people think I am right now, nursing her through some mysterious illness." The kayak moved through the water. "I never told my mother about you until a few weeks ago. She popped in on me on her way to Mexico. I showed her your picture, that one of you with your shirt off, holding a bottle of beer. She looked at it and said it made her feel sorry for Malcolm."

Willy made a snorting kind of laugh. "I would've thought she might feel sorry for the one who didn't get the girl."

"Well, it ought to tell us something about ourselves that I thought she ought to feel a little sorry for me." Some seconds passed and she said, "The problem is, after the thing or not-thing between Malcolm and his assistant, my everyday life began to feel fatuous and . . . flimsy. First at work and then everywhere I went, I'd be thinking things like, *Too much is too much,* or *Enough is enough.*" She went on in this vein for a while longer, then she sighed and smiled at Willy. "I began having these terrible migraines and just wanted to sleep all the time."

They were perhaps a hundred yards from shore when Willy

said, "You know, I wouldn't beat myself up too much, Judith. If we were honest about it, our lives are all fiascoes. There really isn't anything of importance except maybe who gets handed your heart and what they do with it. And just so you don't spend a lot of time fretting over it, even that may be pretty meager." A few seconds passed. "We're just small, Judy. All of us, even though we do stuff every day of the week to distract ourselves from the fact, it's still true. We're just little and small and maybe if we have some backbone we do a few things worth doing and then we're gone."

He cut the power and let the kayak glide toward the dock.

—⁓—

Willy was dying, Judith understood, but at what rate was hard to guess. She'd seen the array of pill bottles on his chest of drawers and presumed they were designed to suppress pain, or at least palliate it, but who knew? She didn't ask and Willy didn't tell. One day in the boathouse, in the midst of a game of Othello, he suddenly laid his chips down and said he was just going up to his cabin to rest a bit. He stood heavily and stared at the door for a moment before he stepped toward it.

"You okay?"

"I am, yeah. Just feel a nap coming on." He had his hand on the doorjamb. "Give me a few minutes and I'll come back and beat the pants off you." He waggled his eyebrows, but it seemed more a faded image of frisky implication than implication itself. From the window, Judith watched him take the trail up to the cabins. Twice he stopped and took in the view, or pretended to, before proceeding on. Finally he turned out of sight and Judith kept staring at the place he had last stood.

At Wind Cave, after sitting alone at its source, they had gone on a disappointing tour that began some distance away, with a ride down an elevator that gave onto a lighted concrete pathway through the cave. The tour's only authentic moment occurred when the ranger turned off all the lights and the hand you held in front of your face could not be seen. When Judith had turned round to touch Willy, he wasn't there—he'd moved away to look at something just before the lights had gone out. That was what she thought of now, with Willy out of sight: the strange panic she'd felt in the black darkness of that cave when she'd reached her hand to the spot where Willy had just been.

The next two or three days were uneventful and often pleasant. "So, Willy," she said one afternoon while they floated on the lake, "you want to tell me what the *C* stands for?"

He gave her a questioning look and she said she was referring to his middle initial.

"Oh that. Well, I might want to, but I can't."

"I figured you'd say something like that."

He gave her a wry, genial look. "Well, you know, I can't help it." He grinned. "It comes from a time when I believed honor twirled the planet."

They were quiet for a few moments, and Judith became suddenly aware of the absence of bird chatter. She also couldn't remember when she'd last seen ducks on the water. She began wondering what would happen to her and Willy if they just stayed into the winter.

Willy said, "What's funny is two or three years must've gone by before Deena even thought to ask about the middle initial."

Judith said she would've asked the first day. At the reception, in fact.

"Well, if it's a comfort, when I did tell Deena, she wasn't impressed."

"So why don't you just tell me and give me one less thing in the world to worry about."

"I don't think you're that worried, to be honest about it."

She laughed. "Okay, not that much. Curious would be more like it."

He didn't speak, and she looked up at the sky: pale blue with wide streaks of white. "I love this little lake," she said, "and I love this kayak and I love the company I'm keeping."

She hadn't intended to say all this when she'd begun the sentence, but there it was, hanging in the still cool autumn air. He was quiet. She kept looking up at the sky.

Finally she said, "Sorry. I don't know . . . something just came over me."

"That's okay," he said, but his voice sounded oddly brittle.

She hadn't been looking at him and now she did. His face was stiff, and his head was turned, his eyes squinting fixedly off, his jaws clamped, holding things in, willing the water brimming in his eyes not to slip free. And then a little bit did break free and he had to wipe it away. "God damn it," he said between clenched teeth. He coughed. He didn't seem to need to cough, but he coughed his wheezy cough, and then he threw the switch and had them moving through the water again.

The following day, or perhaps the next, Judith walked down to the shower. It had been a hazy but not discernibly cooler day, yet the water in the black tank was barely warm. It surprised her; for half a minute she extended her hand into the stream of water, hoping for it to warm up. She quickly washed her hair, but goose bumps kept her from shaving her legs. She toweled off quickly and was glad to get up to the summerhouse and stand by the fire. The next day's shower was, if anything, colder. She became more and more aware of the camp's strange quiet; she heard now only the occasional call of a bird, and imputed to it the worry of a creature abandoned. Nighttime temperatures slipped below pleasantly chilly, and Judith seemed to tighten with the cold. She wore more layers of clothes, and even sitting close to the fire at night, she needed to turn up the collar of the lined denim jacket. She didn't mention the cold. Neither did he.

That night while she lay curled to Willy's back, a wind came up, and then a strange persistent creaking. She expected it to stop, but it didn't.

"Willy?" she whispered.

"Mmm."

"What's that creaking?"

"The trees."

"Why?"

Seconds passed. He seemed not to want to say it, but he did. "From the cold," he said, and Judith, pulling herself tighter to his back, felt herself beginning to brace against a weight she couldn't see.

The next morning the pine needles crackled with hoarfrost. The toilet seat in the privy was so cold she kept herself raised just above it to pee. Throughout the day, the wind blew, the trees swayed, and there were sudden shiftings of shade and light. The cold was piercing. The suddenness and thoroughness of the change was shocking to Judith. The sound through the trees, usually flutish, had turned deeper in timbre, more like that of an oboe.

They spent the day playing board games near the fire in the boathouse. They didn't cook a noon meal, but instead ate venison salami and crackers and kept playing cards. Willy cracked almonds and tossed shells into the fire. Once, staring at his cards, he said, "Boy meets girl, boy loses girl." He looked up. "Not much of a story, I guess."

She said, "How about girl meets boy, girl loses boy, girl finds boy and is happy she did."

Willy gave a quick laugh. "Is that what we've got here?"

"I don't know," she said, laughing herself. "I thought so until you had to laugh at the idea."

A while later, shuffling the cards, he said, "Here's the thing, Judy. Here's the thing we have to look at and accept. For you, I was a chapter—a good chapter, maybe, or even your favorite chapter, but still, just a chapter—and for me, you were the book."

"No, no, Willy, what you're saying about me—that's just not true," she said, but she didn't say what she thought was the truer, darker truth: that, to use his metaphor, he *had* been most of the book, but she had been too careless or self-absorbed or oblivious to know it, and it was too late to change the ending.

After they finished their game of casino, Willy fetched two new logs and fed them into the fire. He went to the stack of board games and brought Monopoly back to the table. She'd never liked Monopoly—the game always felt like it went on forever—but that now seemed its very attraction. They set up a folding table for it, and each of them bought scattered properties here and there and never mentioned the idea of trading deeds to complete monopolies. Neither of them wanted to win. They wanted to keep talking and playing and looking at the fire. They left the game in place on the table when they went up to the summerhouse to huddle close to the fire and prepare their supper.

The trees creaked all through the night. Judith lay awake and felt as if she were going very slowly to a funeral. She curled tightly into his back, knowing that he, too, wasn't sleeping and wouldn't soon be. Finally she whispered his name. "Willy?"

He didn't answer.

"I think it's getting close to time."

For a little while he didn't answer. He didn't move. Finally he said, "I know." Then: "This wouldn't be the place to get caught for the winter."

"I could come back when it's nice again. In May or June. When I'm not working."

446

In a lower voice, as if from far away, he said, "Don't, Judith. Don't say things."

"Okay. But still. I could."

The next morning over breakfast, he gazed off toward the lake and said, "Day after tomorrow, then?"

She didn't answer, but then he was looking at her. She made so small a nod she wondered whether he'd see it, but he did. He must have. He seemed about to say something, but he didn't. He slowly turned away his eyes.

He kept cooking but stopped eating. In the boathouse, they put away their game of Monopoly and began a thousand-piece jigsaw puzzle featuring a color-tinted postcard of Crow Butte, to the west of Rufus Sage. Without talking, they laid out the edges and worked their way inward. It was slow going—the pieces were minute and the colors muted. Once, straightening her back, Judith read aloud the insert provided by the Omaha Public Library. According to their account, the pictured butte was the site of a legendary battle between the Crow and Sioux Indians in the fall of 1849. The Crow, outnumbered and pursued by the Sioux, abandoned their mounts and scaled the butte, where they stayed for three days, building fires each night, singing and dancing in mockery of the Sioux on the ground below. At dawn on the fourth morning, the Sioux found rawhide ropes dangling from the tops of the butte, signaling the escape of the Crow by walking through the Sioux camp.

"Ha," Willy said when Judith finished reading. "You can't say those Injuns weren't wily."

Judith, collecting and separating those pieces with pale green in them, kept thinking of the Crow on an autumn night, scaling silently down the sides of the butte, dispersing into the night, playing their little trick on death.

That night, and the next, Judith didn't start in her own bed but waited until Willy had gone down to his, then turned off her

447

lantern and walked down and crawled in beside him, letting him fold his arms around her and pull her toward his bulk. She had no interest in sexual relations, and neither, seemingly, did he. She wondered whether he slept, and if he did, how lightly, because every time she awakened or stirred, he was awake, whispering, "You okay?"

Yes. She always said yes.

The next day, they moved the puzzle closer to the fire. They had most of the foreground pines and clustered pieces of the rocky outcropping at the base of the butte. While turning a piece this way and that, she said, "You know, I could just stay on."

He looked up at her. "Stay on and do what?"

"Help out." She couldn't keep her eyes on him then. "Be with you ..."

"Like hospice, you mean."

She looked back and saw his rigid expression. "No—"

"Because we've got hospice out here in the hinterlands. We're real up-to-date."

"I don't know, Willy, I just meant ..." Her voice trailed off. She had no idea what she just meant.

"Look, Judith," he said, his voice gentler now, "this isn't a winter camp. It's a summer camp. That's all it ever was."

"I'll come back next summer, then. We can meet here next summer. I don't know how, but I will."

He nodded, but his look was neutral. "Know what you could do this time, before you leave?"

"What?"

"Draw me a sign."

He found a piece of three-quarter-inch plywood about the right size, and white primer. They put out a note for Batch asking for a small brush and pints of gray, yellow, and blue enamel. "Cobalt blue, tell him," Judith said, and Willy said, "Instead of periwinkle?" which he pronounced *perrywinkle,* and turning she took him in and tried to save the image because there he was and he was smiling and he was Willy.

Willy painted the plywood with the primer, both sides, and she made layout sketches on paper. He wanted it to say Camp Blue Moon, and she decided on a bluish moon smiling over the buttes with the camp name off to one side in block letters that from a distance might suggest rough carving. Between coats of paint, they fiddled their way toward the center of their Crow Butte puzzle and played casino and ate and talked and waited.

She cooked a beef goulash that night, and afterward they had peach cobbler. Willy tasted everything, and commended it, and seemed genuinely pleased that her touch with the Dutch ovens had improved so much, but he consumed little. When they finished, he fed the fire and stared at the flames.

Finally he said, "Tomorrow, then."

He explained the arrangements. Batch had confirmed her reservation with Frontier for an evening flight to Denver and then on to Los Angeles. Batch would be there to collect her in the late afternoon, which would leave plenty of time for the drive up to Rapid City.

"Okay," she said. It was almost paralyzing, how little she wanted to leave. "What day is it?"

"Saturday."

Which meant she would get back to Los Angeles late Sunday night, after everyone was asleep.

He said, "Does it feel to you like Saturday night?"

"No," she said. "But it's been a long time since Saturday night felt like Saturday night." She looked at him through the dark and said in a fond voice, "I remember when Thursday afternoons felt like Saturday night."

He exhaled deeply and said, "Me, too." Then: "A long time ago."

That night they sat up by the fire until at last a mist lay over the camp like a damp membrane. Moisture gathered and dripped from the trees. It felt good to settle deep into the flannel sheets of Willy's bed, but for hours she could only lie still and pretend to sleep. She had the feeling he was doing the same; when he slept his wheeze was more pronounced, and tonight there was no pronounced wheezing. Still, far into the night, she felt herself finally giving way to sleep.

When she awakened she was aware first of Willy's absence, then of the empty coldness of the cabin and the pale light filtering through the mist. Only then did she remember that this was the day she was to leave, and the effect was sudden, and puncturing. She put her head back onto the pillow until she heard a series of sharp rapping sounds. She went to the window. Willy was attaching their new sign to the side of her cabin, the first flat surface likely to be seen upon entering camp.

She dressed and put on the denim jacket and walked up.

"Looks pretty good," she said.

His face when he turned to her seemed unnaturally bright. "It does, doesn't it?" Then: "Hungry?"

He'd evidently been up a while. He'd prepared a big breakfast of baked eggs and bacon, and unlike on the past two days, he joined her in eating, finishing off his egg and toasting a second piece of bread, spreading it with his chokecherry jelly. Dew dripped from the trees and the beams of the summerhouse. Judith gazed toward the lake, where mist rose from the water.

"Don't you worry," Willy said with insistent good cheer. "Sun's going to work his way through. It will. You'll see."

"That'd be nice," Judith said.

All her life she had arranged to leave places in the early morning so she could avoid the strange ambivalence of being fixed somewhere she was ready to leave. But she found herself comforted by the small reprieve Willy's arrangements afforded her, and his cheerful deportment was an odd surprise. When he began whistling as they laid in a few more pieces of their puzzle, she said, "My God, Willy. Are you happy to be getting rid of me?"

He'd been whistling that old song, the one he always used to whistle, but now he stopped. "No. I'm not. But in the night I vowed I'd be grateful that you came out here, to see me, when it wasn't an easy thing to do. I didn't think I should let my personal feelings overshadow that fact."

They made the noon meal together in a Dutch oven—a beef, rice, and mushroom soup dish—and he ate a good portion of that, too. She wondered if he'd turned some kind of corner, might in fact be getting better, cheating death, stealing down from the surrounded butte in the dead of night—a preposterous hope, she knew, but she was able to nurse it along until, around 1 P.M., his movements began to slow, grow heavier, as if he could no longer avoid the weight of the day's intentions.

"You want to take a little nap?" she said, and he actually laughed.

"On your last day?" he said. "With the sun shining?"

This wasn't quite true. Its pale form could just be made out through the mist. But it seemed important to Willy that the weather be considered good enough for one last spin around the lake, and Judith liked the idea, too, so she said nothing about the bleakness.

She walked down to the shower and retrieved her brush and shampoo, then began tucking clothes into her big leather bag. Willy tapped at the door and said, "Better get down to the lake if we're going to do it." He stepped into the room, carrying her watch. "Might need this back in civilization," he said. He looked around. "Room's going to miss you."

"And vice versa," she said, using his old line.

When she resumed pressing clothes into her bag, he took down the denim jacket from its horseshoe hook. He seemed to be doing

451

something—going through the pockets—but when she looked up, the jacket was folded over his arm and he was extending it to her. "You should take this," he said. "Seeing it on anybody else would just be a disappointment."

She thought about declining it—where would she put it?—but said, "Thanks. I've gotten pretty used to it."

She zippered her bag.

He untwisted a mint, popped it into his mouth, and managed one of his smiles. "We're okay," he said. "It's okay." He'd looked at her watch before laying it down, and now he checked it again—later she would remember how, for the first time since she'd arrived, he seemed actually concerned with the time—then headed down to the boathouse to fit out the PowerYak.

"Snacks?" Judith called after him. He didn't seem to hear her. She'd thought they might sit bundled up on the boys' dock for a bit and have a last talk of some kind.

By the time she carried snacks down to the dock, the planks were still wet but the mist had given way to an overlay of purple-gray clouds. Willy had made the kayak ready, as well as the snub-nosed dinghy, which was a surprise. He walked from the boathouse with his arms through two life vests, one old and one new. He handed the bright orange one to her, kept the dingy one for himself, and began fiddling with a knot, trying to loosen it, and as he stood there, he began to sway, and she was suddenly overcome. She didn't say anything. She stepped forward and pressed into him. She'd grown to expect the faint scent of liquor, but the smells she detected now were of pine and wood smoke and peppermint.

"You smell like Christmas," she whispered. She pressed him tighter, trying to keep herself from crying. "Like Christmas when Christmas still meant something."

They stood like that a long time, not speaking at all, and then finally Willy stepped back. "Better git if we're going to git," he said, and pulled the old vest over his flannel shirt, tying the straps, snugging it tight. She glanced at the dinghy with oars fitted into the oarlocks. "We going in that?"

"I was thinking of it, but changed my mind." He didn't make a joke about less rowing. He didn't joke about anything. He merely eased himself into the kayak and held the edge of the dock to steady the boat for her. He reversed the motor, and a moment later—it felt like a kind of exhalation—they were gliding silently out into the water.

They skirted the entire perimeter and came upon a doe, maybe the same one they'd seen before, and she raised her head and swiveled her ears, then went back to browsing. It was cold, but here and there the sun found its way through the clouds. Judith watched as a stand of pines on the far shore shone vividly green, then, as the clouds shifted, dimmed almost to gray. Gradually a space of water toward the middle of the lake took on a kind of preternatural illumination. Willy noticed it, too, and as they moved silently toward it, Judith felt as if they'd found a secret passage into an exquisite painting. When they slipped into the sunlight, Willy switched the motor off, and for a moment it seemed as if the entire world had stopped turning—she thought of the day years before in Rufus Sage when she and her father had stood in the wintry silence on Main Street staring at the building that had once housed Feister's Western Wear.

Willy's face was almost glowing. Maybe it was the light. But maybe, she thought, it was the nature of the moment—maybe she seemed radiant, too. They let their eyes settle into one another until at last she was afraid she would say something too big or too rich for the moment, so she said nothing and began to sort through the small cooler at her feet.

"Would you like salami and crackers?" she said.

When she looked up, she caught him gazing back toward the

dock, but he turned now to her. "No, but thank you," he said, softly and almost formal-seeming.

Judith was unwrapping a tube of crackers when the sun slid away and within her mind there occurred something she would always think of as a silent explosion. Something was wrong. She stilled her hands and looked up. Willy sat there staring at her with his radiant smile, and something was terribly wrong.

"Hello!"

A voice from some distance.

A man stood at the dock's edge. A man who looked like Malcolm.

"Hello!" he called again in Malcolm's voice.

Judith turned back to Willy.

He still smiled, but it was more than a smile, it seemed some strange expansion of smiles, so that this was the first one and the last one and every one in between. Then his eyelids closed and opened in a long, languid blink, and everything slowed and broke into distinct particular moments: his smile contorting now, twisting into an expression childlike and wanting and wishful, and then the slight parting of his lips to speak, but he couldn't speak. He closed his mouth and reopened it as if to try again, but nothing passed his parted lips. He drew in air then, a long slow draft of it, and as he slowly released it, he gave up on speech and his eyes, slightly watery now, brightened again, and his smile turned odd and anxious and expectant, the kind of smile, she would think later as she replayed the scene again and again, that you might see when someone is about to present you with a heartfelt gift he isn't sure you will like or will use or will even understand, and then, smiling in just that way, he spread his arms to his sides and took hold of the gunnels and simply and surely heaved his shoulders and weight to one side.

As the kayak capsized, Judith gasped and squeezed her eyes and

454

mouth closed against the water's sudden, ferocious cold, then popped back through the surface, drawing great gasps of air. The kayak floated keel up. The gunnels seemed sealed to the water.

"Willy?" she called. "Willy?"

She swam to the other side—nothing, nobody—then inhaled and tried to dive but couldn't. Frantically she unclasped her vest, shrugged it off, and dipped under the gunnel and felt around in the cavity of air beneath the boat.

He was not there.

She dived again, eyes open, but saw nothing in the dark opaque water, and she resurfaced again, yelling now. *Willy. Willy, Willy, Willy.*

Again and again she dived, seeing nothing, knowing she would see nothing, until finally, when she burst up through the water, there was the dinghy, and Malcolm in a quiet voice said, "Judith?"

6

Batch Batten arrived while Judith was still trying to warm herself in front of the fire in the boathouse. He had the grasping aspect of a man who had been told to appear at a precise time without being told what to expect when he got there. After taking in the scene—Judith hunched and sopping, Malcolm close and attentive—Batch seemed to be looking around for Willy.

"Willy drowned," Judith said. Her voice sounded dull and far away, as if it were not her own.

Batch Batten stared at her.

"He's dead," she said. "You need to get the police or somebody."

After he left, Malcolm tried to coax information from her, but she just kept her place by the fire and sat staring out at the lake. Time passed—how much she had no idea—but it startled her when Batch appeared with two policemen, one of whom looked at Judith for only a split second and said, "Well, well. Judith Toomey."

She looked at him dully.

"Chief Seers," he said.

She could see it was true. Gray hair and a little more jowl, but unquestionably Chief Seers.

"So Willy Blunt drowned," he said, keeping his eyes on her. Malcolm might not have existed.

Judith nodded.

Chief Seers said gently, "Why don't you tell me about it?"

She did, as best she could, while Malcolm stood listening. When she finished, Chief Seers gestured toward the bright orange vest lying wet on the floor. "And you were wearing that life jacket there?"

Judith said yes.

"And he was wearing one, too?"

She nodded. "He couldn't swim," she said.

"His was fastened up good?"

Again she nodded. "But it wasn't like mine. It was an old one with ties instead of clasps."

She kept the blanket around her and led him to the other old vest, which hung on the exterior wall on the boathouse. Chief Seers took the vest down and experimentally pressed his thumbnail into it. It gave way, and wearing still his imperturbable expression, Chief Seers looked out toward the water.

"What?" Malcolm said.

Seers's eyes barely grazed Malcolm. He scanned the porch and instructed his deputy to fetch a fishing rod he'd spotted leaning against the rail, then Seers walked with the rod and the old safety vest down to the dock. While the others watched, he hooked the strap of the vest to the line and swung it into the water. It lay momentarily on the surface, darkening, the water wicking quickly through it; then, shockingly to Judith, it was drawn quickly down into the water. When Chief Seers reeled it back up, dripping, the fishing rod nearly doubled with its weight. They all looked at it lying there on the dock. Judith bent to lift it. It felt like a wet rock. It had sucked in the water and kept it.

In a low flat voice, Chief Seers said, "Who picked the life jackets when you went out?"

Judith looked up at him. "Willy." Then: "He must've . . ."

Chief Seers looked at Judith, then at the smooth surface of the water. So Willy had gone out wearing an anchor, and he had known it. Someone had to say this, and it fell to the chief. "Guess Willy Blunt decided to sink himself," he said. He looked at Batch Batten, whose expression was stricken. "You got to hand it to him, Batch. Neat and clean like this."

There was little to discuss or do after that. The only difficulty derived from Judith's request that the body be recovered. Chief Seers took a deep breath and said, "Well, the body'll float in a few days if it slips that vest. 'Course, that's a big if." He told her that her affidavit was really all they needed to confirm the death as accidental. That in a case like this the county wasn't in a position to pay for dragging a lake.

"I will," Judith said. She knew she should have said, *We will,* but she hadn't.

Seers gave her a look. "Why would you want to do that?"

It was the snapping turtle, that was why, but she said, "I wouldn't want his family to have any doubts what happened. A death without a body . . ." She let her voice trail off.

The chief was studying Judith when Malcolm asked how much dragging a lake was going for these days.

Chief Seers seemed to respect Malcolm for asking, and for the first time he gave Malcolm a thorough look. The chief ran a cupped hand over his mouth and chin, considering. "Neighborhood of a thousand dollars a day," he said. "Can't imagine more than a day or two on it. Might even get a diver to do it. Finds the body fast, you'd save a little money there." Then, not looking at Judith, but certainly for her to hear: "Won't be pretty when we find him."

A few still seconds passed.

A low wobbly voice said, "Dear God, Willy. Dear God almighty." It was Batch Batten. He was staring across the water,

458

swaying slightly and hugging folded arms to his chest. He looked cold and abandoned, a man who might fall to his knees in prayer.

Chief Seers turned to Judith and Malcolm. "No real reason for you California folks to stay on here. We'll take your statements in town. After that, you're free to go as you please."

By the time the paperwork was completed, it was after 5 P.M. Malcolm went down the hallway to the bathroom, and while Judith and the police chief stood alone, he said, "You know, Willy was a good fella straight through, even with the drink." Judith didn't know what to think or say. She had her hands in the pockets of the denim jacket and she just stood there trying to keep from breaking apart. The chief in his low flat voice said, "I ran into Willy a while back. He wasn't long for this world. He knew he was going to go, and he got to go on his own terms. What you did here was good, helping Willy through and all."

Judith felt a stiff thinness shell over her face. She couldn't speak, but she began shaking her head. No, she wanted to say, no, no, no, helping Willy to die was not what she'd come to do, was not what she'd ever intended to do. She heard an opening door, then Malcolm's heels on the linoleum hallway. Judith kept her face squeezed tight and turned toward the front door of the station house. Behind her she heard Malcolm thanking Chief Seers for all he'd done, saying how impressed he was with the professionalism he'd found out here in the hinterlands, losing, Judith knew, what little credibility he'd gained in asking the price of dragging a lake.

On the curb, Malcolm made a claim for himself. He was hungry, he said. He'd driven all night. He had to eat. When she slid into the car and glanced toward the police building, Chief Seers was standing a few feet back from the window, looking out in his sphinxlike way, but she knew what he saw: two people from California about to drive away in their late-model black Jaguar. His head dipped in a slight nod.

459

They found a coffee shop on the highway. Malcolm ordered a flatiron steak, and when the waitress said it came with onion tanglers, he said, "But perhaps not on this occasion." Judith ordered only coffee and toast, then turned and looked across the highway toward the back of the abandoned Starlight drive-in theater, where one night she and Willy Blunt had gone to watch a James Bond movie. A long time ago.

When Malcolm's salad arrived, ladled heavily with the blue cheese dressing he'd requested on the side, he looked from it to her in search of a shared distaste for the here and now, but Judith lowered her eyes. She had not asked Malcolm a single question since he'd appeared at the encampment, but now, without looking at him, she said, "How did you get here?"

He had received a phone call. The caller, who had identified himself as one Batch Batten, informed Malcolm that he knew where his wife was. Malcolm in turn had informed Batch Batten that his wife was in San Miguel, Mexico, with her mother. Here Malcolm composed a small rueful smile. "Batch Batten said, and I quote, 'No, she ain't.' He told me you were at a camp near Rufus Sage, Nebraska, and I needed to come pick you up." Batch had made arrangements to meet Malcolm at the north entrance of the Rufus Sage Municipal Park at 1 P.M. and no later. Malcolm had driven all night and at 12:45 the next afternoon had been waiting for Batch Batten, who drove him close to the camp and, at exactly 1:30, pointed him in the right direction. "Then," he said, "I hiked to the camp and wandered down to the dock just in time to see my wife and a strange man floating idyllically in a canoe that would shortly thereafter capsize and drown the stranger with whom my wife had been canoeing."

Judith asked nothing further. The real question—why Willy had wanted Malcolm there—was one only Willy could have answered. For his own amusement? To personally hand back his wife to

460

Malcolm? To force the Malcolm who had glanced past him as he sat on the concrete bench on the Stanford campus to take another look? Or—and this was the one to which Judith was most insistently pulled—to reveal her, though to whom she was never quite sure.

They left Rufus Sage. By the time they passed through Crawford and Harrison, Malcolm had given up trying to draw Judith into conversation, but in Wyoming, between Lusk and Douglas, he had offered certain information.

He said, "Leo Pottle and Lucy Meynke called every day the first week you were gone, then Leo stopped. Lucy called a few days beyond that, but then she, too, desisted."

Judith sat enclosed in the denim jacket and stared out at the vast plains, at the stretching shadows and paling light. Dusk soon, she thought, and then dark. The lake would be dark.

Malcolm said, "Milla has a new boyfriend. Theo Lane, by name. He's an all-state water polo player, some kind of physics whiz kid, and I don't know what-all." Malcolm forced a stiff laugh. "After Milla went through the complete résumé, she said, 'I don't see how you can objectively disapprove of him.'"

Theo Lane, former boyfriend of Torry McQuaid, Judith remembered almost unwillingly.

A mile or two farther down the road, Malcolm said, "There's something I don't think I've told you."

Judith said nothing. She wasn't waiting for what he said next because she didn't care what he said next. She was merely saying nothing.

Malcolm said, "Francine is no longer working for me. She's in Boston, working for a bank there. She told me about the job offer a while back. She asked whether I thought she should accept it. I told her she should, and she did."

After each of these sentences, he had paused to consider the next.

461

He, too, fell silent then. Judith kept her head turned away from him, toward the window. It was a flat treeless landscape without interest except for the occasional antelope feeding in the day's last light. Deer can jump fences, but antelope can't, or won't, she couldn't remember which. Willy had told her, a long time ago. How it was a failing that often cost them their lives.

By the time they reached Casper and turned southwest toward Muddy Gap, it was fully dark, and with nothing but the faint illumination of the dashboard, they were able to withdraw into even deeper silence. She should have been sleepy—she'd barely slept the night before—but she couldn't sleep. Malcolm stared ahead, Judith stared out her side window, and every now and then a distant lighted farmhouse passed through her field of vision, a farmhouse where, she imagined, a family had drawn together at the end of the working day and was sitting down to a meal.

It was after 10 P.M. when they came into Rawlins from the north, and pulled into a Conoco station. While Malcolm pumped gas, Judith walked over to an odd car installed along the road for promotional purposes. It was long and white and featured two opposing front ends. To Judith, it suggested a kind of vehicular tug-of-war, but painted on its side were the words, *Perkins Conoco— Always Moving Ahead.*

Judith was cold, and pushed her hands into the pockets of the denim jacket. One day, searching for tissues, perhaps, or for coins, she would notice a small, secured pocket sewn into this jacket's lining, and find within it the ring with the small diamond inset, the one he had given to her long ago in a distant land, and had given to her again. It would afford her a pure moment of solace, and even a fleeting sensation of reunion, but that moment was months away. Now she stood, hands in pockets, staring numbly at a car with two front hoods facing in opposite directions.

"Ready?" Malcolm called.

He suggested they find a room, sleep a few hours, and get an early start, but Judith shook her head decisively (the thought of it, asking for single beds or sharing one with Malcolm), so they returned to a public park they had passed and Malcolm found a place for the Jaguar at the dark end of the parking lot. He switched on the door locks, reclined his seat, and fell asleep with his mouth open. Finally Judith dozed, too, and upon awakening was sorry to see where she was and to know why she was there. The comparison to a runaway girl being returned to her foster home came into her head. She opened the door, the dome light flashed on, and Malcolm shot up from his seat. "Where are you going?" he asked.

"Bathroom." She was surprised how dull and fossilized her voice sounded.

She found a cinder-block bathroom littered with toilet tissue, cigarette butts, and Wendy's wrappers, the floor wet with who knew what. She hadn't used a flush toilet since Batch Batten had picked her up at the airport in Rapid City, however many days ago that was, and she took no pleasure in using one now. As she walked back toward the car, she slid her wristwatch over her hand and laid it on the next picnic table she passed.

Inside the Jaguar, Malcolm had fallen back asleep. When she tapped on the driver's-side window, he again bolted awake, this time with an expression of apprehension. He lowered the window.

"I'll drive," Judith said. "I'm not sleepy."

Malcolm said he was fine now, he would keep driving, and really, she thought, who could blame him? She wouldn't trust her either.

They drove on and on. When he found cafés for breakfast and lunch, she ordered dry toast and tea, then, finishing before he did, went out to wait by the car. He forced the issue for supper, so at a restaurant in St. George, she ordered soup with her toast. It was twilight when the car sped through the Virgin River Gorge, and it turned dark again as they crossed the desert. Traffic piled up in Las Vegas, and again someplace to the west where the highway narrowed from three lanes to two. They were soon crawling along so slowly that Judith had to fight the urge to get out and walk. Four-wheel-drive vehicles exited from the interstate and appeared to be bouncing across the desert itself, the beams of their high-mounted headlights fluttering above the dark landscape. "Lunatics," Malcolm said, sounding tired and testy, and Judith, staring out, said nothing. The word *positraction* came unbidden into her mind.

The house from her father.

The summer camp from Willy.

The years before Milla went away to school.

These were the elements at hand, and Judith, staring out at the lights of the straggling cars crossing through the desert, wondered what, if anything, might be built from them.

When finally they crested the Cajon Pass and turned into the San Bernardino Valley with the vast expanse of shimmering lights spread before them, the dashboard clock read 2:17.

"Okay," Malcolm said. "Okay."

He seemed desperate to be home.

Judith felt numb. The touch of her finger to her chin barely registered. She pinched and tugged her cheek and was surprised how rubbery her skin felt. The freeway signs and sights seemed only artificially familiar, as if she'd before viewed them only in movies and travelogues, was now finally coming to visit, and found everything depleted. She closed her eyes and left them closed until the car slowed and they pulled into the driveway of their house, which, too, seemed only strangely familiar. The garage door rolled quietly closed behind them.

"There," Malcolm said, as if a discouraging task had finally been completed.

Judith got out of the car and went inside and walked to Camille's room. On the wall, the crescent moon was lighted. Camille was asleep. She'd gone to bed with wet hair; she'd covered her pillow with a bath towel. Judith used the step stool and slipped into the bed, and Camille turned toward her and said in a sleepy, whispery voice, "Hi, Mom, is that you?" and then, without waiting for an answer, or perhaps already finding it in Judith's shape and smell, the girl shifted and her breathing fell again into the rhythms of sleep. Judith thought then that she, too, might sleep, but she couldn't sleep. She closed her eyes and could not sleep. The scene played again and again and again, unchanged and unchangeable. The bright watery eyes, the crooked smile, the slight parting of the lips as if to speak.

Acknowledgments

I would like to express my gratitude to the National Endowment for the Arts for their support during the writing of this book; to Mary Jo Markey for her help with the minutiae of film editing; to Barbara Myers, Orval and Mary Weyers, and my cousins—the former Moore girls—Susan Vastine, Nancy Fisher, and Jenny Hughson, for their help with Nebraska-based details; to Jack Duckworth, Gary Fisher, Randy "Bird Man" Lawson, John L'Heureux, Fred McNeal, Michael Sykes, Ted Vastine, Diane Wilson, and Tobias Wolff for stray facts and observations that found their way into the book; to Jim Hall and Dana Reinhardt for their critical assistance; to George Ledbetter and his staff at *The Chadron Record* for supplying me with old newspapers and a quiet room in which to read them; to Peter Matson, Judy Clain, and Michael Pietsch for their belief in the book and assistance in bringing it into print; and finally to Laura, for everything, *A* to *Z*.

A RELIABLE WIFE

Robert Goolrick

COUNTRY BUSINESSMAN SEEKS RELIABLE WIFE.
COMPELLED BY PRACTICAL REASONS.
REPLY BY LETTER.

Rural Wisconsin, 1907. In the bitter cold, Ralph Truitt, a successful
industrialist, stands alone on a train platform waiting for the woman
who answered his newspaper advertisement. But when Catherine
steps of the train she's not the woman that that Ralph is expecting.
She is both complex and devious. And, haunted by a terrible past, she
is motivated by greed. Catherine's plan is simple. She will win
Ralph's devotion. Later, she will leave him as a wealthy woman.
What Catherine has not counted on however is that Ralph might have
plans of his own for his new wife . . .

'Full of gothic twists, it's an irresistible
tale of skewed seduction'
Daily Mail

'High drama evolving out of avarice and lust'
Guardian

978-0-349-12236-6

SWEETSMOKE

David Fuller

The American Civil War is in full flame, and tobacco plantation slave
Cassius Howard finds he must risk everything to learn the brutal truth
concerning the murder of Emoline Justice, the freed black woman
who secretly taught him to read and who once saved his life.

Against an epic backdrop and with fleeting moments of redemptive
passion, Sweetsmoke captures brilliantly the daily indignities and
harrowing losses suffered by slaves, as well as the turmoil of a
country waging countless wars within itself, and the lives of myriad
people fighting for freedom.

'Meticulously researched and beautifully written,
Sweetsmoke resonates with unforgettable characters
and is a gripping story of loss and survival'
Robert Hicks, author of *The Widow of the South*

'Captivating'
New York Times Book Review

978-0-3491-2153-6

THE SWEET AND SIMPLE KIND

Yasmine Gooneratne

'Loyalty (and the damnable lack of it in his wife) was
the thought uppermost in the mind of Sir Andrew Millbanke
as he looked down at Lady Alexandra's dead body,
spread-eagled on the paved pathway of the Residency.'

And so begins an engrossing and dramatic family drama, set against
the backdrop of Ceylon's bumpy evolution into Sri Lanka, as the
Wijesinha clan struggles to balance its staunch political ambition
against the ignominy of an embarrassing family scandal. And when
two young family members, cousins Tsunami and Latha, meet and
become firm friends, no one can guess that their triumphant friendship
will be played out over the passing years against both the best and the
worst the newly independent Sri Lanka can offer, as these two smart
and westernised young women pursue their own personal freedoms.

'There is much to commend in the author's refusal to pander to
commercialism and in her obvious integrity. As one of her characters
comments: Jane Austen's observation of society was part critical, part
amused. That quality is evident her'
Elizabeth Buchan, *Sunday Times*

978-0-349-12174-1

Now you can order superb titles directly from Abacus

☐ A Reliable Wife   Robert Goolrick   £7.99

☐ Sweetsmoke   David Fuller   £7.99

☐ The Sweet and Simple Kind   Yasmine Gooneratne   £9.99

The prices shown above are correct at time of going to press. However, the publishers reserve the right to increase prices on covers from those previously advertised, without further notice.

─────────────────── ⬭ ABACUS ⬭ ───────────────────

Please allow for postage and packing: **Free UK delivery.**
Europe: add 25% of retail price; Rest of World: 45% of retail price.

To order any of the above or any other Abacus titles, please call our credit card orderline or fill in this coupon and send/fax it to:

Abacus, PO Box 121, Kettering, Northants NN14 4ZQ
Fax: 01832 733076   Tel: 01832 737526
Email: aspenhouse@FSBDial.co.uk

☐ I enclose a UK bank cheque made payable to Abacus for £ . . . .
☐ Please charge £ . . . . to my Visa/Delta/Maestro

Expiry Date ☐☐☐☐   Maestro Issue No. ☐☐

NAME (BLOCK LETTERS please) . . . .

ADDRESS . . . .

. . . .

. . . .

Postcode . . . . Telephone . . . .

Signature . . . .

Please allow 28 days for delivery within the UK. Offer subject to price and availability.